THE LADY OR THE TIGER

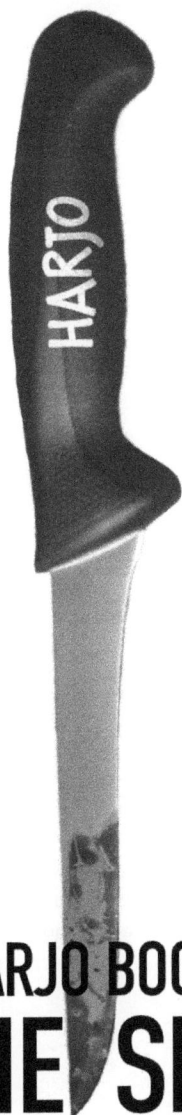

HARJO

JOSIE HARJO BOOK TWO
CATHERINE SEQUEIRA

THE LADY OR THE TIGER

Copyright © 2024 by Catherine Lamm

Cover design by Angela Caldwell

Cover copyright © 2024 by Barcelos Publishing, LLC

Published by Barcelos Publishing, LLC, Sacramento, CA, USA

The Library of Congress Cataloging-in-Publication Data is available upon request.

ISBN 9798988723172 (trade paperback)

ISBN 9798988723189 (hardback)

ISBN 9798988723196 (ebook)

Our books may be purchased in bulk for promotional, educational, or business use. Please contact your local bookseller for more information.

First Edition: October 2024

Printed in the United States of America

Novels by Catherine Sequeira

<u>Josie Harjo Series</u>
If You Hear Hoofbeats
The Lady or the Tiger

<u>Stand-alone Novels</u>
The Before and The After

To every veterinarian who struggles with depression.

If you're reading this, you're not alone,
because your fellow vets are by your side.

We love you and need you.

If the dedication didn't give you a hint, this novel deals with some heavy shit, including depression and suicide.

Help is available. Call 988 from any phone in the United States.

We don't want to lose you.

CHAPTER
ONE

The students were stacked around the dead dog like rubberneckers at the scene of a gnarly car crash. None of them wanted to be there, yet their faces were twisted with horrified fascination.

Taking stock of the six students, I braced for action.

I secretly fretted that there might be a barfer or fainter on rotation because, yeah, that was a thing.

One of them took an obvious swallow, throat bobbing, and my eyes danced to the garbage bin. It was within fetching distance, but I still might be too late.

Trying to snap them out of it, I asked, "Okay. Who wants to cut?"

They shifted uncomfortably and avoided eye contact. The ever-present crooning of Hank Williams spilled from the necropsy floor speakers, filling the awkward silence.

As future vets, a dead animal typically wasn't something they *wanted* to see. And from experience, I knew that most of them *definitely* didn't want to participate in eviscerating one. But anatomic pathology was a required rotation, and there was a lot to cover over the next two weeks. They needed to suck it up.

"Anyone?" I nudged again.

Dustin shot me a smirk from across the room. He'd been a technician on the necropsy floor long enough to know how things went down. My chances of getting a volunteer were slim to none, and he knew it.

Y'all should be thanking your lucky stars, I almost blurted.

It was still hot as Hades outside, and we were bound to get a rotten steer in at least once during their rotation. As soon as they got a deep

1

whiff of that *parfum de bœf mort*, they'd be looking back to this dog nostalgically.

The carcass in front of us was a damn good start to the rotation: nice and fresh. Small enough that they wouldn't get a hoof to the face. No risk of rumen contents slopping into their boots. They should've been more appreciative.

I needed to give them a bigger push, or we'd be here all day. If it had been just Dustin and me, we'd have this dog done in less than thirty minutes. With the students on rotation, the necropsy was going to take at least two hours. If they didn't get a move on, we'd be late to lunch, and I'd miss out on whatever delectable dessert Carol had brought in today.

Eager to get the ball rolling, I held one of the student knives out to the group. Thankfully, no one took a step back.

No one moved forward, either; the knife sat in my hand in the center of the group like a leper.

One of the students coughed lightly.

I couldn't help a surge of defensive disappointment. Anatomic pathology was a pretty chill rotation. There were no rounds at the crack of dawn and no treatments late at night. And, with the very rare exceptions, there were no emergencies. I hadn't called the students in on the weekends since I started at the lab six years ago. And yet they acted like it was agony being here.

"Come on, now. You can't screw it up if it's already dead," I prodded.

One brave soul finally said, "I'll do it."

My first victim.

Maniacal laughter echoed through my head.

"Mackenzie, right?" I asked.

"Yes, ma'am," she replied with a thick Oklahoman drawl.

Mackenzie was built like a tank. She had practical, short, blonde hair and bright blue eyes. I vaguely remember her saying she want-ed to be a mixed animal veterinarian when we did intros this morn-ing. She'd definitely be able to hold her own against a pushy large animal.

I handed her the knife. "Thanks for volunteering." Turning to the other students, I added, "Y'all will get your chance."

Was that a threat?

Maybe.

One savvy student clutched the paperwork, daring anyone to pry it out of her cold, dead hands. Having the paperwork designated her as the scribe, which meant she could get out of the 'ole choppy-choppy.

Her pale skin had a gray tinge to it.

Yeeeeeah, she might be a fainter.

I wracked my brain, trying to remember her name.

Sarah? I guessed.

I took a long look at Maybe-Sarah, trying to decide if I was going to have to catch her before she hit the epoxied floor. She was petite with dirty blonde hair. Her skin was way too pale, but her eyes seemed sharp. Her muscles were clenched tightly enough that I figured she was maintaining sufficient blood pressure and probably wouldn't pass out. Given her look of dread, it was probably a good thing she was applying for a small animal radiology residency.

I tossed Maybe-Sarah what I hoped was a reassuring smile.

She gulped.

"Ready?" I asked the group.

It was absurdly rhetorical, and we all knew it.

Mackenzie clung to the knife, looking a bit lost.

To break the ice, I turned to Maybe-Sarah and asked, "Please remind me of your name?"

"Sarah," she said, barely above a whisper.

I patted myself on the back for remembering correctly.

I wasn't great with names, and it bugged the crap out of me. Former students would come up to me at conferences all buddy-buddy. I'd recognize their faces, but I couldn't for the life of me remember their names. I'd plaster on a smile and pretend I knew who the hell I was talking to. Proclaiming "Go Pokes" and flashing a pistols-firing hand signal was a popular and safe response.

Sarah would probably be happy to hide behind the paperwork the entire rotation.

I tried to ease her out of her panic. "Can you read the history again for us?"

We'd briefly discussed the case in the conference room before trundling out onto the necropsy floor. Because the students looked like deer in the headlights, I figured a refresher was in order before I pushed Mackenzie into the deep end, hopefully with the knife blade pointed *away* from her.

"The patient is an eleven-year-old, male, mixed-breed dog," Sarah read from the form. "He started vomiting and developed bloody diarrhea over Labor Day weekend. He was found dead this morning."

"Did that history come from the vet school?" one of the students asked with a hint of snark.

Emma, I recalled.

She was hard to forget.

Despite her bitchy tone, her question was a valid one. Anyone could submit bodies to the state diagnostic lab for a necropsy, whether it be an owner, a vet, or whatever. Large animals, like horses and cows, were our bread and butter. We'd get dogs and cats, too, but most of them came over from the teaching hospital.

Sarah looked at the form. "Looks like the owner brought it in. There's no vet listed."

Emma snorted and rolled her eyes.

It was no surprise that Emma's immaculately groomed, blonde locks dangled past her shoulders in wild abandon. Students with that kind of attitude tended to think they were above everything and everyone else. One foray into a dead steer, and she'd learn. Hair tended to pick up flecks of blood and rumen contents. I secretly hoped she'd go home smelling like death at least once this week.

Trying to ignore Emma's sass, I asked the group, "Based on the information we have, what are your differentials?"

I saw eyes light up around me as everyone started building a list of possible causes of vomiting and bloody diarrhea. Despite being out of their element on the necropsy floor, veterinary students couldn't help themselves when asked to prove their knowledge.

"Intestinal bacterial infection? Parasites?" a student offered hesitantly.

Harper?

Maybe-Harper was the tallest of the students, thin and wiry. Her straight hair was pulled into a long ponytail. Though I could only guess her name, I placed her face with her background. She'd grown up on a horse ranch, was an avid equestrian, and wanted to be an equine vet.

Despite tracking equine medicine classes, she was spot-on with her small animal differentials.

I nodded. "Yep. What else?"

The group waited through the uncomfortable silence. I wondered if Emma's oppressive holier-than-thou attitude was putting a damper on the vibe.

"Come on, y'all," I nudged. "You know this."

"Pancreatitis?" Mackenzie suggested. She flashed a worried look at Emma, who, thankfully, kept her snorts to herself this time.

"Good answer," I confirmed. "Garbage-can-gut with pancreatitis is high on the list, especially after a holiday. What else?"

I made eye contact with Emma, who just looked down her nose at me, twirling her blonde hair around her finger.

Emma obviously fancied herself the Queen Bee. She wanted to be a small animal vet, but she wouldn't last long with that attitude. Reality was waiting for her, and it was holding a bat.

Another student reluctantly spoke up, "Can't some toxins do that?"

"No way this is a toxin, Kassidy," Emma scoffed with yet another eye roll.

Did this chick take lessons from Real Housewives? *What the hell?*

My eyes narrowed, and I shot Emma with my laser death rays. To my dismay, they bounced right off her.

Turning back to Kassidy with what I hoped was an encouraging smile, I said, "Yes, toxin ingestion can cause bloody diarrhea. Do you know which ones?"

"Um, I'm not sure," Kassidy answered.

"Anyone know?" I looked around the group, and they shook their heads.

I couldn't help but feel a bit disappointed. There'd been an aflatoxin outbreak in dog food a few years ago. The affected dogs had presented with bloody diarrhea and failing livers. I knew for a fact our toxicologist extraordinaire, Dr. Sandy Bishop, taught this in her toxicology class, along with a handful of other toxins that could cause those signs. She was one hell of a teacher and would be mortified that they couldn't remember even one toxin that could do this.

I could only hope that it was the sight of a dead dog in front of them that was chasing away the factoids buried deep in their gray matter.

"Okay. Homework," I said, all business. "During lunch, look up some toxins that can cause vomiting and bloody diarrhea in dogs."

I looked down at the semi-stiff labrador mix lying left-side-down on the cool, metal table. I ran through my own differential list, making sure we hadn't missed anything.

Glancing back to the students, I added, "One more thing we should consider is neoplasia."

"Psh," Emma said dismissively. "The history said the dog just got sick. Cancer doesn't do that."

Yeah, reality is coming for her with a bat. And I might be the one holding it.

I tried to behave myself, even though I wanted to strangle the little snot. She was going to be a thorn in my side the entire rotation.

I plastered on a smile that didn't reach my eyes.

"History is important. But you shouldn't let it bias you," I said, chiding her despite my best effort to moderate my tone. "It's possible the dog was sick for a while, and the owners didn't notice. Or, it's possible that whoever wrote the clinical history didn't think it was important to mention that the dog had lost a lot of weight recently or something. The clinical history is just one piece of the puzzle."

Emma didn't look convinced. Instead, she tossed me a look that pretty much said I was an idiot.

Shrugging off her RBF, I moved on. "Let's get everything opened up first and see what we find. Then, we can talk through what samples to collect. Depending on what we find, we may need to take sections for microbiology or PCR."

Mackenzie stepped up to the table to get started.

"Wet down the surfaces first," I suggested. "It'll make it easier to clean up after."

Maybe-Harper moved forward to help. She grabbed the hose sprayer and gently wet down the stainless steel table around the dog. The water flowed down the slight slope to the sink at the end.

As she was doing that, I went to track down my knife. I felt naked without it.

I made a quick trip over to the secret drawer of treasures and pulled my baby out. The pathologists' knives were kept locked away when students were on the necropsy floor. Most students could dull a knife lickety-split, and it would be impossible to get a good edge back on it. The six-inch necropsy knife was the tool of the trade, and I wasn't about to let my baby get abused.

My knife was resting next to those of the other pathologists, with "HARJO" spelled out in white on the black plastic handle. I pulled it out, feeling reassured by the grip in my hand.

I headed back to the group, keeping my knife handy.

Mackenzie grabbed the front leg and brought the knife forward.

"Wait," I advised, "don't forget to do your external exam."

"Seriously?" Emma said, incredulous. "It's not like this is CSI."

I bit back a retort. Better not to engage. Gerald had taught me that.

Instead, I said, "You never know what you'll find. It's important to get in the routine of checking everything systematically."

Mackenzie put her knife down and checked the oral cavity. She then ran her hands along the length of the dog's body and stopped in the left axilla.

Her eyebrows creased. "I think I found something."

I reached in to feel it. There was a discrete, freely movable, soft mass just below the skin's surface.

"Good catch," I complimented her. "Everyone, come palpate this."

I stepped back as the students reluctantly shuffled up to feel the mass. Even Emma grudgingly complied.

7

Her face flushed, and her lips pressed into a line as she silently stepped back.

Told you, I thankfully didn't snark out loud.

"Is that a lipoma?" Kassidy asked after her turn.

"It has the same texture as fat. So, yeah, that's my guess," I answered. "If you found this during a physical exam, what would you do?"

"Stick a needle in it?" Mackenzie offered.

I nodded and flashed her an approving smile. "That's what I'd do. If you see fat cells, then a lipoma is highly likely. If you hear hoofbeats, think horses, not zebras. That being said, I've seen mast cell tumors hide in lipomas, especially in obese dogs. So, even if you think it's a lipoma, it's important to keep an eye on it if you don't remove it."

I grabbed my knife and made a quick nick through the skin and into the mass. Glistening fat popped out. "This one's probably a lipoma. See how it looks like normal fat?"

The students nodded. Mackenzie reached forward to touch the cut surface with her gloved hand.

"It's greasy, too," she said, rubbing her glistening thumb and forefinger together.

"Once we get going, make sure to get a section of that for the formalin jar," I advised.

Mackenzie nodded.

"Thanks. I think you're good to open him up now."

All the students had been taught how to do a necropsy in their third year of veterinary school. As a refresher, senior students were asked to watch a how-to video before their first day on rotation. *The Necropsy Book*—affectionately known as "the little gray book"—was also recommended but rarely purchased or read. Regardless of all the pre-work, the students always balked on the first day of the rotation.

Watching a video was one thing. It was a whole other bag of beans when you had a dead animal sitting in front of you, and it was your job to cut it open.

Mackenzie held up the dog's front leg and ran the belly of the knife over the skin, making me cringe inwardly. Using the knife like that resulted in zero incisions and instantly dulled the edge. It was fairly common for students to try to use a knife like a scalpel, even though it wasn't right.

I moved to Mackenzie's side quickly. "It's not surgery. Don't be shy. Make a stab incision, and then cut forward and back. Use the belly of the knife whenever you can." I mimed with my knife as I spoke.

Mackenzie picked it up quickly and was able to reflect the right front and back legs without further injury to the knife's edge. Getting into the groove, she cut back the skin and muscle of the abdominal wall lickety-split.

I was pleased to realize she must have done her homework; she knew the general motions and only needed some minor redirection to improve her overall execution.

Knowing the flow of a necropsy and always anticipating our needs, Dustin passed Mackenzie the loppers. She crunched through the ribs, pulling the thoracic wall back to reveal the heart and lungs.

Kassidy and Maybe-Harper had stepped back and were talking quietly. Sarah was still perched on the stool next to the dissection table, clutching the submission form like a shield. Emma stood firm with her judgy face, poised to critique Mackenzie. The last student, whose name I failed to recall, had wandered over to the adjacent dissection table and was sitting on a stool with her hands in her pockets.

"Hang on a sec," I instructed Mackenzie once both cavities were open.

I glanced up at the other students and waved them closer to the table.

"Come have a look. You always want to pause and check the body cavities before diving in. Does anything look out of place or abnormal?"

There were a few thoughtful seconds as everyone peeked in. Only the *shick, shick, shick* of Dustin putting a fresh edge on a few student knives could be heard over the soft sounds of the music.

Pointing to the mid-abdomen, Mackenzie said, "The fat looks a little red here."

"I agree," I said, pleasantly surprised at her observational skills. "Sometimes, autolysis can change the color of the abdominal adipose tissue. Because this dog is fairly fresh, it's probably real and not an artifact from rot."

Mackenzie pulled a couple of loops of small intestine aside, tracing the red area. "Looks like it's focused on the pancreas."

"Yep. See those white dots?" I asked, and she nodded. "What do you think that is?"

Kassidy leaned in bravely, her shoulder-length, brown, curly hair secured in a ponytail and her glasses firmly set on her nose. "Pancreatitis, maybe?"

Kassidy wanted to be a small animal vet. I figured the idea of pancreatitis was exciting enough to get her to inch closer to the table.

"Mhm. That's what I think it is. I bet dollars to donuts this is a case of post-holiday pancreatitis."

Sadly, we had a case like this following just about every holiday. People had parties, dogs got fed stuff they shouldn't normally eat, or they raided the trash can, and then, the poor little things popped with a roaring case of pancreatitis. I'd even seen situations in which a Houdini cat opened things up and walked away, letting their housemate snarf everything down and get sick. Sometimes, as in this case, it could be lethal.

Cats plotting the downfall of their canine housemates? Never.

I smiled to myself at the thought before returning to the case. There were a few more pieces that needed to be sussed out.

"What else should we be looking for?" I prodded.

"Enteritis, maybe?" Mackenzie asked.

My eyebrows shot up. I favored the Socratic method of teaching and expected speedy answers, but I was still caught off guard when she landed the correct answer on the first go.

Mackenzie is on her game.

Trying to hide my surprise, I said, "Exactly. We'll collect samples for histology and look at everything under the microscope to be safe. We'll also send some of the intestine to the PCR lab for a diarrhea screen to look for anything infectious. It could be a two-fer if this guy got into the trash can."

"Why choose PCR over culture?" Kassidy asked.

Emma snorted. "Because Dr. Richter runs the microbiology lab, right? Who wants that creeper touching anything?"

Then, to my disbelief, she actually flipped her hair with a gloved hand and smirked, one eyebrow cocked.

Sure, she was right; Gerald Richter was indeed the lab's resident creeper. But Emma hadn't earned the right to talk shit about him. That was reserved for those of us who had to share a workplace with the troll.

"Now, now," I reproached, frowning at Emma.

I figured I'd try my laser death rays once more. If they weren't effective, I'd have to break out the 'ole Manson lamps: the look reserved to express disdain at only the most abhorrent behavior.

"To answer your question, Kassidy," I continued, trying to get us back on track, "PCR is faster. Plus, culturing gastrointestinal contents can get pretty messy. Once an animal dies, the gut bacteria start throwing parties, and it can be hard to pick out significant organisms from post-mortem overgrowth. You can get false positives and false negatives. PCR is cleaner."

Dustin, hearing the conversation, had moved over and selected some Petri dishes from the cart. He started labeling containers with a Sharpie pen for sample collection.

He'd been a necropsy technician since I started at the state diagnostic lab six years ago. He was *incredible* at his job, and even though he never had any formal veterinary medical or pathology training, I'd learned a ton from him. He was just a smart dude who soaked things up like a sponge. With over twenty years of experience on the necropsy floor, he'd had a lot of time to learn through osmosis.

His tall frame towered about a foot over the students. He wore the same get-up as the rest of us: coveralls and rubber boots. The cut of his hair was neat and short. Despite the risk of getting bits and bobs in it, he sported a well-groomed beard. He said his wife, Dolores, liked it that way. He'd always be quick to add that if she could live with the smell of dead animal coming home on him, the least he could do was rock the beard and hairstyle she was fond of.

As Mackenzie removed the organs, I parsed them out to the hesitant onlookers.

I handed the liver to the budding equine vet. "It's Harper, right?" I ventured.

She nodded, taking the liver.

The kidneys went to Kassidy and the spleen to Emma. Sarah remained clutching the paperwork. I left the gastrointestinal tract for Mackenzie since that's where the main lesions were expected to be.

I waved the last student over to work on the pluck.

"What's your name, again?" I asked.

"Tessa," she answered quietly.

Her hands were still in her pockets, and her shoulders were hunched. She had straight black hair pulled into a messy ponytail. Her eyes were shrouded with deep purple bags. A faint sour smell wafted off of her, almost like a cow's breath when it was in ketosis. The way she looked made me think of Sisyphus, pushing that damn rock up the hill every day just to see it roll back down and have to repeat it all. Over and over.

I couldn't remember what she wanted to do after she graduated. My mind kind of slid over her. She was the antithesis of Emma.

"Let's do the pluck together," I said to her, moving the lungs, heart, trachea, and esophagus over to another table in a giant blob.

I trusted Dustin to hold down the fort with the rest of the students. I felt like Tessa needed some one-on-one time.

I handed her a set of scissors. "Run the esophagus and trachea first."

She took the scissors and went through the motions in silence.

I placed a student knife on the table for her. "Then, bread-loaf the lungs." I squeezed the lung lobes lightly. "The lungs should be soft and feel a bit like bubble wrap. Make sure to palpate them."

Tessa did as instructed and collected a sample for histology. Then, I walked her through opening the heart and collecting the rest of the samples. She warmed up after a bit, slowly getting lost in the work. Even though she went through the motions, she still seemed only half there, and I felt a sliver of discomfort.

As everyone was finishing up, I pulled the students together to run through the case. "Who can summarize everything for me?"

Mackenzie raised her hand, and I gave her a nod.

"There's evidence of acute enteritis and pancreatitis," Mackenzie answered. "We found a bunch of partially digested, raw, fatty chunks in the stomach, along with some bits of wrapper. I think he probably got into the garbage can."

She then rattled off the common bacterial infections that could be contributing to the enteritis as well as the cascade of biochemical events that led to the eventual death of the patient.

Impressed, I couldn't help but raise an eyebrow. This woman knew her stuff. I made a mental note to circle back to talk with her about career goals. She'd make a damn good anatomic pathologist.

"Excellent summary." I flashed her an approving look. "Okay," I continued. "Everyone will need to write up a necropsy report for this case. It's due tomorrow morning."

"All of us? Is that *really* necessary?" Emma whined.

"Yes, all of you. It's a way to practice."

"Are you even going to use them?" she complained. "This is just a waste of our time."

Hell no, I wasn't going to use their reports. It was important to get this report out today so the owner wouldn't worry. Also, it was the students' first day on the necropsy floor, and their reports were going to be a mess.

That didn't mean they could get out of writing it up, though. I'd seen enough botched necropsies and subsequent threadbare reports from general practitioners. I wasn't releasing students into the wild without at least trying to give them the toolset to make me proud.

"Y'all will be doing necropsies in your clinic or on the farm, whether you think you will or not," I advised. "It's important that you know what samples to collect and how to report your findings, especially if the animals are insured."

Emma crossed her arms and pursed her lips.

"We could get legal cases, too, right?" Mackenzie asked.

"True, but I would recommend sending legal cases to a third party. If that isn't possible, call your local diagnostic lab before opening an animal up. Those cases can get really messy, really fast. You don't want to get sued."

All of the legal cases that had passed under my knife flitted through my brain, and my stomach lurched. I was grateful I'd never had to testify in court.

I looked around at the fidgety students and could tell they were antsy to go.

"Okay. That's it for this morning. Thanks, everyone. Let's clean up, and then, you're free to go to lunch." I clapped my hands once to get them moving.

"Isn't *he* supposed to clean everything up?" Emma groused, gesturing to Dustin.

Mackenzie and Kassidy exchanged an irritated look. Sarah looked embarrassed.

Apparently, this was Emma's MO. I felt bad for the students; there was nothing worse than having a dickwad in your rotation group. Chances were, they'd be stuck with her for most of the school year. Poor things.

I decided to ignore Emma for now. I plugged the sink at the end of the necropsy table, squirted some soap in, and started the hot water.

Taking my lead, the students went about bagging what remained of the dog for private cremation. Even the withdrawn Tessa chipped in. They made quick work of it, scrubbing the table down as the sharp smell of disinfectant filled the air. With the table squeaky clean, the students started to leave, queuing at the footbath to scrub their boots.

Before she could escape, I called Emma over. She flipped her hair and audibly huffed. I barely managed to keep myself from shaking my head. I couldn't believe a twenty-something vet student was acting like a high schooler.

"Look," I said, trying to keep the irritation out of my voice. "I know you're only doing this because this is a required rotation, and you don't want to be here. While you're on the necropsy floor, you need to behave appropriately. That includes treating Dustin and the other lab staff with respect. He isn't your maid."

She rolled her eyes.

Seriously, she did it so often that she could probably lift weights with her ocular muscles.

"You won't get far on that high horse," I admonished. "The techs and the office staff—they're the ones who make a clinic or lab run smoothly. You need to treat them with respect and be humble. Otherwise, you'll find yourself hopping from one job to another. It's a small world, and everybody knows each other. You don't want that kinda attitude to follow you."

She let out an exaggerated sigh and said, "Yes, ma'am," without a modicum of sincerity.

I could tell my words were falling flat, and it wasn't worth the fight.

"See you after lunch," I said, dismissing her.

She flounced off, tromping through the footbath without scrubbing her boots.

Once the door slammed closed, I shot a glance over at Dustin, one brow raised. He gave me a knowing half-smile and shrugged his shoulders.

"Sorry about that," I said, embarrassed by Emma's behavior.

"Ain't your fault, Doc. Some people just think they're better than the rest of us."

I sighed. "Yeah, well, that attitude will last all of ten seconds out in the real world."

"No doubt," he replied, and we bumped fists.

With another heavy sigh, I scrubbed my boots in the footbath and followed the students out.

I could already tell it was gonna be one hell of a week.

CHAPTER

TWO

Despite the slow start, we managed to finish the necropsy just in time for lunch. With a hustle in my step, I changed into my civvies, grabbed my food, and headed to the breakroom.

It had been an odd morning. Having the students on the floor was usually pretty fun. But this group just felt *off*. I wasn't sure if it was the overall group dynamic or just one or two bad apples. I needed some time with my work buddies to cleanse my mental palate.

Dustin had beat me there and was already seated at our usual table with Zoe and Anna.

I flopped into an open spot with an inward sigh of relief.

"Hey, y'all," I said, trying to keep my tone light.

"Hey, Josie," Zoe replied, clearing space for me to set my lunch down.

I pulled out a salad chock full of late-summer veggies from the garden, along with a small container of almonds and a water bottle. After popping the lid off the salad, I dug in.

Seeing my meal, Anna teased, "You're lucky Carol's out today. She'd have a fit."

Dustin huffed a laugh.

Carol worked in the front office and saw it as her duty to make sure that everyone ate a week's worth of sugar and fat in one sitting. She was a great cook, but she doled out diabetes like a religious fanatic passing out conversion pamphlets. It was her daily routine to wring her hands over my meal and try to push cookies, brownies, or whatever baked treat she'd brought in that day.

If I was honest with myself, I loved it and could hardly ever resist.

With a twinge of disappointment, I caught up with the conversation and felt Carol's absence at the table. Obtaining one of her delectable items was my sole purpose for rushing off the floor today.

Sigh.

"Where is Carol, anyway?" Zoe asked.

Even seated, Dr. Zoe Smith was taller than the rest of us, Dustin included. She was about my age, with broad shoulders and long blonde hair that was always perfectly styled into a braid, bun, or ponytail. She wore stylish jeans, closed-toed flats, and a pink blouse. She was one of the other anatomic pathologists in the lab, having joined the team about a year or so after Dr. Tom Lang and I started.

"Carol took a long weekend," Anna answered.

Eyebrows went up around the table.

Carol *never* took time off.

"She's not thinking about retiring, is she?" Dustin asked doubtfully.

"Good lord, I hope not," I answered, verbalizing what everyone was thinking.

Carol was a mainstay at the lab. She'd been there forever and was well past retirement age. She was the first voice that vets heard when they called in; everyone in the state knew and loved her. She was training up her replacement, James, but he was fresh out of high school and still had a lot to learn. The lab wouldn't be the same without her.

"I haven't heard her talking about retirement," Anna mused. "I think her grandkids were in town for Labor Day."

Anna worked in the receiving department. Being the center of everything in the lab, she was always up on the goings-on.

"Still," Dustin said, "it ain't like her to take time off. I can count on one hand how many times she's missed a day in the twenty-some-odd years I've worked here."

He was right. I'd only been at the lab for about six years, and I couldn't remember coming in on a day when Carol *wasn't* there. I hoped all was good with her. Sadly, I wouldn't be surprised if something serious happened, and she'd kept it to herself, not wanting to bother anyone. That was just her way.

As if sensing my dark thoughts, Anna changed the subject. "What were y'all up to this weekend?"

"Oh!" Zoe turned to me. "I took your advice and finally got around to trying okra. Jayden and I bought some from the farmer's market."

"And?" I asked, hopeful. I adored okra and tried my darndest to convert every single one of my friends.

"And it was absolutely *disgusting*," she replied and feigned a gag. Anna smiled.

Dustin laughed and asked, "How'd ya make it?"

"I didn't cook it." She shook her head, eyebrows raised. "You know I'd burn the house down trying. Jayden found a recipe on YouTube. But...*blech*. It was so slimy. We had to throw it straight in the compost bin. I don't know how you eat that stuff, Josie."

"Okra's tasty," Dustin said. "It just needs to be prepped right."

Dustin liked to add okra to the deer chili he made.

Dustin's deer chili...yummm....

I realized I might be drooling. I took a bite of my salad to give my salivary glands a reason for their existence.

To my astonishment, Anna chimed in, "I agree with you, Dr. Smith. Okra's nasty."

I flashed Anna a look of abject horror.

"Don't you blaspheme in here," I teased.

Everyone at the table laughed.

"Okra can be amazing," I continued wistfully. "Fried okra, pickled okra, barbequed okra with just a dash of salt. Yummy. You just have to show it the proper respect or else it'll go slimy on you."

Zoe didn't look convinced and feigned another gag.

Dustin patted Zoe on the back, grinning. "Tell you what, Dr. Smith. The next time Dolores and I come over, I'll bring some okra and teach Jayden how to cook it up right. It'll be tasty."

Zoe and Dustin were tight. I knew if anyone could convince her that okra was actually a gift from the gods, it would be him.

"Only if Dolores makes her pulled pork recipe," Zoe conceded.

"Deal," Dustin said, grinning.

With plans made, Zoe looked to me. "How were the students this morning?" she asked, hopeful.

With a friendly smirk, I raised an eyebrow at her rhetorical question.

This early in the school year, the students were typically super green. Dustin and I would be spending most of our time making sure they didn't cut themselves and teaching them the basics. The sweet spot was right around February or March. Then, the students had enough knowledge and experience to rock it, but senioritis still hadn't set in.

"It's a pretty good group," I answered, my optimistic tone falling a bit flat.

Sure, there was usually someone with a ginormous ego on each rotation, but had any of them ever been as bad as the Queen Bee? I wasn't convinced.

I tried to brush off my instinctive dislike of Emma with little success.

"The student who led the necropsy was pretty good," Dustin added. "I could see her goin' into pathology."

Grateful to move on to a brighter topic, I said, "Yeah, she was on her game. Mackenzie is her name." I turned to Zoe. "You'll wanna keep an eye on her."

Next week, Zoe would be working with the students for the second half of their rotation. She could pick up where I left off and maybe further encourage Mackenzie to consider pathology. Zoe was a fantastic mentor.

"She's that good?" Zoe asked, not unkindly.

"Maybe." I shrugged noncommittally. "She wants to go into mixed animal practice, but she has a way with pathology."

"She handled a knife pretty well after a bit of instruction," Dustin added. "She didn't pale none at the sight of blood, neither."

"She *did* pick it up pretty fast," I conceded. "But some folks just want to try their hand as a general practitioner before they specialize."

"Did you ever practice?" Anna asked, looking to me.

"Oh, gosh, no. I hated surgery. I was always worried I was gonna kill the animal. That's why pathology was perfect for me. I couldn't mess them up if they were already dead."

Anna waved a hand in the direction of the necropsy floor. "But you don't shy from anything out there."

"Blood from a living animal is different. Cutting into them when their chest is moving with breath, and their skin twitches when the scalpel bites in...." I shivered. "It's hard to explain. When they're dead, you can just *feel* the difference."

Worried that I grossed them all out, I looked around the table. Everyone was nonplussed. Blood, feces, and body parts were a daily thing around here. I shouldn't have been surprised that they all happily chewed through their meals.

"How 'bout you, Dr. Smith? Did you practice before you became a pathologist?" Anna asked.

"No way." Zoe shook her head emphatically. "By the time my third year of vet school rolled around, I already knew I wanted to be a pathologist. I just went through the motions to graduate and then swore to never treat a living animal again. I take Nita to a *real* vet for anything she needs."

We all laughed.

I knew exactly what Zoe meant. Except for vaccinating Yersi and Chula, I left any treatments to someone who actually liked working on live animals.

"Mackenzie does have potential." I directed the comment to Zoe. "I'll circle back with her this week and keep you posted. Even if she wants to practice first, she might come back to pathology later."

"Sounds good," she said, eyes excited. "I always like nurturing the next generation. Like a pathology godmother. But instead of a pink ball gown, it's a pair of boots and coveralls."

I pictured her out on the necropsy floor with a knife instead of a wand, converting students to anatomic pathology with a shower of bone flecks. Something that was half-laugh and half-snort burbled out of me, and I practically shot food out my nose. She was cracking me up.

Zoe smiled knowingly at me.

It was fun to work with a student who shared our love for the mystery of dead things. Since they were fairly few and far between, we couldn't help but get amped when we stumbled across one. Zoe also loved nurturing students; I was glad that Mackenzie landed a week of pathology with her. If anyone could convert her to the dark side, it would be Zoe.

My thoughts turned to the rest of the student group.

"There's another student, kinda quiet," I continued. "You gotta pull her in to get her to participate. Her name is Tessa—long black hair."

"She looked like she'd just come off a bender," Dustin chimed in.

"Yeah, she didn't look too hot. Maybe she's got the morbs," I mused.

"What on Earth is '*the morbs*?'" Zoe chuckled.

"A brief period of melancholy. It's a saying from the late 1800s or whatever. I just like the sound of it: 'the morbs'. I mean, doesn't that sound cool? Reminds me of 'morbid.' All spooky and stuff."

"You are such an uber-nerd, Dr. Harjo," Anna said playfully.

"Official, card-carrying," I replied with a self-assured nod.

"Hopefully, she isn't sick," Zoe mused. "I am fed up with having a cold all the time. Maybe I should wear a mask next week."

"I don't think she's got a cold. She just looks...." I gestured my hand to Dustin, asking him to fill in the blank.

He shrugged. "There's somethin' there. I just don't know what."

"She probably just needs a good night's sleep and some serious hydration," I said, feeling like I was making excuses.

I always fancied myself as being able to read people fairly well. But I couldn't put my finger on what was wrong with Tessa.

"This afternoon's gonna be slow," Dustin said, crunching on his chips.

"Yeah," Anna agreed. "Nothin's come in."

"Hmm." I pursed my lips in disappointment and started noodling over my options.

We usually saw a pretty steady flow of dead animals come through the door. On any given day, at least one or two carcasses would roll in. The one dog we finished this morning might be all that we got today. Or, we could get slammed this afternoon.

I wasn't sure which I preferred. Slow days were a blessing and gave pathologists a moment to breathe. But it was different when students were on rotation. I wanted enough bodies to keep them busy, but not too many that we'd be working late. Two or three was usually perfect.

If nothing else came in today, I'd have to make a tough call. I could be cool and let them skip out early. That'd earn me some serious brownie points. Or, I could be a wicked witch and make them sit through two or three hours of PowerPoint slides. Given that it was the first day, I might be stuck doing the latter. I felt a twisted duty to make sure they knew some of the basics before I pushed them out into the world.

With a resigned sigh, I decided to split the difference.

"If nothing comes in by the end of lunch, I'll probably torture them with some slides for about an hour and then cut them loose."

"Sounds good," Dustin said. "I'll come getcha if something rolls in."

With the afternoon plans sorted, the conversation shifted to the weather. Despite the exclamations about the pleasant temps in this week's forecast, I still couldn't shake the feeling that a storm cloud was looming.

The last time I'd felt this way, a dead horse from JW Ranch had shown up at the door, dragging me into one of the roughest cases of my career. That was only a month ago, and I was still in recovery mode.

Too bad the universe didn't give two shits about my mental state.

***

After lunch, Zoe and I walked back to our offices, chatting idly and blissfully unaware that a wolf was waiting to pounce.

"There you are," a shrill, masculine voice interrupted.

My heart sank, and my muscles tensed.

Gerald exited his office to intercept us, an oily smile plastered on his face.

Despite his relatively thin frame, he somehow managed to block the hallway in such a way that we'd either have to twist sideways to awkwardly sidestep around him or brush against him to move past.

I shivered in disgust at the thought.

"I've been looking for you, Dr. Harjo," he said sternly.

My stomach clenched, and I cringed.

I didn't hate many people, but I *loathed* this guy. Gerald was our resident troll, and we all dreaded having to interact with him, especially the women.

The guy had come to the lab with full tenure—an unusual move by our boss, Fran. Because of that and a couple dozen publications, he thought he was all that and a bag of chips, strutting around the lab like he owned the place.

Sadly, he kind of did.

Fran was a limp noodle when it came to controlling his behavior. He ran rampant, his acts of sexual harassment and bigotry left unchecked. His behavior was so disgusting that it was only under duress that I would admit that he was actually good at the science part of his job.

Being good at his job doesn't excuse being a shitass.

"I need to discuss a case with you," he pressed.

I scrambled to think of which case had pending microbiology results and drew a blank. I had a hunch an attack was coming and wondered if that was the storm I'd sensed earlier.

"Which case is that?" I was forced to ask, the hallway cooling with the iciness of my tone.

Gerald's beady, brown eyes narrowed, and Zoe tensed next to me.

"Which case?" he repeated mockingly and crossed his arms. "Accession 43500679. Why didn't you send samples from that case to my lab?"

"Huh?" I stumbled, trying to catch up.

"The necropsy from this morning," he chided, trying to make me feel small. "Why didn't you send the intestine in for microbiology?"

I felt a jolt of surprise.

What the hell? I finished that case less than an hour ago. How does he even know about it?

Then, I felt a flash of stupidity for being surprised.

Of course, he knows. This guy is a legit stalker.

As my mind spun in circles and his sneer spread, Zoe rescued me.

"That's Josie's case," Zoe snapped. "Why do you always have to be in everyone else's business and question their decisions? Why don't you focus on your own work?" She fluttered her hand at him before placing it on her hip, chin up.

It was a challenge.

The air crackled, and Gerald's predatory gaze shifted over to Zoe. The hunt was on, and a faint smile danced around his mouth. Of all of the people in the lab, he was particularly brutal to her.

"Why do *you* spend so much time pretending to be a woman? Maybe *you* should focus on work. It was just the other day that I had to fix a case you botched."

Zoe's entire body went deathly still. The tension was now thick enough to cut with a knife.

He waved his hand dismissively from her head to her toes. "Without this distraction, you could demonstrate some true dedication to your work and the quality of the results provided at our lab. It is our responsibility to ensure that every case receives superlative service."

Zoe's face flushed with anger. I was legitimately worried that she would smack him.

He pressed on, "That's why I follow up on *all* of the cases that come through. Like accession 43500679. It's my duty to ensure that our clients receive the best care."

I jumped in. "Gerald, would you just cut it out?" I shook my head in disgust.

My comment was enough to pull his attention toward me. He flashed a smug look, sensing a small victory. Zoe was still tense as all hell, but I took her clenched hands as a sign that she wasn't going to slap him.

"As I said, I'm concerned that the correct tests were not ordered. With a case of enteritis, you should be testing for *Salmonella*, *Clostridium*, and *E. coli* at a minimum."

Oh, sweet baby Jesus. The splain was strong with this one.

I let out an exhausted sigh.

We'd been here less than a minute, and I'd had enough. Gerald just had a way of poking at me and constantly questioning everything I did. He did this to every woman in the lab and was indiscriminate with his attempts at supremacy.

I took a deep breath before I answered, trying to modulate the anger in my tone. The more irritation I showed, the more he'd get off on it.

"Yes, Gerald, I'm well aware of what causes enteritis in dogs. The PCR test I ordered will do just fine in ID'ing any infectious agents."

His face grew stony at the jab.

He was very protective of his lab and hated seeing sample volume shift over to the PCR department, which was run by Dr. Manuel Rodriguez.

I'd like to say that I'd forgotten how sensitive he was, but I'd be lying.

"PCR is a very limited test," Gerald sneered. "It's only a matter of time before you miss a diagnosis because you rely too heavily on that modality."

His voice was defensive now, and I felt a surge of malevolent joy.

Sensing an escape, Zoe said sarcastically, "Thank you for the advice. We'll be on our way now."

Gerald seemed to concede the battle in hopes of winning the war and shifted his body to let us pass.

Zoe and I grabbed hands and gave each other a light squeeze. We'd made it together. Maybe not entirely unscathed. But at least Zoe hadn't laid the beat down on him in the middle of the hallway. Any physical pain she inflicted on him would only come back tenfold in the form of political punishment. She couldn't risk it.

I squeezed her hand again and gave her a reassuring smile as we parted ways at my office door.

***

Back in the sanctuary of my office, I took a few deep breaths to shake off the Gerald ick and recenter. I was still a bit jittery from the adrenaline dump.

I had about thirty minutes before the students would be back from their lunch break. I needed to get my shit together.

I busied myself with writing the report for the pancreatitis case and hit *send*. It felt good to get that checked off my list.

After releasing the report, I grabbed my laptop and ducked down to the small teaching conference room. When I walked in, the students were already huddled around the table, snacking on the last bit of their lunches.

Tessa sat in a chair pulled off into the corner. She wore a gray hoodie over a set of rumpled coveralls. The hood was pulled up over her messy black hair. Deep bags hung under her eyes, and her cheeks were sunken. I wondered if she'd eaten.

A tingle of worry started to build.

The gloomy room didn't help. It was small with off-white, scuffed walls, no windows, and a buzzing fluorescent light that seemed to drain the life out of everyone. Two uneven tables were pushed together and surrounded by a mashup of rickety chairs. A projector sat in the center, pointing at a beat-up pull-down screen.

Fran said the lab was too broke to spruce the room up. I made a mental note to talk to Zoe and Tom, maybe pass the jar to collect some money to cheer it up ourselves. Having a nice place to meet might help the students enjoy the rotation a smidgen more.

"Hey, everybody," I said and grabbed an empty chair. It screeched across the floor as I slid up to the table.

The chatter died down, and everyone turned to me.

"We don't have any new cases," I announced.

This was met with several smiles and a few soft *yesses*.

The response was expected but still made me smirk.

Veterinary students paid out the nose to attend school, but not all of them wanted to milk every second of learning out of the system. I knew they wanted an afternoon off, a chance to chill before they started the real hairy rotations. They seemed happy enough to be up to their eyeballs in debt and still coast this afternoon.

"We'll go through a PowerPoint for the next hour or so," I continued, determined for them to learn regardless of their reluctance. "If nothing comes in, y'all can dip early."

"Thank you, ma'am," Harper said.

Emma huffed.

After dimming the lights. I powered up the projector and plugged my laptop in. I found the slide deck and put it in presentation mode. An image of a dark red, smooth, lobed organ filled the screen.

I channeled my inner Socrates.

"Tissue from a cat. What's the organ?" I asked the group.

"Liver," Emma said curtly and rolled her eyes like I was asking her the answer to two plus two.

I pursed my lips and bit my tongue.

It was fairly common to have a designated know-it-all on each rotation, but I was pretty sure Emma's reputation exceeded all expectations. I'd bet money the faculty knew exactly who she was and prayed she wouldn't land on a rotation when they were on duty. People tended to actively avoid toxic personalities like hers.

"Yes, it's the liver," I said, trying to keep a neutral tone despite my irritation.

Though the question of organ identification seemed like a simple one, some students had a hard time identifying the organ outside the body. When looking at lesions, it was the first thing we asked all students, even pathology residents. I didn't need someone like Emma making people feel stupid if they didn't know what it was.

"What do you see?" I asked the group.

When describing a lesion, we wanted to hear things like color, distribution, size, what it looked like on cut-surface, etc. And if they could touch it, we'd also want to know the texture. It was pretty hard to tick all of those boxes. How they responded now would determine whether I would have to do the "orange exercise" with them tomorrow, where I'd be asking them to provide an adjective to describe the orange until we'd exhausted the list.

"Ummm..." Mackenzie chimed in. "There's a diffuse nutmeg pattern?" Her upward inflection indicated that she wasn't sure, even though she was spot-on.

"Correct. The alternating pale tan and red areas are classic for a nutmeg pattern. What things cause that?"

I looked around the table, trying to make eye contact. The students fidgeted quietly, avoiding my gaze. Even the Queen Bee sat with her arms crossed tightly over her chest. Tessa stayed hunched back in the corner, picking at her nails, eyes heavy-lidded.

"What hepatic architecture does the nutmeg pattern highlight?" I asked, reframing the question.

"The hepatic lobules," Emma said in a petulant tone.

"Yep." I caught Emma's eye. "So, why might different parts of the hepatic lobule have different colors?"

Emma looked away, unsure of the answer, and huffed to imply that my question was dumb.

"Doesn't that happen when the blood pools?" Harper asked.

"Yeah," Mackenzie chimed in. "Like with chronic passive congestion—heart failure and stuff. Is that what this is?"

"Could be," I answered. "In a cat, that's most likely. This patient had hypertrophic cardiomyopathy with subsequent heart failure. What other organ should we check in a case like this?"

The puzzle pieces were starting to fall into place for those at the table, and I saw realization fill their faces. Except for Tessa; she remained reticent.

"Thyroid?" Kassidy tossed out, hopeful.

She was spot-on, and I felt a flush of joy. I wondered if she might go for an internal medicine internship. She'd be good at it.

"Exactly," I answered her with a smile. "This was a case of primary hyperthyroidism due to a functional thyroid adenoma with secondary hypertrophic cardiomyopathy. Heart failure resulted in hepatic congestion and the nutmeg pattern on the liver. Great job, everybody."

We talked about the liver slide a bit longer, running through other differentials. I kept throwing questions at them as we moved on to other pictures from different cases.

Mackenzie continued to knock it out of the park, with Kassidy holding up second. Harper and Sarah occasionally chimed in. Emma's contribution consisted of a series of loud sighs, eye rolls, and exacerbated answers.

Even though Emma was annoying as hell, Tessa was the one I was the most worried about. She stayed hunkered in her corner, silent, fidgeting with the edge of her sweatshirt.

I'd only failed a student once, and that was for not showing up to the rotation. But Tessa was so checked out, it was like she wasn't there. Maybe Dustin was right, and she'd had a rough weekend.

Even though I hoped she'd be more engaged tomorrow, I still couldn't shake the feeling that there was more going on with her.

An hour of PowerPoint slides and several yawns later, I knew I'd lost my battle with the postprandial lull. Sarah had even started the sleepy head-bob.

With no new cases, I released the students early.

I still had a weird taste in my mouth from the day and was worried about what the rest of the week might hold. That damn black cloud was looming again.

Back in my office, I checked my phone and was delighted to find a text from Armand.

Happiness surged through me.

Black cloud be damned.

Armand had swept into my life via my best friend, Laila. He was a plant biologist from Romania on a sabbatical at Oklahoma State University. Since Laila was a senior faculty member in the plant biology department and was in a similar area of research, she'd been hosting his visit. I'd been Laila's plus-one at a department event about a month ago and ended up talking with him for hours.

We'd clicked instantly. Since that evening, I just couldn't get enough of him.

I unlocked my phone to read the text.

> Miss you. What's your weekend looking like?

> I'm on call and have breakfast with Aunty on Sunday.

> I'm free otherwise. Want to hang out?

He thumbed up my text.

> Friday? I should be back before dinner.

Even though he'd stayed over last Saturday, I was bummed I'd have to wait almost an entire week to see him again. Friday felt like it was *ages* away.

I didn't have a choice, though. He was in the field up in the panhandle for the week and was a good five- or six-hour drive away.

My heart swelled, knowing that I'd be his first stop on his return to Stillwater.

> Friday sounds good. Want to come to my place? I can cook for you?

> Sure. What can I bring?

> Yourself

I added a kissy face emoji.

A heart popped up on my text.

My stomach fluttered. I couldn't wait to see him again.

Armand was incredibly intelligent, got my jokes, and didn't mind when I smelled like a dead animal. My cat, Yersi, also approved, which was a rarity. Armand was a keeper, and I was positively head over heels for him.

I tried not to think about the fact that he'd have to skedaddle back home to Romania in two months when his sabbatical was up.

Nope. Those nasty thoughts are going into a small box and getting buried down deep.

My goal was to soak up as much of him as I possibly could, every chance I had.

My excitement built at the thought of having him over on Friday. It meant that I could cook for someone, which I loved. It also meant that we'd be able to play some tabletop games, a hobby we both shared.

I set my phone down and couldn't help but smile.

If I were extra lucky, he'd stay the night again. That's when the best games were played.

CHAPTER

THREE

I woke up Tuesday morning feeling like I'd been hit by a two-by-four. I'd gone through the motions of feeding Yersi, getting myself ready, and driving to work. But after pulling into the parking lot, I lacked any motivation to leave the car.

Delaying my entry into the building for as long as possible, I sat in the driver's seat for a few minutes.

I wasn't sure why I felt so out of it. I usually loved coming to work; each day brought more puzzles to solve. I also liked working with the students.

So, why was I so apprehensive? Was it dealing with Emma's arrogance? Tessa's apathy? Or something else?

It could be Gerald, too. Don't forget that turd nugget.

As if sensing my negative thoughts bouncing in the ether, my phone binged with a text from Laila. She always had a sixth sense regarding my moods and knew when I needed cheering up.

> Thinking about you! How's your week going?

I responded with a shrug emoji.

> Feeling off but it'll pass. How about you?

> I'm good but worried about you. Want to call or hang out?

Nah, I'm good

It was nice to know that she cared, but I was having a swell time wallowing in my mopiness. Plus, I was feeling oddly weepy. The tears were lingering just on the edge, and I was worried that hearing Laila's voice might push me into the red zone.

I had the students today. I had *Emma* today. I needed a solid game face this week. Sniveling and handwringing were *not* allowed.

My phone binged again with another text from Laila.

What are you up to this weekend?

Armand is coming for dinner Friday and I have brunch with Aunty Sunday

I'm also on call

Wow. Your schedule is packed.

Want to have lunch sometime this week?

Maybe. I have students this week. Can I keep you posted?

Absolutely! I'm around.

Thanks for being there

I sent her a heart emoji before dropping my phone into my purse with a sigh. I leaned back in my seat and closed my eyes.

A loud *BANG* echoed on the roof of my car, scaring the ever-loving daylights out of me.

I jerked forward. My heart racing, I dipped my head to look out through the windows. In my rearview mirror, I caught a glimpse of Gerald's slim form casually retreating up the steps and into the lab.

What a prick.

It wasn't the first time he'd done that to me. It was fairly routine for him to screw with me at least once in the morning, either while in the parking lot or the hallway. It was like his espresso shot for the day. One would think I'd be used to it by now.

I took a few deep breaths to calm myself before heading in. Now, I was on the verge of being tearful *and* frazzled. I truly hated that shitass.

The walk to my office was thankfully uneventful, and I ducked in, closing the door behind me. I put my stuff away and sifted through my tea drawer.

With my mug, tea, and steeper in hand, I ventured forth to the breakroom. I already had two cups of caffeinated tea in me, but I just knew I was gonna need at least one more cup to make it through the morning. It was one of those days.

I rounded the corner into the breakroom and almost spun a 180 to high-tail it back out of there. King Troll was patiently waiting by the coffee pot as a fresh batch percolated. His back was to me, and I still might've been able to make a clean escape.

I grimaced.

My choices were to knowingly put myself in Gerald's presence or venture forth without the life-saving effects of caffeine. It was a choice between two evils. I decided to suck it up. No one was getting between me and self-medication today.

Hearing me walk in, Gerald turned around, and his blue eyes locked on me. He was around six feet tall and lean. His short, thinning, dark brown hair was meticulously slicked back. He was wearing a long-sleeved dress shirt and khakis. Though his appearance wasn't all that intimidating, I'd learned from years of harassment that this man was a heavyweight when it came to dishing out nastiness.

"Good morning," he said. Though his tone was polite, his facial expression told the truth.

His gaze was piercing, and his eyes sparkled with excitement. A few small wrinkles of glee tipped the corners. He'd enjoyed toying with me in the parking lot and was plotting his next move.

"Morning," I answered, unable to keep the thread of angst out of my voice.

Unfortunately, the hot water dispenser was right next to the coffee pot, and I'd have to enter the blast radius.

He stood his ground, and I awkwardly leaned around him to fill my cup. I set it on the counter as I measured out the tea into my steeper.

"You're looking out of it today, darling," he said without an ounce of sympathy or care.

It wasn't the first time that I'd wondered if the guy was a sociopath.

Since I couldn't think of anything polite to say back, I ignored him.

As most misogynists tended to do, he filled the silence. "You better look sharp. You have students on rotation, and there's a sensitive case for necropsy this morning."

I jerked my head up in surprise.

If it had been anyone else, we could've had a nice chat about whatever fresh pile of crap was waiting for me and strategized next steps. But I was stuck with *Gerald*, and this shitass was using the knowledge as ammunition.

Seeing the look on my face, he said smugly, "Oh? You didn't know?"

He was relishing the moment. Basking in it, even. Knowledge was power to him, and he hoarded it.

I fought back the bile in my throat.

"I'm on my way to check in with Dustin," I replied.

Did I sound defensive?

He flashed me a smile, but his eyes narrowed like a predator.

Damn it. I'm pretty sure I sounded defensive.

"Have fun today," he smirked.

I grabbed my tea, steeper still sitting in the cup, and fled the room. The students would arrive in an hour, and I needed more deets on this "sensitive case" before they swooped in.

I did *not* have a good feeling about today.

Dustin's office was empty, but a steaming mug of coffee was on his desk. I set my cup next to his and tried the necropsy floor. Sure enough, as I neared the entrance, the muffled sound of "Honky Tonk Blues" greeted me. When I swung the door open, good 'ole Hank Williams spilled over me loud and clear.

The room was pristine. The cool metal of the tables glistened with polish. Frothy bubbles coated the surface of the recently refreshed footbath. The sharp tang of disinfectant filled the air.

I'd always had a place in my heart for a crisp, clean necropsy floor. There was just something about it that made me mime a chef's kiss.

Dustin was singing along off-key, restocking the equipment carts that sat alongside the three small animal necropsy tables.

Not wanting to get fully decked out in a lab coat and shoe covers, I leaned through the door.

"Mornin', Dustin," I called out.

He turned the music down and came over.

"Good mornin', Doc," he said with a friendly smile.

I looked around the room, puzzled.

Both the small animal necropsy tables and the hydraulic large animal table stood empty. If an animal had come in overnight, Dustin would have laid it out first thing so that he was ready to go when the pathologist came out. The empty room stood in stark contrast to Gerald's threat of a "sensitive case."

"Anything come in?" I asked.

"Yes, ma'am," he said with a nod.

My heart sank.

"Just one," he continued. "Josh brought it in late last night."

My eyebrows crinkled. There was more to this, and it wasn't the fact that the person on-call received an animal after hours. We'd occasionally get stuff in overnight and on the weekends. That's why we had folks like Josh and a few others covering on-call shifts for us.

Seeing my confusion, Dustin added, "It's a tiger."

Ohhhh....

All the pieces fell into place. Though I hated to admit it, I realized Gerald was right; this *was* a sensitive case.

It also became abundantly clear why Dustin hadn't put the animal on the table. This case was going to cause quite a stir.

Technically, anything that wasn't a primate could pass through our doors for necropsy; primates required several levels of biosecurity that our lab just didn't have. Still, ninety percent of our cases were domestic animals. Occasionally, we'd get the odd wildlife species. Large exotic species—like a friggin tiger—were *rare*.

To add complexity to the situation, zoos, aquariums, and animal sanctuaries were often fairly protective of when and how they announced the death of an animal in their care. This could get ugly, especially with the students on rotation.

Damn! The students!

"Is the tiger in the cooler?" I asked.

"Yes, ma'am. I've got it stashed under the shelf in black bags."

The lab had a huge walk-in cooler where carcasses were stored before and after the necropsies. The large animals hung from hooks on one side. The offal bins, both empty and filled with innards from previous large animal necropsies, were stored on the other side. Small animals were kept in tagged baggies on open shelves along the back wall.

A tiger was damn big, and I figured Josh must've had to use the hoist to get it in the cooler last night. I wondered how Dustin had managed to bag it and stash it. That was smart thinking.

Out of sight, out of mind.

"Want me to lay it out on the table?" he asked.

I pursed my lips, thinking. "Not sure, yet," I answered.

I wasn't worried about doing a necropsy on an exotic species; I was just anxious about having the students out on the floor at the same time. It'd be hard to keep them from taking pictures or gossiping about it with their buddies.

There was also the problem of the glass window that looked out from the receiving department and onto the necropsy floor. Any rando dropping a sample off could see what we were working on.

"Want the paperwork?" He gestured with his chin to the hanging file holder on the wall.

"Yeah, thanks."

I pulled the sheet of paper out and read through it.

Tora was a fourteen-year-old, female tiger. She'd been at the Tiawah Animal Sanctuary for over ten years. A year ago, she'd been diagnosed with mammary carcinoma.

The way the history read, it sounded like her death wasn't unexpected. That lowered my level of anxiety fractionally.

"Let me go look this up before we bring her out," I said. "I'll be right back."

I dropped the form back in the holder and headed back to my office.

Bowing before the almighty Google, I searched "Tiawah Animal Sanctuary" and "Tora." Sure enough, there was already a social media post from the sanctuary. A picture of a large, majestic tiger was captioned:

Our beloved Tora passed away last night after a battle with cancer. She will be missed!

I felt a wash of relief.

Knowing that the sanctuary had already announced Tora's death, I was no longer concerned about keeping everything hush-hush. It also helped that her battle with cancer was already public. That made everything ten times easier.

I just had to keep people from doing dumb shit, like taking selfies with the poor thing.

I headed back to the necropsy floor and leaned through the door to chat with Dustin. "I just checked, and Tiawah already announced Tora's death. I think we're okay doing the necropsy with the students. We should probably close the blinds, though. I don't want anyone thinking they can steal a pic or something."

"Roger that," he replied.

He walked over to the large window facing the receiving area and dropped the Venetian blinds in a *swish*.

"I'll be back out with the students at nine," I said, trying not to sigh. I'd need a lot more tea to face this morning.

I was still nervous about bringing the students out, but performing a necropsy on a tiger was a once-in-a-lifetime opportunity for them.

"Sounds good," he said with a nod. "I'll make sure she's ready for y'all."

I started to close the door and then quickly popped my head back out.

"The form didn't say what they wanted to do for disposal." I paused and chewed my lip.

Large animals typically went to the renderer after necropsy—at least, that was the procedure until they stopped picking up carcasses in a couple of months. But Tora wasn't just any 'ole large animal. I suspected Tiawah Animal Sanctuary would want some, if not all, of her back.

Better to be safe than sorry.

"I'll give 'em a jingle and figure out what they want to do," I said.

He gave a salute, casually acknowledging the comment before grabbing the controller for the hoist to bring the tiger out. The *whir* chased me out the door.

I headed back to my office with my tea in hand. I still hadn't taken a single sip. If I didn't properly maintain my caffeine levels, I was going to crash hard.

I sighed, picked up the phone, and dialed the sanctuary.

I pressed my thumb and forefinger between my brows as the phone rang in my ear.

"Hello. You've reached Tiawah Animal Sanctuary. How may I help you today?" a pleasant voice answered.

"Good morning, this is Dr. Josie Harjo from the state diagnostic lab. I'm calling about Tora. Is there someone I can speak to about her?"

"Oh, poor Tora." She paused. "Yes, ma'am. Hold, please."

The sound of bland hold music trickled out of the phone.

I grabbed my pen and started tapping the desk. It was an annoying, nervous habit I hadn't been able to break.

After a click, a deep voice laced with a thick Oklahoman accent said, "This is Liam Brown. Is this the lab?"

"Yes, sir. This is Dr. Josie Harjo from the state diagnostic lab. I'm calling about Tora." After a beat, I added, "Sorry for your loss."

"She'll be missed. She was an old lady, and we knew it was comin'. But it's still been a rough go," he responded solemnly.

Though tigers weren't the cuddly type, most of the staff who provided care for the animals developed a strong bond with them. Tora's death was expected, but I could tell the pain still echoed through everyone who worked there.

"I saw her pictures on social media. She was very beautiful."

He laughed lightly.

"Yes, ma'am. She sure liked to pose for the camera. We're open to the public two days a week, and she'd always come right to the front of her habitat. The guests loved lookin' at her. She was an excellent ambassador."

He coughed lightly as if fighting back tears.

"The kids 'round here all know her," he continued. "They're gonna miss her, too."

My heart tugged.

"I am so sorry for you and the community. I'm sure she had a wonderful life with y'all there. I bet she captured a lot of hearts and minds."

"She sure did," he said, sounding a bit better. He cleared his throat. "Well, now. I'm sure you didn't call to hear me go on and on about Tora. How may I help you today, Dr. Harjo?"

I fumbled, trying to find the best way to broach the subject.

Exotic animal parts were highly regulated. Occasionally, zoos, aquariums, and sanctuaries asked for some of the parts to be returned for educational use; the rest would be incinerated. I couldn't find a polite way of asking what he wanted done with her remains. Because Tiawah had the permits to house live tigers, I assumed they also had the permits to keep the tiger parts after death.

"I know this is difficult, but I need to know if you would like anything returned after we complete the necropsy."

I bit my lip, hoping I hadn't offended him.

Most people who ran the larger zoos and sanctuaries could switch to business mode and talk about the tough topics in times of crisis. But Tora seemed particularly beloved, and discussing the disposition of any remains was always touchy.

"Oh," he sighed. "I asked Devon to tell y'all what we wanted done when he dropped her off last night. I apologize for that. He must've forgotten. We're all a little distracted."

"Completely understandable," I replied.

"We'd like the pelt, claws, and skull back, if possible," he continued. "We have a small education center. Tora will be able to continue her ambassador work there."

I nodded, even though he couldn't see me, and made a note on the sticky pad. These were common parts used in education; I was expecting this request.

"Our necropsy technician is very talented and can get the pelt for you. He has a lot of experience with this and will make sure everything is collected respectfully. He'll collect the claws and skull, as well."

"I 'preciate that. Thank you, ma'am."

I hesitated before continuing. There was still the matter of cleaning the gore off.

Dustin had the skill to gather all of these items for Tiawah, but prepping all of the materials to be handled by the public would require advanced taxidermy. Though Dustin preserved deer hides at home, he didn't have the chemicals, the space, or the time to clean up the tiger pelt at the lab while on the clock.

Not to mention the fact that the pelt alone was probably worth over twenty grand. A tiger pelt was a far cry from a deer hide. We had to make certain we didn't mess this up.

My pen started tapping faster.

"We can return those items following the necropsy, but...we don't have the facilities to make them ready for the public. Do you have someone who can do that for you?"

To my relief, he answered matter-of-factly, "Yes, ma'am. We have a local taxidermist that we use. Just give us a jingle when everything is ready. I'll send Devon back out to pick it up."

"Sounds like a plan. Everything should be ready in the next day or two."

"Thank you, ma'am."

I had one more question to ask, and it would be the most difficult. Even though I frequently talked to people about the disposition of remains, this case was different. My stomach clenched.

"Um, we still have the matter of the rest of the remains. Would you like those returned?"

"Is it possible to have her cremated?" His voice was laced with hope.

"She's fairly large...but we do have one facility that cremates horses. They may take her. Do you know if they'll need a permit to handle the cremation?"

Because of the impact of illegal trade on the wild tiger populations, tiger parts were highly regulated. I didn't work with exotic species often enough to know if a crematorium would be allowed to process the remains without a special permit.

Liam saved me by replying. "I'll look into it. May I have their number?"

"Yes, sir." I dug through my resource binder, found the number, and read it off to him. "If you'd like Tora cremated there, please call the lab back. You can just leave a message, and we'll make sure everything is taken care of."

"Thank you, ma'am. I 'preciate all you're doin'."

"You're welcome. We'll be doing the necropsy shortly, and you should have the full report by the end of the day."

He thanked me again, and we traded pleasant goodbyes.

I set the phone down with a sigh.

Ugh.

I hated it when Gerald was right.

Today was going to be rough. I was working on an endangered species, and we had to collect several highly valuable items. I had to somehow get this necropsy done and teach the students while also making sure no one wandered out onto the floor to catch a glimpse of the tiger or—even worse—took pictures to post on social media.

My mind swirled deeper.

Social media posts would be a disaster. We might even get animal rights protesters out front if that happened. Fran would have my ass.

Aunty's reassuring voice filled my mind: *Deep breaths. Little steps. Eyes on the prize.*

I chugged my tea, hoping the caffeine would kick in before the students showed up. I needed every bit of *oomph* to summon the power of Grayskull and get 'er done.

CHAPTER
FOUR

Several cups of black tea were keeping my eyes open, but my dang corneas still felt dry and grainy. Exhaustion pressed in, making every action feel ten times more difficult.

I sat at my desk, tapping my pen, waiting until the last possible moment to meet the students. Anxiety was curling around my spine, and I couldn't put my finger on the cause.

The tiger necropsy should be a cakewalk.

Dustin would do most of the cutting. And with a diagnosis already in the bag, we'd just go through the motions to collect samples. Something as cool as a tiger would also keep the students interested and engaged.

I knew all of this, yet the sneaky, selfish part of me was still being irritatingly petulant. I was starting to doubt my ability to keep the students in line with such a "sensitive case."

Fucking Gerald.

I wasn't sure if the apprehension I was feeling was because of the sliver of doubt he'd stabbed under my nail this morning or my intuition trying to raise the alarm. The logical part of me was repeating that there was no reason to be nervous.

I closed my eyes, took three deep breaths, and laid my pen down.

It was time to get going.

I strapped on a fake smile and headed to the conference room.

"Morning, y'all," I said as I walked in.

My attempt at a cheerful and energetic tone was unconvincing.

I chewed my cheek. I'd need to get a better game face on if I was going to control the situation today.

"Morning, Dr. Harjo," Mackenzie replied.

Harper, Kassidy, and Sarah turned to me and echoed a greeting. Tessa had her head tucked into her folded arms on the table and appeared to be sleeping.

Emma didn't acknowledge my existence. Instead, her eyes were locked on her phone, where her reflection gazed back as she touched up her makeup.

Makeup. On an anatomic pathology rotation. Really?

Bless your heart, I thought and then instantly felt like an asshole.

I needed to rise above that shit, even though I was tired.

"Please put your phones away, and let's get started," I instructed.

Harper tapped Tessa lightly. She raised her head groggily and rested her chin on her palm. She still looked awful, deep bags hanging like purple bruises beneath her eyes. I was amazed she managed to keep them open and focused on me.

And I thought *I* was tired.

I took a seat and slid the submission form into the middle of the table. "We have one case today."

Emma was still glued to her phone, now picking at individual strands of hair and arranging them around her face. Getting her attention was like trying to pull Narcissus from the pool.

I pursed my lips in irritation. I wasn't used to this type of behavior from veterinary students and felt at a loss on how to get her to behave like a considerate human being. This needed to be nipped in the bud.

Trying a more direct approach, I said, "Emma, please put your phone away."

Avoiding eye contact, she made a few last adjustments to her hair and put her phone down before rolling her eyes. She tilted her chin up and smirked with her eyebrows raised.

I tried to keep my face neutral. I figured ignoring her mini-tantrums might be the best way through this week.

I pushed the submission form to Kassidy, who just happened to be seated closest to me. "Will you read it for us?"

Kassidy looked at the paperwork briefly before her eyes snapped back up. "A tiger?!"

"We have a tiger today?" Mackenzie asked, excitement lighting up her eyes.

Kassidy and I both nodded.

"Yes, ma'am," I answered.

Eyebrows went up around the table. Harper turned to Tessa, grinning, and gave her a friendly nudge with her elbow. Tessa responded with a slight smile. Emma continued to look bored.

"How often do you get something like that?" Mackenzie asked enthusiastically.

"Not very. We don't see many exotic species. Y'all lucked out." I turned to Kassidy. "What's the history say?

"Oh. Yes. Ummm...." Refocused, Kassidy held up the form, scanning it. "Tora is a fourteen-year-old, female tiger. She was diagnosed with mammary carcinoma three months ago. She was found dead yesterday afternoon."

"If they knew it had mammary carcinoma, why even bother with a necropsy?" Emma quipped. "Seems like a waste of time."

My hackles instantly went up.

Mackenzie furrowed her brows and said defensively, "I think it's kinda cool."

"Yeah," Harper said, jumping in. "I've never seen a tiger up close before."

"The only thing a dead tiger is good for is their claws. I bet they'd make some sick jewelry." Emma pursed her lips. "Or maybe the pelt could be used for something."

Shocked silence filled the room. Even I was at a loss for words.

Emma caught the death glares from the other students. She used the first two fingers on each hand to push her primped locks back from her face and over her shoulders.

"What?" she asked rhetorically, tilting her chin up. "Geez. It's already dead. It's not like it matters."

How had I not heard about this woman before now? Somebody should've warned me. Students like this had reputations that transcended the divisions between departments. Unless....

She must come from a rich family.

47

I cleared my throat to buy a second to collect my thoughts. I wanted to smack the bitch but figured that was not the best course of action.

Sometimes, being a role model sucked.

Trying my best, I said, "Trafficking of wild animal parts is the reason some species are endangered. The last thing we want to do is put more items out there."

She didn't look convinced.

"Plus, it's illegal. Federal offense," I added pointedly.

She glared at me, unphased.

Figuring it was a losing battle, I pressed on. "Even though we know Tora had a mammary carcinoma, we'll need to do a full necropsy and collect all tissues for histology, even if they look normal."

There were a few crinkled eyebrows.

"It's because preserved tissues from tigers are scarce," I added. "We collect everything in case they're needed for future studies. A database of tissue."

"What types of studies would they use normal tissues for?" Mackenzie asked, leaning forward on her elbows.

I shrugged in a friendly way. "Who knows what they'll need them for down the line? Maybe they want to look at thyroids. And they want samples of normal thyroid from at least thirty tigers as controls. It might be difficult to accumulate that many control samples for some species. So, we just hang on to them in case they need the samples later. We'll be collecting just about everything today—even muscle, skin, nerve, and bone marrow—the stuff you might not normally sample during a typical necropsy. We'll process them all and store them as paraffin-embedded samples, should they be needed later."

Mackenzie nodded thoughtfully. "How long can you keep them for?"

Geeking out a bit, I answered, "If kept at the right temp and humidity, the paraffin blocks can last more than fifty years. When I was a veterinary student, I was pulling blocks that were almost seventy-five years old. The biggest issue is space to store everything. With the exotic species, we keep them for as long as we can."

I looked around the table, trying to make eye contact with everyone. Tessa still had her eyes open, which I took as a good sign. Emma was listening, even though she was acting bored.

"The tiger necropsy will go a bit different," I began. "The sanctuary wants the pelt, claws, and skull returned."

"What do they want them for?" Sarah asked with genuine curiosity.

Harper answered, adding helpfully, "They use things like that for education. You know, when you go to the zoo, or whatever, and they have items out for kids to touch and stuff. Like that."

"They should just sell that stuff instead," Emma huffed. "Those things are worth a *ton*. They could make money for the sanctuary that way."

She was so wrong it hurt. But a debate would go nowhere.

"Anyway," I continued, trying to brush off her comment, "because they would like these items returned, Dustin will be opening the carcass. He has a lot of experience field dressing deer and will make sure the pelt is removed correctly. He'll parse out organs for y'all to work on in teams."

There was relief on a few faces. As cool as a tiger was, most of them would rather not be the lead on the case. Except for Mackenzie. I suspected she'd be fine jumping right in.

There was one more important rule for the day, but I wasn't sure how to approach it. Given how rare a tiger necropsy was, I knew they'd be texting their friends about it no matter what I said. But I was crossing my fingers and my toes that no one was stupid enough to take pics or, heaven forbid, selfies with the tiger. Cell phones weren't allowed on the necropsy floor, but that didn't stop students from sneaking them out anyway.

Part of me said they were all adults and should know better. Reminding them might come off as condescending. Then, after a glance at Emma, I realized it *had* to be discussed.

"One important thing," I said. "No phones on the necropsy floor. Period. Absolutely *no* pictures of the tiger."

I made eye contact with Emma.

Emma frowned, and her eyes narrowed. "Our phones could get stolen if we leave them in here."

"It'll get covered in blood on the necropsy floor," Mackenzie quipped.

She was getting bold. I felt a flash of pride, and a smile tugged to free itself.

Emma glowered at her.

"If you're worried, you can leave your things in my office, and I'll lock the door," I offered the group.

Emma snorted with a mocking cringe. "No, thanks."

A tingle of adrenaline raced through my veins.

"We're fine with leaving our stuff here, Dr. Harjo. I'm sure everything will be fine," Harper said kindly, trying to defuse the situation.

"Yeah, we understand," Mackenzie agreed, giving Emma the side-eye.

"Thanks for being cool about it," I said, directing my comments toward Harper and Mackenzie. Turning back to the rest of the group, I added, "Okay. We'll meet out on the floor in fifteen minutes."

I rapped my knuckles lightly on the table, signaling for everyone to get a move on.

As I left the conference room to change into my coveralls, I felt a hint of apprehension build, and my stomach clenched.

Emma was going to be a problem.

I'd gambled, thinking a necropsy on a tiger would be a wonderful experience for the students. With any other group, it might've been fine. But I couldn't shake the feeling that allowing Emma to participate was a huge mistake.

Too late now, dumbass.

***

On the necropsy floor, the soft sound of "The Angel of Death" spilled from the speakers and was discordant with the excited chatter of the students. There was an infectious buzz about the room. Even I was finding it hard not to be awed and a little electrified by the large predator before me.

The tiger was stretched on its left side on the hydraulic necropsy table. Her head was massive, and her sharp teeth were obvious below her stiff, black lips. Her large whiskers were pushed askew by the cool metal table. Her coat was beautiful and lush; I found it hard not to run my bare hands over it just to feel it without gloves on.

Dead animals had a distinct stiffness and emptiness that was hard to describe; I could just *tell* they were dead. Even though Tora's body had that characteristic vacant feeling, there was still a magnificence about her that was impossible to ignore.

I made my way over to Dustin, who was straightening his knife on the steel with a familiar *shick, shick, shick.*

"Ready, Doc?" Dustin asked.

"Yes, sir," I said with a nod. "I let the students know that you'd be on point. Time to channel your mad dressing skills."

Dustin tossed me a friendly salute and went back to working his knife.

"Okay, everybody," I called out loudly.

I motioned the students forward so they could hear me.

Thankfully, the chatter died down quickly, and all of the students shuffled closer. Emma was up front, leading the pack, her arms crossed. Tessa was in the back, her sweatshirt on over her coveralls and hood pulled up over her greasy hair. The rest of the students were practically bouncing on their toes.

"What's the first thing we want to do?" I prompted the group.

"External exam?" Mackenzie offered.

"Correct. You want to get started?"

A few of them moved over to the tiger, led by Mackenzie, and began the external exam. This included looking at the tiger from head to tail for any evidence of wounds, scars, masses, or anything else abnormal.

Emma ran a gloved hand over the chest. "Wow, the fur is so thick and soft."

The comment lacked the usual snark. I felt a twinge of hope that maybe she did have a soul.

The other students mobbed forward to pet the tiger with their gloved hands.

"This is so cool," Kassidy said, touching the whiskers.

I was doing my own once-over and spotted a few things. I understood how the tiger was distracting—it was a unique experience—but we had a job to do.

"Okay, y'all," I said, drawing everyone's attention. "Back to work. What do you see?"

Their focus returned to the necropsy, and they started examining the body.

"I think there's a mass down here?" Harper said. Her hands were palpating the tiger's abdominal area near the legs. Her eyebrows were creased with doubt.

I ran my hands over the area. Sure enough, there was a firm, roughly two-centimeter, multilobulated mass beneath the skin that felt semi-attached. On closer examination, I noticed it was adjacent to a nipple.

That's the money-maker.

Stepping to the side, I said, "Everyone, come palpate this."

The students queued up.

"What do you feel?" I asked.

"A hard mass in the mammary gland," Emma said, her tone laced with condescension. She had a way of making it seem like every question I asked or thing I said was incredibly stupid.

Nope, she doesn't have a soul.

"Isn't the mass technically 'firm?'" Mackenzie blurted innocently.

Emma directed a scowl at her, and Mackenzie flinched.

"Yes, it's 'firm,'" I answered. "We reserve 'hard' for things like bone."

Emma let loose a *Beavis and Butthead* laugh.

Irrationally annoyed that she was co-opting something that wholeheartedly belonged to my generation, I frowned. Trying to move past it and get back into teacher mode, I pulled one glove off.

"A good way to remember is…'hard.'" I touched my forehead. "And 'firm.'" I touched the end of my nose. "And 'soft.'" I touched my lips.

"Mammary tumors can be hard if they have bone or dense cartilage in them. But this one is firm."

"Mammary tumors have *bone*?" Emma scoffed.

"Yes, a mixed tumor can produce cartilaginous and osseous matrix," I replied, trying not to snark. "Why is this one firm?"

Blank stares greeted me, and a few students shifted uncomfortably.

"My guess is that there is a prominent scirrhous response," I answered for them. "All of the fibrous tissue is making the mass firm. That's probably why it feels semi-attached, as well."

I stepped forward again to palpate the remaining mammary glands. Finding nothing, I added, "I suspect this is the primary. But we'll see what we find once we get her open. Who's our scribe?"

Sarah raised her hand.

Hadn't she scribed yesterday?

I was gonna need to shuffle things around a bit, or she'd be hiding behind paperwork the entire two weeks.

Resigned to her keeping the position today, I asked, "Can you take notes on the mass, including which gland it's in?"

Sarah nodded and stepped forward to count the mammary glands, making notes.

"You'll also want to palpate the local lymph nodes to see if any of them are enlarged," I advised the group.

I quickly kneaded the skin along the mammary chain, searching for subcutaneous lymph nodes before checking the inguinal and popliteal nodes. I stepped aside to let the students try.

After everyone had a shot, I said, "I didn't feel any enlarged lymph nodes, but we'll still collect them to check for metastasis."

A couple of the students nodded in understanding.

Dustin had finished with his knife and silently watched us. I caught his eye, and he gave a slight nod. He'd noted the location of the mass and would make sure to dissect it out in one piece as he was removing the pelt.

"Okay, everybody," I gestured over to the small metal tables to the side, "go ahead and grab a knife. Split up into two groups. Dustin and

I will bring over the bits and bobs as we work our way through the carcass."

The students split off as instructed.

There was an awkward shuffle as they all avoided being grouped with Emma. They eventually sorted themselves into two groups of three.

Since Dustin would be doing the cutting, I moved to the back of the tiger to assist, wetting down the table and dropping the running hose on the ground.

The room was hushed as the students watched on. The music was turned down to a whisper.

Dustin raised the table to waist height and moved to face the tiger's lower chest.

In an act of sacrilege, Dustin made a straight incision from the thoracic inlet at the throat down to the pelvic symphysis between the legs. In doing so, he was breaking one of the ten pathology commandments, but it was necessary to remove the pelt correctly.

From there, he carefully held the skin in one hand and used the belly of the knife to separate the skin from the underlying soft tissues. He moved slowly and methodically, conscious of its value.

"This is a beautiful pelt," he said thoughtfully.

"Yes, it is," I replied, slightly hushed.

Using the hoist, he artfully worked the pelt away from the underlying tissue. Once he was finished, I carried it reverently across the room and out of the way. Later, we'd wash and dry it before packaging it for the taxidermist.

Back on the necropsy table on her left side, Tora was looking less like a tiger. With the precious pelt removed, we could revert to the doctrine, and I held the front leg back as Dustin cut the attachments between the scapula and the body. I pulled the leg toward me, reflecting it to my side of the table. Then, he moved to the rear, doing the same with the back leg, which fell toward me with a *pop* as the round ligament of the hip joint was cut.

Dustin removed the mammary mass, which I bussed over to the first table.

"Make sure to measure all three dimensions and describe the cut surface," I advised the students before heading back to help Dustin. They bent over the mass and got to work, Sarah scribbling notes.

Dustin made quick work of it, opening the abdominal and thoracic cavities faster than I could blink. As organs were removed, I passed them to the students to dissect.

With the cavities emptied, Dustin asked, "Need anything else before I finish up?"

I ran through the checklist in my head. "I'll need the inguinal lymph nodes and any you come across in the subcutis."

If the tumor had spread, it was likely to have gone to the local lymph nodes first. I needed to have a gander at those both grossly and under the microscope.

"Oh, and can you grab me a section of skin?" I continued, pointing to the small bits left around the paws.

"Yes, ma'am."

"And a bit of muscle, bone marrow, and sciatic nerve, please."

He nodded before collecting the samples and dropping them in the formalin bucket for fixation.

I moved over to look through the organs with the students.

At the table with the thoracic organs, Mackenzie, Sarah, and Kassidy were chatting. Sarah still clutched the notes, and Kassidy was assisting. As the designated "cutter," Mackenzie had done an excellent job making her way through the heart and lungs of the pluck. I was once again impressed by her skill and interest.

I moved up next to her, palpating the lungs. "What did you find?"

She went into full nerd mode to describe the metastasis in the lungs. "There are a dozen white, firm masses scattered throughout the lung, ranging from three millimeters to one centimeter in size."

She pointed to the cut surface of one of the lung lobes. "On cut section, the masses are homogenous and firm."

"Excellent," I said, unable to hide my smile of pride. The force was strong with this one. "Anything in the heart?"

"No, ma'am."

I inspected the different parts of the pluck. She'd done an excellent dissection. It looked like she'd collected samples of everything for the formalin jar, too, which was awesome.

"Just to confirm, everything is sampled, right? Even the trachea and esophagus?"

"Yes, ma'am. I only took one section of each of the normal structures. For the heart, I took the T-piece, the right ventricle, and the left ventricle. I took several sections of the lung because of the masses."

I peeked into the formalin bin at her table. The samples were all of the right size, less than one centimeter wide, which would allow appropriate fixation in the formalin.

Damn, Mackenzie is better than some pathology residents!

"Excellent job," I said, flashing her an appreciative smile.

She blushed.

"What's he doing?" Sarah asked, slightly horrified, looking over at Dustin. The blood had fled her face.

I moved closer to her. I was pretty sure she wasn't a fainter, but one could never be too careful.

Dustin had removed the head. With the skin removed, it looked pretty gruesome, and I couldn't blame her for feeling queasy. Our job was not for those of the faint of heart.

"They've asked for the skull back, too. It's a good educational tool, especially when talking about adaptations of carnivores. It's a way to engage the public and a good lead-in to talk about conservation. He'll collect the claws, as well."

Sarah was still looking white as a sheet but nodded slightly after a visible gulp.

And please, no barfing, either. I silently crossed my fingers.

With the relevant parts removed, the whirring of the hoist and clack of the chain pulling tight around the tiger's leg filled the room. The carcass rose from the table, and Dustin operated the controls to follow it back into the cooler.

The claws sat in a small pile next to the pelt.

It was a bit unnerving, even for me.

I couldn't help but hope that Tora's contribution would help reach young minds and inspire people to protect tigers in the wild. It might even be the nudge that people needed to *not* buy illegal tiger parts, like pelts and claws.

With the carcass stored safely in the cooler, Dustin hosed the pelt down and draped it respectfully across the bandsaw table. He carefully rinsed the claws and set them to the side. It would take several hours to dry before he could pack them up. Otherwise, the items might mold while they waited for taxidermy.

I moved over to the other student group, where the abdominal organs were being dissected. Harper slowly worked her way through the organs, knife-in-hand. Emma stood over her shoulder, like an evil shadow. Tessa sat hunched on a stool with her hands in her pockets, watching with hooded eyes.

Though Emma was, by far, my least favorite student, Tessa's oppressive apathy was edging her into second place.

The organs sitting on the table were a mess and had been hacked to bits. The students clearly hadn't followed protocol.

"What did y'all find over here?" I was trying to be upbeat, but I couldn't hide the bit of annoyance in my voice.

Harper spoke up, looking slightly embarrassed. "There are spots in the liver." She pointed with her knife. "Everything else looks fine."

I made my way through the organs. The "spots" were actually metastases of the mammary tumor. I called Sarah over, and we worked on describing them for the report. The other organs looked normal grossly, despite being mangled.

"Please review *The Necropsy Book* over lunch," I prompted and then explained how the liver, kidneys, spleen, and GI tract *should* have been dissected.

Harper blushed, and Emma huffed. I strongly suspected that Harper knew the correct procedure, but Emma had misdirected her.

As for Tessa, she'd just checked out; who knew what she was thinking?

I peeked in the formalin bin with some trepidation. Sure enough, large chunks of tissue that would take forever to fix lay clumped on the bottom.

"The tissue-to-formalin ratio should be 1-to-10," I chided. "There's way too much tissue in here. It'll just rot, and nothing will fix."

I dug the tissues out of the formalin, the sharp, chemical scent making my eyes water and likely killing brain cells.

All in a day's work, I guess.

I rinsed the tissues off with water to reduce the fumes. "The sections should be about this size."

I selected a piece of liver and whittled it down to demonstrate the correct dimensions.

"That's what I said," Harper whispered to herself.

Emma, hearing her, fumed.

After getting all of the pieces shaved down, Harper and I plopped the smaller sections back in formalin.

I called everyone over for a huddle. "Okay, who wants to summarize the case for us?"

Mackenzie jumped in, walking through a spot-on description of the primary lesion as well as the metastases in the lung and liver.

"Excellent job." I looked up at the clock. "Let's clean up and then break for lunch. If you haven't turned in your report from the pancreatitis dog yesterday, please email that to me before the end of lunch. Let's meet back in the conference room at one. Depending on what we have this afternoon, we'll see who writes up this case."

The students went about cleaning up their respective tables. I couldn't help but notice that Emma was acting busy but wasn't actually doing anything.

I frowned, unable to hide my disappointment.

As the students stepped through the footbath to leave the floor, Queen Bee chimed in. "Such a shame to see such a gorgeous pelt wasted like that."

The door slammed behind her, and I glanced at Dustin in disbelief.

He was just shaking his head, going through the motions of tidying up.

"Need any help?" I offered. There was still the hydraulic table to clean.

"I got it, thanks."

"I know the pelt has gotta dry, but we may want to bag it up sooner rather than later." I nodded to the door the students had just passed through. "Not sure I want them back out here with it if we get anything else in this afternoon."

He gave me a nod and shifted the hose to wash the last of the blood away.

CHAPTER

FIVE

I collapsed into my office chair, feeling a bit huffy and antsy.

The tiger necropsy had been relatively cut-and-dried. I hadn't seen anyone taking selfies with Tora—thank goodness. And even though Emma was a raging brat, the rest of the students were well-behaved. I couldn't put my finger on why I was feeling so unsettled.

My fingers twirled, tapping my pen on my desk.

Resigned, I dropped my pen and booted my computer up. I had just enough time to knock out the report for the Tora case before heading to lunch.

I didn't think the folks at Tiawah would be waiting for the results with bated breath. But getting the case out would be a distraction. Plus, it always felt good crossing something off my list.

After hitting the release button, I was still feeling a bit down.

Between Gerald and Emma, all of my "nice" was just about tapped out for the day. I thought about hiding in my office for lunch but decided to head to the breakroom. Some of my coworkers were cool, and they might share enough positive vibes to help me make it through the rest of the day.

In the breakroom, Anna and Carol were already camped at a table, and I grabbed a seat with them. It was nice to see Carol back, and not just because of the box of treats in front of her. I hadn't realized how much her absence yesterday had thrown me.

"Welcome back, Carol. Did you have a nice weekend?" I asked as I set my lunch and reusable water bottle down.

The happy wrinkles around Carol's eyes creased as she smiled. "Yes, ma'am. I had a lovely weekend. Thank you kindly for asking."

Pushing a plastic container toward me, she said, "Would you like some brownies? I made some for the grandkids and had leftovers."

Sure, ya did, I thought with a smile, knowing that she'd deliberately made extras to feed everyone in the lab.

She popped the lid open, and the delicious smell of rich dark chocolate wafted out. Saliva filled my mouth, making me feel like one of Pavlov's dogs.

With that smell, I had no choice; I had to partake. I selected a small one and set it on a napkin next to my lunchbox.

"Thank you, Carol," I said. "They smell amazing."

She nudged it closer. "Have another."

How could I resist?

Anna flashed me a knowing smile.

Just as I placed a second one on my napkin, Dustin and Zoe joined us, Dustin trailing an extra chair.

"Oh, brownies!" Zoe said with excitement.

Carol shifted the box over. "Take as many as you want."

Dustin and Zoe helped themselves.

"We missed you yesterday, Carol," Zoe said cheerfully. "We had a heated debate about okra. It wasn't the same without you."

Carol grimaced.

"That's not fair!" I declared. "We all know Carol dislikes anything green, whether it's okra or not!"

"Just sayin'. One more tick in the 'nope' column for okra," Zoe said with a self-satisfied smile, raising one of her eyebrows.

"These brownies are so much better than okra," Anna said, reaching over to select another one.

"Mhm," Dustin hummed in agreement.

"I can't argue with that," I conceded. "Thanks for bringing them in. They're delicious."

The brownies *were* amazing. The rich dark chocolate exploded across my taste buds. There was a hidden swirl of raspberry jam that added just the right amount of tartness. They were also the right amount of chewy that made a brownie a brownie and not chocolate cake.

I might just eat five more of these and skip the salad I brought altogether.

It was just one of those days.

Sensing the vibe, Anna asked, "How was the tiger this morning?"

"You had a tiger?! Jelly!" Zoe said, licking the chocolate off her fingers. "I had a lion when I was a resident, but I've never done a tiger before."

"Same here," I said. "It was a first for me. I'm usually not one for exotic species. But there's just something about the large carnivores."

"Did you let the students join you?" Zoe asked.

I nodded, mouth full of my second brownie.

"What a cool experience for them," she said.

"Honestly, I was a bit worried about having them out there, especially with some of the personalities that we have on rotation this week. But Tora's death wasn't a surprise, and Tiawah had already shared it on social media. I didn't have a good reason to keep them off the floor."

"They could've posted something stupid on TikTok or, like, taken pictures with the tiger or something," Anna mused. "I know they're vet students and all, but they can still make stupid choices."

"Hopefully, I made it clear that no phones were allowed before we went out. I didn't see anyone take any pictures. Did you?" I arched an eyebrow at Dustin.

"No, ma'am. Everyone was respectful," Dustin answered. After a beat, he added, "Except for the Queen Bee. She's somethin'." He whistled in disbelief and shook his head slightly.

I shrugged.

"She's a bit of a..." I caught myself before I cussed in front of Carol, "...twerp," I finished. "Could be worse, I guess."

Dustin looked unconvinced but nodded with a slight frown. "Yeah. Could be worse."

"Is she really that awful?" Zoe asked with doubt in her voice.

Zoe always thought the best of people—a fact that repeatedly surprised me. After all that she'd been through, I was shocked she wasn't more jaded. Being a transgender woman who had very striking masculine features, she got endless heaps of shit for embracing her true self, especially in Oklahoma. Despite the side-eyes, rude comments, and even one instance of battery, she still had a big heart and was eternally optimistic.

I struggled to find the right words and ended up saying, "She's just the typical privileged brat. She talks a lot of crap but doesn't actually do anything evil."

Dustin raised his eyebrows skeptically and pressed his lips together.

"What?" I asked, seeing his face.

"I'd keep an eye on her if I were you. She's shady."

"Really think so?"

He nodded.

I trusted Dustin, but I wasn't sure about his assessment. I'd been around my fair share of shady people, and Emma didn't fit the bill. She just thought she was better than everyone else. Sure, people like that could do damage in their holier-than-thou way. But shady? No, I didn't think so.

I shrugged noncommittally.

A loud cough sounded behind me, and I practically jumped out of my chair. Everyone around the table looked up.

Gerald towered over us.

"The tiger pelt is lying out in the open on the necropsy floor," he chided. "That's worth quite a bit of money. It's extremely unwise to keep it out where anyone can see it. You should be more careful."

We stared at him, trying to process all of the words tumbling out of his mouth.

His gaze skated around the table, as if looking for the sense of shame that he'd hoped to impart.

Coming up empty, he pressed on. "It's negligence to leave it out."

Sick of his shit, I sucked my teeth.

Wrong choice.

His icy glare shifted to me. "Did you grow up poor? Is that why you don't understand the value of things?"

The entire table was deathly silent.

My chest went tight with rage.

This fucker always knew where to poke. And he'd done it twice today. I wondered if he had sensed how tired and grumpy I was this morning and was coming back for more when I wasn't at my best.

Carol shifted uncomfortably and cleared her throat, pulling her brownies closer to her.

My mind raced, trying to figure out how to respond without stooping to his level.

Dustin saved me.

"As always, Dr. Richter, your concern is noted," he said, acting nonchalant, his face neutral. The small creases of tension around his eyes were the only tell that he was mad as hell. "The pelt needs to dry out before we bag it," Dustin continued. "Otherwise, it'll mold."

"What do you know about handling precious items like that?" Gerald snarked. "You lack formal veterinary training. Do you even have a high school diploma?"

Dustin lowered his sandwich and leaned back, muscles stiff.

The women around the table traded a glance. It was unlike Gerald to attack men, and we were all a little shocked.

I was also worried that Dustin would jump up and deck him.

Instead, Dustin didn't say a word. He simply sat there, strong hands resting firmly on the table in front of him.

It was a full-on, silent showdown, and tension built around the table.

"Oh, Gerald, what do you know?" Zoe laughed uncomfortably. "Dustin is an expert huntsman. He'll make sure everything is taken care of proper-like." She waved her hand dismissively.

Gerald tensed. "Y'all better hope he does. The last thing this lab needs is to be responsible for destroying a valuable object that belongs to one of our most treasured clients."

"I'm sure it'll be fine," Carol said in her grandmotherly voice. "Dustin's been doin' this for as long as I can remember. He's the only one who's been here almost as long as I have. He knows what he's doing."

Sensing a dead end, Gerald switched tacks. "If the pelt is going to be so expertly prepared, then it's at risk of being stolen. Items like that are highly valued on the black market."

Zoe snorted a small laugh. "How would you know?"

"Do people really do that? Sell pelts on the black market? How would you even do that in a place like Stillwater?" Anna asked, slightly aghast, her eyes wide.

Anna was a keeper, so I didn't judge her naiveté.

Gerald, sorely deficient in self-control, scoffed. "Are you serious? *Of course,* people sell illegal items on the black market. I'm sure someone like Dustin, with his record, would know the exact people to contact."

I felt the color drain from my face and glanced at Dustin. My mind was whirling with what Gerald had said.

Dustin had a record? Like a criminal record? Or... like what?

I had no clue what Gerald was alluding to.

Dustin was utterly still, his eyes locked on Gerald and shoulders tense with fury.

Gerald squirmed under his stare and turned to a softer target: me.

"It'll be your fault, Pocahontas, if something happens, especially since you know exactly *who* works here," he hissed, waving a hand at Dustin. "It would be wise to be more diligent and responsible. Consider yourself warned."

He must've intended that as a mic drop because he abruptly turned and flounced off.

What the hell?

"Why does he do that?" I asked in a hushed voice.

Dustin sighed heavily, face stony. "Who knows."

"He comes at people like a honey badger," Zoe said, shaking her head angrily. "Running around, snapping at everyone."

"More like a scrawny rooster strutting around, pecking people," I snarked.

Carol squeaked a laugh, and just like that, the tension broke.

"Don't take none of that personal, Dustin," Carol said, reaching over to squeeze his arm. Turning to me, she added, "And you don't listen to him, neither. I've been here for ages, and people like that don't last long. Y'all just stand together, and this, too, shall pass."

***

A knock sounded on my office door as I was putting my lunch containers away. It was way too polite to be Gerald, but I still reflexively flinched.

"Come in," I called out.

Harper peered around the door. Her eyebrows were pressed together in worry over dark, shaded eyes. Now that she was in her regular clothes, I realized how thin she was.

"Dr. Harjo?" she said hesitantly. "Do you have a second?"

I couldn't help but feel my heart sink. I could tell by her face that she wasn't here for anything good. I didn't have the energy for any more drama today.

"Sure, come on in," I said anyway.

I gestured to the seat across from my desk.

I kept my office pretty tidy, and she slipped right into the guest chair after dropping her backpack at her feet.

She still seemed uncomfortable, with her legs pressed tightly together and her hands tucked under them. I could see her chewing on the inside of her cheek.

"What's up?" I asked, leaning forward and trying to keep my body posture relaxed and welcoming. I normally liked helping students, but I was sure my face had a dash of RBF today. I didn't want her to think my grumpiness had anything to do with her.

After a beat, she quietly said, "I'm worried about Tessa."

I tried to hide my surprise.

It wasn't often that students came to me concerned about one of their peers. Veterinary students were usually pretty tight and supported each other. This was new territory for me.

Tessa, in her disheveled apathy, was already on my radar. I'd had an eye on her since I'd first met her. But in more of an

I-might-have-to-fail-this-student way versus actual concern for her welfare.

Shame on me.

Flailing a bit, I said, "I've noticed she looks tired. Is something going on at home?"

Harper's shoulders relaxed just a tad, but her hands stayed firmly tucked in. "She doesn't want to talk about it. But I know she got kicked out of her apartment because she couldn't pay rent."

"Oh, no," I said, feeling a crushing empathy.

Couldn't pay rent? Damn.

Vet school was extremely expensive. Most students started vet school already shackled with debt from their bachelor's degree. Though most loan repayments could be deferred when they were in vet school, the interest on those loans kept ticking up. And more time in school just meant more loans. I knew some students who graduated with over half a million dollars in debt. There was no realistic way they could make that back, especially on a general practitioner's salary in Oklahoma.

The rich snobs would say, "Just get a job." All that did was show their utter lack of understanding of what veterinary school required.

And complete lack of empathy.

Between in-class and study time, it was virtually impossible to hold down a job when in veterinary school. Some students could pad the bank ever-so-slightly over the summer. But it was never enough to make it through vet school debt-free. Unless you had a rich benefactor, a vet student was graduating with both a DVM and a huge IOU.

Harper coughed lightly, drawing me out of my thoughts. "I offered for her to come stay with me. She said she was fine." Harper hunched her shoulders a bit and continued, "I think she might be sleeping in her car. I just...I just don't know how to help her, and I don't want her to fail. And...."

Gentle tears started.

I scooted my chair around the desk and gave her a half hug. "Thank you for looking out for her. She's lucky to have a friend like you."

She finally released a hand from beneath her legs and held mine. "I'm just worried she's going to do something stupid. She owes a lot of money, and we've got another year before we graduate. I think all her loan money for this semester is already gone to pay her tuition."

I squeezed her hand.

"Is she a suicide risk?" I asked, a sinkhole opening in my chest.

It was a legitimate question. Veterinarians had one of the highest suicide rates of all of the professions, sharing a place in the top four with police officers, medical doctors, and dentists. The crippling debt was one contributing factor. Another was downright nasty owners.

Tessa's lack of self-care was a big red flag. Her persistent apathy was another. I needed to know how serious this was.

I'd lost a former veterinary student, Nathan, to suicide three years prior, and I still felt the weight of that. He'd always seemed happy and been a ray of sunshine. He was good at hiding his agony. When they found him dead, we were all shocked. To this day, I still brooded on which small clues or what opportunities to help him I may have missed.

No way in hell am I going to lose one more person to suicide.

"I don't know," Harper answered. "But I'm worried. Something is really, really wrong. I don't know how to help her."

"Do you think she might be willing to talk to me? Or should I talk to Admin?" I asked.

Harper tensed. "Please don't go to Admin. They don't care about us. They just want our money."

I was surprised at her bluntness, but I couldn't disagree.

I gave her hand another squeeze. "Okay, no Admin. I'll pull her aside this afternoon and see what I can do."

I was tired and grumpy today, but I absolutely had to make space to address this. I certainly didn't want Tessa sleeping in her car. More importantly, I didn't want her to think suicide was the best way to manage what she was dealing with.

"Thank you, Dr. Harjo."

We hugged again before she grabbed her backpack and left with a shy wave.

Damn. Today had been heavy. And it wasn't even over yet.

CHAPTER

SIX

After lunch, I made a quick stop at the necropsy floor to see what the afternoon would hold, and a stiff horse was waiting on the table.

Hopefully, it isn't anything too wild.

I had enough on my plate today, and the caffeine had completely worn off. I allowed myself a moment to wallow in my grumpiness.

Taking the submission form with a sigh, I went to the conference room.

The students were arranged around the table in a repeat of this morning, as if they'd followed a seating chart. Four of them were chatting casually with a few laughs. Emma was busy with her makeup.

Because, I mean, who doesn't freshen up before digging into a dead animal?

The huff of laughter in my head was cut off when I caught sight of Tessa.

My stomach clenched.

She was hunched off to the side, biting her nails, the hood of her sweatshirt hiding her face. She looked like a homeless drug addict. After what Harper had shared with me this morning, at least one of those no-so-nice labels was probably true.

Suicide risk, a dark voice whispered in my head.

Echoes of regret from my inability to help Nathan pricked my heart.

I needed to catch Tessa *today.* See if there was anything I could do to help. Make sure she knew she wasn't alone.

I must have been standing there, looking stupid, because the conversation had died down, and the students were staring at me expectantly.

I pulled myself up by the bootstraps and plastered on a canned smile. The tension in the skin around my eyes reminded me how fake it was.

"Good afternoon," I said, grabbing a seat. "Have a good lunch?"

There were a few nods around the table.

With the nudging this morning, I'd received necropsy reports for the dog from everyone but Tessa. I thought about nagging her. But with the black cloud looming, I decided there was a bigger elephant in the room that needed to be addressed first.

And in private.

I directed my next comment to the group at large. "Thank you for turning in your reports. I'll provide feedback by end-of-day today. For the rest of the rotation, we'll pick a lead for each case, and the lead will write it up. We'll rotate through everyone. Who wants to write up the tiger from the morning?"

Mackenzie's hand shot up.

"Great. Thanks, Mackenzie. You're on the tiger." I flashed her a smile of gratitude for volunteering. I was grateful I didn't have to pull any teeth over that one. "We have a horse this afternoon. Who would like to lead the case and write that one up?"

The students glanced at each other.

"I'll do it," Harper said.

Harper seemed ever-so-slightly interested. It wasn't too surprising given her plan to go into equine medicine. But just because someone liked treating a species didn't mean they liked cutting them up. I appreciated her stepping up to the plate.

"Great, thank you. Who wants to scribe?"

Sarah's hand shot up.

"You've scribed the last two cases. Let's give someone else a shot."

I looked around the table. Emma sat with her arms crossed, emphatically resisting anything that might remotely look like an offer to help. Tessa remained completely tuned out.

"I'll scribe," Kassidy offered.

"Thanks." I passed her the submission form. "Want to read it for us?"

She grabbed the paperwork and quickly scanned it. "The patient is a six-year-old, male quarter horse. And then, it just says, 'colicking before died.'"

"That's it?" Harper asked. "Is there any information on if there were any gut sounds? Or if there was reflux? Did they try mineral oil?"

Kassidy scanned the form yet again as if willing more words to appear.

"Nope. Nothing else," she replied. "Just 'colicking before died.'"

"Geez," Harper said, eyebrows creased. "I wonder if they even had a chance to work it up. Who submitted the case? The vet or the owner?"

"Um," Kassidy stalled. "Looks like the veterinarian submitted it."

I chimed in, "Unfortunately, it's pretty common to get sparse histories. I know it gets super busy in-clinic, and everyone is always crunched for time, but it's really important to take a sec to provide a complete history to specialists, pathologists included. It helps us put the pieces together and start building a list of differentials."

Emma made a *pfft* sound.

"The vet I used to work for said that he didn't give pathologists any history because it would bias them," she said smugly.

An abrupt belly laugh escaped before I could stop myself. "If you had your druthers, wouldn't you prefer to have a clinical history before you treated a patient or performed surgery?"

It was a leading question, and several heads obediently nodded around the table. Emma blushed slightly.

Maybe I should have felt guilty for embarrassing her, but I didn't.

"Sure, there'll be times when you have to make a best guess, like in shelter medicine or with some emergencies," I continued. "But if you can get a history, it's just one more piece to help solve the puzzle. It's the same thing for pathologists."

"So, that whole 'it'll bias you' thing is just a myth?" Mackenzie asked, braving Emma's wrath.

"Do you let histories bias you in the exam room?" Another rhetorical question that was met with shaking heads.

I was standing strong on my soapbox, and they were just begging for more proselytizing.

"Sure, I take what's on the form into account," I pressed on. "But I always try to go in with an open mind. If someone sends me a mass that they think is a lipoma, and I see a mast cell tumor, I'm not going to ignore the fact that I see a mast cell tumor. If anything, because I have that history, I can add something in my report about why my findings are different from what was expected."

Their eyes hadn't glazed over yet, so I plowed forward. "The necropsy procedure is the same, no matter what, but the samples I collect or tests I run might change based on the clinical history. Plus, if the vet has a differential that I've ruled out, I like to address that in my report. Ruling things out is just as important as finding the right answer."

I paused to let the words settle. Most of the students seemed to be noodling over what I'd said.

Sarah spoke up. "Aren't there times when you can give too much info, though? I worked in the radiology clinic last summer, and some vets would send the entire patient record to the radiologists. That seemed like a little much."

I shuddered. "Yes. That's definitely too much. A lot of specialists don't have the time to dig through twenty pages of vaccination records, annual exams, or whatever. I wouldn't send the entire record unless a specialist specifically asks for it."

"So, what should we include, then?" Kassidy asked.

I glanced at the clock. This was an important topic, but I didn't want to be here until midnight, either.

"At a minimum, I'd like to see a list of the clinical signs, duration, if there was any response to treatment, and what the vet's differentials are. But some cases need to be teased out more. I had a case just a month ago; this guy brought in a dead horse, and it wasn't until I questioned him that I learned that several horses had also died. He didn't think of including that on the form."

Harper's eyebrows shot up. "That's *kinda* important," she said.

I nodded.

Kassidy ran her finger along the form, making sure she hadn't missed anything. "Oh! It looks like this horse was insured."

"Good catch. Anyone know what we need to do differently for insured animals?"

"Record and take pictures of any markings?" Harper offered.

She's going to be a great equine vet. I smiled inwardly. I loved seeing students grow into their roles—find that perfect career that slipped on like a pair of comfy shoes.

"Yep. We'll look for lip tattoos, markings on the head and limbs, any brands, that kinda thing."

I looked up at the clock again. We needed to get a move on.

Turning back to the group, I asked, "Given the limited history of colic, what are your differentials?"

"Obstruction, torsion, displacement. Likely GI-something," Harper answered, fast as lightning.

"Yep. That's what I'm betting."

Emma snorted.

"Have something to add?" I asked her.

"Nope," she replied bluntly, sneering.

She was actually sneering. Like full-on *Mean Girls* sneering.

Boy, she's something else.

I filled the tense silence. "Nine times out of ten, a colicky horse will have gastrointestinal disease. If you hear hoofbeats, think of horses, not zebras. But we can't completely rule out disease in another organ system until we get in there. We'll just have to see what we find. Once we get it open, we'll want to take a good look at everything before we pull stuff out. Any questions before we go?"

A few students shook their heads.

I rapped my knuckles on the table. "All right, then. Let's meet out on the floor in about fifteen minutes."

***

The students were right behind me when we stepped out onto the floor in our coveralls. "Lost Highway" was warbling from the speakers.

"Is it possible to turn this awful music off?" Emma asked, hands held dramatically over her ears.

Despite her bitchy tone, Dustin obliged, his lips pressed firm.

He's such a nice guy, I thought. I probably would've ignored her or told her to suck it up.

Could Hank Williams 24/7 get annoying? *Yes*. Was the music obnoxiously loud? *No*. It made Dustin's time at work more enjoyable, so we all just rolled with it because we absolutely adored him.

Apparently, Emma didn't have the good grace to do the same thing.

I caught his eye and sent him a questioning look. He shook his head slightly.

I'm not sure if I would've acquiesced to Emma's demand. But with the shake of his head, I figured he'd rather turn the music off than fight a petty squabble with a spoiled snit.

Clenching my teeth, I moved over to the horse and waited for everyone to gather around the table.

Dustin had already wet everything down. A hose was positioned on the floor below the opening of the lip in the table, ready to wash away any split blood.

"Let's get started with the visual inspection," I instructed.

The students moved around the horse to complete the external exam.

"Don't forget to check the mouth," I advised.

Sarah stepped forward and peeked in.

"Any lip tattoos?" I asked.

She shook her head.

"There's a brand." Mackenzie pointed to the right rump.

"It also has a white blaze on the forehead and white up to the left fetlock," Harper noted before turning to Kassidy. "Can you write that down?"

Kassidy scratched down some notes.

Dustin had the Polaroid camera in hand and started snapping off shots of the identifying marks for insurance.

With the external exam completed, I nudged the students to get started. "Harper, since you're writing it up, you get to cut. Grab a knife."

She picked up a student knife and hesitated. Mackenzie moved in to help, offering encouragement and advice. I stepped back, keeping an eye out but letting them teach each other. Dustin did the same, moving the hose around to get better coverage.

Even with Mackenzie's help, it took Harper about twenty minutes to reflect the right front and back leg. Another fifteen minutes later, the skin was removed, the subcutis glistening under the bright lamps.

I cringed when Harper used a stabbing motion to cut through the abdominal muscle. A resulting *fzzzzzz* echoed through the room, followed by the smell of partially digested feed.

Harper's face turned bright red as she stepped back.

"Don't worry about it," I said, trying to reassure her. "It's not surgery. Just remember where you nicked it so we can make sure it doesn't spill out into the abdomen later."

"Yeah, but how can we tell the difference between where I cut it and a true rupture?" she asked, worried.

"A pre-mortem rupture will be red around the edges." I waved my hand in the direction of the fizzing hole. "With this, there won't be any color change. It'll be fine. Just a bit messy."

Harper finished reflecting the abdominal muscle. With the abdominal cavity opened, she stabbed the diaphragm, and a second rush of air sounded through the room. This was a sound we wanted to hear; the negative pressure in the thoracic cavity meant it had been intact.

Harper and Mackenzie worked in tandem, using the loppers to chomp through the rib cage.

"This is a workout," Mackenzie said with a slight laugh, sweat beading on her forehead.

To my immense surprise, Sarah stepped forward.

"Here, I'll help," she offered.

She even had color in her cheeks this afternoon. Maybe getting her out from behind the paperwork had been a good call.

Together, and with significant effort, the trio removed the right thoracic wall.

Emma sat back, content to let others do all of the work.

Harper swiped her arm across her forehead.

"Okay, let's stop for a sec and have a look," I advised. "What do you see?"

Mackenzie stepped forward and ran her gloved hands over the large intestine. She gently pressed on the cecum, looking at the left dorsal and ventral colon tucked beneath.

"Looks normal," Emma said from the back.

Mackenzie rubbed some fine, light tan strands off the surface of the cecum. "There's fibrin. That's not normal. But everything is in the right place so far."

Emma glared at her.

"What's the morphologic diagnosis for that?" I asked, pointing to the fibrin strands.

The students shifted and avoided my gaze, even Mackenzie.

"Mild, moderate, or severe?"

"Mild," Harper said.

I nodded and asked, "Distribution?"

"Locally extensive," Mackenzie added. "Right? It's concentrated around the intestine but not on the liver that I can see."

"Works for me. I could go with 'diffuse,' too." I shrugged. It was splitting hairs at this point. "And what's the chronicity?"

"Acute?" Mackenzie offered.

"Yep, now turn that into a morph," I nudged.

"Mild, locally extensive, acute fibrinous peritonitis?" Mackenzie guessed.

"Perfect!" I flashed a smile. "Now that we've confirmed that everything is in the right place, let's pull the GI tract out slowly and look for the cause of the inflammation. Watch the nick. There's nothing worse than GI contents spilling into your boots."

Well, maybe finding dried blood on your elbow on a first date with a phenomenal person was worse...but I wasn't going there.

Mackenzie stepped back to let Harper take the lead. I could still tell that she was eager to get in there but was deferring to Harper. She had that natural curiosity that was gonna make her a bomb-ass pathologist one day. For the fifty millionth time, I made a mental note that I needed to have a chat with her and see if I could turn her to the dark side.

After Tessa.

I needed to deal with that first.

I snuck a glance at her. She was standing at the back of the group, sweatshirt pulled down over her gloved hands. Deep bags shadowed her eyes. She looked like she was carrying one hell of a load.

As I noodled over the best way to approach her, Harper called out, "We found it!"

My attention shifted back to the horse, and I moved between the students to have a look.

The cecum and colon had been pulled out onto the table. With these larger structures removed, we could now thoroughly examine the small intestines that had been hidden below. A large section was bright red to purple with clear lines of demarcation between the affected and unaffected areas.

"Looks like a torsion," Mackenzie said, leaning in. Unable to help herself, she followed the mesenteric attachments down into the sea of bowel loops. "I feel it! There's a knot down here."

She left her hand in and moved to the side so that her classmates could find and palpate the twisted segment.

Harper and Sarah stepped forward for a go at it. Even Kassidy put the paperwork down for a feel. Emma stood firm, hip cocked and arms crossed, defiant to the end. Tessa, as usual, was completely tuned out.

Not wanting to bother fighting either of them, I said, "Okay. Let's get all of this out."

The urgency to meet with Tessa today was gnawing at me. I didn't want to be mucking around in horse guts as the students piddled around for three hours.

Harper did a fairly good job of getting the guts out. Her cuts were surprisingly precise and confident. She quickly cut the mesenteric attachments, and the intestines were pulled from the waist-high table and onto the floor with a *splat*.

She'd make a good surgeon.

Dustin helped the students pull the GI tract away from the table where it could be dissected on the floor. With the horse taking up the bulk of the table, it was easier to spread the seventy-plus feet of intestines on the ground to get a good look at everything.

Harper continued removing organs and parsed them out to her peers. Then, she took point on the GI tract, leaning over the endless loops of bowel spread out on the floor. She quickly found the small ball of fat that had caused all of the trouble.

"Here it is," she called out. "There's a strangulating lipoma in the mesentery."

Sure enough, when unwound, a wedge shape of discolored mesentery formed a blazing arrow to the lump of fat that dangled on a thin stalk.

I called the rest of the students over to see.

"What's your morphologic diagnosis?" I asked.

Harper stood from her crouched position as the wheels turned.

"Pedunculated lipoma," she offered.

"Yeah, that's the mass, though. How can you put it all together with the intestine?"

"Um...strangulating lipoma with segmental intestinal congestion?" I could tell she wasn't sure.

"Close enough. I'd probably add 'necrosis' in there somewhere. With all of the fibrin in the abdomen and the purple tinge to the tissue, I'm thinking this segment had started to die before the horse did."

Harper nodded.

"Does anybody know why it looks dark red and is well-demarcated?" I asked.

Once again, I was met with blank stares.

I gestured down to the fatty mass. "The gut twists around the lipoma. The pressure is enough to collapse the thin-walled veins, but not enough to collapse the arteries. So, blood pumps in but can't get out. That's why it looks dark red."

I pointed to the wedge shape of red in the mesentery. "The triangular shape here reflects the blood supply to the segment that was affected." I pointed to the discolored intestinal segment. "And here, this piece is starting to die. That triggered a whole cascade effect, including the fibrinous peritonitis."

There were a few slow nods.

Mackenzie pointed to the lesion with her knife. "That's cool how sharp that line is."

I smiled inwardly. *Yep, pathology is in her blood.*

"We've got our answer, but we're not done yet. Let's get the rest of the organs finished and get cracking on cleaning up."

The students hustled back to their respective duties.

Tessa had been working on the liver. I wandered over to give it a once over.

"What did you find?" I asked, trying to sound cheerful.

"Nothing. Looks normal," she said. Her tone was curt but not entirely rude.

"Did you get a piece for the formalin bucket?"

She nodded.

"Cool beans, thanks. I'll help you clean up."

I carried the liver to the offal bin and then returned to help her scrub down the table. She went through the motions, but I could tell that both her mind and her heart were not in it. It wasn't the same detachment Emma had. It was more like she was on auto-pilot and her mind was entirely somewhere else.

"You doing okay?"

She nodded ever so slightly, but she kept her head turned down, focused on slowly washing the blood off the table.

"Do you want to talk about it?"

She shook her head.

Arg, I shouldn't have phrased it that way.

Worried that I had somehow closed the door to discussions, I nudged ever so slightly. "Harper is worried about you. I am, too."

"I'm fine," Tessa said, sounding *far* from fine.

"After we clean up, come by my office. Okay?"

She stiffened.

I kicked myself.

I was totally messing this up. Now, I'd made it sound like she was in trouble and had to report in.

I quickly added, "I just want to see if there is something I can do to help."

"I'm fine," she said again, firmly this time, still not making eye contact.

"Okay. I hear you." I paused but kept my hands busy cleaning. "I'd still like to talk to you. You're not in trouble or anything. I just want to check in."

Was I being too pushy? Yes, I probably was. Damn it.

"Yes, ma'am," she said noncommittally.

At a loss for words, all I could think of to say was, "Thank you" before I fled like a coward.

I'd royally screwed the pooch during that conversation. I'd made a promise to myself to not bumble my way through it when she came by my office later. I wanted to help her, not come off as a nanny.

With the room pretty much tidied up, I brought the students together for one last huddle.

"I think we're all cleaned up?" I asked the group, taking quick stock of the tables.

Everything looked fairly neat and tidy.

Sarah pointed across the room and said, "The tiger pelt is still out."

"That pelt is *so* gorgeous," Emma said admiringly.

"Dustin will put it up before he leaves tonight. I was talking more about the horse."

"Where do you even store something like that?" Emma asked.

"Huh?" I responded, not following her line of thinking.

"The tiger pelt. Where do you even keep something like that so it doesn't get ruined?"

That's an odd question.

"Um. We'll keep it in the cooler until the sanctuary comes and picks it up." I fumbled through the answer.

"Won't that make it smell?" Emma asked.

"Is that safe? There's no lock on the cooler, right?" Mackenzie added.

It'll be your fault, Pocahontas, if something happens, Gerald's voice echoed in my head.

I felt like I was in front of a firing squad.

Uncomfortable with the direction of the conversation, I said, "The taxidermy chemicals will crush any lingering dead animal smell. And the lab is locked up. It'll be fine. Plus, not many people know the parts are even here."

"Except us," Kassidy chimed in, her cheery tone discordant.

I saw Dustin's eyebrows go up from the other side of the group, and I felt a tingle of worry.

"Everything will be fine," I tried to reassure everyone.

Wanting to get as far away from this topic as possible, I said, "Don't forget: Mackenzie, you're writing up the tiger, and, Harper, you're writing up the horse. Please email your reports to me before we start tomorrow." I gestured to the students who had skated today. "The rest of you will be writing up the next few cases that come in."

I looked up at the clock. It was a few minutes past 4 P.M.

"You're excused for the day. Enjoy your evening."

I tried and failed to catch Tessa's eye.

I was getting increasingly concerned about her and didn't want her to skedaddle without checking in. She avoided eye contact and followed the pack through the footbaths to get changed.

"You good out here?" I quickly checked in with Dustin.

"Yes, ma'am. Just gonna put the pelt away and shut things down for the day."

"Thanks. I gotta go catch Tessa before she leaves. I'm worried about her."

"Me, too," he confided. "She's been off since the start of the rotation. That's more than a rough weekend of partying that she's carrying on her shoulders. You go on. I can handle everything out here."

CHAPTER

SEVEN

After dressing in my civvies, I rushed to the conference room to catch Tessa. All of the students were busy packing up and chatting.

Except for Tessa. She wasn't there.

My heart sank.

"Is Tessa still changing?" I asked.

The students looked around at each other, and Kassidy shrugged. "I haven't seen her."

Harper moved to the back of the room, pushing chairs in. "Her backpack is gone. She must've left." Her face was etched with worry.

"Good thing, too," Emma sniped. "That woman needs a spa day. She looks awful."

Emma pulled her backpack on and then used the first two fingers on each hand to fold the yellow waves of her hair artfully around her face.

"I'm leaving. Bye, y'all," Emma said with a flitter of her fingers. She slid past me through the door.

Not wanting to draw too much attention to Tessa's plight, I thanked the group and headed to the locker rooms. We had two all-gender bathrooms that sat side-by-side. Each room had a set of eight lockers along the wall, a sink, and a shower.

Both of them were empty.

I'd somehow missed her.

I went back to my office and slumped in my chair. I picked up my pen and started tapping it on my desk. I held a modicum of hope that maybe, just *maybe*, she'd come by my office.

The worry was still chafing at me.

Had Tessa even changed out of her coveralls before she'd sped out of the lab? Surely, she'd know better than to leave without changing. It was a big no-no to wear gear off the floor and out into the real world; she'd be a walking fomite. Thankfully, the tiger and the horse probably weren't carrying anything super scary.

But still.

She'd have to be pretty flustered or out of it to leave in bloodied coveralls.

I sighed, pen twirling through my fingers.

When I started chewing on my cheek, I realized that I was in a full-blown anxiety loop. I took a few deep breaths, trying to identify the root of my angst.

It wasn't the fact that Tessa had worn her dirty coveralls out of the lab. It wasn't even that she ghosted me. I didn't know what it was.

Tap, tap, tap. My pen bobbed.

I went back to the beginning.

Tessa had started the week looking a bit rough and ready. Somehow, she looked even worse today. Something was eating at her, and I was afraid it was going to devour her. Like a dragon.

Or like a tiger.

I dug deeper into that line of thought.

I'd initially blown Tessa off and even toyed with the thought of failing her. Harper's concern had flipped that on its head. Ever since she'd come to me, I had, rightly or wrongly, assumed a personal responsibility for Tessa's welfare.

I'd lost one former student to suicide, and it still ate at me, hanging like a permanent shroud of guilt and despair.

As a vet student, Nathan had worked part-time for us on the floor for three years, serving in Dustin's stead on the weekends, after hours, and when Dustin took time off. I'd loved working with him; he'd been a natural on the necropsy floor. I'd tried to convince him to do a pathology residency, but he was dead-set on going into general practice.

After graduation, Nathan moved back to his hometown and joined a small practice outside Tulsa. I'd get the occasional email and send one back, checking in on him. I'd never given up hope that I could loop him back into pathology someday. From the outside, he seemed like a happy person with a great job.

But who truly knew what was happening on the inside?

A year went by, and the emails petered out. That was kinda how it was. Most students fade after graduation. I might see their name on a submission form. Or, they might pop back up as a resident in the vet school. But most of them just went their own way.

I didn't think anything of it until I saw the obituary.

At the age of twenty-eight, he'd killed himself.

The hardest part about the whole situation was that he'd never shown even a hint of the depression he was feeling. He'd always been bright and cheery. If you'd asked me back then, I never would have thought in a million years he'd commit suicide.

See, that's the thing.

A lot of people struggle but still put on a game face for everyone else. They have a veneer of cheer and are good at keeping those meticulously crafted masks from cracking around people who know them well.

I never figured out why he'd done it, and there was no way in hell I was gonna ask his family or friends. And, at the end of it all, the "why" didn't matter. He was still gone.

I knew suicide was common among veterinarians. But the whole thing hadn't become *real* until Nathan.

Maybe that's why the present situation was messing with my head.

I couldn't let the same thing happen to Tessa.

Agitated and unsure of what to do next, I decided I needed to pick Zoe's brain.

In addition to her day job, Zoe served as an advisor at the vet school. Because she was so awesome, students from all walks of life came to her to ask for advice, not just those who were assigned to her. At least once a week, there'd be a student in her office. She'd helped several students through rough spots in the past and might have ideas on how I could help Tessa.

I knocked on her door and entered after she called out, "Come in." Seeing me, she beamed. "Hey, Josie. What's up?"

Zoe's office had that perfect balance of order and flare. Everything was obsessively organized. Her desk was clear except for a tidy stack of cardboard flats filled with microscope slides. Behind her, medical books were arranged by subject on a small shelf. Everything else was tucked away in file cabinets and drawers. Her degrees were framed and hung on the far wall.

The meticulous placement of her work items was balanced by splashes of color from pictures of family and friends, a pride flag, and healthy plants spilling out of handmade, colorful pottery. Because she was a hardcore fan, there were also anime magnets arranged artfully on the metal file cabinets. She even had a bobblehead doll from some obscure anime I'd never heard of before.

I normally liked hanging out in the organized chaos that was Zoe's workspace. But today, the normal cheer of her office fell flat.

I crumpled into a chair.

When she saw my face, her smile turned to concern. "What's going on?"

"I need your help."

Her eyebrows creased, and her shoulders tensed. "Is it Gerald?"

"Huh?" I said, confused for a moment. "Oh, no. Believe it or not, it's not Gerald."

She leaned back, relaxing a tad.

"It's about a student."

"The Queen Bee?"

"No, another one. The one who looked like she'd been on a bender."

She nodded, giving me space to collect my thoughts.

"She looks super tired. I'm pretty sure she hasn't changed her clothes. She participates, but it's the bare minimum. And not the usual apathy we get from students who just don't want to be there. You know? It's different. Like she'd totally checked out."

I started to feel anxious and fidgety. Without my pen to fiddle with, I felt lost, and my sewing machine leg started up instead.

"Anyway, her friend came by today and said she was worried about her. Sounds like she got kicked out of her apartment and is sleeping in her car. I think she might be a suicide risk."

Zoe's face softened, and her eyebrows creased in concern.

"I asked her to stay after so I could connect with her. But she ghosted me. And no one saw her leave."

"Dang," Zoe said sympathetically.

"Yeah, kinda freaking out."

I started chewing on my nails, caught myself, and tucked my hand under my bouncing leg.

"After Nathan...." I left the unsaid words hanging between us.

She sighed sadly. Nathan also weighed heavily on her. Maybe even heavier than with me. She was great at connecting with students, and I assumed she took it as a personal failure that she hadn't recognized the signs.

She leaned forward. "What's your gut telling you? Can this wait until tomorrow?"

I looked deep into my heart.

Something was terribly wrong with Tessa. We could all see it. It would've been easy to write her behavior off as a hangover that first morning. But with two full days under my belt and the warning from Harper, I couldn't brush it off.

But is it urgent enough to call in reinforcements?

I was less certain about that.

"Maybe?" I offered.

Zoe ran a hand through her hair, eyebrows still creased. "I would normally recommend a welfare check, just to be safe. But she's unhoused, right? So, we don't even know where she is?"

I nodded sadly. "According to Harper, yes."

"Do you have her phone number?"

I shook my head.

Sometimes, we'd let the students off early and collect their cell phone numbers in case we needed to call them back in. I hadn't needed to ask for that yet; it'd been too slow these last two days.

"Admin should have it," she suggested.

"Harper asked me not to go to Admin."

"Hmmm." Zoe pursed her lips.

Admin always loomed like a monster hiding deep in the forest, ready to pounce on innocent Little Red Riding Hood. It was a place where students went in with a need or a concern and left in tatters.

The students didn't trust them, and neither did Zoe. She'd had her fair share of fights with them over student welfare. I'd always admired her bravery; fighting so hard without tenure was a huge risk. But she always stood up for what was right, demanding that people be treated honestly and fairly. She was likely Norma Rae holding up that union sign. Damn anyone who might try to bully her into silence.

She sighed again, bringing me back into the moment. "Yeah, if you go to Admin for a phone number, there'll be fifteen pages of paperwork. And they'll insist on knowing why. There's obviously more to the student's story. The last thing we want to do is make it worse by putting her on their radar."

My heart sank a little.

I could see where this was headed. I knew what she was going to say before she even said it, and I felt sick to my stomach.

"I'd ride this out overnight," Zoe continued. "See how she looks in the morning and grab her then. Send the other students out to get started with Dustin so she can't dip again."

Seeing my shoulders slump, she added, "I'm sure it'll be okay. Don't let this eat at you. You've done what you can. That's more than most. Somebody like Gerald probably wouldn't even notice something was off."

Having more heart than Gerald wasn't saying much. But her words did make me feel a tad better.

As I stood up, she came around her desk to give me a hug. After releasing me, she kept her hands on my shoulders and dipped her head to make eye contact. "It'll be okay, Josie. Trust me."

***

I pulled into my driveway a smidgen after 5 P.M. with a sense of guilty relief.

My little one-bedroom was my sanctuary and was proudly guarded by my main man, Yersi. His cat-meatloaf outline was visible in the window. When I unlocked the door, he hopped down and wove around my legs, meowing for dinner.

Just the feel of his tail sliding across my calves made me smile. My shoulders relaxed just a tad.

I was still exhausted, grumpy, and anxious. But Yersi always made everything just a little bit more bearable.

I tossed my keys down on the entryway table next to the stack of books that were waiting to go back to Aunty Molly on Sunday.

I could totally use a dose of Aunty right now.

Aunty was my rock. Growing up, it'd been just me and my mom. When she'd passed, Aunty had leaned in. She was my cozy aunt, friend, and mentor all bundled into one amazing woman. Our usual Sunday brunch couldn't come fast enough.

Meow, yowled Yersi, bringing me back to the present.

Having reminded me of my current obligations, Yersi made a bee-line to the kitchen. I followed him and pulled out a can of cat food.

His meowing intensified, transitioning from irritation to exuberant excitement. The cat food plopped in his dish, and he buried his face quickly, with an appreciative *merf*.

With his royal highness taken care of, I headed outside to tend to the chickens.

The backyard was muggy, and the insects were singing. The air felt thick, and clouds hung heavy in the sky. It didn't feel like tornado weather, but I wouldn't be surprised if it rained.

I brushed the lavender by my back door, and the air filled with its scent. The chickens, excited to see me, started clucking softly, pacing the door of their Eglu.

There were a couple of hours of summer daylight left, and it would be a while until the major predators came out. I decided to let the girls roam the garden for a bit. With the Eglu door open, the four of them skittered out, eager to scratch around the yard.

I refreshed their water and scattered some chicken feed in the mulched pathways between the arching flowering bushes and trees. They fluttered over in enthusiastic half-runs with flapping wings.

I checked on the veggie garden, which was still growing strong in the shade of the house. I brushed the straw back and stuck my fingers in the dirt. With potential rain coming in, I turned the drip system off. It was damp enough that it would make it even if the gray clouds just passed right over, selfishly holding everything in.

I picked a few snap peas and crunched on them as I checked on the other veggies. The broccoli was coming along nicely. The lettuce was going bonkers. I may have to serve a salad when Armand came over to make sure it all got eaten. If not, I'd toss it to the chickens.

Yersi meowed through the glass at the back door, eager for some outside time, despite the heat. He was an indoor-only cat unless I was outside with him; killing the local wildlife was entirely off-limits at Casa Harjo. Though he'd never admit it to the other cats in the neighborhood, The Black Death only slayed canned food.

I grabbed my half-eaten pint of mint chocolate chip ice cream and left the door open so he could join me outside.

With a *merf*, he leapt into the cushioned patio chair next to mine and proceeded to take a post-meal bath, front foot swiping gently across his tongue and then his face. He took pride in keeping his black coat panther-esque.

I took a bite of the ice cream, feeling the coolness across my tongue and the mint tickle the back of my nose. I sighed deeply, finally feeling my shoulders fully relax.

I was in my happy spot.

As I polished off the last of the ice cream, my cell phone started to ring from the house. I was surprised to feel my stomach lurch in concern.

What the hell am I so jumpy about?

Duh, Cher Horowitz's valley-girl voice echoed sarcastically in my head.

Oh, yeah...that....

Digging through my purse, I found my phone and answered before checking who it was. I was definitely acting weird—I usually avoided personal calls like the plague, unless it was Aunty, Laila, or Armand. People knew if they wanted to talk to me, they should text.

It was too late now; I'd already answered. "Hello?"

"Hey," Armand's chill, masculine voice answered.

I instantly relaxed and almost melted into a puddle. "Oh, hey, babe."

I made my way back outside and slumped back into the patio chair.

Yersi hadn't moved at all and was still sprawled out like he was ruler of the kingdom.

"You sound out of breath. Bad time?" He had a Romanian accent that was so deliciously sexy.

"Oh, no, it's fine." I waved my hand even though he couldn't see me. "I was just outside and had to run to catch the phone. What's up?"

"I just wanted to hear your voice," he answered. "I miss you. Friday feels far away."

My heart fluttered.

"Yeah, it does. I miss you, too. How's the field treating you?"

"Not bad. We're all crammed in a trailer out in the middle of nowhere. But Desmond makes sure we're well fed. They've got an interesting system set up out here. I'm taking a lot of notes."

During his sabbatical, Armand was rotating through different labs and spending time out in the field with different research groups. His area of interest was drought-resistant wheat. This week, he was out in the panhandle. They grew various strains of barley and sorghum out there, which were inherently fairly drought-tolerant. But the researcher he was working with this week was testing some heirloom strains of oat, selecting hardier species. The panhandle was the armpit of Oklahoma, and I felt bad he was stuck out there in a trailer.

I'll have to make sure he has a warm welcome back.

I grinned to myself as my mind swam through the gutter.

"What've you been up to?" I asked, trying to climb back out.

"The field is the field."

I could practically hear him shrug.

"One good thing: there's a fellow footballer here. He brought a ball, and we get to kick it around after work."

"I didn't know you played football."

That must be why his legs were so awesomely muscled.

Did I just drool?

"Not your kinda 'football.'" He laughed. "The *real* football. The football the rest of the world plays."

"What's *my* kinda football?" I teased.

"Go Pokes, Boone Pickens Stadium, and all that. How can 'Poke' be used as a noun, anyway?"

I barked a very unladylike laugh. "It's short for 'cowpoke.' Like a cowboy."

"Ohhh...Pistol Pete. I see it now."

"*Exactly.* Be careful talking trash about Pistol Pete. And don't *dare* say anything about soccer being the real football on campus. They'll tar and feather you in orange."

It was his turn to belly laugh.

I smiled. It felt great to hear him laugh.

"They invited me to play *football* with them this weekend. It'll be nice to get back out on a real pitch again."

"Glad you found something up in the panhandle worth your while," I teased, smiling.

"Yeah." He laughed with me.

"Seriously, though. I'm glad you're having fun up there."

"Me, too. Looking forward to coming back and having a real shower, though. It'll be nice to see you on Friday."

"Ditto. I have the students this week, but I should still be back home by six. When do you think you'll be back?"

"Mid-afternoon. It'll give me time to shower and change."

"Perfect."

I could practically smell the pleasant aroma of his aftershave already: never too strong—just a faint whiff—enough to remind me that there was a hot guy next to me.

Yeah, I'm drooling.

"How about you? Any cool cases?" he asked, bringing me back from fantasy land.

"Uh, yeah. I had some great teaching cases: a dog with pancreatitis, a tiger with metastatic mammary carcinoma, and a horse with a GI torsion. Enough to keep us busy, but not too crazy."

"A tiger? Wow!"

"Yeah. I've never had a tiger before. It was pretty cool. Amazing opportunity for the students, too."

"What was it like to necropsy a tiger?"

"Um...this might sound cheesy, but it's kinda awe-inspiring. Seeing a magnificent predator like that and being able to touch it.... It's hard to describe."

He made a *hmmm* of agreement.

"I'm a bit jealous," he added through a smile. "Did the students appreciate the experience?"

"I think so."

Except for Emma, I added in my head. I wasn't sure anything could please the Queen Bee.

"How's it with the students back?"

I hesitated before answering, and he caught it.

"I'll take that as a 'not so good.'" The inflection of his tone was questioning.

I'd been talking about how excited I was to have the students back—I liked working with them. But this week had been a rough start.

"Strikes and gutters," I answered.

It was an inside joke, and I smiled at his soft laugh.

"I've got an amazing student who should seriously consider becoming a pathologist. You know when you have one of those students who just...." I snapped my fingers, even though he couldn't hear it. "They just get it."

"Yes, I know exactly what you're talking about. Do you think she wants to go into pathology?"

"Not sure. I plan to pull her aside before the week is over. And Zoe has them next week. I already gave her a heads-up. She's a great mentor. A lot of students come to her for career advice."

"So that's the 'strike.' What's the 'gutter?' Want to talk about it?"

A heavy sigh escaped despite my best intentions.

"One of the students is a total Queen Bee...probably the worst student I've ever had."

"Queen Bee?" he asked, confused by the colloquialism.

"Someone who always gets their way, thinks they're better than everyone else, likes to run the show, privileged—you know."

"Like a teenager," he said, laughing.

"Exactly! A loaded, teenage, cheerleader...except she's in her mid-twenties, and we'll be releasing her out into the wild in less than a year as a veterinarian."

I shook my head in disappointment.

"At least you only have to work with her for a few more days," he offered.

"I guess," I responded doubtfully.

I took another deep breath, not sure if I wanted to bring up Tessa. I chewed on my lip for a second before continuing. As if sensing I needed a moment, he didn't fill the space.

"I have another student I'm pretty worried about. She showed up yesterday like she'd been rode hard and put up wet. We were all joking that she probably partied all weekend. But she showed up today in the same clothes, looking like crap. She's sleepy and detached from the group, too."

"Hm," he said with a hint of concern.

"One of her friends came by and asked me to talk to her. She's worried the student may be a suicide risk."

He sighed heavily.

"I tried to catch her after we cleaned up for the day, and she'd already taken off. I'm just worried about her."

I thought about where I was at that precise moment: sitting comfortably at my own home, eating ice cream with my cat, and talking to someone who cared about me.

Where was Tessa this evening? Had she eaten? Was she sleeping in her car tonight? Was she even still alive?

"Well..." he started slowly. "There's not much you can do tonight. I think you just have to catch her in the morning."

I couldn't help but feel like the comment was dismissive, and my hackles went up.

"Umm," I hesitated.

I shouldn't blame Armand for brushing past Tessa's situation. He hadn't seen the full picture. He didn't know about Nathan or the high suicide rate in veterinarians.

He hadn't *seen* her. Or tried to interact with her.

Plus, he wouldn't patronize me like that, I thought. *He's not Gerald.*

"If you saw her...something is definitely up. A black cloud. A heavy load. Like...." I fumbled for the right word.

"Like she has a *moroaică* feeding on her?" he filled in.

"Moro-ika?" I repeated back, shamefully mangling the pronunciation.

"*Moroaică*," he said again. "They're not *strigòi*—you know, the classic vampire—but similar. They're ghosts—spirits—that draw energy from people."

I was surprised he knew a monster that I didn't. For someone who wasn't into horror flicks, he sure knew his malevolent beings.

"I thought you didn't like spooky stuff?" I teased.

"I don't. My *mamaie* told stories before bed. They scared the hell out of me. Between the *strigòi* and *vârcolac*, I'm surprised I picked a job where I work outside all of the time."

I laughed sympathetically. "Yeah, Aunty *still* does that. Even as an adult, she tries to scare me with stories of *Lofa*. He's a big hairy monster, like Bigfoot, that skins people alive. Some of those stories scarred me for life."

We shared another laugh.

My smile dropped, and I sighed. "Anyway, the situation with the student...It's more like she's carrying an *obariyon*—a *yōkai* from Japanese mythology. They hop on someone's back and weigh them down, getting heavier and heavier until the weight is too much, and it crushes them. It's like that. Like her load is too hard to carry, and it's killing her."

"Ah, I see."

"I know I can't do anything tonight," I continued. "It's just hard with my hands tied. I'll be fretting until I get eyes on her tomorrow."

"Understandable," he said with genuine empathy. "Anything I can do to help?"

What I really needed was a hug. But that wasn't going to happen with him five or six hours away.

"Nah, I'm good," I lied. "Thanks, though."

My face was sweaty against the phone. Thinking about Tessa had brushed away the dash of calm that I'd felt sitting outside, and the anxiety crept back in.

"Anyway, I gotta get going. I need to get the chickens locked up and stress-eat some more ice cream. Call you tomorrow, maybe?"

Sensing that I needed space, he replied, "Sure. I'm here whenever you need me. Night or day. Just call, and I'll answer."

I could tell he was still worried about me.

Trying to reassure him, I answered, "I appreciate it. I'll be fine. Don't worry. Talk soon."

We said our goodbyes, and I hung up the phone.

With a sigh, I crawled out of the patio chair and chased the girls back into their Eglu. I then grabbed my empty ice cream container and shooed Yersi inside.

All that ice cream on an empty stomach was making me feel icky. I thought about eating a real meal, but after staring inside the fridge for a full minute, eyes glazed over, I decided to say, "Fuck it." I ended up taking a shower and going to bed early, feeling as grumpy as I had when I'd started the day.

CHAPTER

EIGHT

A shrill beeping yanked me out of sleep.

My hand flailed around on the bedside table, desperate to make the dying cat sound go away. My phone thumped to the floor with the alarm still blaring.

I leaned over the bed and fumbled around on the screen until blissful silence filled the room. Hanging halfway off the bed, my fingers dangling on the floor, I felt my lids go heavy.

I really, really did *not* want to get up today.

A slightly malevolent and oddly inquisitive *merf* interrupted the silence. The bed shook lightly, and the covers pulled tight with Yersi's weight.

The *Jaws* theme song began in my head.

How could a cute little cuddle muffin of a cat actually stomp—yes, *stomp*—when he was annoyed? This time, said stomping was up and down my back.

I laid there like a slug. It was my only defense.

Unfortunately, he quickly saw through my ruse.

He let out a deep, scratchy, incredibly annoying yowl. It was time for his breakfast, and he wasn't having any of this sleeping-in nonsense.

I rolled over, brushing him off my back. "Cut it out, dude."

This was answered with another deep yowl. He hopped off the bed and stood in the doorway, just out of spray bottle range, and resumed his incessant meowing.

I let out a deep sigh and sat up.

With a *merf* of victory, he dashed into the kitchen, knowing I wouldn't be far behind.

I rubbed my face, trying to wake up. I felt puffy and gross.

Why the hell am I so out of it?

The smoldering burn of cramps answered my question.

Fuck.

Aunt Flo had checked in.

My period was like a werewolf, eating my uterus apart every month. I could choke through the pain provided I had enough ibuprofen on board. Aunty jokingly called them my blue Tic Tacs.

The worst part was that I bled like a stuck pig. And it was *a lot.* Like, I'd put a new tampon in, stand up, and blood would soak my jeans as soon as I zipped them up.

I'd seen a doctor about it but was instantly brushed off. "Just part of being a woman," he'd said. In other words, he was telling me to suck it up because he couldn't possibly understand how lame it was to have a period ravaging your body every month.

Sigh.

Back to the situation at hand. Here I was, bleeding everywhere and on duty with students. The last thing I needed was dear, sweet Emma pointing out that the blood on the ass of my coveralls wasn't from a carcass.

Stop whining. Suck it up and get your ass out of bed.

I should be grateful I hadn't bled on the sheets last night. Those stains were always a bitch to get out.

After a trip to the bathroom, I shuffled into the kitchen, ignoring Yersi and working on the most pressing needs first: I needed caffeine, ibuprofen, and food. In that order. Yersi would have to wait a hot second.

Let's just say he was *not* pleased with that arrangement.

I did my best to ignore him as I slugged around the kitchen.

Less than thirty minutes later, I had one cup of black tea down and meds onboard. Yersi and I had both been fed. Another three cups of tea were sitting in my to-go mug. Gerald wasn't going to ruin my day in the breakroom this morning; I was bringing my own supplies.

I can do this.

I stood in front of the mirror, taking stock.

Though having to dress a certain way always chafed, I knew that looking well-put-together had a power to it. I needed that extra strength today.

It was going to be rough. I'd have to navigate Queen Bee, biting my tongue, making sure I didn't say something spiteful. Or smack her. That was definitely a no-no regardless of how evil she was behaving.

And then there was Tessa.

That conversation needed to happen today. No matter what.

Even with my cramps tugging painfully at my stomach and making me feel faint, I whined to myself.

Despite feeling awful, I looked pretty good in my curvy jeans and fitted blouse that hugged my narrow waist. Forgoing the usual dangling, beaded earrings, I put small studs in. I also skipped wearing a bracelet or a necklace.

I brushed my hair, parted it down the middle, and pulled it into a tight ponytail. As usual, I skipped makeup; I had this thing against dousing myself in chemicals because some ad told me I needed to. Plenty of people loved me, and it had nothing to do with whether or not I wore makeup.

I took stock of my reflection.

With a start, I realized I'd dressed like I was expecting a fight in the schoolyard.

Maybe I am.

***

On the way to work, I blasted my power song, feeling the bass shake the poor wimpy speakers of my Prius. The caffeine was starting to sing in my veins, and the ibuprofen had tamped the cramps down to a dull ache.

Yeah, I got this, I kept reminding myself.

Throwing my shoulders back, I grabbed my purse, my lunch, and my to-go tea before heading into the lab. I made it unscathed to my office without hide nor hair of Gerald.

I dropped my stuff off and went to find Dustin. The faint sounds of his usual music coming off the necropsy floor helped me pinpoint exactly where he was camped out.

I opened the door and called out, "Morning, Dustin."

He looked up, gave me a nod in greeting, and turned down the music before heading over. "Morning, Doc."

I nodded my chin over to the carcass of a large golden retriever lying stiff on one of the small animal necropsy tables. "That it so far?"

"Yes, ma'am. Mast cell tumor from the vet school."

I grabbed the submission form. "Thanks. I'm gonna brief the students and send them out. I have to speak to one of them privately first. Go ahead and get started when they come out. I'll be close behind."

"On it," he said as he gave a friendly salute.

Dustin was a good egg and more than competent; he was a master at his trade. The dude only had a high school diploma...*and possibly a criminal record?*

That unpleasant Gerald-nugget was still bouncing around in my head.

Whatever his past, Dustin knew more than most veterinarians and even some pathologists. And he shared that knowledge willingly in a humble way. The students would be in good hands with him while I met with Tessa. I also trusted he'd save any lesions for me to have a gander at.

"You gonna talk to the rough-'n-ready one? What's her name again?" Dustin asked, drawing me out of my thoughts.

"Yeah. Tessa."

"I saw her come in this morning. She's still looking pretty bad. Maybe even worse."

A confusing sense of relief washed over me. If he saw her this morning, she was still alive. *That* was a win.

I knew we weren't out of the woods. But it was one day at a time with these things, and I'd be grateful for each one of them.

He saw all of those thoughts pass across my face, and he smiled in a soft, reassuring way.

"You're doing right by her, checkin' in and all." He gave a small nod of approval.

We exchanged an air knuckle bump, his gloved hand stopping millimeters away from my bare one.

***

About thirty minutes later, I was feeling a tad more confident. My cramps were almost silent, and the caffeine was doing its job. With the submission form in hand, I headed to the conference room.

The students were all there, in the same seats they were in yesterday.

I smiled inwardly.

Students were creatures of habit. We all were. All our vet school lectures were in the same classroom, and everyone pretty much stayed in the same spot *forever*. People would get mighty pissy if anyone moved around and claimed another seat. That was what happened when a bunch of type-A personalities were shoved into a high-intensity environment. Everyone could get a little bit Milton Waddams sometimes.

Staying true to form, Emma was using her phone to touch up her makeup. Tessa was slumped on the table, face buried in her crossed arms. The other students were chatting quietly.

Seeing me come in, Mackenzie said, "Good morning, Dr. Harjo."

"Mornin', everyone. Y'all have a good evening yesterday?"

A few nods around the table. Tessa remained face down. Emma was still entranced by her visage.

Harper tapped Tessa lightly. She picked up her head, face groggy and slightly confused. She was in the same coveralls and hoodie as yesterday. I couldn't help but wonder if she stank.

By the time my attention focused back on Emma, she'd put her phone down and was staring at me, arms crossed and one eyebrow arched. Her hostile posture got my hackles up, but at least I wouldn't have to chew her ass about her phone.

I placed the submission form in the center of the table. "We have one necropsy so far today. A dog from the vet school. Who hasn't taken point on a case yet?"

I knew exactly who hadn't led a case, but I wanted to see who would fess up. Their type-A personalities kicked in, and all the relevant hands raised around the table, even Tessa's.

"Who wants to take this one?"

"I'll take it," Sarah said. I could tell she was just resigned to the fact that she was going to have to get bloody at least once during these two weeks.

"Thanks. Want to read the history for us?"

Sarah grabbed the submission form. "The patient is a ten-year-old, spayed, female golden retriever. The patient had a mast cell tumor removed from the right thorax six months ago. She re-presented about a month ago with decreased appetite and weight loss. FNA of an enlarged axillary lymph node revealed metastatic mast cell tumor. The owner declined another round of chemo and elected euthanasia when the symptoms progressed."

"*Pfft*. This is just like the tiger. They already know why it died. This is such a waste of time," Emma complained.

I gritted my teeth.

Each body was a gift, a chance to learn. Even a dog with a common type of cancer was something this spoiled brat should appreciate.

I bit back a nasty retort and decided to ignore her.

"What will we be looking for?" I asked the group, avoiding Emma's glare.

Mackenzie tossed Emma a skittish glance and answered, "Metastasis in other organ systems?"

"Yes. Where do we want to be looking?"

The room started to warm up a bit, and Kassidy answered, "Regional lymph nodes. Maybe the liver and spleen?"

"Yep, those'll be the most common sites. We'll still check everything. Even the bone marrow. I've seen mast cell tumors met there before. The oncologist will want to know how far it spread."

"Why? The dog's already dead," Emma snarked.

Holy cow, she's something.

"Emma..." I started.

Please, shut up.

"Cut it out," I said instead.

She rolled her eyes and picked her phone back up.

The other students shot me looks of sympathy.

I pressed on, "We'll also want to ID the previous surgery site and collect that. The oncologist will want to know if there's any residual tumor there. Any questions?"

The students shook their heads. It was a pretty easy case.

I was already planning on bumping any case that came in this afternoon to tomorrow. A dead animal could usually wait overnight in the cooler. I'd make an exception for an outbreak situation, but that was about it.

If I could just get through this day without bleeding through my tampon, that would be a win.

"Let's head out, then. Dustin will get y'all started. I'll be a sec."

The students shuffled out, with Tessa bringing up the rear.

"Tessa?" I called quietly to her.

She turned to me, eyes dull and encircled by deep bags.

"Can I talk to you for a minute?"

Her body tensed.

"I'm glad to see you today. Harper and I have been worried about you. I tried to catch you yesterday. Wanna sit?" I gestured to the table.

She stuffed her hands deep into her pockets, and her shoulders scrunched up in a slight flinch. I didn't sense any hostility. It was more a deep, overwhelming despair with a hint of fear.

I'd had friends growing up who looked like that. It usually meant the adult figure at home was drunk or high all the time. There was frequently a degree of physical abuse, too. Invariably, there was neglect: not bathing, maybe not eating, and not caring about school. Just another good person thrown to the wolves. That being said, I wasn't used to seeing vet students looking the way Tessa did.

I didn't want her to feel trapped, so I sat down. The door was clear. She could easily leave if she wanted to. Or, she could sit down with me.

It would be her choice; I wasn't going to be a wolf.

Keeping her hands stuffed in her pockets, she sat on the edge of the seat, her spine so crooked it touched the back of the chair. She avoided my gaze and seemed to shrink beneath the hood of her sweatshirt.

I could smell her now—the cloying scent of rotting clothes and sour BO. There was also a whiff of ketones; she was burning fat.

I didn't know where to start. I wasn't trained to manage these situations, but I knew I had to do something. I just hoped I didn't make it worse.

Trying to keep my posture relaxed and non-threatening, I said, "I'm worried about you. Wanna talk about it?"

She shook her head.

"That's okay. You don't have to."

I paused and chewed the inside of my cheek. I wanted to make sure she was safe with a roof over her head, food in her belly, and a shower. I didn't want her to feel shame, though. I wasn't quite sure how to phrase anything.

"Harper said you might need a place to stay. If you want, you can crash at my place for a couple of days. My house is tiny, but you can sleep on the couch."

Trying to lighten things up, I added, "I have a super bossy cat, though. He might try to cuddle you to death. So, I can't guarantee a good night's rest."

I forced a small laugh.

She didn't laugh back, but the corner of her mouth turned up ever-so-slightly.

I felt a thread of hope.

"The offer is there. We don't have to talk or anything. Just a safe place for you to hang. I have like fifteen gallons of ice cream in my fridge you're welcome to if I don't stress-eat them first."

I let the silence stretch between us. I wanted to give her a reassuring pat or even a hug. But I didn't want to spook her, either. I clasped my hands to make sure I respected her personal space.

"The offer is there. Think about it. Harper cares about you. I care about you. We just want to make sure you're okay. I'm here if you need anything. I'll check in before we finish up for the day, and you can let me know what you want."

She let out a deep sigh. I couldn't believe a sigh could sound so anguished.

"Thanks," she said softly.

I felt a small victory at the sound of her voice. I didn't want to push my luck, though.

I stood and said, "Let's head out."

She stood a second later and followed me out onto the necropsy floor, the sound of "I'm So Lonesome I Could Cry" washing over us.

***

By the time Tessa and I tromped through the footbath, the other students already had the dog's thoracic and abdominal cavities open. I was pleased to see that the students were learning quickly. Dustin didn't have to do much other than keep an eye out to ensure that no one cut themselves. By enforcing the one-knife-at-a-time rule, he ensured the students didn't cut each other diving into the same carcass.

Seeing me walk in, Dustin gave me a chin nod. The baton was passed in that gesture, and I stepped over to assume my duties as no-bloodshed-monitor. Tessa followed behind me, hands still stuffed in her pockets. She perched on a stool next to the necropsy table.

"What'd y'all find so far?" I asked.

"We found the surgical scar," Sarah answered. "It's in formalin. We found a few big lymph nodes, too."

I pulled the lid back on the formalin container. The strong chemical scent made my eyes water and burned my nose. The students had done a good job collecting the samples. A large section of skin about the size of my palm sat at the bottom. Three large lymph nodes that had been butterflied bobbed slightly.

"Perfect. Did you all get measurements on those lymph nodes?"

"Yes, ma'am," Kassidy said.

I traded a gloved knuckle bump with her and said, "Excellent. Thank you. What'd you find inside?"

"We haven't gotten very far," Sarah said, slightly embarrassed.

"You've done a great job. Don't worry." I pointed to the spleen. "That looks a bit swollen. Let's get some impression smears of that. It'll be good practice."

I didn't see anything else too exciting at this point. But as sick as the dog was, I was sure I'd find stuff microscopically; this was a case I'd have to trim in for histology.

"All yours," I said, stepping back to let them get back at it.

The students went to it, with Sarah in the lead. Even Emma got off her high horse for a moment to chip in. To my disappointment, Tessa remained outside of the group, hands still glued in her pockets, slouched on the stool.

It was almost 11 A.M. by the time they finished. When we started to clean up, I handed Tessa a scrub brush, which she took without comment. With the slight nudge, she helped out.

After the room was clean, we rounded up, and Sarah summarized the findings.

Tessa was still despondent. I felt like I hadn't made it through to her yet and was getting increasingly worried.

On a whim, I offered, "I was thinking of ordering pizza for everyone for lunch. What do y'all think?"

If I had the students on the last day of their rotation, I'd typically order lunch for them. Zoe would have the honors next week with this group. But I was hoping that pizza would cheer Tessa up. If nothing else, at least it would get some calories in her.

"That would be amazing! Thank you, Dr. Harjo!" Mackenzie exclaimed.

"Yeah, thank you, Dr. Harjo," Harper added.

Sarah and Kassidy smiled and nodded their heads. Emma smirked. Tessa looked like she hadn't even heard me.

Four out of six wasn't too bad.

"What kinda pizza do y'all like?" I asked.

"Anything," Mackenzie said.

"Can we order a veggie one? No onions?" Kassidy asked.

"Sure," I answered.

"Plain cheese, please. If that's okay." Sarah requested shyly.

"How 'bout you, Dustin?" I asked.

"The usual. Thanks, Doc."

That meant a Meat Lovers. With his order, it was a good balance of options.

"Okay. I'll get this order in. It should be here around noon. See everyone back in the conference room then."

After changing, I placed the order.

Splurging, I added breadsticks, a family-size salad, cookies, and drinks. I figured maybe I could get Tessa to take some leftovers.

An hour later, we were back in the conference room in our civvies.

The thick, tomatoey smell of pizza filled the air as the students dove into the food. Even Emma grabbed a slice and nibbled at it delicately. Seated next to Dustin, I worked on my pile of veggie pizza and salad.

"Thank you for lunch, Dr. Harjo. This is tasty," Harper said.

This was followed by a few more "thank yous" from around the table.

"Pathology may end up being my favorite rotation." Mackenzie directed the comment to me as other conversations resumed around the table.

My heart swelled just a tad.

"Because of the pizza bribe?" I teased.

Mackenzie flushed a little, embarrassed, and I instantly felt guilty.

"It's the vibe," she pressed on. "Everyone is super chill and nice. And the cases are interesting. It seems like a cool job."

"It's definitely a cool job." I nodded. "Don't get me wrong. There are rough days. Like the animal cruelty cases or a rotten steer that's been baking in the Oklahoma sun for three days."

Dustin gave an empathetic grunt.

"But," I continued, upbeat, "I still love it. Are you thinking of going into pathology? You'd be good at it."

"Maybe." She flushed again. "I don't particularly like surgery. Cutting something that's alive...I don't know. I just didn't realize it would be so hard."

"Ya can't screw it up if it's already dead," Dustin chimed in, repeating my favorite mantra. "That's the beauty of necropsies."

"And we always figure out what happened, even if it is a little too late," I added with a grin.

Mackenzie smiled. "You don't have to deal with crazy owners, either."

I felt a hold-my-beer moment coming.

"Depends on where you work," I replied. "Here, anyone can bring a carcass in. And we have to interview the submitters. I've seen my fair share of difficult owners. They're usually tied up in grief, and the interviews can occasionally go sideways."

Dustin nodded sagely.

My thoughts drifted to Adam Williams, who'd been just a little shady when he'd submitted the Shadowhawk case a month or so ago.

"Really?" Mackenzie asked. "Sideways how?"

"You'd be surprised. 'Member that Texan?" Dustin said, turning to me.

"Oh, geez, the guy with the decorated coffin?" I asked, recalling the dude perfectly.

Dustin nodded and took a bite of pizza. "Yup. That guy."

I nodded my head slowly, remembering the day.

Seeing the exchange, Mackenzie said, "Okay. You *have* to tell the story now."

Dustin laughed lightly and looked at me, one eyebrow raised.

I cleared my throat. "Welp," I started.

Sensing a juicy story, the students around the table hushed and turned their attention to me. Emma was practically salivating, eager for the gossip. Even Tessa looked interested. It was a captive audience.

"It was some holiday or another," I continued. "We were all getting ready to go out for lunch as a group. Before Anna could lock up, this guy rolled in holding a small coffin—a fancy one to bury people in—baby-sized. It was painted black with pictures glued to it and rhinestone decorations and all."

"Aww. That's actually kinda sweet," Kassidy said.

"Yeah, he really cared about his dog. But that's not the crazy part." I paused for dramatic effect.

"He'd driven about six hours up from Texas. He'd tried to get the diagnostic lab down there to help him, and they'd refused."

"First red flag," Dustin chimed in and took another bite of pizza.

I nodded. "The dog had died about a month prior. The owner just couldn't bear not knowing what happened to his pet. So, he dug it up and brought it in."

"Second red flag," Dustin added.

"He was adamant his vet killed his dog and wanted us to prove it. He wouldn't let us cut it open, though. He said we were only allowed to swab the inside of the dog's mouth to see if the vet killed it or not. 'Like in them TV shows,' he'd said."

"And there it is." Dustin nodded and pointed a finger.

"What?!" Mackenzie exclaimed incredulously.

"Did he really think that would work?" Kassidy asked.

"Poor Dr. Lang. He tried to explain it to the guy. The man just got more and more angry. He started shouting and put his hand on his sidearm."

Eyebrows shot up around the table.

"I remember we were all so worried the guy would shoot Dr. Lang that we delayed going to lunch. We didn't want to leave him alone in the lab with the guy."

Shaking her head in disbelief, Mackenzie asked, "Then what happened?"

"Dr. Lang held his ground. He somehow managed to talk the guy down," I replied.

"What did you find in the dog?" Mackenzie asked. "Or was it too autolyzed?"

"Oh, no," I answered. "The guy wouldn't let us touch it. But he left without putting a bullet in Dr. Lang. We figured that was a win. He just took the coffin and headed off into the sunset."

"Wow...I wonder if he just kept driving to find another lab or if he went back home," Mackenzie mused.

I shrugged.

"Think about that dog's vet," Sarah said, white as a ghost. "The person he blames for the dog dying. *That's* who needs to be worried."

I couldn't help but nod sadly. She was right. Tom had somehow made it out unscathed during his interaction with the owner. But who knew how that man would feel when he returned home with his dead dog after driving for who knows how long, frustrated, angry, and buried in grief?

I thought telling the story would be fun. Instead, I felt a little grimy making fun of someone who wasn't handling a tough situation well. I could tell the story wasn't sitting right with others around the table either and instantly wished I told the lotion story instead.

"Anyway, when owners care deeply for their animals, death can bring out the worst," I said, trying to smooth things over. "I think we just saw the worst of that guy that day."

I made eye contact with Mackenzie. "And anatomic pathologists deal in death. So, even though we don't have owners who are going to bully us about the bill or try to get us to prescribe opioids for their pets that they'll end up taking, we do get our fair share of difficult folks passing through. There are only a few jobs in veterinary medicine where you don't have contact with owners."

"There's so much James Herriot leaves out," Mackenzie said dolefully.

I barked a laugh. "Yes, the days of James Herriot are *long* gone. But there are still a ton of awesome owners. Those folks and the patients we help—that's what gets us through."

Thankfully, conversations drifted to lighter topics from there. Relaxed chatter between Harper, Sarah, Kassidy, and Mackenzie kept things pleasant for the rest of the meal.

Toward the end, Dustin leaned over to me.

"Thanks again for buying lunch, Doc," he said. "It was a pleasant surprise. Good to see the students enjoying it, too."

He nodded his chin slightly at Tessa with a smile and gave me a knowing look. She was slowly working through a plate heaped with food.

"Yep, good to see everyone enjoying their meal," I replied with a relaxed smile.

I knew Tessa still had a long way to go. But this was one step in the right direction.

CHAPTER

NINE

Everyone was leaning back in their chairs, bellies stuffed with pizza. We'd all eaten seconds, and there was still a ton of food left.

Maybe that's a good thing?

I couldn't help but glance at Tessa. She'd packed away a crap ton of food. Now, she was deep in her postprandial lull and looked like she might fall asleep.

"Y'all want any more?" I asked the group.

Heads shook around the table.

"Thanks again for lunch, Dr. Harjo," Harper said.

"Yeah, thanks," Mackenzie added.

"You're welcome. The leftovers are up for grabs. Whatever you want. Just make sure to write your name on it. There's a fridge in the breakroom where you can stash it if you need to. Anything you don't want, I'll leave out—it'll get cleaned up by others in the lab."

The students went about packing their doggy bags.

"I'll take what's left to the breakroom, Doc," Dustin offered.

"Thanks."

I stood and tossed my paper plate and napkin in the trash. Suddenly, I felt the uncomfortable reminder that I needed to change my tampon. Like, immediately.

If I didn't make a quick escape, things were going to get ugly fast.

Turning to the students, I said, "I have the weekly lab meeting right after lunch. Let's meet back here at two and see what we have for the afternoon."

There were a few nods of acknowledgment.

I fled the room. The last thing I needed was for everyone to think this was a reboot of *Carrie*.

Refreshed, and with my circulating ibuprofen levels topped up, I headed for Zoe's office in the hopes that she was back from lunch already. I was fretting over my initial conversation with Tessa and wanted to bounce some things off of her before the lab meeting.

I peered through the small window into her office and knocked lightly. Spotting me, she waved me in.

"Hey, Josie. How're you doin'?" she asked with a smile.

She turned from her computer and rested her hands in her lap.

"Hey, Zoe. Pretty good. Have a sec?"

"Sure, what's up?"

I grabbed the seat across from her and sighed deeply, letting some of the tension go. I'd been pretty damn worried about Tessa. But seeing her stuff herself at lunch had brought hope.

"I want to pick your brain about the student I talked to you about yesterday: Tessa," I started.

Zoe encouraged me to continue with a nod.

"I caught up with her this morning," I pressed on. "She was super cagey and didn't want to talk. I didn't press her."

I paused to catch Zoe's eye, seeking reassurance.

"That's the right approach," she responded. "It's about opening a door and creating a safe space. If you push too hard, she might just shut down and cut everyone out."

Feeling a bit more confident, I continued, "I let her know that there are people who care about her and want to help. I offered to let her stay at my place tonight if she needed to."

Zoe's eyebrows shot up.

My gut clenched.

"What?" I asked, worried, feeling like I'd pushed a granny down to get the new iPhone.

"I'm just surprised you offered to let her stay with you. That was kind. I'm not sure if I'd let a stranger stay at my place."

I paused to reflect and then shrugged one shoulder. "She's a vet student. It's not like it's some dude hitchhiking on the side of the road."

I must've sounded defensive because she quickly put her hands up in surrender. "I'm not judging you; it's just very generous." She paused a beat before continuing, "How'd she respond to the invitation?"

"She didn't say anything. I just threw it out there and gave her time to think about it." I chewed on my cheek. "I was worried she wasn't eating, so I bought everyone lunch today. She actually ate, though, and made a to-go box with the leftovers."

"That's a great sign," Zoe said hopefully.

"Yeah. It was nice seeing her a bit more animated. Dustin noticed it, too."

"See! You're doing right by her. Just keep checking in and let her know you care. I'll keep an eye on her next week."

"Is there anything else I can do?" I asked, feeling way out of my depth.

My sewing machine leg started up. I wondered where all the energy came to power that bad boy, seeing as my uterus was sucking all of the life out of me today.

"If we need to, we can try to figure out what her next rotation is and give the faculty a heads up," Zoe offered.

"Harper asked not to involve Admin," I reminded her, getting nervous and feeling slightly protective.

Zoe waved the worry away with her hand. It might've been rude if it'd been anyone else.

"I'm not talking about Admin. Just passing the baton between people who can keep an eye out and check in. It helps that Harper is looking out for her, too."

I nodded, picking up what she was putting down. "Thanks, Zoe."

She got up and came around the table to hug me. "We'll make sure she's okay. Don't worry."

***

A few minutes before the lab meeting, I debated hiding in my office. I wasn't feeling it today and wished there was a way that I could skive off.

I didn't bother trying.

Gerald would hunt me down and give me heaps of shit if I didn't go. He made a habit of playing the evil nanny.

What a shitass.

Resigned, I grabbed my stylus and iPad and headed out.

Once a week, the heads of the various labs and the pathologists would meet to discuss any lab-wide updates and pick one another's brains about weird cases. It helped to have more than one uber-nerd noodling over the more difficult ones. The Shadowhawk case was a great example of that; it was a stinker of a case, and I couldn't have made it without Sandy.

I took a seat sandwiched between Zoe and Tom. We were a wall of pathology. Opposite us sat Sandy, Manuel, and Gerald. Fran, the director of the lab, sat at the head of the table.

The meeting started like any other one. I doodled with my stylus, hoping I could skate through. Boy, was I wrong.

Fran cleared her throat, and the light chatter died down. "Good afternoon, everyone. I don't have any general items to share today. Shall we go around for departmental updates? Sandy?"

Sandy fidgeted absently with the reading glasses hanging around her neck. "Not much happening in toxicology. We're seeing an uptick in blue-green algae, but other than that, it's status quo."

Fran nodded. "Manuel?"

"The flu testing seems to have slowed down a bit. We're still getting a lot of samples, but I don't think we'll need any more overtime."

"Great. Still not seeing any AI cases come through the floor, right?" She looked over to the pathologists.

We all shook our heads.

"Excellent. We may be through the thick of it, then. Gerald?"

"Our superlative performance continues from last week. Our turn-around-time remains excellent, and our volumes are steady." A smug smile curled his lips, and he crossed his arms.

Fran nodded and turned to us. "How about pathology?"

Tom, Zoe, and I exchanged glances before Tom spoke for us. He'd been on duty last week and had the latest and greatest.

"Just the usual," Tom said.

Gerald snorted. "How is a tiger 'just the usual?'"

"A tiger came in?" Fran asked, laser-focused.

A large carnivore was kind of a big deal, but I didn't think it was meeting-worthy. Tiawah had known she was sick and already knew why she died. It wasn't a huge mystery or anything that needed to be kept hush-hush. Leave it to Gerald to make a mountain out of a molehill.

"Yes. It came in from the Tiawah Animal Sanctuary. She was an older tiger with mammary carcinoma. It was expected and had already been announced on their Insta account," I answered, trying to talk Fran off the ledge.

"You let the students out there with *a tiger*. That was very irresponsible," Gerald chided. He shook his head at me like I was a naughty child.

Zoe stiffened. Her eyes narrowed, and she leaned forward.

Hold up a minute, motherfucker, I imagined her saying.

"Please enlighten us, *Gerald*. How is allowing the students on *pathology* rotation to perform a *necropsy* irresponsible?" Zoe challenged him.

We all felt the tension crackle in the room.

Gerald messed with all of the women in the lab; that was his thing. But there was some serious bad blood between Zoe and him.

A sly leer spread across his face, and his chest puffed out.

He was loving this. A thread of worry twisted in my gut.

"Well, with a high-profile case such as an endangered species, it would be prudent to do the necropsy with as little fuss as possible. The students were probably out there taking pictures with the dead body. I'm most concerned about that beautiful blonde one. She seems like just the type."

Zoe bristled. "I am certain that Dr. Harjo did not allow students to take pictures of the tiger," she practically hissed. "We don't let them take pictures of *any* case."

"Hmmm," he said with mocking doubt. "What would you know? You have your own problems that you clearly have not addressed."

Sandy cleared her throat, preparing to step in to break up the fight.

"Why are you always in everyone else's business?!" Zoe practically shouted. "Just stay in your damn lane."

Her fists were clenched on the table, knuckles white.

"Everybody calm down," Fran chided. Though her comment didn't specifically call anyone out, she was looking directly at Zoe.

Of course, she corrects Zoe and not Gerald, I thought bitterly. *So much for solidarity against the tyrannies of evil.*

Underneath the table, I put a hand on Zoe's leg in warning. Gerald was baiting her, and I could feel the trap start to close. The last thing I wanted was for her to get reprimanded for defending me.

I worried for my friend. Gerald had tenure, and she didn't. It put him in a position of power, and he knew it. He could get away with being a dick. Zoe needed to watch herself.

She leaned back in her chair, fists still balled in front of her.

"Zoe's right," I said, trying to modulate my tone even though I felt the rage building. "We don't let students take pictures on the floor. I reminded them again before the tiger necropsy. Dustin and I kept an eye on them. Everyone was polite and respectful."

Gerald's eyes narrowed. "You kept your eyes on the students the *entire* time?"

"Yes, Gerald. We were with them the entire time. No one took any pictures."

Did I sound condescending? Maybe. Was I worried about that? Absolutely not.

Seeing him plotting his next move, I quickly added, "Again, the tiger had been sick for a while. Tiawah had posted about her death before they even brought her in. I made sure we weren't risking a media leak before I invited the students to participate. We don't see exotic species very often. This was a unique experience for them."

It killed me that I was starting to sound defensive.

Fran's nod confirmed that my decision was the right one. I felt a flood of relief that I tried to keep from spilling over into my body language. I needed to show a strong, confident front.

I thought we were done, and then, Gerald dropped his last bomb.

"You seem *very* certain. But what about the tiger pelt and claws? Those are extremely valuable. They could be sold for a significant amount of money." He flitted his fingers. "Now, all of those girls know about it. One of their boyfriends may be one of those criminal types."

There was so much wrong with that statement, I was at a loss for words.

The tension built again. Manuel shifted uncomfortably.

Gerald had a gleam in his eye, and I knew he wasn't finished. He wanted to lord this over me and then gloat when he was done.

"It's pretty irresponsible," he continued. "Now, all of the students know those items are just sitting there in the cooler. *Unlocked.* Anyone could waltz right in there and steal them."

As if everything wasn't already tipping sideways, the avalanche began.

Zoe snorted. "It's more likely that *you'd* steal them just so you could blame one of those poor women."

"*Actually*, more likely that you'd steal them to pay for your next cosmetic surgery," Gerald sniped back.

Zoe's fist hit the table, startling the ever-loving daylights out of me. Fran's eyes went wide.

Zoe's pale skin flushed red with anger. "Would you just *stop* it? All you do all day long is just pick on everyone. Just STOP IT!"

Everyone froze as shock settled over the table.

We all thought Gerald was a dick, and he constantly pushed everyone's buttons. Even though he'd been picking on me this time, Zoe had finally had enough and lost her shit.

And she'd done it in front of everyone.

Fuck.

"No need to get violent," Gerald said with a Cheshire cat grin. "I know you may want to be a woman, but clearly, you have the build of a man. All of that strength." He gestured to the table where her clenched fists rested.

He leaned back in his chair with his arms crossed and waited for Zoe's next move.

I shot a look at Fran: *Are you going to stop this, or what?*

Fran's face was ghost-white, and her expression was unreadable. I wasn't sure if she was angry, aghast, completely lost at how to handle the situation, or all of the above.

Silence spread through the room as everyone struggled to decide what to do next. There was a stillness. Like the eye of a storm. Or like everyone was afraid to move because they might get jumped.

Maybe there *was* a reason I'd worn studs and a ponytail today.

Sandy was the one who saved us.

She leaned forward, posture relaxed. "Why don't we just call the meeting here? Some issues need to be worked out. But now, I think we all need to take a moment."

That was enough to pop the bubble of tension.

Gerald jumped out of his seat and stormed out of the room like a petulant child.

Fran coughed, fussing with some papers and avoiding eye contact with anyone.

Sandy came around the table to hug Zoe before leaving. Tom patted Zoe on the back, and Manuel sent a look of support.

I grabbed Zoe's hand and gave it a squeeze.

Leaning over, I said quietly, "It's hot as hell outside, but let's go for a quick walk anyway."

I saw tears fill her eyes as she nodded, letting me lead her outside.

***

I used every possible minute to hang with Zoe before I had to get back to meet the students.

We made a slow loop down Farm Road, through the heart of the campus, and back to the lab. The insects were all abuzz, filling the comfortable silence that spread between us.

She didn't want to talk, but the walk still seemed to do her some good. Her mood went from fuming to smoldering, which I viewed as a small win. She was still pretty rattled, but her hands were no longer balled into tight fists.

With some coaxing, I convinced her to take the rest of the day off. She deserved an afternoon away from the abuse at work.

I just hoped Fran didn't come down on her for what happened. Someone couldn't be blamed for lashing out when they were hounded to their breaking point.

Fran might be forced to reprimand her.

The whole system sucks.

I was still feeling frazzled after the walk, my head caught in an anxiety loop. I took some deep breaths and wiggled my toes, trying to escape it.

Yeah, that's not gonna happen.

Resigned to the fact that I was just going to have to suck it up, I took the one submission form for a case that had come in over lunch and quickly read through it.

My heart sank.

Even though I'd wanted to push any real work to tomorrow, we needed to get this one done today.

I slogged back to the conference room to meet the students, somewhat resentful.

Everyone was back at their usual spots at the table. The postprandial lull must have kicked in because most of them were chilling in their chairs and messing around on their phones. I couldn't help but feel a sliver of disappointment at seeing Tessa with her head buried in her arms on the table. Hopefully, she was finally getting some rest on a full stomach, rather than slipping back into the dark corner she had been in before.

"Afternoon, everyone," I said, knocking my knuckles on the table as I sat down.

Tessa raised her head groggily. The other students put their phones away, even Emma, which was a bit of a shocker. She usually liked to wait a minute or two to fuck with me and let me know who she thought was in control.

"We've got a fetus this afternoon. Should be quick and easy. Who hasn't done a case yet?"

"I'll do this one," Kassidy offered.

I passed the form over to her. "Thanks. Want to read us the history?"

"It's a third-trimester bovine fetus that was found today. Not much else on the form." She huffed, shaking her head, and put the paper down.

"That's pretty typical," I sighed. "Did they at least say if it was dairy or beef?"

I was pretty certain it was beef; we were in Oklahoma, after all. But there were a few dairies around.

"Um...breed says 'Angus.' So, beef."

"What other info would have been helpful?" I asked the group.

"It'd be good to know how many other cows had lost their calves, if there are any infertility issues, if this dam has lost a calf before...lots of stuff," Mackenzie answered.

Daaaammmmmnnnn, I heard Smokey's exclamation of appreciation in my head.

Mackenzie was on it, getting more confident with each passing moment. I felt a surge of pride.

"Exactly. All of that info would help us narrow down the differentials," I said appreciatively and flashed her an encouraging smile.

I wanted her to join the pathology ranks so bad it hurt.

"With cases like this, we often don't see any lesions," I continued. "We'll take samples for an abortion panel and test for the common viral and bacterial infections. Fair warning: Those tests often come up negative. These cases can be frustrating."

"Does that mean we won't figure out what caused it?" Harper asked with curiosity.

"To be honest, probably not. It's pretty rare to figure out the cause of fetal loss when we only have the one fetus. We can look for malformations and check for infectious diseases. With the infectious stuff, a negative result doesn't entirely rule it out."

I looked around at the students. "What's another sample that would've been useful in ruling out an infectious cause?"

The students avoided eye contact, each hoping that someone else would speak up, even Mackenzie.

"Blood from the dam, at a minimum," I said, too tired to not feed them the answer. "If there are more fetal deaths or infertility in the herd, submission of blood from affected and unaffected dams would also be helpful. Plus, if this is an abortion storm, testing other fetuses increases our chances of figuring this out."

Their eyes were glazing over. I tended to soapbox a bit about reproductive pathology; it was my favorite.

I cut things short. "Anyway, this should be an easy one. Just sample collection. Let's get cracking, and then, everyone can go early if nothing else comes in."

With that announcement, the students scurried to get out onto the floor.

Being the amazing dude that he was, Dustin already had everything prepped for us. One of the small animal necropsy tables had been wet down, and the fetus was laid out. He'd even pre-labeled all of the containers to collect samples for viral and bacterial testing.

I thanked my lucky stars for such a great necropsy technician; the guy was a rockstar.

The students arranged themselves around the table.

"Ugh, that is disgusting," Emma said, reflexively covering her nose.

Yeah, good luck with that.

I'd admit, all fetuses were pretty nasty. They almost always had a strong metallic smell with a hint of rot. Not much could mask that unique scent.

This fetus was about five to six months along. The hair coat wasn't fully developed, and it had a bright, hot pink tinge that was reminiscent of the late 1980s. It was also slimy. Inside wouldn't be much better; the organs would be uniform in color, poorly developed, and mushy.

Kassidy stepped up to the table, scalpel in hand, grimacing. I could tell she was kicking herself for volunteering for this one. Sure, performing the necropsy would be pretty lame, but the report would be easy, so I didn't have a lot of pity for her.

"Before we get started, what's missing?" I asked.

The only reply I received was the shifting of eyes to avoid my gaze.

"Placenta is the most important organ to sample in any fetal or neonatal death," I answered for them. "It's also the most forgotten. Or the dam eats it."

Emma's face went pale, and for a moment, I thought she'd barf up her pizza.

I'd admit, I got a sliver of joy seeing the Queen Bee turn green.

I fought a smile.

"Looks like Dustin has all of the containers labeled for you," I continued. "It'll be pretty routine. Just collect everything in formalin, as per usual, and collect fresh samples as per the labeled containers."

I stepped back to let the students dive in.

Sarah, Mackenzie, and Harper all moved forward to help Kassidy. Emma stood to the side, undershirt pulled over her nose, still whining about the smell. Tessa assumed her usual position: perched on a stool with her hands stuffed in her pockets.

With the rest of the students distracted, I took the opportunity to talk to Tessa.

"How was lunch?" I asked, opting for an easy question to break the ice.

"Pretty good," Tessa said softly. "Thank you."

"Glad you enjoyed it. I think the others did, too."

We watched the other students for a minute as I groped for what to say next.

Out of desperation, all I could come up with was, "How're you feeling?"

She shrugged one shoulder, and I could feel her shutting down.

"That's cool. We don't have to talk about it. The offer is still there: If you want to crash at my place tonight, just swing by my office after you get changed."

I wanted to give her a hug, but I wasn't sure it would be welcomed. Instead, I nudged her slightly with my elbow and smiled before joining the rest of the students.

***

Later, as I was typing up the gross reports for the day, a knock at my door dragged me out of my pathology rabbit hole.

"Come in," I called out, turning from my computer.

"Dr. Harjo?" Tessa asked timidly, leaning her head through the door without opening it all the way.

"Hey, Tessa. Come on in."

She snaked around the door, closing it behind her softly, and grabbed the seat across from me.

"What's up?" I asked, trying to keep my voice soft and welcoming.

"I...um..." she stuttered, shifting uncomfortably in her seat.

I kept my mouth shut, giving her space to finish her thought. I could tell she didn't want to be here, and what she was going to say next was very difficult.

Her face flushed dark red. "I don't like takin' handouts or nothing. But"—she cleared her throat—"if the offer is still there...is it cool if I stay on your couch tonight?"

My heart sang with joy. I was positively delighted that she felt brave enough to accept the offer. I felt even better knowing that she'd be safe tonight.

"Absolutely. My cat and I would love to have you. Here's my address."

I wrote my address and phone number on a sticky note and passed it to her.

I'd wait until she offered me her number or texted me rather than ask for it. I was walking on eggshells here, and the last thing I wanted to do was spook her.

"I should be home a little after five. Come over any time after that."

"Thanks, Dr. Harjo," she said softly with a thread of shame.

I bit back the reflexive "You're welcome," worried it would come off as patronizing.

I couldn't see her face. She held the sticky note with two hands and was looking down at it. She obviously felt bad about asking for help. I racked my brain, trying to figure out how to offer support without it feeling like charity. It was something I needed to work on.

Instead, I said, "I'm glad to have the company. Yersi can be *quite* the demanding fur muffin."

She chewed her lip and stuffed the sticky note in her pocket.

Welp, I screwed that up.

"See you tonight," I said, fumbling.

"Yeah. See you later," she said.

She stood and slung her bag over her shoulder. She left without another word, closing the door lightly behind her.

I sat back in my chair with my eyebrows crinkled, feeling a foreboding sense of uncertainty.

CHAPTER

TEN

I'd never been so grateful to see a piece-of-shit sedan parked in front of my house as I was when I pulled into my driveway that evening.

The rust bucket was positioned in the shade of the large ash tree in my front yard. All of the windows were rolled down. The driver's seat was leaning back and filled with a rumpled lump of clothing that I could only assume was Tessa.

I parked my car in the driveway and exited the sanctuary of the air conditioning. The heavy atmosphere of the late Oklahoma summer swept over me. Sweat instantly beaded in my pits.

Tessa must be baking in there.

I wondered why she hadn't camped out in the arctic air conditioning of the conference room in the lab. Embarrassed, maybe? There were also plenty of other places she could have hung out on campus that were indoors and didn't require a purchase.

My stomach clenched.

Something's not right.

Ripping the Band-Aid off, I headed over to her car.

The sedan was a trainwreck. The driver's side mirror was held on with duct tape, and there was a long, jagged crack in the windshield. There was a pretty serious dent in the trunk; it looked like someone had gone at it with a baseball bat, and I was shocked it even stayed closed. The edges of the wheel wells looked like sharp, jagged teeth dipped in rust.

The backseat was filled with large, black trash bags, various shapes pressing haphazardly against the plastic. A threadbare backpack sat on the passenger seat. Books and notebooks were scattered across the passenger-side floor.

This mess likely represented all of her earthly items, and it was exceedingly depressing.

"Tessa?" I called out, unable to keep the apprehension out of my voice.

The person in the driver's seat didn't move.

I stepped out into the road and approached the driver's side window.

Tessa was curled in a fetal position, bare feet tucked up on the seat. She was still in her coveralls, dried blood flecks splattered on the cuffs. Her sweatshirt was balled under her head like a pillow. Her dirty hair was matted with sweat, and there were wet rings under her armpits.

"Tessa?" I said again, now in full-blown panic mode.

Her chest rose slightly with a deep breath.

I felt my shoulders release. For a moment there, I'd thought she was dead.

I knocked lightly on the driver's side of the car.

She didn't wake.

Worried that she was heading toward heat stroke, I reached through the open window and lightly tapped her shoulder.

"Tessa?" I said, a bit louder this time.

She jerked awake, a fearful reflex. Her eyes were blurry and confused.

"Tessa, it's Josie. Want to come inside?"

She blinked a couple of times, still foggy. Nodding slightly, she pulled the lever to bring her seat up with a jerky *thump*.

I stepped back so that she could open the door. "Can I help with anything?"

She shook her head. "Sorry...I fell asleep."

"All good. Come inside. It's roasting out here. We can get your stuff later."

I wanted to get her inside and get some water in her ASAP. She looked dreadful. Though I didn't think she was in full-on heat stroke, she unquestionably looked like she had heat exhaustion.

She opened the door. A *ding, ding, ding* chimed as she rolled up the windows.

She put one foot on the asphalt and quickly jerked it back, hissing. "Shit!"

Yeah, she's totally gorked.

She wasn't acting like she was drunk or high—just incredibly tired and not thinking straight. Her normal brain function was out of whack. I was sure that once she was hydrated, showered, fed, and rested, she'd regret putting her foot on the hot road...and probably mortified that she'd cussed in front of me.

Spotting some flip-flops in the back, I opened the rear door and handed her the pair. "Here."

She slid them on her feet before retrying her exit from the car.

I slowly walked up the path to my house, keeping pace with her. I wasn't sure she'd make it without passing out.

Yersi sat in the front window, eyes wide and curious. Hearing the key slide into the lock, he jumped down and started meowing at the door.

"Come on in," I encouraged her. "Sorry about Yersi. He's gonna be a turd until I feed him."

She shuffled in behind me.

Seeing a stranger, Yersi stood about three feet away. He let out a long yowl and started sniffing the air.

Well, that's odd.

Yersi was usually pretty brave with strangers, acting more like a dog than a cat. Instead of running away, he typically came right up for the smell test. If they passed, he'd rub his face on their legs. If they failed, he'd let out a judgy *merf* and show them his ass as he walked away.

I'd never seen him cautiously hang back like he was doing now.

I felt the hair on the back of my neck prickle.

What the hell? Why was I so edgy? She was a vet student, for heaven's sake. It wasn't like I picked up some rando off the road to let them sleep on my couch.

"Have a seat," I offered, sweeping my hand toward the living room. "I'll grab us something to drink. What would you like? Water? Iced tea? Lemonade?"

"Anything is fine, thanks," she said, sinking into the couch weakly.

Figuring she could do with some sugar, I poured two glasses of lemonade—made from lemons from my garden—and plopped in several ice cubes.

"Here." I handed her the glass.

She cradled it with two hands and took a long sip before leaning back. "Thank you."

"It's pretty hot out there. Are you okay?"

She nodded.

"Is there anything else I can get you?"

She shook her head.

Yersi hopped on the end table next to the couch with a *merf* and sat, tucking his tail around his feet. He stared intently at Tessa, the tip of his tail slapping up and down.

It made a very faint *thump, thump, thump* in the silence of the room.

"Well, *mi casa es su casa*," I said, trying to make up for Yersi's complete and utter lack of hospitality. "I only have the couch, but I'll bring out some blankets and a pillow. The bathroom is back there." I pointed down the hall.

I watched as she took a couple more sips of the lemonade. She was still wet with sweat, and her face was flushed, but her eyes were less dazed. She looked over at Yersi.

He glared back, all judgy like the mean girl from *Clueless*. If a cat could hold a thumb and forefinger in the shape of an L on his forehead, he'd be doing it.

I chuckled uncomfortably, mortified by his behavior. "That's Yersi. He runs this place. He thinks he's all that, but he's just a dork."

She held a hand out to him.

He leaned forward to sniff her fingers and then sat back, shifting the weight on his front feet. His tail continued beating its rhythm on the side table.

I couldn't shake the feeling that something wasn't right.

"Honestly, I'm shocked that he's not screaming for dinner," I blubbered.

She smiled and took another sip of her drink.

My anxiety was creeping in again. I was getting antsy and needed to move.

I set my glass down on a coaster and lightly slapped my hands on my thighs. "Speaking of which, I should probably feed him before he starts plotting a poop-on-my-toothbrush act of revenge."

Am I speaking from experience? Uhhh, yeah.

"Want any help carrying your things in?" I offered.

"No, thank you," she said, not unkindly.

"Okay. I'll get His Royal Highness fed and get started on dinner. Any food preferences I should know about?"

She shook her head slowly. "I'm good with anything, thanks."

I hadn't been planning on company tonight, but I'd figure something out. My fridge was relatively full, and I was pretty sure I could miracle a salad out of what was in the garden.

Seeing me stand, Yersi finally remembered what time it was and ran to the kitchen with an excited *meow*.

"Mind if I use your shower?" Tessa asked shyly.

"Help yourself. There are fresh towels in the cabinet under the sink."

"Thank you again, Dr. Harjo," she said, her voice catching.

I tossed her what I hoped was a reassuring smile. Her eyes were turned down, and I wasn't sure she caught it.

"You're welcome anytime," I said. "Dinner should be ready in about twenty or thirty minutes. Make yourself at home."

***

Trying to shrug off the apprehension dancing along the edge of my feelings, I pawed through the fridge to see what I could patch together for dinner.

There was enough leftover homemade potato salad to feed us both, with an option for seconds. I also had some leftover sliced tri-tip that was still red enough that a quick warm-up in the oven wouldn't turn it into rubber. I could pair that with some veggies from my garden and serve cookies for dessert. Seeing the meal come together in my head, I threw the meat in the oven and grabbed a bowl to harvest the veggies.

Before I headed out, I glanced around for Yersi, knowing he'd want to join me.

He'd wolfed down his dinner, and his food bowl was empty. Normally, he'd be taking a kitty bath on the chair at the end of the counter by now. Today, he'd just disappeared.

"Yersi. Kitty, kitty," I called, my hand on the knob to the back door. No response.

My stomach clenched.

Something was assuredly off. Yersi *never* missed a chance to come outside with me and survey his kingdom. If I so much as deigned to go in the backyard without him, he'd yowl at the door until I acquiesced.

My thoughts went to what Zoe had said about my "generous" offer. Maybe I'd been a little rash?

Trying to shake off the weird vibes, I went into the backyard solo, figuring Yersi would hear the door and start demanding that I use my primate advantage to open the inconvenient barrier in his territory.

Once I stepped outside, the peace of the backyard settled over me. The anxiety still growled in my mind, but I could tuck it back into the corner when I was in my safe place.

Seeing me, the chickens clucked excitedly inside their Eglu. I fed them and changed their water. But I didn't let them out for a scratch in the yard. My worry was already sky-high, and I didn't want the added stress of them outside without supervision.

After collecting the eggs, I moved around to the raised beds. The lettuce was still growing strong, enjoying the shady spot on the side of the house. I harvested enough for a mixed salad. There were still some snap peas left that I plucked, planning to sauté them with some garlic. I wanted to make sure that Tessa went to sleep with a full belly tonight.

The sound of the shower greeted me when I came back inside. My shoulders relaxed slightly, knowing she was finally taking a moment for self-care.

It nagged me that Yersi was still MIA. He'd not only skipped his usual post-meal bath, but he'd also ignored the fact that I went outside without him.

I chewed my cheek, and my eyebrows creased.

"Yersi?" I called out, unable to hide the nervousness in my voice.

I checked around the living room: *Nada*.

I stopped short when I turned into the hallway.

Yersi was standing guard in front of the bathroom door. The only movement was the steady flick of the tip of his tail.

"As of someone gently rapping, rapping at my chamber door," I whispered the line from Poe's poem.

Another prickle of apprehension arced up my spine.

Yersi was an excellent judge of people. When he'd first met Laila and Armand, he'd taken to them right away, claiming their laps as soon as they sat down. The few other folks I'd brought home, he'd taken one sniff and disappeared.

This silent sentry act was freaking me the fuck out.

"Yersi," I called in a neutral tone.

One ear flicked back in acknowledgment, but he didn't move.

I didn't want him creeping Tessa out.

"Yersi," I called again, this time a bit louder.

His tail flicked once with irritation and then went back to the slow, steady tapping.

Defeated, I slunk back to the kitchen to finish dinner.

Just as I was laying everything out, Tessa shuffled into the kitchen. She was wearing a rumpled t-shirt and sweats. Her hair hung limp and wet, leaving dark imprints on the shoulders of her shirt. Bags still hung heavy around her eyes, but there was a tad of color in her cheeks.

Fidgeting with the edge of her shirt, she asked, "Can I help?"

"We're all set. Thanks for offering, though. Have a seat. Would you like a refill on the lemonade?"

"Yes, please."

I topped up her glass and set it in front of her before joining her at the table.

"Help yourself," I said, gesturing to the food. "Hope you don't mind leftovers."

"This is great, thanks," she said quietly before reaching to serve herself.

She filled her plate shyly, and I could tell she was holding back. I'd be pushing seconds on her if I could.

The silverware clinked on serving plates and bowls, filling the silence. I let it settle between us as we both took a few bites. Tessa remained focused on her plate, shoulders hunched, left hand laying in her lap and right hand using a fork to push food around her plate.

Hoping to break the awkward silence, I sighed contentedly and said, "I fucking *love* potato salad. Like, obsessed with it. Good potato salad is the cure for *anything*."

Her eyes shot up.

I'd taken a risk dropping the f-bomb; that wasn't tolerated by a lot of folks in Oklahoma. One time, I'd made Carol squeak—literally *squeak*—when I'd accidentally dropped an f-bomb in the front office. Ever since then, I kept my work face tightly strapped on when in the lab.

I was hoping that cursing might help relax things a bit and make me seem less like an authority figure.

I saw a glint in her eye, and the corner of her mouth turned up in a slight grin. "Yeah. Potato salad is pretty dope. Thanks again."

I took a couple more bites, taking a sip in between to try to slow myself down. I'd already cleared half my plate, and she'd barely eaten anything.

"You're going into mixed animal practice, right?" I asked, attempting to break the ice.

Most students could talk for days about what they wanted to do when they were done with vet school; it was the easiest way to get someone gabbing.

"Yeah. I kinda have to." Her voice was oddly resigned.

"What do you mean 'you have to?'" I asked, trying to catch up. I wasn't used to an answer like that, and it caught me off guard.

"I've got a ton of debt. I need to work in rural medicine to get some student loan relief. I'm not like Emma or those other rich folks."

Her face turned bitter. She pushed her food around on her plate.

Frowning, I nodded in understanding.

Not many people wanted to work in rural medicine. Many ranchers didn't want to spend money treating their animals; it just ate too much into their margins. Many rural vets spent a lot of time just trying to convince people to give their herd vaccines or send a dead animal in for necropsy.

Plus, it was just damn hard working out on the ranch. My large animal medicine professor had finally hung up his hat when he'd had to deliver a calf in a foot of snow at 2 A.M. by the lights of his pickup truck. My large animal surgery professor had been kicked by a horse and had her kneecap shattered. That pretty much ended her career in the field. Work like that was rough on the body.

Folks like Charlie Anderson from Willow Park Mobile were few and far between. Being past retirement age, he was one of the few holdouts. Once those old-timers finally kicked up their boots, there'd be no one left to treat the livestock.

In an attempt to fill the void, the USDA had set up repayment programs that absolved some student debt if veterinarians worked in rural practice for several years. The intentions were good, but what it ended up doing was turning the poorest vet students into wage slaves, forcing them into jobs they didn't want.

Their bright eyes and bushy tails soon faded as the reality of what they'd signed up for sunk in.

I had a feeling Tessa knew what she was walking into but had no other choice.

Hoping she wouldn't lose that spark, I asked, "If a fairy could magic the debt away, what would you do?"

She snorted, making me smile. It was nice to see her have enough energy to *snort*.

"I *want* to be a behaviorist. Do a residency. Do research." There was a slight sparkle in her eye. "I did a summer project with Komodo dragons at the Oklahoma City Zoo. We were looking at responses to different types of environmental enrichment. It was a lot of fun."

It was the most I'd ever heard her say.

I smiled, trying to encourage her to keep going.

Instead, she shrugged one shoulder and frowned. "But a residency will have to wait. I'll need to work to get this monkey off my back first."

I empathized with her. Almost all of us left vet school with heaps of debt. And residencies barely paid enough to live on, much less pay back a six-figure student loan.

I'd taken a big financial risk by going straight into residency. And, once I'd finally finished and gotten a real job, I'd had to live an impoverished lifestyle to get my debt paid off. It had *not* been pleasant.

"I had a ton of debt, too. I'm not going to lie; it was a struggle getting it paid off. But I'm glad I did a residency. Don't give up on that dream. Even if you have to wait a few years for it."

She sighed and nodded.

"How long will you have to work for the Veterinary Medicine Loan Repayment Program?"

"Um. For every twenty-five grand, it's three years of service."

I did the quick mental math. For the average hundred and fifty thousand dollars of debt, it would take eighteen years in service to pay that all off.

Eighteen years.

And that was assuming she didn't have more than a hundred and fifty grand in debt.

"Wow, that's a long time," I blurted before I could stop myself. I'm sure she knew *exactly* how long it was and that it would feel like forever.

"Yeah. It pretty much sucks."

She paused, poking at her food. Her lips were pressed together, and I could tell she was trying not to cry.

"What about the military?" I offered.

The military needed veterinarians, similar to human medical doctors. They even had scholarships to help people through veterinary school. And if someone missed that boat, they had repayment programs if they signed up after graduation. This also came with a commitment to service, though.

Another form of wage slavery.

I loathed the system. Equal opportunity, my ass.

"I tried for the military scholarship, but my grades weren't good enough. I might join after, but...." She left the thought hanging.

I put my hand on her arm and gave it a light squeeze, letting the silence stretch.

Then, the dam broke.

"Even with the loans, I don't have enough to live. I used to work nights and weekends. But with rotations, we have to be available twenty-four seven." She looked up quickly to see if I'd taken offense. "Not pathology—this rotation has been cool so far. But you know what I mean."

I smiled sadly in understanding.

"With the other rotations, we're on clinics all day, seven days a week, and then, we have to do treatments in the evening. Then, we have to take turns being on call for emergencies at night. Like, when the hell are we supposed to even sleep?"

She shook her head and sighed dejectedly. She looked like what little energy she'd pulled from the meal had been sucked right back out of her.

I gave her arm another squeeze and sat back in my chair.

"Loans don't cover everything," she said quietly. "I have to work to pay all my bills."

I could tell she was holding back—but I could put two-and-two together. No one wanted to admit they didn't have a place to live, but she'd all but said it with her circumstances and current financial situation.

I could tell she wasn't looking for advice. Nor did she want me to solve it for her. She just needed to vent.

Tonight wasn't the night to start problem-solving. I knew there were some resources on campus. I'd just need to dig them up and connect her with them before the end of the week.

"You're welcome to stay here for a bit," I said. "I'd enjoy the company. I might sucker you into a tabletop game or two for payment."

She pointed to Yersi, who was sitting three feet away, still studying her like a creepy, possessed puppet. "Not sure if your cat will let me," she said with a soft laugh.

"Psht." I waved my hand dismissively. "The Great Slayer of Canned Food will just have to deal with it."

She laughed and then looked up to catch my eye. "Thanks again, Dr. Harjo."

"Call me Josie—you've met my cat. We're on a first-name basis now."

CHAPTER

ELEVEN

The next morning, my body clock woke me before Yersi did. I groggily patted around on the bed for the black fur demon but came up short.

I sat up, bleary-eyed, and sent my senses through the house.

Worry slivered around my shoulders.

On the rare occasions that Yersi slept in, the change in my breathing pattern from asleep to awake was like Pavlov's bell, and he was up and at 'em, meowing for breakfast.

As concerned as I was, I had to pee, and I could tell that I was just about to bleed through my tampon. I quickly threw a robe over my oversized t-shirt, went through the motions to relieve my aching bladder and prevent the house from looking like a crime scene, then shuffled into the main part of the house.

I self-consciously ran my fingers through my hair. I could pretend like I was just trying to look better for my guest, but in reality, it was just my anxiety once again getting the better of me. My cramps tugged, echoing my angst.

"Yersi?" I called out quietly, not wanting to wake Tessa up. "Kitty, kitty?"

Silence answered me.

A glance around the kitchen and dining room turned up nothing. I moved into the living room. Tessa's form made a large mound, buried in a thick quilt, that moved up and down with the slow breathing of deep sleep.

To my astonishment, Yersi was curled up in the nook of her legs.

Seeing me, he raised his head and offered a slow blink.

This was so unlike Yersi that I was at a loss for what to do. I just stared at the two of them like a creeper.

Shaking off the heebie-jeebies, I decided to let them sleep. Yersi must've felt that Tessa needed some extra TLC, and I didn't want to interfere with the healing process.

Anything was better than that spooky *Raven*-tapping he was doing last night.

Hoping to let them rest for at least another fifteen or twenty minutes, I decided to take my shower and get dressed before starting breakfast.

Even with the warm water pattering on my shoulders, I still couldn't fully relax. I was way out of my element with this Tessa situation. I never knew if I was saying the right thing. I figured it was a win that she was alive, showered, and sleeping.

Then, there was Yersi. His weird behavior was throwing me off.

The anxiety edged in again.

Deep breaths. Little steps. Eyes on the prize.

The most important thing right now was to make sure that Tessa was safe and that she could see a path forward.

With my wet hair tightly braided and my civvies on, I ventured back into the front of the house and set the water to boil. I bustled around the kitchen, popping bread in the toaster and scrambling some eggs for the two of us.

About halfway through, Tessa wandered in with Yersi padding softly behind her, tail alert.

"Morning," I said.

"Good morning," she replied, voice soft.

"Sleep okay?"

"Yes, ma'am. Thanks again for letting me stay."

"Anytime." I gestured to the eggs in the skillet. "I made some eggs and toast. Interested?"

She nodded shyly. "Yes, please. Can I help at all?"

I shook my head. "I'm just about finished. Thanks, though."

She sat at the table. Yersi circled once around her legs, and she stretched down to pet him from head to tail.

Deep bags still hung below her eyes, and her shoulders were hunched like she was wearing a backpack that weighed a hundred pounds. But there was more color in her cheeks, and she looked more animated. I felt better knowing that a good night's sleep had helped just a tad.

"What would you like to drink? I have hot tea but can make coffee. I have some OJ in the fridge, too."

"Tea would be nice, thank you."

I pulled another cup out and measured leaves into the steeper.

As if realizing an egregious error, Yersi's tail went stiff in the air, and he paused mid-step. He then trotted over to his food bowl and let out a pitiful yowl.

"Yes, yes," I answered, slightly exacerbated.

I left the eggs to cook in the skillet and plopped some food in his bowl.

He scarfed everything down in zero-point-five seconds, making an appreciative *merf* around a bite.

Tessa laughed softly. "He's cute."

"Yeah, when he's not making biscuits up and down your back at four in the morning," I teased, trying to feel normal.

I slid the eggs onto two plates next to the slices of toast and bussed everything to the table. I fished around the fridge and pulled out the butter and some strawberry jam, placing them in the center. Two steaming cups of black tea rounded everything out.

"Thank you, again," she said softly. "I appreciate all you're doing for me."

"Any time. You can stay as long as you need to," I said, feeling a slight tug.

It was an offer I wasn't a hundred percent behind. I liked my space, and I wasn't sure I wanted a guest sleeping on my couch for an indefinite period. But the strong desire to make sure that Tessa was going to be okay won out.

Covering up my doubt, I pointed at Yersi, who was back to sitting about two feet away from Tessa, watching her with his ever-twitching tail.

"Besides, Yersi wouldn't let you just leave without making sure you're in a good spot."

Tessa smiled softly. She held her hand down to Yersi, rubbing her two fingers against her thumb and making soft kissing sounds.

With a *mrrp*, Yersi sashayed over to her and rubbed against her hand.

She didn't meet my eyes, but I knew she was considering the offer to stay longer.

"I may take you up on that—but only for a day or two," she added quickly. "I'm looking for another place. It's just hard when I don't have a job."

Student loan disbursements happened at the start of the semester. I wasn't sure how much money she had left, but I could only assume it was paltry. According to Harper, Tessa hadn't been able to pay rent. I wasn't sure how she was going to be able to find another place until her next loan check came in.

"Do you mind if I ask around? See what options you have? I'm pretty sure there are some housing resources on campus. Dr. Smith might have some ideas."

"That'd be cool. I appreciate it." She didn't sound optimistic.

Eyebrows furrowed, she poked at the eggs on her plate.

"I just don't know what to do," she continued. "I'm thinking I may have to request leave so I can get my feet underneath me."

She fought the tears filling her eyes.

I was fairly certain that taking time off would only make things worse by dragging everything out longer. Getting her some emergency housing and finding a way to muscle through it might be her best option.

"There might be a way through without taking leave," I said, sounding more hopeful than I felt. "We just need to find the right path."

She smiled, but it was laced with doubt.

"Give it a day or two," I advised. "I'll ask around and see what I can find."

"Thanks for doing all this for me," she answered.

"Happy to. I got your back."

✳✳✳

Tessa had acquiesced when it came to camping at my place, but pride got the better of her when it came to driving into the lab together. She insisted on taking her own car.

And that, my friend, was how I walked straight into a shitshow all on my lonesome.

I pulled into the lab parking lot distracted by the constant nagging of my cramps. I'd been so caught up in everything "Tessa" that I'd forgotten to pop ibuprofen this morning.

I just hoped Aunt Flo would take a hint and skedaddle off before Friday. Armand was coming over, and it'd been an entire week since I'd seen him last.

Damn! Armand!

I fished my phone out of my purse and texted him.

> Are you available for a quick call?

The message showed as delivered but unread. I waited a few beats and then continued texting.

> I know ur busy in the field. Just wanted to give you a heads up that I have a student staying at my place. She may be there on Friday. Long story.

> ...

> Ur still welcome for dinner.

145

I knew I needed to connect with him later to make sure he understood what he was getting into this Friday. There was nothing worse than showing up for a date night and finding a third wheel.

I couldn't help but feel bummed by the timing of it all.

Since we'd started dating about a month ago, we couldn't keep our hands off each other. That being said, I had a strict no-messing-around-with-guests-in-the-house rule. Both Tessa and Aunt Flo counted as house guests.

Sigh.

Just as I tossed my phone into my purse, a loud thump on the roof of my car startled me.

It took a millisecond for me to realize that Gerald was up to his usual games. I looked up to shoot daggers at him.

I was surprised to see him looking grim, his usual leer replaced by a deep frown.

"Better get in the lab, Pocahontas," he said firmly. "You seriously messed up this time."

He pulled my door open.

I couldn't believe it. He'd *actually* pulled my fucking door open, acting like a dad punishing his daughter who'd turned up at home after curfew and smelled like booze.

What the hell?!

"Get off my fucking car, creeper," I hissed before I could stop myself.

I couldn't say his flinch didn't give me a small amount of satisfaction.

I snatched my stuff and stood quickly. "What is *wrong* with you?!"

Startled by my uncharacteristic resistance, he took a small step back.

I turned my back on him, closed my door, and hit the button on the key fob. My car made a *thump* when the locks slid home.

Gerald recovered quickly, following hot on my heels into the lab to keep chewing my ass.

"I told you that you needed to lock those tiger parts up. Now they're *gone*, and it's because of your negligence," he squeaked after me.

I halted dead in my tracks and turned to him. "What?" I asked, off balance, certain I'd heard him wrong.

He stopped short, almost crashing into me.

Pointing a finger at me, he pressed on, "You! The tiger pelt and claws have been stolen because of *you*."

"What?" I repeated stupidly.

Say "what" again, motherfucker! I chided myself, unable to resist channeling my inner Jules as a form of self-flagellation.

"They've been stolen!" he practically shouted, exacerbated.

With a sinking feeling, realization dawned on me. The idea of the tiger parts being stolen was so outlandish that I was having a hard time wrapping my mind around it. Finally, my brain caught up with everything, and I felt a sliver of dread.

Just as Gerald puffed up to have another go at me, a beater sedan pulled up next to us.

Relief washed over me when I recognized Tessa. It gave me the perfect excuse to turn away from Gerald and try to figure out how to escape this ambush.

She must've seen my face and Gerald's body language. Women had a knack for knowing when another woman needed a lifeline.

She rolled down her window. "Good morning, Dr. Harjo. Do you have a minute? I'd like to ask you a question before we meet in the conference room."

Gerald stepped back, face red and hands clenched.

I could have kissed her.

"Sure!" I said, sounding way more cheerful than I should have.

When I turned back to Gerald, he was already storming off.

Tessa pulled into a slot nearby and got out of her car.

"You okay?" she asked quietly. "Dr. Richter was acting kinda scary."

"Yeah, I'm good," I said, lying through my teeth.

After a beat, she added, "For a second there, I thought I was going to have to tase him."

That was such an un-Tessa-like thing to say, I blurted a laugh, letting the last bit of adrenaline flutter out.

She looked at me out of the corner of her eye and shrugged.

The shy, ashamed Tessa of the last three days wasn't anywhere in that shrug. It was a shrug that said, "I'm not going to take any shit." It was a shrug that said she'd been around the block, and she was *done* with that hot mess.

Under her cloak of despair was one tough woman.

"Thanks for the lifesaver," I said gratefully.

"Anytime. I got your back, Dr. Harjo."

With that, Tessa flashed me the biggest, most energetic grin I'd seen the whole week.

I felt a surge of hope.

And then, it was instantly washed away.

As soon as we crossed the threshold into the lab, she threw the hood of her sweatshirt over her head, stuffed her hands in her pockets, and hunched her shoulders.

"See you in the conference room, Dr. Harjo," she said, nodding her chin once at me before ghosting off.

A bit shaken from the rollercoaster of emotions coming off her, I headed straight for Dustin's office to check in. Something had gotten Gerald in one hell of a tizzy, and I needed to figure out what was going on before I faced the rest of the students this morning.

Dustin was seated at his desk, mug of coffee cool and untouched, phone clutched in his hand.

I tapped my knuckles lightly on the doorjamb before walking in. He looked up at me, the skin around his eyes wrinkled with tension, and waved for me to have a seat.

"Yes, sir," he said into the phone, voice firm and official.

I started chewing on the inside of my cheek, my leg bobbing. Wretched anxiety. It was like that friend who was always around that you hated but didn't have the heart to tell them to get lost.

"Yes, sir," he repeated into the phone. "The building is locked at night, but we don't have a lock on the large animal cooler. Yes, sir, that's where the items were stored."

My heart sank.

Gerald's words came back to smack me in the face, and all the pieces fell into place.

Dustin frowned deeply, listening into the phone. His chest rose with a deep, angry sigh.

"Yes, sir. I can send over a list of everyone with access." There was a long, tense pause.

"Pardon me?" he said, sounding completely befuddled. "My boss, sir?"

He coughed uncomfortably and shifted in his seat. "Yes, the director of the lab is Fran Jones.... Yes, I can transfer you. Just a minute, please."

He pressed a few buttons on the phone to transfer the call and then hung up before making a live introduction.

He turned toward me, his face filled with defeated fury.

I raised my eyebrows in a question.

"The tiger pelt and claws are missing, and the cops are acting like I took them."

"What?!" I scoffed. The idea was so ridiculous that I couldn't keep the laugh out of my tone.

He took another deep, belly breath, nostrils flaring. His hands clenched the armrests of his chair, knuckles white.

"Rewind—start from the beginning," I coaxed. I was trying to remain chill and talk Dustin off the ledge, but I felt the buzz of stress ringing in my muscles.

This is serious. Like, career-ending serious.

He cleared his throat. "I came in this morning, early, like usual. The histology technicians were here—you know they start before me."

I nodded. The histology technicians worked staggered shifts; two of them started an hour or two before everyone else came into the lab.

"The alarm was already off. But I still had to buzz in."

The public could enter through the front door, but only between the hours of eight to five. And even then, they couldn't get past receiving. Outside of those hours, we had to use our badges to get in and out of the lab. Everything sounded normal so far.

"A body came in overnight—Josh brought it in. I went into the cooler to get eyes on it...you know...see if it was gonna be a rotter."

I nodded again. I always wanted to know what awaited me that day. If it was gonna be a stinker, it gave me time to mentally prepare. The *parfum de bœuf mort* had a tendency to stick.

"I could tell someone had been in there, moving stuff around. I just knew something was up." He shook his head. "I checked everywhere. I even emptied the offal bins to make sure I hadn't accidentally tossed the pelt and claws in one of 'em. I swear they were on the third shelf when I closed everything down yesterday."

He looked down at his desk and started pushing a pen around. "As soon as I noticed the stuff was gone, I called the cops."

"How did Gerald know?" I blurted.

His eyes shot up to lock on mine. "What?"

"Gerald ambushed me this morning, saying the tiger parts were stolen. He was all up in my face about how I was negligent. Did you talk to him?"

Dustin shook his head slowly.

"How did he know they were gone, then?" I asked, agitated. My sewing machine leg started up.

Dustin sucked his teeth. "It's classic Dr. Richter. He was probably snooping around, trying to get the one-up on someone. All y'all know he's like that."

"I guess," I said doubtfully.

Gerald *did* like to be up in everyone else's business. But it was usually about cases, like trying to splain us about how we should test for something or how we failed to think of a differential.

This was different.

"What did the cops say?" I asked.

He sighed heavily and his shoulders sagged. "They ain't tellin' me nothing. They were treating me like I was stupid for not lockin' 'em up better. Then, they started acting like they suspected me. Wantin' to talk to Fran."

I snorted. "That's ridiculous."

"No offense intended, but it doesn't matter what you say about all this, Doc. I'm thinkin' I might need a lawyer."

I started feeling all momma-bear protective of him and was about to go on a rant when he stopped me with a look.

He was right.

My shoulders sagged.

"Okay. So, what do we do now?" I asked.

He shrugged. "Go open up that cow that came in overnight."

***

I left Dustin's office feeling completely off-kilter. A bomb had gone off this morning, and I was still blinking in shock and picking brains out of my hair.

It was Fran's job to deal with this mess; that's what she got paid the big bucks for. I decided to drop this turd in her lap, take some deep paper-bag breaths, and put my game face on for the students.

And I'm on the rag. And I have a suicidal student staying with me. And I miss Armand. And, and, and....

I was switching pretty fast between my pity pot and my anxiety loop. I paused outside Fran's door and took a deep breath before going in.

I probably should've knocked because she looked up, startled, when I burst in.

She was standing hunched next to her desk, purse still over her shoulder and car keys in her hand. The phone was glued to her ear, held by her iron fist.

Her eyes narrowed almost infinitesimally before she waved me in to sit down.

"Yes, sir. I'll need to call you back. I just got in, and I need to get a better understanding of the situation."

She paused. "Yes, sir."

She grabbed a pen and wrote something on a sticky note before saying a polite goodbye and hanging up.

A tense silence filled the room as she slowly put her keys in her purse before stuffing it under her desk. Then, she slid into her chair. Clasping her hands together, she rocked back and turned an icy glare on me.

"Quite a bit of excitement this morning," she prompted.

I wasn't gonna take the bait and waited for her to say something that required a response. I couldn't care less if she was my boss.

She pursed her lips and leaned forward.

"My morning started with Gerald informing me that the tiger parts were stolen. Then, I'm barely in my office, and I have an Officer"—she looked down at the sticky note— "Watts calling me, asking some very detailed questions."

Officer Watts? I felt my mind scramble around, trying to place the name.

Then, in a classic lightbulb moment, I connected the dots. He was the cop involved in the Shadowhawk case.

What are the chances?

Stillwater was a small town, but not *that* small.

Fran coughed lightly, jerking me back to the conversation. "Care to fill me in?"

I started picking absently at the peeling armrest on the guest chair.

"I just found out and don't have a lot of information yet," I said, feeling entirely unhelpful. "Dustin said the cooler looked tussled this morning and realized the pelt and the claws were gone. He called the police right away. I wanted to check in with you to discuss next steps."

She looked down her nose at me as if I was the source of all the turmoil in the lab. "Those items are extremely valuable. I'd say about forty to fifty grand worth of items were stolen from this facility. Add on the fact that it's illegal to be in possession of these items without the proper permits in the first place. We're looking at one felony, if not more."

"Yes, ma'am. I'm aware." Irritation crept into my voice; I wasn't going to let her shift the blame to me.

"This makes the lab look incompetent. I don't need this right now."

Yeah, no kidding.

"Has anyone contacted the owner yet?" Fran asked. "Where did the tiger come from again?"

"Tiawah Animal Sanctuary. And no, ma'am, no one has called them. We all just got in. Dustin called the cops immediately—which, in my opinion, was the right thing to do. I came to you first thing to discuss an action plan."

My voice was laced with cool anger. I needed to be careful.

"I can call the owner if you'd like," I continued. "But I think it might mean more coming from you."

Her eyes narrowed.

Part of me felt bad about flicking this booger, but it really would be better if she called. It was possible this drama could make the news. She'd have to work with the head of the sanctuary on messaging.

A look of resignation pulled her mouth down. "I'll ask Carol for the information and call them shortly. Do not tell *anyone* until we figure out how we're going to message this."

I cleared my throat. "Um. You know Gerald has probably told everyone already."

"Damn it," she said, more to herself.

She knew I was right. The entire lab would know within the next hour, if they didn't already. I didn't want to get blamed for that along with everything else.

She sighed. "I'll pull everyone together for an all-hands meeting after I make some calls. Until then, don't talk about it, and tell others to keep their mouth shut if they start yapping about it."

"Yes, ma'am," I answered.

With that, I made my escape, happy to have fled her office without any more tasks lumped onto my plate. I needed to get my game face on for the necropsy this morning and then get the students out of the lab for the rest of the day.

Today was going to be mighty unpleasant.

CHAPTER

TWELVE

The nervous chatter of the students hit me like a brick when I entered the conference room.

Apparently, the gossip had already trickled down to them, and everyone was abuzz. The drama had even been enough to pull Emma away from her usual primping-in-front-of-the-phone time.

My eye twitched.

I was severely under-caffeinated, my uterus wouldn't stop reminding me that it was cleaning house, and this crap with the tiger was gnawing at me.

I grabbed a seat and pushed the submission form for the cow into the middle of the table. "Okay, everybody. Let's mellow out a bit."

Everyone turned to look at me.

"Is it true that the tiger pelt and claws were stolen?" Sarah asked, slightly aghast.

I cleared my throat uncomfortably. "Unfortunately, yes...they're missing."

Eyes went wide around the table.

"Isn't that like a felony or something?" Harper asked.

"Yeah, I think it is," Kassidy responded.

"How would you know?" Emma said with a retort. "Have a rap sheet we don't know about?"

"It's a *tiger pelt*," Mackenzie said, stepping in. "They're endangered. I'm sure it's regulated."

"Yeah, it has to be a felony," Harper mused.

"A felony?" Sarah said in a hushed voice, eyes wide. "What's going to happen to the person who stole it?"

"Oh, my God, Sarah. You are so naive," Emma scoffed.

The comments were flying around the room like a ping-pong ball, and I could barely keep up.

I coughed loudly to get everyone's attention.

All eyes swiveled back to me.

"Look," I said firmly. "Right now, all we know is that some items are missing."

"Psht." Emma sniffed, rolling her eyes. "Some ghetto-ass person stole them. Probably that necropsy tech. We all know it."

The chatter started back up as they argued back and forth about the penalties for getting caught stealing something that valuable. They quickly slipped into a tangent about the legality of even having it in their position and landed on how one would even attempt to sell something like that all in a matter of seconds.

It was like trying to control a flock of squawking parrots.

"Hey, everybody," I interrupted again, trying to regain control of the conversation. "Listen. Let's take it down a notch. Out of respect for Tiawah Animal Sanctuary and the director of this lab, cut it out with the speculation and the gossip."

I made eye contact with each and every person around the table.

Sarah flushed, as if embarrassed. Harper, Kassidy, and Mackenzie appeared to be taking my words seriously. Tessa had her chin resting on her folded arms but still appeared to be listening.

Emma, on the other hand, narrowed her eyes and crossed her arms.

"Please don't share any information about the case or the missing items with anyone, I pressed on. "It should be Tiawah's decision on if, when, and how to share any information publicly."

Emma smirked.

I raised one eyebrow. "Emma," I said sternly.

She waved her hand dismissively. "I'm just sayin', y'all aren't going to be able to keep this quiet."

A tense silence filled the room, and the other students held their breath, waiting to see how I would respond.

I was starting to get pissed and it came through when I said, "I'm asking *you* to keep this quiet. Are you going to be able to do that?"

She waved her hand again. "Fine. Whatever."

I wanted to slap her. Instead, I took a deep breath.

Before I could move on, a look of horrified realization spilled across Sarah's face as it drained of color.

"Oh geez. Do you think the police are going to want to talk to us?" she asked.

All of the students tensed.

"Why would they want to talk to us?" Harper asked, too innocent for her own good.

"They can talk to my lawyer," Emma huffed and flipped her hair.

A lawyer?! WTF?

Dustin had said that word, too.

A sliver of dread slipped down my spine.

Do I need a lawyer?

The blame tended to land on people of color. And my skin was just brown enough to be on the radar in Oklahoma. I could feel myself being pulled into yet another anxiety loop.

Desperate to move on, I said, "I understand everyone is worried. But right now, we have a job to do. We've got a cow to necropsy. Let's focus on that."

Feeling the need to dish out some evil, I quickly added, "Emma, I think you're up to lead."

I'd read the history already, and I knew this cow was going to be a stinker. I couldn't help but feel a hint of glee knowing that the Queen Bee would have to wash her hair a few times to get the smell out. She deserved it, the privileged little snot.

"What about Tessa?" Emma whined. "She hasn't done anything all week."

I saw Sarah's wide eyes bounce back and forth between Emma and me. Clearly, this was turning into a show. Though Emma was right about Tessa, I just couldn't let her win.

"Tessa will scribe for us today. She can lead the next case that comes in."

I knew I shouldn't be playing favorites, but I couldn't help myself.

Emma's face turned bright red, but she shut up, which was my number one goal at the moment.

She snatched the paper and read through it. "It's an adult Holstein. Developed vaginal discharge post-calving and died three days ago."

Exacerbated, her arms dropped with a dramatic *thunk* on the table. "Three days ago?!" She turned to me, miffed. "Seriously?"

I shrugged. "All part of the job."

Inside, I was laughing like Mr. Burns.

"Even though the carcass was in the fridge overnight, you might want to tie your hair back," I added. "The smell of death tends to stick."

This time, I couldn't keep the glee out of my voice, and her eyes narrowed.

"What are your differentials?" I asked the group, ignoring her eye-daggers.

"Probably metritis," Mackenzie offered.

"Yep, I'd bet dollars to donuts its metritis. We should still go in with an open mind and check everything. Make sure you check the mammary gland for mastitis, too. That often gets missed, but it's important in dairy cattle. Depending on what we find, we'll probably collect samples for culture."

Eager to get them out on the floor before the chatter built back up, I rapped my knuckles once on the table. "All right, let's head out."

***

About fifteen minutes later, the students were hunkered around the cow, everyone too chicken to get started.

I didn't blame them.

A putrid, cloudy discharge was weeping from the vulva. The abdomen was green-tinged—never a good sign on the rot-spectrum. The soft tissues were also crepitus with post-mortem gas production, forcing the legs into the air.

I grabbed one of the student knives and handed it to Emma. "You're up."

Taking several steps back, I added, "I'd recommend decompression first. Stab the abdomen to let the gas out."

The other students joined me outside of the splash zone.

I couldn't help a tiny smile from creasing my lips. This was glorious!

I tried to catch Dustin's eye and share the Queen-Bee-torture-joy, but he was otherwise occupied. He was standing back, hands in his pockets, eyebrows creased, and a frown pulling the sides of his beard down.

It all came crashing back.

I couldn't ignore the missing tiger parts. Dustin was heaping all of the blame on himself, and it was torture watching him shoulder that stress.

A loud hissing sound followed by a squeal of horror pulled me back into the moment.

Emma had tried decompression, but she'd also hit the rumen just right. The soft tissues were fluttering with escaped gas, spitting small flecks of partially digested feed onto her face and coveralls.

"Oh, God! Disgusting!" She dropped the knife on the table, yanked her gloves off, and ran to the sink to wash away the small bits that had stuck to her face.

"Come on, now," I chided. "No need to be dramatic."

Chuckling in my head, I decided to throw her a bone. I grabbed my knife and worked in tandem with Dustin to get the cow opened up.

After the abdominal and thoracic cavities were opened, I gestured to Emma. "Your turn. Finish it up."

I'd already gone above and beyond to help her out. She could take it from here.

While the students had at it, I washed my knife and arms.

I pulled Dustin to the side.

"How're you doing?" I asked softly enough so that only he could hear.

"It is what it is," he replied.

His face said something different; he looked crushed.

I felt a surge of worry.

"Anything I can do to help? Want me to go through the cooler again? Another set of eyes?" I offered.

He shook his head. "No. Thanks, Doc. I've been through it three times already. I took everything off the shelves and emptied all the bins. It ain't nowhere."

"Did anything get picked up for cremation?"

Once, during my residency, the necropsy technician had given an amputated leg to the crematorium, thinking it was a carcass. I couldn't imagine how someone could confuse a leg for an entire body. Dustin would never do something like that. He was too meticulous. But accidents could still happen.

"No, ma'am. Everything was there yesterday when I closed up. Only person who's been in there since is Josh. When he brought that cow in." He gestured to the carcass with his chin.

"Josh didn't even know the tiger was in there," I said, doubtful.

"*Everybody* knew it was in there," he countered.

I could tell he was mad at the situation and not at me, so I didn't take it personally.

He sighed. "But Josh didn't take it. He's a good kid and had no reason to."

"Yeah," I agreed without a lot of data to back up my position.

I hadn't crossed paths with Josh often. He was an animal science student who worked on call on nights and weekends. When I worked with him on the rare off-hours case, he seemed like a stand-up guy.

That's what they said about Bundy, I thought, startling myself.

My thoughts were getting pretty damn dark.

Dustin continued, "If Josh was gonna steal it, you'd think he'd do it on a day when he wasn't bringing a carcass in. Be kinda stupid to do otherwise."

I took a long look at him. I'd never seen him carrying such a heavy burden before.

"This isn't your fault, you know," I said softly.

He kept his eyes locked on the ground.

I nudged him playfully until he looked at me. "It isn't your fault. There's nothing any of us could have done differently. We'll let the cops sort it out."

He sucked at the bottom of his mustache.

"Dude. Seriously. I've seen way worse. Trust me."

The corner of his mouth turned up. I'd shared the stories of the necropsy tech from my residency with him before, and he'd been equally shocked.

"You've been here forever. If this is the worst thing that happens...." I shrugged, letting him fill in the blanks.

He leaned his head down and sucked on his mustache again.

"Come on." I gave him another gentle nudge. "Let's go save Queen Bee from the Bog of Eternal Stench."

That got a slight smile, and he pulled himself up by the bootstraps to assist Emma.

I watched the students bounce around the organs like little bees, the inescapable stench of the rotten cow burning my nose. It was good to see Dustin knee-deep in guts and Tessa more engaged today, but I still felt like we were all walking on a tightrope.

A small lean to one side, and someone was gonna go *splat*.

I just had to hope the splat wouldn't be me.

***

Emotions were tense after the stinky cow, and talk quickly returned to the missing tiger parts as we were cleaning up. Even with gentle reminders, I couldn't get the students to knock it off.

With each comment, Dustin's expression grew more clouded. The cow necropsy had been a distraction, even if unpleasant on the old olfactory bulbs. All the gossip just dredged everything back up again.

By the time we wrapped the necropsy up, it was 11 A.M. Even though it was early, I decided to excuse the students for the rest of the day. I just couldn't be around their incessant speculation and chatter.

Dustin also needed a break; the more they talked, the deeper into the darkness he slipped.

With the students out of my hair, I hid in my office, pretending to do work.

I was caught in a loop and needed Laila's help to get out of it. I shot her a quick text.

> I know its short notice but want to meet for lunch?

> Hey! Nice to hear from you!

> Sure I can meet up. Where and when?

> I need to get out of here. I'll come by your lab at noon?

> I didn't bring food. Can we go to the commons?

> Sounds good. Thank you for always being there for me!

She hearted my text.

At fifteen to noon, I ducked out of the lab and trekked across campus to the plant biology building. The air was wet and heavy, the ever-present, oppressive Oklahoma heat hinting at rain while the insects sang loudly.

Despite the weather, I always enjoyed the walk over to Laila's lab. The red-brick buildings with white trim were separated by ancient trees sprawled over expanses of greenery. It was a gorgeous campus, one where every building was thoughtfully designed to blend into the other structures, some of which dated back more than a hundred years. This was in stark contrast to other universities, like UC Davis, where it looked like architecture students vomited all over campus. The buildings there were almost as discombobulated and confused as the culture of that little college town.

The hall of the plant science building was busy with students, and I had to surf against the tide to Laila's lab. I found her in her adjoining office, clacking away at her keyboard. I knocked lightly on the doorjamb.

"Hey, Josie!" She beamed. "Two secs."

She saved whatever she was working on and put her computer to sleep before getting up to fold me in a hug.

Well, I guess it was more like *I* folded *her* into a hug; she was tiny, but her hugs were so reassuring.

"Thanks for coming out on short notice," I said with a hint of relief.

"Any time!" She grabbed her wallet and phone before saying, "Shall we?"

We followed the tail end of the student swarm out of the building and wound our way to the commons. It was going to be pretty busy this time of day. But Laila was there; she always made things better and cheered me up.

We wove through the line at Zest, grabbing gyros. The Commons was packed, but the hustle and bustle were a great distraction. Students were spread like peanut butter through the building, backpacks and laptops sprawled across tables. We wove our way through, finding an empty booth in a relatively quiet corner.

"So, what's up?" Laila prompted. "Wanna talk about it?"

I hesitated, trying to collect my thoughts. I didn't know where to start. I just knew that the anxiety was building up, and it was going to explode everywhere soon.

One of my fellow residents had described it as holding a beach ball just below the surface of the pool. You hold it down until your arms shake. It gets harder and harder, and then, the tension is too much, and the ball bursts out of the water and into your face. Between all the stuff with Tessa and the tiger, I saw a beach ball bitch-slap in my near future.

I needed Laila to help me hold the damn ball down because the problem sure as shit wasn't going to be solved anytime soon.

"I have students on the floor this week," I started and then fumbled again, not sure where to go from there.

Do I talk about Tessa? The tiger? These two conflicting worries were raging around my head. It was like the story about the lady and the tiger; I didn't know which door to open. Deep down inside, I knew either one was probably going to bite me in the ass.

I picked the lady.

"I've got a vet student who's having a rough time—just got kicked out of her place and is sleeping in her car."

Laila's eyes went wide as saucers.

"Yeah, I know. She started rotation looking tore up, like she'd been on a bender. One of her friends came to me and explained the situation. Said she was worried she might kill herself."

"Dang, Josie," Laila said softly and stopped eating. "Isn't suicide super common in vets?"

I nodded, my lips pressed together.

"Anyway, the first day I tried to talk to her—that was Tuesday—she ghosted me," I continued. "Yesterday, I finally pinned her down. I felt bad cornering her. But I was really worried she might do something stupid. I offered to let her stay at my place. I was honestly shocked when she took me up on it."

"That was super nice of you," Laila said, reaching across the table to give my wrist a squeeze. "Did you figure out what was going on? An abusive boyfriend? Money? Drugs?"

I shook my head. "I didn't want to poke too much. I just wanted to make sure she lived through the night. Get her showered. Get some food in her."

Even though I was feeling sick to my stomach, I took a tasteless bite of my gyro and forced it down. It gave me a moment to think.

"She did talk about student loan debt and how she has to work in rural practice to try to get some of the debt waived. She wants to be a behaviorist but thinks she might have to let the dream go. So, money, maybe?"

"Hmmm," Laila responded, face neutral.

"I invited her back tonight."

A flash of surprise flitted across her face.

"What?" I asked, slightly defensive.

She shrugged one shoulder, leaned forward, and picked up her gyro again. "You just really like your space, and your house is tiny. It's nice of you to welcome her like that."

"What choice do I have? If she were to do something, I'd never forgive myself."

The comment hung between us. Laila knew about Nathan's suicide. She knew it weighed heavily on me even though he and I had already lost touch when it happened.

She smiled at me sadly as she chewed her bite of gyro.

"Anyway," I said, brushing the icky thoughts away by waving my hand in the air. "Yersi's weird with her. So, that's throwing me off, too."

"Weird, how?"

Laila only knew Yersi's two settings; he either loved you or he hated you. Yersi *loved* Laila and stuck to her like Velcro when she came over for game nights. And she'd heard about the *hate* from failed date stories. This third Yersi setting was new to both of us.

"It's kind of like a reluctant affection?" I frowned. "He watches her all the time. Just sits about two feet away. But then I found him sleeping on her this morning."

"At least he isn't scratching up her shoes," Laila teased, referencing one disastrous adventure when I brought a guy home about three years ago.

Yeah, Yersi hated *him.*

I should have listened to the cat. That guy turned out to be a total dick.

I barked out a small laugh, and Laila beamed.

"Back to the student, though," Laila said around another bite. "I think you're doing the right thing. You just need a path for her into her own place. You know what they say about long-term guests. Especially ones sleeping on your couch, weirding your cat out."

"Yeah. Do you know of any emergency housing on campus or something like that?"

She shook her head regretfully. "I haven't had to help a lot of students with money issues."

"No worries. I was also going to ask Zoe to see if she has any ideas this afternoon."

"That's a great idea!" After a beat, she added, "Sorry I couldn't be of more help. When you find out what resources are available, can you let me know? It might come in handy *when* I become Chair."

"*When*?" I felt a surge of happiness. "Laila!"

She put a hand up in surrender, her other one still holding the remnants of her gyro.

"When were you going to tell me?!" I exclaimed.

Laila had been in a head-on fight with this total asshole, Ian Murray, for the position. I'd met the guy and could attest to the fact that he was definitely *not* someone who should be leading a department. He had the social skills of a hyena, and that comparison was a bit mean to the hyena.

"It still isn't sealed. But I'm the only candidate selected for an interview. Rumor has it that the interview panel is more of a formality." She shrugged, bashful. "I just found out. And you sounded like you needed an ear today. Anyway, back to your student.... When you find out what's available, can you let me know? I want to set up a mini-resource center for students, even if it's directing them to other locations on campus to get the help they need."

"You can't just wave that accomplishment away, Laila," I chided playfully. "That's awesome! Congratulations! I'm so happy for you. You're going to be an amazing Chair."

She smiled shyly.

"And yes," I continued. "I'll let you know what Zoe says. I can't go directly to Admin. Both the student staying with me and her friend seemed almost scared when I offered that as an option."

Laila shook her head in disappointment. "See? That's why we need positive spaces for students to go where they'll feel supported and not penalized for the crap they're going through."

"Yeah. At least the vet school has Zoe. She's not in the main building, but I see students come by her office all the time, even if it's just to chat. She's a keeper."

"Yes, she is," Laila agreed. "I wish I had more people like that in my department."

I smiled affectionately at her. Laila was so humble she didn't even realize that *she* was that person in her department. This time, I reached across and gave her arm a squeeze.

"Thanks for listening," I said. "I just needed to get away for a minute. Get my head on straight."

"Totally get it. Glad I could help."

CHAPTER

THIRTEEN

It was like wading through mud on my way back to the lab. Lunch with Laila had pulled me out of my spiral. But I still felt like I was perched on the edge of a sucking drain, feeling the tug of the water at my toes—a threat to pull me right back in.

I did *not* want to go back to the lab today.

To make matters worse, the walk back was uncomfortable. The sun glared down, and the damp afternoon heat was pressing in. The buzzing of the cicadas had gone from singing to screeching.

I pulled the loose end of my shirt and waved it, trying to avoid a boob sweat line.

Even though the walk back sucked, it still went too fast. Before I knew it, the lab loomed before me.

I'd never realized how clunky the cement block of a building looked—how unwelcoming it all was. A brief desire to just get in my car and go home washed over me. My cramps seconded the motion.

But I had obligations. I couldn't walk away from this mess.

Sigh.

As I pushed through the front doors, a cold wash of air slammed into me, making me shiver.

I'd barely stepped over the threshold when James from the front office fluttered over.

"Dr. Harjo! I'm so glad I found you." He was practically wringing his hands.

James was young and fresh out of high school. He was a classic Oklahoma cowboy: skinny with stiff jeans, a button-up short-sleeve shirt with snaps, and a rim around his hair from his cowboy hat. His momma had raised him right, and he didn't wear it inside. He was our Carol-in-training.

"Hey, James. What's up?" I tried to sound casual, but dread was tracing up my spine.

"Fran is holding an all-hands meeting in"—he pulled his phone out of his back pocket and checked the time—"now. She sent me to find everyone."

He chewed his lip and continued, "We're meeting in the large conference room. It has to be about the tiger, right? Who do you think stole it? Was it one of us?"

It was weird seeing him in a state of panic; James was typically super chill.

Before I had a chance to answer, his eyebrows bunched up, and he said, "I still have to find Dr. Lang. I gotta go. I'll meet you there."

With a quick wave, he skittered away, cowboy boots clacking on the linoleum.

I stood there, stunned. Everything had escalated a hundredfold over the lunch break. The reality of the situation was finally hitting me. This wasn't just something that had gone missing from the necropsy cooler. The objects were of high value, and people were on the hunt for a scapegoat. If this wasn't handled right, it could turn into a political bloodbath.

My hands itched for something to fidget with as the stress built.

I followed the sounds of heated conversation down the hallway to the main conference room. At least I'd excused the students for the afternoon. The vibe of the lab was all out of whack. I couldn't imagine trying to manage them and whatever circus awaited me up ahead.

The large conference room wasn't much bigger than the one where we met the students, and the twenty-some-odd employees were stuffed into the space. It was standing-room-only by the time I'd arrived.

I tucked into a corner next to Dustin and crossed my arms.

His expression was unreadable. "Hey, Doc."

"Hey, Dustin." I nodded to the rest of the people in the room. "Quite the excitement, eh?"

He sighed heavily. "Yep."

"We'll wait a few more minutes for any stragglers and then get started," Fran announced in her lecture voice.

The atmosphere was electric, and there was a faint whiff of BO. People whispered to each other, expressions ranging from worry to excitement.

Except for Gerald. He looked smug.

"Do you think Josh took it?" a hushed voice asked. "He was in the cooler overnight when no one was around."

I looked down to see Noah, one of the histology technicians, seated in front of me. He was leaning over toward Lenny from toxicology.

"No way. Dr. Smith thinks it was Dr. Richter. Look at him over there." Lenny gestured with his chin toward Gerald.

He wasn't wrong. Gerald looked like he'd put his hand in the cookie jar and gotten away with it.

But still, Gerald? Seriously?

On closer examination of the other lab folks, I noticed that several people were giving Gerald the side-eye. To my horror, a few were even looking at Dustin the same way.

I'd never seen a group of people go feral so fast. It was like *Lord of the Flies*.

Kill the pig. Cut her throat. Spill her blood.

I wasn't sure if it was the thought or the air-conditioning that caused goosebumps to break out on my arms.

Dustin's face was stony. I wanted to give him a nudge of support but wasn't sure it would help.

Dr. Lang came in, squeezing in next to me. James zipped in right after him.

Seeing them enter, Fran stood at the head of the table. "Okay, everyone! Quiet down, please."

An expectant hush spread through the room.

"We might be shy one or two folks, but let's get started." Fran cleared her throat. "As I'm sure y'all are aware by now, the tiger pelt and claws are now missing from the pathology department. Dustin has scoured the cooler, and they haven't been misplaced."

Gerald snorted loudly.

A quiet buzz picked up again as people whispered to each other. My palms started to sweat. Dustin's face went pale.

"Please," Fran said, holding out both her hands, palms-down, patting the air as if to tamp down the gossip. "Please, keep it quiet."

The whispering died down again, but just barely. The herd was spooked and ready to bolt. Fran was losing what little control she might've had.

"We're also certain that they were not accidentally disposed of," she continued. "Because the missing items are highly valuable, Dustin has done his due diligence and has contacted the authorities."

Dustin shifted, and his biceps clenched as he crossed his arms tighter. Saying his name repeatedly was making him seriously uncomfortable.

Fran was oblivious to the damage she was doing and stumbled on. "I spoke with the police this morning. Now, *I* trust everyone in the lab and know that none of *my* employees would have stolen the items. However, the police are not convinced."

The room erupted in chatter. Already, alliances were being drawn, and people were casting accusatory glances across the room. It was like the Capitol folks placing bets on the Hunger Games.

Jesus, Fran. Couldn't you message this any better?

Normally, just about everyone in our lab got along, mainly due to the unifying dislike of our resident troll. Against Gerald, everyone else looked pretty damn cool.

But Fran's words had dropped a big, fat bomb into the room, dissolving the thin web that held us all together.

Fran looked around, stupidly surprised by the effect of her words. She tried to regain control by tamping the air with her palms down again.

"Everyone! Please!" She had to raise her voice over the cacophony. *How can twenty-ish people make so much noise?*

Dustin and I stayed in the back, arms crossed, silent as lambs.

"Everyone!" Fran said again.

The room quieted, but whispers were still being traded by a few of the technicians.

"As I said, given the value of the items, the police will be coming tomorrow to interview everyone. And I mean *everyone*. If you have any on-call or part-time employees not in the meeting today, please make sure that they make themselves available tomorrow." She looked up at Dustin. "That includes the student who was on call last night."

Dustin nodded tightly to acknowledge the command. But he clenched his jaw. I'd never seen him this tense.

"Now, I'm also asking that all of you—*all of you*—do not talk about this outside of work until this is resolved. That includes your families."

I couldn't help a *pffft* from escaping as I scoffed softly.

There was no way in hell people weren't going to talk about this. It'd start at home, hushed conversation over the dinner table. Feeling safe after crossing that first line, their BFF would come next. Then, it would devolve into a bar conversation with their buddies.

We couldn't even keep the drama within the pathology team. Asking people not to talk about it at home was stupid.

This is a complete disaster.

"I'm also asking that you not discuss this at work, either. There is enough speculation going around the lab already. Please remember that we are all friends here. Now is the time to come together."

Her kumbaya attempt fell flat, and conversations picked up around the room again.

"Are there any questions?" She was floundering now.

Gerald's hand shot up.

Despite her inability to control the overarching situation, Fran knew well enough not to give Gerald a platform.

She looked around the table hopefully. She might have been able to deflect if there was another person with a question. She frowned slightly when no one else raised a hand or spoke up.

"Yes. Dr. Richter?" she finally said, resigned.

"Clearly, there has been a gross act of negligence that resulted in these items being stolen in the first place. What repercussions are planned for those responsible?" He blatantly gestured to Dustin and me.

A hush fell across the room. All eyes turned to us, rubbernecking.

Heat rose in my cheeks as my adrenals dumped a fresh batch of epinephrine. The blood fled Dustin's face.

I tried to remind myself that the whole wide-eyed observance of a trainwreck was just hundreds of years of evolution; they couldn't help themselves.

It didn't work. I felt a small fire of resentment building.

Fran finally spoke through the uncomfortable silence. "Once we resolve the immediate situation, we will start looking at options to better secure the large animal cooler."

She'd tried to sidestep the question. But Gerald, being Gerald, just couldn't catch a social cue, even if it slapped him in the face.

"That's not what I meant," Gerald pressed. "If people did their jobs correctly, we wouldn't be in this situation. That needs to be addressed."

Fran sputtered, stunned by the direct, inappropriate question in front of such a large audience.

Most employees looked back and forth between Fran and Gerald, eager for the next move. The others seemed uncomfortable or embarrassed, shifting in their seats and avoiding eye contact.

Before the silent showdown could end, Zoe stood from her place at the table and moved to leave the room.

"Thanks for holding this session, Fran," she said casually. "I need to get back to work."

It was the lifeline that Fran needed to try to regain control of the mob.

Fran cleared her throat. "Yes, we'll call it there. If anyone has questions, they can come to my office. Thank you, everyone."

Gerald's shoulders went stiff, and his face became unreadable.

The stress spread through the room as everyone shifted to leave, chairs scratching across the floor. Worried conversations picked back up.

Dustin and I waited for everyone to exit. I nudged him with my elbow and caught his eye.

"Don't listen to that idiot," I said, quietly enough that only he could hear.

His face grew cloudy. "I don't know, Doc. I gotta bad feeling about this."

***

After the meeting, I could tell that Dustin wanted to be alone. He wasn't mad at me; he just needed space. We parted ways in the hall with polite "see ya's."

I was also in a terrible headspace, but I couldn't hide in my office this time.

Tessa and the tiger were vying for my attention. Even with all of the kerfuffle over the missing items, I still needed to sort everything out with Tessa. I was hoping to resolve one issue so I could focus on the other.

I decided to try to make the most of the afternoon and catch Zoe. She might have some leads on housing, emergency funding, or some other resources for Tessa.

My light knock was answered with a "Come on in."

I closed the door behind me and sat down across from Zoe. She had a sad, resigned smile.

"This stuff with the tiger...geez," she said with a sigh.

"Yeah...ummm..." I started, shifting in my seat.

I absolutely *did not* want to talk about the tiger right now. Especially after Fran's explicit instructions not to. It didn't matter that Zoe and I were tight.

"I'm actually here about a student. Do you have a sec to talk? I can't deal with the tiger mess right now." I waved my hand, batting away the negative thoughts.

Her face softened. "Which student?"

"Tessa. The suicide risk."

She nodded, remembering. "How can I help?"

"Well, I don't know the full story. But she doesn't have a place to live right now. She's living out of a beater car with all her stuff in trash bags in the back."

Zoe's eyebrows shot up.

"Yeah, I know." I paused to chew on my cheek. "Anyway, I let her crash at my place last night."

"Again, that was incredibly generous of you," Zoe said with an appreciative look. She knew how small my place was and that having a student crash on my couch was a borderline imposition.

Trying to shrug off the compliment, I replied, "You would've done the same."

Zoe arched one eyebrow doubtfully but didn't say anything.

"I offered to let her stay for a bit until she gets things sorted. I get the impression she's pretty strapped for cash, so I'm not sure when she can get back into a place of her own again. Do you know of any place where she can get help? Like a roof for a bit until she gets more financial help?"

She pursed her lips, thinking. "Hmmm..." she said, turning to her computer.

I sat back and kept my mouth shut while she worked her magic. The speedy clacking of her keys filled the silence as her hands sped between her keyboard and her mouse.

"Yeah, here we go." She leaned back in her chair. "There's a women's shelter in town. But it might be full and difficult for her to get into. She might have more luck with the options on campus. There's a section of Bennett Hall that's reserved for emergency housing. That's probably the better option if she's open to it."

She grabbed a sticky note and wrote a number down before passing it over. "Have her call this number. If they have an opening, she could have a place as early as tonight."

I took the note and fidgeted with the edges. "Thank you, Zoe. Given the drama at the lab today, I excused the students for the afternoon. But I'm pretty sure she'll come back tonight to stay again. I'll pass this along as soon as I see her."

"Do you have her cell number?"

I kicked myself.

"No," I answered.

She'd stayed at my place last night; we now had a legitimate reason to trade numbers. But she still hadn't texted me after I'd given her mine. And I'd been so distracted that I'd forgotten to ask for her number.

After a beat, I added, "I wonder if she even has a working phone. It's possible that it's been shut off, and she's too embarrassed to say anything."

Zoe's eyebrows creased with worry. "Wow. It's really bad with her, isn't it?"

"Dude, she's living in her *car*." I nodded sadly. "Yeah, I think it's that bad."

"And she still doesn't want to talk to Admin? They might be able to get her an emergency grant to help get through this last year."

"I can ask her again," I answered with a thread of skepticism. "But I sense that there's a serious lack of trust there."

"Well, if she accepts emergency housing on campus, there'll be main campus folks who can connect her with resources, including a free cell service plan, meals, that kinda stuff. They probably have some short-term loan options, too."

I let out a deep sigh. "Thanks, Zoe. I'm really worried about her and want to help her as much as I can."

"That's 'cause you're a rockstar." She flashed me a supportive smile. "I'll dig a bit more later today and see if I can find anything else for her. I'll text you if anything else comes up."

"I'm glad you're on rotation with her next week," I said. "If she has a place to stay by then, it'll help having you around to make sure she's okay."

"If they even let students back in the lab," Zoe quipped. "Fran was pretty agitated about this whole tiger thing."

"You really think they'll cancel rotations until it's sorted?" I asked, flabbergasted.

"I don't think they'll cancel them. But they might have us just run through PowerPoints in a conference room across the street or something to keep the students off the necropsy floor. I haven't seen everyone this freaked out before."

I tried to shrug it off. "It's a small lab, and not a lot happens here. It makes sense that people are all in a tizzy about it."

Dustin's words crept into my thoughts. *I got a bad feeling about this.*

My stomach clenched.

Zoe looked doubtful. "I think Fran's gonna sic the cops on the students, especially poor Josh."

I knew we were toeing the line when it came to Fran's command about not talking about the situation, but I couldn't help myself. "Yeah, but *Josh*? I mean...*really*? He's been working on call for us forever. It doesn't seem like something he would do."

"I agree." She arched an eyebrow and pursed her lips. "I wouldn't be surprised if it was Gerald. The guy's morally dubious as it is. The damn tiger is all he can talk about. He's like an arsonist calling the fire department and standing to watch them put the flames out."

Gerald *had* ambushed me with the news, waving it in my face. And he seemed to know before anyone else did...maybe even before Dustin.

But that didn't feel right either. He was a misogynist of the highest order and a giant prick. But stealing? It didn't fit.

I still had no clue who had taken it—not even a best guess. I wasn't going to point any fingers until I had hard evidence.

I tried to shake the swirl of thoughts from my head. I didn't want to deal with any more of the tiger shit today.

Before I had a chance to redirect the conversation, Zoe added, "He may have even done it just to get you in trouble."

"I don't know," I said slowly, feeling uncomfortable and not fully understanding why.

Zoe sat back and crossed her arms. "You always think the best of people. That's what I love about you. But the more I think about it, the more it makes sense. I'm sure it's him. I bet he took it as a way to punish you. And maybe Dustin, too. Though he's usually not as much of a dick to men. All this bluster." She waved her hands in the air. "That's just a cover."

Uncomfortable with the finger-pointing, I cleared my throat awkwardly in reply and shifted in my seat.

"That'll be up to the police to sort out," I fumbled.

Zoe snorted. "Yes, it *will*. I can't wait for that blood-sucking tick to finally be pulled out of this lab's ass."

I liked Zoe wholeheartedly; she was a good soul. And I hated Gerald like everyone else. But I didn't like where the conversation was headed. Gerald did a lot of messed up stuff, which I was more than happy to call out. But until there was proof that he was guilty of stealing the tiger parts, I wasn't gonna cast stones.

"Thanks again for the housing lead, Zoe." I stood, hoping to end the conversation politely. "I'm gonna go check in with Dustin and try to button everything up so I can boogie early. It's been a rough day."

After a brief hug, I closed Zoe's office door behind me with a knot of dread building in my stomach.

People were picking teams in this tiny little lab. Pretty soon, they'd be lining someone up in front of the firing squad. I hoped Dustin and I could just come out the other end in one piece.

***

Dustin sat at his desk, worrying the edge of his beard with his right hand and rocking anxiously in his chair.

"Hey, man," I said, grabbing a seat across from him. "You doing okay?"

His lips pursed, and he shrugged a shoulder. "Okay enough."

I'd never seen him this stressed, and it was freaking me out. He was supposed to be the rock, the source of the calm, cool logic that kept us all grounded. Not much shook Dustin. For the umpteenth time today, I wondered if I should be more worried about what was going on.

"Anything I can do to help?"

He snorted. "Find me a good lawyer."

My laugh quickly stopped short when I realized he hadn't meant it as a joke.

"What makes you think you need a lawyer?"

179

He looked at me incredulously. "Seriously?" he asked, not unkindly.

Gesturing from his head to his boots, he continued, "Look at me." Then, he counted off on his fingers. "I have access. I have the experience. I hunt. I know the right people to sell this kinda stuff to."

Sitting back with a huff, he shook his head dejectedly. "I'm fucked." Realizing he cussed, he quickly added, "Pardon the language, Doc."

"Fuck that," I replied, waving my hand dismissively and cracked a smile.

His mustache twitched slightly. It wasn't a smile, but it was close.

"Look, dude. I know you didn't take that stuff. I'll defend you to the end." I reached over and squeezed his arm. "It'll all sort itself out. It's just a bit crazy in the lab now. People have nothing better to talk about."

"I'll feel better when I have a lawyer. I'm not talking to the cops again without one."

He was drawing a line in the sand, and I felt a twinge of empathy for the poor cop who was gonna try to interview him tomorrow.

"Fair enough," I conceded. "Do you know anyone?"

"Nah."

He tossed me a hurt look that was difficult to read.

Sure, I knew Dustin was from a bitterly poor family. He'd scratched his way out of rural Oklahoma, being the only one in his family to finish high school, and landed this gig based on his experience and ease at working with dead animals. He'd cleaned enough animals to feed the family, and he knew his way around a knife.

But just because someone grew up poor didn't mean that they didn't know any rich or formally educated people. It also didn't mean that they didn't know a good lawyer.

If they have a criminal record, they might know someone.

With a start, I realized another reason why my comment might have hurt him.

There was no way to apologize without sounding like a total asshole.

I offered help instead. "I think Aunty might know some people. Want me to check with her?"

Aunty knew *everyone*. Surely, she'd have a lead.

"Will they help me, though?" he asked.

The fact that he was white hung between us, unsaid.

I chewed my cheek. "I think if Aunty vouches for you, yeah."

I tried to sound more certain than I felt. Having been oppressed for generations, the tribe had closed ranks to protect itself, reserving resources for its own citizens. Even in the 21st century, I was still treated differently because of my ethnicity and tribal membership. I understood why the tribal leadership invested in our people and our Nation first.

"Well, I'd appreciate any leads you can get," he said.

"I'll let you know what Aunty says," I said, giving him a reassuring smile.

He leaned forward and caught my eye. "You need to get a lawyer, too, Doc."

After seeing the incredulous look on my face, he added, "Seriously. Promise me you will. 'Cause if they ain't sticking it on the poor, white trash guy, they're gonna try to stick it on someone brown. It's the hard fucking truth."

***

Back in my office, I tried to fight back the nausea. My anxiety had gotten the better of me, and now, I was trying my hardest to keep from blowing my cookies across my desk.

I grabbed my cell and called Aunty. I knew we weren't supposed to talk about this outside of the lab, but Dustin's words kept banging around in my head.

You need to get a lawyer.

Those missing tiger parts amounted to a federal crime and translated to serious jail time. It would be a career-ender for a veterinarian.

Promise me you will.

Aunty picked up on the third ring. "Hello, sweetheart. Give me a second to step outside."

I'd caught her on duty at the library. The sound of several doors closing echoed through the phone as she moved to a space where she could talk.

"There now," she said, her voice laced with worry.

I never called her when she was at work. I was sure her heart was thudding as fast as mine.

"Are you okay?" she asked. "I was thinking about you, and then you called."

"Yeah, I'm okay, Aunty. Sorry to worry you. I just need some advice."

"Oh, good." The relief was reflected in her voice. "What's going on?"

"I can't talk about it too much," I started and then decided to throw caution to the wind. It would all come out shortly anyway. "A tiger pelt and claws have gone missing. We think they might have been stolen from the lab."

"Oh, dear," she said, aghast.

"I didn't really think anything of it, you know? Just let the cops do their job."

"Sweety," she interrupted, "this can't be brushed off. You need a lawyer."

My stomach threatened to go rogue again.

I still couldn't believe everyone was freaking out so much over this. We were trained professionals doing our job, and a few items were stolen. Why the hell was everyone running around with their hair on fire?

"It's not that big of a deal, Aunty."

Was I trying to reassure her or myself?

"Josie, dear," she said, voice dead serious. "It *is* a big deal. What if Schedule One drugs were stolen from a veterinary hospital? It would be a big deal, right?"

"This is different." My tone didn't back up the statement; it sounded weak and defeated.

"You know it's not. Highly valuable—and controlled—items were stolen. I suspect it's a felony, given their value."

I nodded, even though she couldn't see me. She was right. I knew she was. I just didn't want to accept it.

"I think Donnie knows someone who can help you," she said, all business now. "Let me make a few calls."

"Thanks, Aunty," I said, resigned. After a beat, I added, "Do you think the lawyer would help Dustin, too?"

Though Aunty had never met Dustin, she knew him through the stories I told about the necropsy floor. She knew he was a good guy and that I would vouch for him.

"Yes," she responded with certainty.

By her tone, I knew she'd be whacking someone with her walking stick if they didn't help both of us.

I smiled with affection. "Thanks again, Aunty."

"Let me get to it and find you a contact. Love you, sweetheart."

"Love you, too."

After hanging up with Aunty, I immediately called Armand.

I wasn't sure why I needed to talk to him right at that moment. I think I just needed to hear his voice. Feel something normal.

To my relief, he picked up.

"Hello, Josie," he answered, the wind muffling his words.

"Hey," I replied, feeling the knot in my stomach unravel a bit.

"I apologize for not being able to call earlier. I was out in the field, and the reception was bad. I saw your text, though. I'd still like to come on Friday if it won't be an imposition."

My throat bobbed.

After a beat, he added, "Everything okay?"

Tears started to fill my eyes.

What the hell?

The events of the last few days had shaken me more than I'd realized. I'd managed to keep my cool with Aunty. But I was on a slippery slope to completely losing it.

I just needed to hold it together for a few more minutes.

"Yeah, it's all good," I said, trying to make my voice sound okay. "Just miss you."

"I miss you, too. Are you sure you want me to come over with the student staying with you?"

Oh, sweet baby Jesus! Please don't cancel on me!

I needed these connections with people like Laila, Armand, and Aunty to see me through this mess. I wasn't sure I could do it alone.

"Yes, I'm sure," I answered. "I just wanted to make sure you weren't blindsided by it."

The wind gusted against the phone mic again.

"Sounds miserable out there," I added.

"It wouldn't be that bad except for the wind. I don't know how people live out here. I feel like every drop of water I drink is instantly sucked out of me."

"One more day, and you can come back to civilization," I said through a forced smile.

"Looking forward to it."

Another gust of wind.

"I'm gonna go," he continued. "I'll see you tomorrow?"

"Most definitely," I answered.

After both calls, my emotions were whirling. I felt a tad reassured but also vulnerable. Like talking to people I cared about had somehow allowed all of the other emotions to spill everywhere.

I quickly tried to stuff everything back into its tidy little box and put my game face on.

I just needed to get the hell out of dodge before any more crap flew my way.

CHAPTER
FOURTEEN

Relief flooded over me when I pulled into the driveway.

I wished I only felt that way because I had escaped work and was finally back at home with Yersi. But if I was honest with myself, a small part of it was because Tessa's beater wasn't in sight. With all of the stuff going on at work, I'd be lying if I said that it wasn't an inconvenience to have her camping in my sanctuary. Those thoughts triggered a hint of shame.

I was definitely going to be snarfing down a pint of ice cream tonight.

I'd made it home early enough that Yersi wasn't waiting in the window. When I unlocked the door, he ran from the back hall with a *merf* sound, tail perky. He whirled around my legs, hoping for an early meal.

After dropping my stuff on the entryway table, I collapsed on the couch, letting the quiet of the house surround me.

I was worried about so many things, I could barely keep track of them all. I fretted over the missing tiger parts and whether Dustin might take the fall. The building tension between Gerald and Zoe was also concerning; if it came to political blows, Zoe would be the loser since she didn't have tenure yet. Hell, I needed to be careful, too, with my own tenure review coming up in about a year. The Tessa situation only added to the angst—just one more thing on my random-crap-to-fret-about list.

There was just *so much* worry. It was overwhelming.

And...Tessa could still show up tonight.

With a sigh, I realized that I probably had to think about more for dinner than ice cream. Even though I loved cooking, just the thought of standing around my kitchen was exhausting.

After a millisecond of hesitation, I decided that there was no way I was cooking tonight. I needed some comfort takeout. There most certainly would still be ice cream after, maybe even the entire pint, but at least I would have offered my potential guest a meal before that.

With another heavy sigh, I crawled out of the couch.

It was still hot out, but I knew some time on my back patio with a good book and the sound of the chickens scratching around the yard would be just the thing. I could see where life took me from there.

***

An hour and a half later, the doorbell pulled me out of my book. A thin sheen of sweat coated my armpits and slicked between my boobs. It was blazing hot out, but sitting in the shade of the pergola with my main-man, Yersi, a cool glass of iced tea, and a good story was exactly where I had needed to be.

The cramps were still nagging at me. But mentally, I was feeling oodles better.

I chased Yersi inside and shuffled behind him to answer the door.

Tessa was there, hands stuffed in her pockets. There was color in her cheeks, but her shoulders were still slumped. I couldn't tell if it was shame at having to come back or if it was all of the life baggage she was carrying.

"Hello, Dr. Harjo," she mumbled.

"Hey, Tessa. Come on in." I stepped back to let her through.

"Thanks."

Closing the door behind her, I offered, "Want something to drink?"

"Yes, please."

I headed into the kitchen, hopeful she would feel comfortable enough to follow me.

"I've got lemonade, iced tea, pop, and water," I said, grabbing a cup out of the cabinet.

"Water would be great. Thank you."

"Ice?"

"No, thank you."

She climbed into a chair at the counter, tucking her hands under her legs. I passed the glass of water to her.

Yersi was being a total weirdo again.

He'd followed us into the kitchen. But instead of climbing into her lap, like he usually would with Laila or Armand, he sat about three feet away, staring at her. His tail was tapping on the floor. It was such a creepy repeat of the night before that I decided to pop a can of cat food an hour ahead of schedule.

The sound of the lid pulled him from his vigil, and he started wolfing down his meal. With the night stalker mollified, I turned to Tessa.

"I hope you'll stay another night." It was more of a question than a statement.

"If that's okay," she answered timidly.

"Absolutely, you're welcome any time," I said, feeling guilty that I didn't mean it and then feeling guilty for lying.

Self-flagellation, anyone?

"I was thinking of ordering Indian food tonight. Interested?"

"I'm okay," she said when she obviously wasn't. "Thank you."

Realizing what the issue might be, I added, "Are you sure? My treat. Plus, I always feel stupid paying a delivery fee for just one. If we both order, I won't feel so bad about it. You'd be doing me a favor."

We both knew I was giving her a way to say "yes" without feeling like she was taking another handout. Just when I thought she would decline again, she acquiesced.

"Okay, then," she answered hesitantly. "Thank you."

"I'm friggin' starving. I'm gonna order now. What do you want?"

"I've never had Indian before. What do you recommend?"

"What?!" I blurted, surprised.

Stillwater was a tiny town, just enough to support two Wal-Marts, but that was about it. The takeout options were pretty slim if you didn't want cheap American fare. Since there was only one Indian place in town, I figured she probably had the menu memorized like the rest of us did.

"I've never had Indian food before," she repeated.

I felt heat rise to my cheeks. I was pretty sure it had nothing to do with a lack of interest in Indian cuisine and more a lack of funds to pay for it.

Open mouth, insert foot, Josie.

Pretending like there was no awkwardness, I blabbered on. "Oh, my gosh. It is so good. I'm gonna order a bunch of stuff so you can try different things. You're gonna love it."

Now, I was gushing like a teenage cheerleader. All I needed was blonde hair and a pair of Uggs, and I'd fit right in at Stillwater High.

I took a deep breath. "What spiciness level do you like?"

"Medium?" she offered, one eyebrow up as if unsure of the right answer.

"I've got you covered."

I'd order everything mild. Many people thought they could handle spicy Indian food because they ordered spicy barbeque sauce at Buffalo Wild Wings. There was a *huge* difference between American "spicy" and Indian "spicy." Some of those dishes could burn going in *and* out; I didn't want her suffering through that.

I grabbed my phone and placed the order. I went all out, ordering several appetizers, curries, and garlic naan.

With dinner sorted, I went back into the kitchen, where Tessa was still nursing her water. Yersi was now sitting meatloaf-style on the chair at the far end of the counter. Thankfully, his damn tail was tucked tightly in; that twitching thing was starting to spook me.

"Food should be here in about twenty minutes. I was think-ing...um." I chewed my lip, trying to figure out the best way to say what I wanted to say next without sounding like a douchebag. "You're welcome to use the washer and dryer when you're here."

Thankfully, she took the offer for what it was.

"Thank you," she answered. "I'd appreciate that. I'll go grab my stuff."

"Need any help?"

Her cheeks flushed. "Naw. I'm good. Thanks."

Grasping at straws, I said, "I've gotta get the chickens locked up and water the garden. I'll be outside if you need me."

We parted ways, and I heard the front door open just as I reached the other door to the backyard.

Expecting Yersi to follow me, I held it ajar. Once again, he ghosted me, uncharacteristically opting to stay inside.

The dude was creeping me out.

I closed the door with trepidation.

After shooing the chickens back into their Eglu, I piddled around the garden. I watered what was left of the summer crops and the surviving lettuce. I contemplated pulling a few of the crops that were reaching the end of their growing season and decided to push it off.

My mind relaxed as I slipped into the routine chores.

With my shirt once again wet with sweat, I went back inside the house just in time to accept the Indian food delivery. I could hear the washer running, and Tessa was back at the counter.

I brought the warm bags into the kitchen, trailing the strong scent of tikka masala. When I opened the bags, the delicious smell of garlic naan wafted over us.

I inhaled deeply and then pushed the bag over to her. "Seriously. You have to smell this. It's like part of the whole experience."

She smiled and obliged, eyes closing as she took a deep whiff of the aromatic steam rising from the bag.

Her eyebrows shot up. "Wow! That smells amazing."

"Right?"

I unpacked the containers and passed her a plate and utensils. Then, we both dove in. To my delight, she tried everything, making happy sounds and exclamations of appreciation. The conversation was sparse as we both ate, but it was still surprisingly comfortable.

After we vacuumed down more than half the food, she leaned back and said, "That was delicious."

"See? Indian food is the best. Which dish was your favorite?"

"Hmm." She looked around at the various have-filled containers. "This one, I think. With the garlic bread stuff."

"Yeah, the butter chicken is pretty awesome. Garlic naan just ties it all together. The curries are even better the next day. Like Chinese food or pizza."

"Oh, no," she laughed. "Pizza is *not* better the next day!"

"What?!" I teased. "It *absolutely* is. Cold. Right out of the fridge."

"Then the fat from the cheese makes that film on the roof of your mouth." She feigned a gag.

"That's the best part! Same with Chinese. Like chow mein the next day." I made a chef's kiss. "You can just taste the oil on it."

She laughed.

It felt *so* good to see her laugh.

"That's fine," I said, eyebrows raised in a mock *whatever* look. "I can eat all the Indian leftovers. You won't need to worry about choking it down."

"Now...wait a minute," she teased back.

We laughed together.

Her smile dropped, and her face turned earnest. "Thank you so much, Dr. Harjo. Seriously. All this means a lot."

"Josie...please.... We've had Indian food together." I flashed her a smile.

She smiled back; it was a deep smile that was reflected in her entire posture. I finally felt like we could talk with no barriers. I guess Indian food had a way of doing that.

I decided it might be safe to venture back into the dark areas. I went to my purse to dig out the sticky note Zoe had given me.

Placing the sticking note on the table between us, I said, "I talked to Dr. Smith today. She has a lead on some temporary housing for you."

Tessa's smile dropped, and I felt my stomach flop.

I didn't have the mad people skills that Zoe did. I was always floundering around like a dufus. My heart was in the right place, but my direct communication style meant I had a charisma of two.

I quickly added, "You're welcome to stay here as long as you need to. Really. I mean that."

I took a risk and leaned over to give her a half hug.

"I just know that some people like their own space. I wanted to make sure you have options. This place is on campus." I slid the sticky note closer to her. "They give students a place to stay short-term on an emergency basis. And they have resources for you. Like to help you get a more permanent place. And food. And all sorts of stuff. They might even have some grants or short-term loans to get you through your senior year. OSU alums are pretty generous and want to see fellow Cowboys succeed. There might be a scholarship for your exact situation. These folks will know about it if it exists."

Feeling myself rambling, I shut up to let her process.

She took the sticky note and rubbed the corner between her thumb and forefinger. Tears filled her eyes.

Returning to my seat, I added, "They won't tell Admin, either. It's just a resource for students."

"I...." She licked her lips and swallowed. "Thank you, Josie."

She said "thank you" so often that I wasn't sure what it meant. I knew she was appreciative and trying to be polite. But I didn't know if I'd hurt her feelings or embarrassed her.

I decided to go out on a limb.

"There's no shame in taking advantage of the resources on campus. It's just like any other thing they have for students, like tutors or resume workshops. We all want to see you get your degree and put this rough patch behind you. If this will help you accomplish that, then"—I shrugged—"why not? Right?"

Tessa was smart, and I could see her thinking through all of the different possible futures. When she pressed her lips together resolutely, I knew she saw that this was the next best step.

"Yeah. I'll check it out," she said, her tone unreadable.

Wanting to get back to the light, postprandial contentment that we had just moments before, I said, "Welp, I'm gonna clean up and watch some Netflix. Wanna join me?"

"Sure," she said, flashing me a soft, genuine smile. "Let me clean up, though, please."

"Fair enough," I said, knowing the feeling.

When someone made you dinner or paid for something, there was always that innate tit-for-tat desire to give back. If cleaning up made Tessa feel a tad better about crashing at my place or me paying for dinner, I wasn't gonna fight her over it.

She got up and started stacking containers in the fridge and wiping down the table.

I patted my belly. "After all that stuff with the tiger, I was thinking I was going to stress eat a pint of ice cream tonight. But that Indian food topped me up."

Tessa remained silent, dishes and silverware clanking as she loaded the dishwasher.

"What do you want to watch? What kind of shows do you like?" I asked.

"Ummm. All kinds of stuff. Except for romance, I guess. I mainly watch stuff on YouTube."

"Do you like spooky stuff?" I asked. "Armand doesn't like horror. I try to binge my favorites when he's not around."

"Like hack-and-slash-horror?"

"Oh, hell, no." I cringed. "I see enough blood at work."

"I don't like that gory stuff, either. But I like tense, thriller, *Alien*-like shows."

"Ripley is *amazing*," I said reverently "Who doesn't want to kick some major ass and then snuggle up with Jonesy after?"

"Awwww, Jonesy. Orange tabbies are the best." She paused before continuing, cups clinking as she loaded them into the top rack. "I always wanted to be like Ripley. Or Furiosa. She was pretty baller, too. Didn't take any crap."

I laughed, and my heart skipped a beat with joy. It was slowly dawning on me that Tessa may be my sister from another mother.

"One hundred percent agree. Some people say they want to be like Princess Leia. And, yeah, maybe in the late seventies, it was nice to see a woman finally holding a gun. But there was still something off about her character. I mean...yeah, she tried to rescue Han, but she ended up in a bikini, chained to Jabba for it. That was like a warning to women to not get too uppity."

Tessa snorted her agreement. "Yeah, but didn't *Alien* come out around the same time as the first *Star Wars* movie?"

"Yeah," I conceded. "I think you're right about that."

"Either way, Ripley beats Leia hands down," she said with certainty.

"Agreed."

I smiled to myself. It was nice to see her come out of her shell. To see her joke a bit and talk about the things she likes. I felt like I was finally starting to get to know the real Tessa.

"Anyway, for tonight," I continued, "I was thinking more of a slow burn, cerebral show with a dash of action. Have you seen *The Fall of the House of Usher*?"

She perked up as she dried her hands on the towel. "Isn't that the series by the people who did *The Haunting of Hill House*?"

"Yup. Which I've watched like five times. That one's real good."

"Yeah, it is. I watched it over at Harper's."

Yes, definitely a sister from another mother.

"I used to be a hard-core *American Horror Story* fan, but the last few seasons have been crap," I said.

"Yeah, they were," she snorted.

"I think *The Haunting of Hill House*, *The Midnight Club*, those ones—that's the new *American Horror Story*. I dare say I might be converted. Let's watch *Usher*, then, since you haven't seen it."

"Cool," she said.

I flashed her a smile as we both grabbed our drinks and moved into the living room. As soon as we sat down, Yersi jumped into my lap and started purring.

I wish the night had ended there, with a belly full of Indian food, watching a kickass show with a fellow horror fan, and The Black Death curled up in my lap.

But the universe had other plans.

A text from Aunty popped up about ten minutes into the first episode. It was the name of a lawyer, and it was like a bitter dessert.

CHAPTER

FIFTEEN

The lab was crackling with energy Friday morning. It was the bad sort of vibe—the kind that filled the hallways with harsh whispers, tense shoulders, and side-eyes.

A cop was on the hunt, and it was weighing heavily on everyone.

As soon as I was through the front door, Fran intercepted me.

She looked like she'd been run over by a pickup truck. Her normally immaculately groomed quaff had barely been brushed. She was dressed in her usual business attire, but her shirt was uncharacteristically wrinkled. Her confident posture was replaced with shifty eyes and wringing hands.

"I've been waiting for you," she said, anxiously.

A glance at the clock in the hall told me it wasn't even 8 A.M. I was early.

What the hell?

"What's up?" I asked, trying to sound casual despite the clench of my gut. I shifted my purse on my shoulder.

"Let's step into your office," she said, ushering me down the hall.

She closed the door behind us with a fatal click.

I set my purse down and flopped in my chair. I was tired already.

"What's going on, Fran?" I asked, not really wanting to know the answer.

She took the seat across from me and leaned forward on my desk. Her hands were clenched so tightly that her knuckles were white.

"We need to find the missing items from the tiger." Her voice was pleading. "As soon as possible."

No shit, I thought, thankfully keeping it to myself.

"I'm certain the police think Dustin is the thief," she said. "They were questioning me quite extensively on his ability, possible motive, and any potential connections to animal traffickers. Can you imagine? Dustin working with traffickers?"

She shook her head and clenched her jaw. Worry creased her brow.

Taking a deep breath, she practically whispered, "It can't be one of *my* employees. That's just impossible."

I agreed; I didn't think anyone in the lab did it. But the way she phrased it rubbed me the wrong way. Fuck if I was going to give her any validation.

I just stared at her, trying but failing to keep my face neutral. The corners of my mouth turned down in a classic Josie-judge-face.

"The Tiawah Animal Sanctuary has been diplomatic about the entire thing," she continued. "But I'm fairly certain they blame me, as well."

Yep, it's all about her.

I tried not to shake my head in disappointment.

Dustin was literally giving himself an ulcer over this. Everyone in the lab was pointing fingers at each other. I was legitimately concerned that Zoe might strangle Gerald before this was all over. And here was Fran, worrying about herself.

I felt my hackles rise.

"How's Dustin?" I asked.

"What?" she asked, head jerking back slightly in surprise.

"Dustin...how's he handling this?" I asked sternly.

She looked puzzled. "Why would I know?"

I practically snorted with disgust.

Dustin was one of the best employees this lab had ever had. After almost twenty years of superlative service, I was shocked Fran hadn't even thought about how he might be doing.

I knew Fran wasn't the best director; she left Gerald's behavior unchecked. But I'd made excuses for her. I figured she was dealing with it behind closed doors and building a paper trail. I thought she had our backs.

Until this moment, I hadn't realized how insanely selfish she was. She didn't have an ounce of empathy for her employees. She probably ignored Gerald's behavior because addressing it might put her own job at risk.

It was the same thing with the tiger situation. She only cared about how the chaos made her look.

Ew.

"Is there something specific you need from me?" I asked, trying to get this conversation wrapped up and her out of my office.

"Yes, the officer wants to speak to you, of course. You'll need to be available for that." She frowned. "But more importantly, you need to be aware that I'm closing the lab to all non-essential personnel until this is resolved."

"Does that include students?"

"Yes, that includes the students on the rotation, as well as all of our on-call students. They will likely be interviewed by the police since they had access, but they should not be in the lab right now."

"Fran...how will we receive any overnight submissions?" I asked. If my tone was a tad sarcastic, it couldn't have been helped.

"I've let the answering service know that all after-hours calls should go to Dustin for the foreseeable future."

I was gobsmacked at how unfair that was. She was putting Dustin on call every night and every weekend until further notice.

I felt a slow, burning anger rise to the surface.

"You can't do that to Dustin," I practically hissed.

Her eyes narrowed.

Realizing my mistake, I tried another tactic. "Why don't we all take shifts? I can cover this weekend."

Her lips tightened into a white line, and I knew I'd misstepped yet again.

Her back straightened, and she stood. "Dustin is the reason we're in this mess. He can shoulder the weight. That's my decision. It's final."

She pushed her chair in to emphasize her point, and then added, "Please make alternative arrangements for the students who are on rotation."

"Yes, ma'am," was all I could say.

After the door closed behind her, I closed my eyes and took three deep belly breaths. People were losing their ever-loving minds. I couldn't believe that something like a stolen tiger pelt and claws would throw the lab topsy-turvy.

Poor Dustin.

My heart ached for him and his situation.

Fran had essentially commanded me to sort out something for the students immediately. But I couldn't move on with the day before checking on Dustin. Grabbing a sticky note with the lawyer's number, I headed to his office.

Two mumbled voices could be heard through his closed door.

I knocked lightly.

"Come in," Dustin called out.

I pushed open the door.

"Come in and shut that thing," Zoe said, waving me in.

The small office was packed with the three of us in it. There was a warm, stuffy feel to the room with a faint whiff of nervous BO.

Dustin was at his desk, chewing on his mustache. His eyes were focused on his coffee cup, which was slowly twirling in circles in his nervous hands. His shoulders sagged.

Zoe sat across from him, eyebrows creased with worry. Her eyes bounced between him and me.

With no place to sit, I awkwardly stuffed my hands in my pockets. "Just checking in on you. How you doin', man?"

Dustin shook his head in defeat and stayed silent.

Zoe answered for him, "He's got a target on his back. Everyone is coming down pretty hard on him."

"Dude, we all know you weren't involved," I offered.

"You and Dr. Smith, maybe," he said gruffly.

Zoe and I exchanged another worried glance.

"Pour your soul into your job for over twenty years, and then this," he practically whispered.

I squatted down next to his desk, trying to catch his eyes. "Dustin."

Placing a hand on one of his arms, I repeated, "Dustin."

He looked up at me, eyes filled with resigned sadness.

"You're not alone." I pointed between Zoe and me. "We have your back. And I'm sure Tom does, too."

"Yeah, we do," Zoe agreed emphatically.

"Look," I said, placing a sticky note with the lawyer's number on his desk. "This is a lawyer that Aunty gave me. I haven't called them yet. But I'm gonna. You should, too."

He looked at me with a faint, defeated smile. "Come on, Doc. You know I can't afford no lawyer."

"But yesterday, you said you were going to get one," I said, confused.

He huffed. "I know I *need* a lawyer. But I can't afford one."

Zoe threw her shoulders back and crossed her arms. "You're getting a lawyer. I'll pay for it."

"I appreciate it and all, Dr. Smith—" he started.

Zoe interrupted, "Nuh-uh. You're gonna call this lawyer. And I'm gonna pay for it. Don't you argue with me."

"I'll chip in, too," I added. "Plus, Aunty knows this person. I'm sure we'll get the hook-up." I squeezed his arm. "Please? Call them?"

He sighed ruefully. "Fine. I can't fight both of you."

It was an attempt at a tease, and I knew he was coming around. I stood and gave him a half hug.

Trying to spare him of further friendly nagging, I switched to business. "On another note, Fran said no students on the floor for the time being."

"What?!" Zoe said.

I saw Dustin's jaw clench. Normally, he'd have dropped his two cents. But he was so stressed and unhappy that he just brooded in silence.

"I'll book a breakout room across the street for today and next week," I said. "I figure we can run through slides with them. They haven't done many necropsies, but they've done enough that they shouldn't have to repeat the rotation."

Zoe nodded.

She was the pathologist on duty with them next week and would have to pick up the teaching duties. If we had a lot of animals come in, it would be pretty rough trying to teach and be on duty at the same time.

"If you get too busy on the floor next week, let me know," I offered. "I can cover teaching or pick up a day of necropsy duty. It's gonna be a bit bumpy, I think."

"Thanks, Josie," she replied.

"Fran also told me that the on-call students won't be allowed in the lab for a bit."

"Seriously?" Zoe said incredulously.

"Yep," I said bitterly. "She told me that you're gonna cover, Dustin. But that's bullshit. I'll call the answering service and let them know I'll cover the weekend. Fran'll never know."

"What the hell? Fran is so unfair." Zoe shook her head. "I'll cover on-call duty next week. Can you let them know, Josie?"

I nodded, heart warmed with Zoe's show of solidarity and support for Dustin.

Zoe reached out and grabbed Dustin's hand. "You call that lawyer. Spend time with Dolores. Don't let this place mess with your head. Got me?"

Dustin didn't respond.

"Hey," Zoe said, dipping her head to catch his eye. "Got me?"

"Yes, ma'am."

He sighed deeply and looked at both of us. "Thanks, y'all. It's nice knowin' y'all got my back."

"Always," I answered confidently. "No matter what."

***

Less than an hour later, I was back in the conference room, about to chase the students out of the lab. When I entered, a hush settled around the table.

Harper, Mackenzie, and Kassidy watched me expectantly. Sarah looked like she was about to pee herself. Tessa was expressionless.

Emma, on the other hand, was sitting confidently with an evil Cheshire cat grin plastered on her face. It was like she knew her wealth made her untouchable, and watching the rest of us peons worry was just entertainment.

Gooseflesh prickled across my arms.

"Good morning," I said, grabbing a seat and trying to pretend like everything was normal.

The students answered with a few mechanical pleasantries.

"Do we have any cases today?" Mackenzie asked hesitantly, noticing that I didn't bring any paperwork with me.

"Well, that's what I wanted to talk to y'all about. There's a lot going on in the lab right now, so—"

"Because someone stole the tiger parts," Emma interrupted.

"Oh, geez," Sarah fretted. "We're not in trouble, are we?"

"Someone's going to be in *huge* trouble," Emma retorted with a haughty sneer, crossing her arms.

"You're not in trouble," I answered hurriedly, trying to regain control of the conversation.

Things were going sideways fast.

"Because of everything that's going on, the lab is going to be open to essential personnel only," I continued. "Students won't be allowed in. Probably for the rest of the rotation."

"See! We're in trouble," Sarah whispered, the color fleeing from her cheeks.

"Not that I'm complaining, but why can't we be in the lab?" Emma snarked. "The stuff is long gone. It's like closing the barn door after the horses escaped."

I couldn't argue with her; it was a surprisingly rational question and comment. My eyes narrowed, trying to figure out her schtick. Why did she even care?

"With the police onsite, things are pretty tense," I said.

It was all I could come up with.

"*Pfft.*" Emma rolled her eyes. "What does that mean for us?"

"Well, that means no more necropsies, to start," I answered.

I saw disappointment flitter across Mackenzie's face. Sarah and Kassidy exchanged an uncomfortable look.

"Will we have to retake the rotation?" Kassidy asked nervously.

"Nope," I answered, trying to reassure them. "We'll work something out for the rest of the time. These are exceptional circumstances. I'm sure Admin will understand."

"Yessss!" Emma said, not even trying to hide her glee.

I flashed her an annoyed look.

"I booked one of the study rooms in the library for today and next week," I pressed on. "We'll still need to put some pathology time in."

Emma slumped in her chair dramatically.

Even though she wasn't going to get rumen contents in her hair, she was still going to have to do work, and it was probably going to be boring. One could only look at PowerPoint slides for so long before going cuckoo for Cocoa Puffs.

"I've got a few things to wrap up over here before I head over," I said. "We'll meet over there at ten and get started."

"What does that mean?" Emma huffed. "What are we *actually* going to be doing, then?"

"We'll run through slides for about an hour. Then, I have a couple of online cases y'all can work through. On Monday, you'll meet Dr. Smith in the same room at nine. I don't know what she'll have for you, but I suspect it'll be something similar." After a beat, I added, "Sorry 'bout all this."

Throwing me a lifeline, Harper said, "It's okay, Dr. Harjo. We understand." Her eyes were soft with empathy.

And maybe a bit of pity?

I wondered how far this story was going to spread and how much damage was going to be left behind.

Like a damn tornado.

"I'll need to chase y'all out of the lab now," I said, getting back to business. "It's gonna be badge-scan-entry only until further notice."

I stood as a signal. Everyone around the table rose and grabbed their bags.

Emma flipped her hair and huffed, "Would've been nice to have known this before I dressed in coveralls."

I held the door open for everyone. Emma flounced through first, the cloying smell of perfume trailing behind her. The others filed through after.

Mackenzie stopped at the door. "Dr. Harjo?"

"What's up?"

She fidgeted with the strap of her backpack, and her cheeks flushed.

"I'm bummed about missing this rotation." She looked around to make sure Emma was gone before continuing. "I enjoy doing necropsies. Is there a chance I can add another week or two as an elective?"

My heart warmed.

She *was* good at pathology, one of those students who just got it. Natural talent, motivation, and interest were a winning combo. I felt bad that she was going to miss out on doing any more necropsies during the rest of the rotation.

"We'd love to have you back. Just check in with Admin. They can adjust your schedule, and I think there's a form I need to sign or something."

Mackenzie beamed with encouragement. "Thank you! Um...one more question. I know I need to get out of the lab, but maybe we can meet sometime? I want to ask your advice about becoming a pathologist, what it's like, stuff like that."

I couldn't help but beam back. Despite all of the other crap floating in my orbit, this right here was what made teaching *awesome.*

"Sure, I'd be happy to talk more. And if you decide to apply for a residency, I can take a look at your application for you. Maybe we can grab lunch one of these days? Just shoot me an email."

"That would be amazing. Thank you so much, Dr. Harjo!"

With that, she practically bounced down the hall with happiness.

With a start, I realized that Tessa had hung behind, taking extra long with her backpack and waiting to catch me alone.

At a glance, she appeared a bit better, with clean clothes and freshly washed hair. Nevertheless, her face looked hollow, and bags tugged at her eyes. Despite the tune-up, she was still carrying one heck of a load, and it was gnawing at her.

"Everything okay?" I asked.

"Yes, ma'am. I just wanted to catch you alone."

She chewed on her chapped lips, pausing to get her thoughts together.

"If it's okay, I'm going to go across campus and check on housing. I'm just saying...I might be back late, is all. But...." She chewed on her lip some more. "I just don't want to impose on you anymore. And it's Friday. And I don't know where to crash this weekend. And I'm not even sure they'll have a spot for me right away...."

She petered off, realizing she was rambling, and her face flushed.

I gave her a half hug. "Take all the time you need. If we aren't in the conference room when you finish up, it means we've wrapped for the afternoon. And if they can't get a spot for you this weekend, please stay at my place?"

She nodded shyly. "Thank you, Dr. Harjo."

"FYI, though, my boyfriend is coming over tonight. He knows you'll probably be there. He's cool with you hanging with us."

"I just appreciate a place to crash. Thank you."

Trying to cheer her up, I said, "I was planning on cooking tonight. But this week just sped by, and there's nothing in the fridge. I'm thinking we'll get food delivered again. Followed by ice cream and a movie. If you like tabletop games, Armand and I usually play one when he comes over. You can join us if you want. Strategy games are always more fun with three people...if you're interested?"

I cocked an eyebrow and grinned.

The corner of her mouth cracked with a slight smile. "That sounds great, thanks."

***

With the students excused, I headed back to my office to call the lawyer. I was carrying a heavy load, too. And if I was going to enjoy my time with Armand and Tessa tonight, I needed to unpack it.

"Hello, this is Colbert Law. How may I help you today?" a perky feminine voice answered.

"Hello, this is Josie Harjo. I'm calling for Ted. Is he available?"

"Yes, ma'am. He's been expecting your call. May I place you on hold?"

"Yes, thank you."

Elevator music floated through the phone. I felt my anxiety build again. I grabbed a pen and started tapping it on my desk.

"Hello, Josie?" a strong, masculine voice asked.

"Yes, sir. This is Josie Harjo."

"I'm glad you called. Ted Colbert, here. A pleasure to meet you over the phone."

"Likewise," was all I could say. My anxiety was nipping at my heels, but it felt good to know I had an ace up my sleeve.

As if hearing everything unsaid, he added, "Wish we'd be meeting under better circumstances. But how 'bout you fill me in, I'll fix this up for you, and we can meet in person with some good news. How's that sound?"

The relief was enough to stop the tapping pen. "That sounds great."

"Molly said something about a high-value theft at your work?"

"Yes, sir. You want the short, short version?"

"How 'bout in the middle?"

"Ummm...." I hesitated, gathering my thoughts.

I could do this. It was like writing a report: Just the facts in a logical order.

"On Tuesday, we had a tiger come in for a necropsy from a local animal sanctuary," I began.

"Necropsy?" he asked.

"An animal autopsy."

"Got it. Go on. Apologies for interrupting."

"The sanctuary asked for the pelt, claws, and skull to be returned. They were going to send them to a local taxidermist and eventually use them for education."

He *hmmed* in response.

"The items were removed and stored in the cooler in the lab. Yesterday, our necropsy technician found them missing."

"Any chance they were lost rather than stolen?"

"Um. Probably not. I've been hoping that was the case, but Dustin—he's the necropsy tech—went over the cooler with a fine-tooth comb. And we hadn't sent anything out to the renderer or for cremation or anything."

He *hmmed* again.

"Anyway, the items are of high value, probably over fifty thousand grand altogether."

He whistled. "And probably require a permit to even have in one's possession," he mused.

"Yes, exactly."

"Have the police spoken to anyone yet?"

"I've heard they'll be around the lab today, interviewing people."

"I assume you haven't spoken to the police yet, then?"

"No, sir. I haven't."

"Don't talk to the police without me there."

"Um...okay. I don't think I'm a suspect, though. I think they're trying to pin it on Dustin."

My pen started tapping again.

"You never know how these things will shake out. It's best if I'm there when they interview you."

"I think the police will want to talk to me today. What should I say when they come by?"

Sure, I'd seen a ton of movies and knew I should just say "lawyer" and fuck-all else. But this was real life in semi-rural Oklahoma. That just seemed *rude*.

As expected, Ted answered, "Inform them that you'd like to have a lawyer present. You can even blame it on Molly and me. Tell 'em we insisted. If the officer comes by your office today, call my cell. I can teleconference in. How's that sound?"

That sounded *great*.

My pen stilled.

If I could crank through my time with the students and get the police interview out of the way, I could go into the weekend with a lighter weight to carry.

"That would be awesome. Thank you, Ted. I appreciate the support."

"Happy to help Molly's *chokka-chaffa* anytime."

"Um. Before we go...I hope you don't mind...I gave your number to Dustin, the necropsy tech, too. I'll cover his bill, of course."

Ted cleared his throat.

I sputtered, "I'm not asking for information about how things are going with him or if he's called or whatever. I'm just giving you a heads-up that he may call you if he hasn't already. And also to let you know that I got his bill and vouch for him and all that."

"Thanks for the information, Josie," he said, somewhat cryptically.

"Thank you again, Ted. I appreciate the support."

"Anytime. Have a pen?"

Uh, yeah, I did.

"Yes, sir."

My pen swung in my fingers to a writing position, and I grabbed a sticky note.

He rattled off his cell phone number. After saying our goodbyes, we hung up.

Thinking of how awesome Aunty was to connect me with Ted, I sent her a quick text.

> Spoke with Ted. Thank you. He's great.

She hearted my text before my phone could auto-lock.

> I'm glad he could help you. His mom and I go way back.

After a few seconds of watching the blinking ellipses, a second text popped up.

> How are you?

> Meh. As good as can be expected. Feeling a lot better with Ted on my team.

She thumbed up the text.

> Armand's coming tonight. I just need Flo to buzz off and I'll be golden.

She sent a laughing emoji.

> Still on for Sunday brunch?

> Of course!

> I'm on call this weekend but can bump any late cases to Monday if I need to.

She hearted my text.

I was feeling warm fuzzies with Aunty on my side. She was my rock, and I wasn't sure what I'd do without her.

CHAPTER

SIXTEEN

My stomach was growling with hunger.

Normally, I'd be on my way to the breakroom, lickety-split, secretly salivating at the thought of the baked treat Carol was invariably going to push on me.

Today, I wasn't so sure. The tension in the lab was palpable.

After returning from the morning's PowerPoint doldrums, I'd caught a glimpse of the black-uniformed figure prowling around the lab, like a harbinger of doom. I'd dodged him so far, but I knew I was on the list and wouldn't skate through the day without dealing with that bit of unpleasantness.

Surely, the cop is at lunch, right?

I pulled my lunch out and set it on my desk, staring at it for a good five minutes as my internal debate raged on. Even if the cop was likely out topping up the calorie tank for the afternoon's inquisition, the lab still had the feel of electric cattle wire.

Wouldn't it be better to show confidence? And pretend that everything was okay? A show of force?

Screw it.

I grabbed my food and headed to the breakroom.

Carol was already there with Anna, a container of snickerdoodles in front of her. She gave me a reassuring smile when I walked in.

"Howdy, y'all," I said, taking a seat.

"Howdy, Dr. Harjo," Anna replied. Her voice was pleasant and casual, but there were crinkles of skin around her eyes. She was putting on a brave face.

"Have a cookie," Carol said, pushing the box over to me.

The smell of cinnamon and sugar was overwhelming, and I caved like I knew I would.

Aunt Flo was a hungry guest.

"Thank you, Carol," I said, salivating.

I selected a cookie and kicked off the meal by snarfing it down in three bites. After a millisecond of internal debate, I shrugged it off and grabbed another.

The normal idle conversation was absent, and a creepy silence stretched through the room.

Anna cleared her throat and leaned over. "Is Dustin okay? I haven't seen him all day."

I wasn't sure how to respond. The polite answer would be that he was doing fine. The honest answer would be that he was struggling to pull the knife out of his back.

Carol saved me by saying, "He's as okay as he can be, honey." She patted Anna's hand and pushed the cookie container over to her.

Anna took one and continued, "I don't know why Gerald is going around telling everyone Dustin did it." The creases around her eyes deepened with worry.

"It's just gossip," Carol answered sagely. "You know how people are. Justice will prevail."

I decided I needed another cookie.

"You're quiet, Dr. Harjo," Anna said. "You don't need to worry, you know. No one thinks it's you."

I felt a slight jolt of surprise at the odd comment.

"I'm not worried about me. I'm worried about Dustin," I replied cautiously. My eyebrows crinkled.

"And Josh," Anna added. "Some of the folks in the lab are betting on him."

"Betting?" I asked, slightly appalled.

"Yeah. There's a pot going around, betting on who took it." Anna pressed her hand to her chest, declaring her innocence. "*I'm* not the one doing it. I was just asked if I wanted to join in."

What the hell?

I was horrified that people were so shallow that they would take bets on who stole the items.

This was a small lab. I thought of my coworkers as a family, complete with the creepy uncle.

"Asked by whom?" I probed defensively.

Anna blanched. "I don't want to cause any more trouble."

Carol snorted. "Dan in PCR."

All I could do was shake my head.

"This is crazy," I practically whispered.

"Yes, it is," Carol said with firm certainty. "I haven't seen nothin' like this."

My mind raced. "People think Josh did it? There's no way."

"I know, right?" Anna said and then added with a shake of her head, "It wasn't Josh."

I was getting really worried that this was spinning out of control. I didn't know who took the items, but I was fairly certain it wasn't a lab employee. It just *couldn't* be.

"The most bets are on Gerald," Anna continued.

This was a slippery slope, and I wanted to steer clear of it.

"I don't know..." I waffled.

It would be just like him to use the situation to stir things up—heck, he was already doing that—but I didn't think he would steal something. That method of torture didn't fit his usual MO.

The speculation was making me uncomfortable. Talking shit wasn't as bad as betting on people with money, but it was close. We were just betting with political capital instead of dollars.

Again, Carol rescued me.

"Those of us who engage in gossiping or talebearing will cause the wrath of God to fall upon us," she said, not unkindly, as she pushed the box of cookies closer to Anna and me.

I took a fourth cookie. "How 'bout that weather?"

***

Stuffed with about fifteen snickerdoodles, I camped in my office for the afternoon, shifting glass across my microscope, apprehension building.

I knew I was on the cop's list. I just didn't know when he'd pounce on me.

When my phone pinged with a text, I flinched.

I pulled it off the charger and unlocked it. To my relief, it was just a text from Laila.

> Just checking in on you. How are things?

> I'm okay. Thanks for looking after me.

I sent her a heart emoji.

> Is the student still staying with you?

> Yeah

> How's that going?

> She's looking better each day.

> Zoe hooked me up with the emergency housing contact.

I texted her the info so she'd have it if she ever needed it for a student. She responded with a thumbs up.

> Were they able to get her in?

> She went by this morning and they said she could get a room starting Monday.

> That's great news! Is she staying with you until then?

> Yep

> I'm glad it's working out. I was worried about her.

I smiled. Of course Laila was thinking about Tessa. She was such a sweetheart, and empathy was woven through every fiber of her being. I was so grateful to have her as a friend. She always made me smile, even with the tiger gnawing at my belly.

> Thanks again for your help

> Anytime! Have a nice weekend. Text me the next time you are free for lunch.

I sent her a thumbs up.

As I set the phone down, I sighed deeply and leaned back, rocking slowly in my chair. I picked up my pen and started fidgeting with it. I felt a ton better knowing that Tessa had a plan and hoped it was the first step on a longer journey. Further, I felt like we might be out of the woods when it came to suicide. She certainly *looked* better.

Despite the small victory with Tessa, the dark cloud of the missing tiger parts still hung over me like a shroud. I just wanted to put it all to bed, get them off Dustin's back, and enjoy my evening with Armand.

As if a higher being had answered my not-wish, a strong knock rapped on my door three times.

Tap, tap, tapping like the damn raven.

I couldn't escape Poe this week.

A shiver ran up my spine.

"Come in," I called out, resigned.

An imposing man built like a brick shithouse pushed open the door. He wore a traditional police uniform, complete with a sidearm. His hair was in a crisp military cut, with gray peeking through the blonde. He had permanent furrows on his forehead and piercing, bright blue eyes. I put him in his late forties.

Seeing the uniform was like hearing the shake of a rattlesnake's tail, and a sense of trepidation washed over me. If I followed the rules and listened to any warnings, there wouldn't be a fuss. But if I stepped wrong, he would bite.

I did *not* want to get bitten.

"Excuse me, ma'am," he drawled in a thick Oklahoman accent. "Are you Dr. Josie Harjo?"

I stood and reached out my hand. "Yes, sir."

He nudged his way in, closing the door behind him, and took my hand. His fist was large, and his rough sausage fingers enveloped mine. His shake was firm but not painful.

"I'm Officer Watts. We spoke on the phone about a month ago regarding another case."

"Oh, yes...the JW Ranch case. Hope everything is okay out there now?"

"Yes, ma'am. But I'm not here today about the Williamses."

No shit.

Thankfully, I didn't blurt that out.

Tread carefully, Josie.

"Do you have a minute?" he asked.

"Yes, sir," I stuttered and gestured to the chair across from me. "Please sit."

I returned to my seat, trying to keep my cool.

"How can I help you?" I asked, hoping I could get through this without having to call Ted.

"I'm here today about the missing items. It's my understanding that you were the pathologist on duty and performed the autopsy on the tiger."

"Necropsy," I corrected him, unable to help myself.

"Mmm...." His eyes narrowed.

My palms started to sweat.

"I'd like to ask you a few questions since you were the pathologist on the case. Is now a good time?"

I cleared my throat, uncomfortable, and started fidgeting with my pen.

Rattlesnakes can get eaten, too, and Ted is my hawk.

"I'd be happy to answer your questions, but I'd like my lawyer present," I said with mock confidence.

His eyebrows lifted ever-so-slightly.

I had to clear my throat again before I continued. It felt awkward and dramatic to ask for a lawyer. "I'm represented by Ted Colbert. He said we could conference call him in. Would you like me to try to call him now?"

The relaxing of his shoulders was so subtle I almost missed it.

"Works for me," he answered.

Maybe the distance of a phone conversation made him feel a little more in control of the situation. And yet, I couldn't help but hear the rattle start to shake.

I called Ted's cell on my desktop phone, setting it to speaker. He answered on the third ring.

"Ted Colbert here."

"Hey, Ted. It's Josie Harjo. You're on speaker with Officer Watts."

"Hello, Josie. Pleasure to meet you, Officer Watts. My name is Ted Colbert from Colbert Law in Ada. I'm representing Dr. Harjo."

Officer Watts leaned forward to speak into the phone. "Howdy, sir. I'm investigating the missing items and just wanted to ask Dr. Harjo some questions. Nothing serious."

"Yes, yes. Dr. Harjo, please only answer the questions that are asked. I'll just listen in," Ted replied.

It was clear from Ted's tone that he'd heard the spiel before, and there was no way he was going to drop off the call until the questioning was over.

It was Officer Watts' turn to clear his throat. He pulled an old-school notepad out of his breast pocket and clicked his pen. He flipped through the notebook, found a page, and rested it on his knee to write. It was positioned in such a way that I couldn't see what he was jotting down.

I *really* wanted to see what was on that notepad, but I couldn't lean over without looking a fool.

"What's your role at the lab?" he asked.

My eyes leaped from the obscured notepad to his crisp blue eyes. He was watching me intently.

I kept eye contact even though I felt like squirming. "I'm one of three anatomic pathologists. We provide necropsy and biopsy services to the region."

That was an easy question, but I figured he was trying to warm me up.

"How long have you worked here?"

"About six years."

"What makes a vet want to cut up dead animals?"

Surprised by the question, I quipped, "Because you can't screw it up if it's already dead."

He barked a laugh, and I felt my shoulders loosen. I managed a small snicker.

"To each his own." He shrugged and looked back to his pad. "What day did the tiger come in?"

I knew he already knew this information but parroted it to him all the same. "The on-call student received it on Monday night."

He flipped a few pages back. "Josh Andrews?"

"Yes, sir. We performed the necropsy on Tuesday morning."

Ted coughed lightly on the speakerphone, and I realized I was offering information that hadn't been asked of me. The laugh the cop and I had shared a moment ago had loosened my tongue. I pressed my lips together and started tapping my pen.

"Who knew about the tiger?"

"Everyone."

"And who was present during the autopsy?"

Necropsy, I thought to myself, annoyed. "The final year veterinary students on rotation, Dustin, and me."

"Do you have the students' names?"

"Yes. Fran said she had already forwarded that information to you," I said, unable to hide my irritation. I knew he had all of these details already. I felt like he was wasting my time...or trying to fluster me.

"Probably. Just want to confirm."

"I only know their first names. I'd have to look at the roster for their last names."

I fished around on my desk. On the first day of the rotation, I'd printed out their names and class pics. I'd also added notes about their preferred pronouns and areas of interest when we'd met.

A pang clenched my heart. I knew the guy had the students' names already. But I couldn't help but feel like I was shifting his attention to them by passing the sheet over.

I reluctantly slid the paper across the desk and narrated, "Ted, I'm sharing the rotation roster with him."

"Thanks, Josie," Ted answered.

The officer jotted the names down, likely planning on cross-referencing them with the list that Fran and the others had provided him.

"Walk me through the autopsy. Anything unusual?"

Necropsy! I wanted to shout.

Instead, I said, "No, sir. Pretty standard." I tried my best not to sound flippant. I wasn't sure how successful I was.

"You didn't do anything differently?"

The *ch-ch-ch* of the snake's tail grated a warning.

"Well," I proceeded cautiously, "we had to break from the usual method to preserve the integrity of the pelt. At the request of the sanctuary, of course. But other than that and removing the claws, which we don't normally do, it was relatively standard."

Ted was silent on the line, and I assumed that meant things were going okay.

"Is it common for people to ask for parts back?"

"Umm...I'm not sure what you mean."

People asked for the return of cremated remains and bodies to be buried all the time. That wasn't unique to veterinary medicine.

"Do people commonly ask for *certain* parts returned?"

"Oh," I answered, the light bulb popping on. "If it's a zoo or wildlife center, then yes."

"Why?"

"For education."

The movement of his pen on the notepad was hypnotizing. I couldn't tell if he was doodling flowers to mess with me or actually writing everything down verbatim. I ached to get my eyes on it.

"Back to the autopsy. Did anyone else come out to observe?"

Necropsy, damn it!

I sighed, feeling perturbed. "No, sir."

"Was anyone aware of the value of those items?"

"It goes without saying, I think."

The irritation was starting to creep into my voice. The questions felt stupid, nit-picky, and patronizing.

"Dr. Smith said that Dr. Richter made several comments about the value of the items." He looked up from his notepad, eyebrows raised.

Officer Watts hadn't actually asked a question, so I stayed silent. I hoped Ted appreciated it.

His eyebrows dropped, and he rested his writing hand on the pad.

"What about Dustin? Did he know the value of the items?" he continued.

I felt my hackles rise.

Ted saved me and said, "My client shouldn't be asked to speculate on what another individual may or may not have known."

Officer Watts reframed the question. "Did anyone comment about the value of the items?"

Gerald and Emma both immediately popped into my head. Even though I didn't like either of them, I didn't think they were the type to steal a tiger pelt and claws. I couldn't imagine Emma entering a cooler of dead animals, digging through the dripping bags, and hauling the tiger pelt out. It didn't seem right. But that wasn't my call.

Regardless, I felt stubborn, and I didn't want to name any names. He could try to shake his tail at me all he wanted to; I wasn't budging.

"There were multiple conversations with several people about the value of the items," I answered. "We're a veterinary medical lab, after all."

"Hmm," he huffed. "Where were the items stored?"

"After the pelt was dry enough to bag, it was placed in the cooler with the claws."

"Who has access to that?"

"During the day, pretty much anyone."

"How about at night?" he pressed.

"Anyone with a badge can get in at night. I think there's a log that can be pulled with that information."

"Could someone potentially come in during the day, with or without a badge, and stay in the lab until after hours?"

Ted's cough echoed through the speakerphone, making me jump. I'd almost forgotten he was there.

"I guess?" I answered hesitantly. "But that would be pretty wild."

"Given that any 'ole person can just waltz in here, why didn't it occur to anyone to lock the items up?"

Gerald's voice echoed in my head. *I told you that you needed to lock those tiger parts up. Now they're gone, and it's because of your negligence.*

I felt my face flush, and I shrugged. "We're a small lab in Stillwater, Oklahoma. That kinda stuff doesn't usually happen here."

Oh, bless your heart, his expression replied.

That was the moment when I really started to get pissed.

"When did you notice the items were missing?" he asked.

"I heard about it when I came into work yesterday," I answered curtly.

"Did you look for them?"

I narrowed my eyes. "Dustin tore the cooler apart several times looking for them. I trust him to do due diligence."

"Oh, yes, Dustin."

What the fuck does that mean?

I felt another flush, this time with defensive anger. I was *done* with this shit.

"How would one clean something like that?" He waved his hand in the air. "A pelt can't be sold like that, can it?"

I leaned back in my chair and crossed my arms. "I wouldn't know."

"Would anyone else in the lab have that information?"

"I don't know."

"What about Dustin?" He flipped a few pages back. "It looks like Dr. Richter said that Dustin is an avid hunter and does some taxidermy on the side. Is that true? He seemed to think that Dustin stole the items."

I felt a surge of adrenaline. *Fucking Gerald.*

"You should ask Dustin about that," I snarked.

Ted, sensing my ire, jumped in. "I think you should have just about everything you need. Right, Officer Watts? If you need to speak to my client again, perhaps we can schedule a time for Josie and me to come by the station?"

I was certain Officer Watts wanted to poke at me a bit more, but he conceded the match. "Yes, sir. I'll be in touch should we have any more questions."

He clicked his pen, placing it in his pocket with his pad. He stood and reached out his hand. "Nice meeting you in person, Dr. Harjo."

Forced by my southern upbringing, I couldn't help but shake his hand in return, hoping he didn't notice how sweaty my palm was.

I flashed him my best fake smile.

"I'll see myself out," he said, pushing his chair in.

As soon as the door closed behind him, I picked up the phone. "Ted? He's gone, and you're off speaker."

"I'm glad you called me, Josie. The good news is, I don't think he's after you. You enjoy your weekend and try not to worry 'bout it. But if he comes by again or calls you, you get me right back on the phone. Okay?"

"Yes, sir," I said, the tension in my shoulders easing. I'd made it out without getting bitten.

For now, at least, an evil voice whispered in my head.

"Thank you, Ted," I added.

"Anytime, Josie. Tell Molly I said 'hi.'"

We said quick goodbyes, and I hung up the phone.

I sat back in my chair, trying to process the last agonizing fifteen minutes. I'd wanted to get this conversation out of the way today. And it was a relief to know that the target wasn't on my back. But I couldn't help but fret about Dustin. I was certain he hadn't done anything wrong, but I felt like I hadn't helped him at all when I'd talked to Officer Watts.

Feeling grumpy, I briefly toyed with the idea of flaking on Armand tonight. I just wanted to mope on my couch, eat a pint of ice cream, and snuggle with Yersi.

But Tessa will be staying there.

I looked deep into my heart and realized I wanted to see Armand anyway. I couldn't be the perky, engaged girlfriend all the time; I was sure he'd understand.

I quickly texted him.

> This week's been crazy. I'm gonna order delivery tonight.

He immediately replied by sending a thumbs up.

I quickly flicked through the minimal options in Stillwater and decided on Greek food, hoping he'd approve. We'd been a couple of times; he always ordered the same thing, and he seemed to like it.

> Greek sound okay? The usual?

He sent another thumbs up. The brevity of his replies was slightly unusual. But I figured it was probably because he was driving or otherwise busy rather than miffed.

With the evening sorted, I stress-ate four more cookies that I'd brought back to the office with me and went back to shifting glass.

A few more hours, and I could blow this joint.

CHAPTER

SEVENTEEN

That evening, Tessa and I were watching the chickens in the backyard, trying to relax, when the doorbell rang.

Yersi streaked past me and let out a hearty *meow* command at the front door. I was expecting both Armand and the Greek food I'd ordered for dinner. Given Yersi's unbridled enthusiasm, it *had* to be Armand.

My heart fluttered with anticipation.

"That's probably Armand. Do you mind locking the chickens up?"

"I'd be happy to." Tessa stood to shoo the girls back into their Eglu before following me inside.

When I opened the door and saw his face, my heart melted. The pleasant smell of his aftershave wafted over me.

I *loved* that smell.

He flashed me a shy, goofy grin. He must've stopped by his place for a shower and a shave because he looked *amazing*. His dark, curly hair was slightly damp and tousled over his forehead. A casual crimson polo stretched across his shoulders and was paired with dark gray slacks and dress sneakers.

I shot into his arms for a long hug.

He'd only been gone a week, but I'd still missed the hell out of him. I had no clue what I was going to do when his sabbatical was over and he went back to Romania.

"I missed you," I said, slightly breathless.

Meow, Yersi purred at our feet, rubbing his cheek against Armand's leg.

Yersi agreed: A week was too long.

Armand's hug tightened slightly, and he took a deep breath, face buried in my hair. "I missed you, too."

It felt so good to fall into a hug. The week had been emotionally charged. It was nice to get grounded.

"Come on in," I said, releasing him and stepping back. "Tessa's putting the chickens away."

He followed me through the house, Yersi close at his heels.

Tessa met us in the kitchen, where we were perched at the counter.

"Armand, Tessa," I said, gesturing to each of them.

Armand stood to shake her hand. "Nice to meet you, Tessa."

The doorbell rang again.

"That must be the food," I chimed in. "I'll go get the door."

With two large bags in tow, I joined them at the kitchen table, where they were already casually chatting. To my delight, Armand and Tessa had instantly hit it off.

Yersi had claimed Armand's lap, purring loudly.

Having slayed the Greek take-out beast, I laid the spread out for everyone. The spanakopita, grape leaves, and Greek salad were shared family-style. For the main meal, Tessa had ordered a gyro with fries. Armand and I had both ordered kebabs with Greek rice.

"I have to ask," Tessa started bravely. "Are you an OU fan?"

"Huh?" Armand replied.

He put his fork down and wiped his mouth with his napkin, catching a bit of tzatziki that had plopped on his chin.

She nodded to his shirt. "You're wearing OU colors, and the bedlam game is tomorrow."

His eyebrows creased, and he looked down at his shirt, still lost.

I didn't know squat about sports, but I lived in Stillwater. It was impossible *not* to know that there was a major American football game tomorrow.

"OU is a college in Norman, just south of Oklahoma City, and their colors are crimson and cream," I explained. "There's a big rivalry between OSU and OU. The bedlam game is when their football teams play each other. American football. They're playing each other tomorrow."

"Just sayin'. It's pretty brave wearin' crimson this weekend, is all," Tessa teased, one eyebrow raised.

"Yeah," I joined in on the ribbing. "You're liable to get jumped."

"Orange is an ugly color," he said, the seriousness of his voice discordant with the smile dancing around his lips.

Tessa feigned shock.

He made a bored face. "I don't follow American football. And this"—he gestured down to his shirt—"is just me selecting a shirt from my closet. If I'm dressing to support a team, it will be a team playing *real* football, and I'll be wearing red, yellow, or blue."

"Watch it, fella. Them there's fightin' words," Tessa said with a friendly grin.

He held his hands up in surrender. "I promise I'll never do it again."

We all laughed. I tossed Tessa a smile, which she returned. It was nice seeing her laugh and play a little.

The conversation shifted to whether football or soccer was the best sport. It was a heated debate but still all in good fun. Knowing nothing about sports, I sat back and enjoyed the ride.

Armand's cheer warmed the house and distracted us both from all the drama. He was great at keeping the conversation going with Tessa. As they chatted, I ate my meal and watched her.

The couple nights of sleep, even if on a couch, had done wonders for her. Her bags were less prominent, and she had color in her cheeks. I still sensed a cloud over her, but the delicious Greek food and conversation had pushed it off to the horizon. It made me happy to see her relax and forget about the heavy weight she was carrying, that damn *yōkai*, even if it was for just a minute.

I'd have to keep my eye on her, though. It'd be easy enough to slip back into depression. Her difficulties weren't going away any time soon. I planned on asking her to check in with me after the rotation was over, even if she just stopped by the office to say "hi."

Assuming the chaos at the lab is sorted, and she's allowed in.

I tried to brush away the dark thought.

I was here with Armand, belly full of tasty food. I'd be damned if I was going to let work stuff press in on the evening.

When everyone seemed to have eaten their fill, I asked, "Want to play a game?"

Given that Aunt Flo was still in town and I had a house guest, a tabletop game was the only game I'd be playing tonight.

"Sure," Armand said, leaning back in his chair, content.

"Yeah, I'm down," Tessa answered, sounding interested. "I'll clean up while y'all set it up."

"What do you want to play?" I asked.

They both shrugged.

"Let's look," Armand said and rose from his chair.

As we left the kitchen, he laid his hand gently on the base of my back and leaned over to whisper next to my ear, "Are you okay?"

Catching his eye, I gave him what I hoped was a small, reassuring smile.

Once out of earshot, I said, "It's been a rough week." And then, to my horror, I felt tears well up in my eyes.

What the hell?

I did *not* cry.

His face flashed with concern. He folded me in another comforting hug.

I pressed my cheek against his chest, willing myself not to break down. I needed to be tough for Tessa—be her rock in the storm. Plus, I'd been through my fair share of shit and shouldn't be this shook up. This crap with the tiger was nothing compared to what I'd been through with my mom dying.

Tessa was safe, for now. And it didn't seem like I was even a suspect in the tiger drama. Why the hell was I freaking out?

Because it isn't over, yet, the dark side of me whispered.

Armand interrupted my inner monologue. "Is it the stuff with Tessa?"

Kinda, I thought but shook my head in the negative.

"Is it Gerald?"

I'd shared the stories of our resident work troll. But damned if I'd cry over anything that shitass did.

I shook my head again.

"What is it?" His voice was laced with concern. "Do you want to talk about it?"

A heavy sigh escaped.

I knew I wasn't supposed to talk about the tiger stuff. I also knew that I'd already overstepped that slightly by talking to Aunty about it. I needed to pack this up and shove it deep down inside. I *needed* to enjoy this night.

I pulled away from the hug and plastered on a brave smile. "I'm good. It's just work stuff. Let's go pick a game."

I probably should've talked it out. Hindsight and all that.

***

Saturday morning, I woke up curled in a ball next to Armand. I snuggled closer to him. He wrapped an arm around me and rested his head on my back.

It was so nice to have him over. He'd only been gone a week, but it had been a rough couple of days.

"Good morning," he whispered, breath tickling across my shoulder.

Meow, Yersi yowled in reply on the other side of the bedroom door.

I groaned.

"Shhh...pretend you're asleep," I whispered to Armand with little hope.

Yersi meowed again and started scratching at the wood.

The little rascal did *not* tolerate closed doors, and it was quite the match last night as he decided between sleeping with us or having free rein to roam the rest of the house. After about four trips to let him in or out, I'd just kicked him out.

He was *not* pleased.

He meowed again, this time sounding like his entire world had shattered. It was a desperate wail of a meow.

I sighed.

Armand's arm tightened slightly around me when I moved to get up.

"Wait a sec," he said softly.

I rolled over to face him. Morning breath be damned.

He was on his side, one arm scrunched under his pillow. His dark, curly hair was tousled, and a five o'clock shadow brushed his skin.

When I caught his heavy-lidded eyes, I felt a tingle and wished I didn't have any house guests.

"I wanted to talk. Have a minute?" he asked, voice soft.

He brushed my hair back over my shoulder, and I shivered.

"Sure, what's up?" I answered, a little breathless.

"I was hoping to speak to you last night. But with Tessa..." he trailed off.

I felt a sliver of concern. I had no clue what was coming next, and my mind assumed the worst.

Yersi had stopped yowling, and it was eerily silent. I could practically see him there with a furred ear pressed to the door.

Armand reached up to smooth the crease between my brow.

"Don't worry," he whispered and smiled.

He used his free hand to lace his fingers gently in mine.

"My sabbatical is going to end in five weeks," he said, voice still hushed.

My stomach clenched. I didn't want to be reminded. I'd been keeping that tidbit locked away because it hurt too much to think about.

"I don't want to go," he continued and squeezed my hand. "I love being here with you. And OSU is an excellent campus. I've learned a lot and could do so much more with the resources they have here. But I can't stay even if there was an open faculty position to transfer into. My visa is strictly tied to the three-month sabbatical."

I felt a slow heat spread across my face and did everything in my power not to start crying. I didn't understand why he was bringing this up *now*. This was the last thing I needed on my plate, especially with all of the other stuff going on.

"Please don't be upset." He leaned forward and kissed me.

The silence spread between us. The absence of Yersi chiming in only made it worse.

"I have a plan, but I wanted to talk to you about it." He gave my hand another squeeze. "I was looking into some options. I found a grant that has a six-month stipend plus a small amount for lab supplies and equipment. I would need to apply for it, and I might not get it."

I tried to push down the burgeoning hope. The world of grants was highly competitive.

"There's also the issue of not having a lab here," he continued. "I talked to Laila about it yesterday. She was very supportive. She said the department could host me. I could use one of the benches in her lab, and they might even be able to bring me on as a short-term fellow or something similar to make the visa application easier. She offered to write a letter to include in the grant application."

I felt a rush of gratitude for Laila. For the millionth time, I wished she was my boss.

As everything clicked together, I realized that there must be a "but" here somewhere.

"That all sounds amazing," I said tentatively. "What about your position back in Romania?"

"I'm not sure. I have a call with my boss on Monday."

"And Ileana?" I couldn't forget his cute dog, waiting for him back home.

"I'm thinking about flying her out here. But I haven't gotten that far yet."

"Wow," I said, trying to process everything.

A look of concern flashed across his face.

I squeezed his hand, and quickly added, "I'm delighted that you're thinking about all this. It's just...it's been a week, and I'm trying to catch up."

The worry was still trapped in the crinkles between his eyebrows.

"Seriously." I kissed him softly. "I don't want you to leave. I've been trying not to think about it. It hurts too much."

He gave me a sad smile.

"There are many things that will have to happen for it to work out." The furrows between his eyebrows deepened. "You think I should apply?"

"Absolutely."

"I'd still have to go home in November. But I'd come back right after the holidays if everything works out."

I snuggled in closer to him, resting my cheek on his chest. "Just come back, okay?"

He kissed the top of my head and said, "I promise."

***

Armand left early Saturday for a pick-up soccer game, and the rest of the day sped by in a relaxed blur. The weather had started to cool from the sauna of summer, and Tessa and I spent most of the weekend outside reading under the pergola. Even though I was a loner at heart, I was enjoying her company, and part of me was going to miss her when she moved into the temporary housing on Monday.

Feeling sun-drunk, I pushed my sunglasses up headband-style, looked over at her, and impulsively said, "You should come with me to brunch tomorrow."

Tessa looked up from her study notes.

Her NAVLE test date was a couple of months away. Her ability to practice medicine hinged on passing that test; she couldn't botch that one up. I admired her for sticking with it despite all of the other stuff heaped on her plate. It was a heavy load to carry.

"Brunch?" she asked almost hesitantly.

"Yeah, I go to my Aunty Molly's house in Ada every Sunday. She cooks food. I eat food. It's pretty awesome." My tone was still light, but I felt an edge of worry that maybe I shouldn't have asked her.

My time with Aunty was typically *my* time. I didn't bring people with me very often. Laila had only been once. Armand hadn't been at all. Sunday was *my* day with Aunty, and everyone knew it was off-limits.

So why did you invite Tessa, dumbass?

I couldn't tell if it was my heat-soaked brain or something else that had pushed me to ask her to join the most private and sacred of family rituals.

It's because you feel sorry for her. You don't want her to feel alone. You don't want to leave her alone.

As if reading my mind, Tessa said, "I wouldn't want to intrude."

Those were the words that came out of her mouth. And I credit her for trying to make them sound genuine. But I couldn't help but notice that there was a hunger there. A desire for something normal, for family, for comfort. I couldn't deny her that.

I waved my hand dismissively. "Not at all. Aunty loves everybody. The only thing you have to worry about is being fed too much."

And it was true; Aunty would see Tessa—stressed and under-fed—and bundle her into the house to take care of her. That was her nature. I'd text her a heads-up, but she wouldn't bat an eye at an extra mouth to feed or a stranger coming over.

"Aunty would love to meet you. And feed you. It's her thing," I added, closing my eyes and leaning back in my chair, trying to look relaxed.

"Sure, I'll come, then...."

I felt the pause. I knew she wanted to fill it with a "What can I bring?" and stopped herself. It was the Oklahoma-polite thing to do. But she didn't have any money.

I decided to dodge the discomfort.

"And don't even think about bringing a host gift or anything. She won't accept it. If we go for a walk, she might ask you to help pick up litter. But that's about it."

"I can manage that," she said with a soft smile. "Thanks for inviting me."

I gave her a friendly now-that's-settled nod and pulled my sunglasses back down to cover my eyes.

***

The drive to Aunty's did *not* go as I'd expected.

I'd thought it was going to be a stiff ride with jilted conversation, the gap between faculty and student yawning between us uncomfortably.

To my delight, the ride was like two BFFs on a road trip. When I'd cued up a playlist, we'd bonded instantly over music. The entire two-hour drive was spent singing along off-key to a breadth of songs that spanned forty years of hip-hop.

Tessa had transformed with the music, and I finally saw the person who was buried beneath the weight and stress of her life.

I was genuinely starting to like her and felt a blooming hope that we could stay friends once this mess was over.

We pulled into Aunty's place, cheeks rosy with joy and goofy grins plastered on both of our faces.

Chula ran to the driveway to greet us, startling the chickens.

"What a cute dog!" Tessa exclaimed, still giddy from the drive.

She kneeled, and Chula came up to lick her face. Tessa gently cradled Chula's cheeks, scratching her airplane ears.

"Oh, my gosh," she cooed. "Aren't you sweet! Out here guarding the chickens, aren't you, girl?"

Chula responded with a tail wag and another lick to the face.

"What kind of dog is she?" Tessa said, still soaking up the doggie cuddles.

I shrugged, pulling a stack of books out of the back of the car. "No clue."

"She looks half coyote," she joked.

"Ha! That's what Aunty says," I said with a grin.

Turning back to Chula, she cooed again, "Yes, you do. Who's a cute coyote girl? Yes, you are."

Chula sat back, panting with a happy dog smile and basking in the adoration.

Tessa stood and came over. "Here. Let me help." She grabbed a few books off the stack in my arms. "What are all these books for anyway?"

"Aunty is a librarian. She checks out like ten books for me every week, hoping one or two will stick." I flashed her a grin. "Just watch, she'll have a stack for me when we leave."

"That's kinda cool. She must think about you all the time."

Her comment gave me pause. I'd never thought about it that way before. Even though my parents were gone and I didn't have any siblings, I still had Aunty. She was *always* there. My rock.

I suspected Tessa didn't have that, and my heart ached for her.

"Yeah. I'm lucky to have her," I said with deep respect.

We schlepped the books to the metal screen door and let ourselves in. The smell of fry bread kissed our cheeks, and my mouth watered.

"Hey, Aunty! We're here."

"Come on into the kitchen," Aunty called from the other room.

We set the books down by the door, next to the stack that was positioned for me to take when I left. Tessa tossed me a knowing look, one eyebrow raised.

"Yep, those are to take home."

She smiled.

Chula's toenails clicked on the wood floor as she followed us into the kitchen.

"Hello, sweeties!" Aunty flashed us a huge grin, wiping flour off on her apron, and came over to fold us into big hugs.

"Aunty Molly, this is Tessa."

"Call me 'Aunty,'" she said as she folded Tessa into a hug.

Before releasing her, she held Tessa for a moment by the shoulders. Her eyes swept over her. A flash of concern crossed her face before she brushed it away with a smile. I doubt Tessa noticed, but I sure as hell did, and my gut clenched.

Aunty had a way with people; she could read them like all of the books in the library. Aunty saw deep into Tessa and saw something that worried her.

We may not be out of the woods yet.

"It's wonderful to meet you," Aunty said.

Aunty's warm smile seemed genuine. What she saw around Tessa couldn't have been that bad, right?

Tessa smiled, blushing slightly at Aunty's attention.

"Come sit," Aunty said, returning to the stove to flip the fry bread in the pan.

Tessa and I moved to the table and made ourselves comfortable. Chula settled next to Tessa, resting her head in her lap.

"What would you like to drink? I think a nice herbal tea might be in order?" Aunty asked.

I looked at Tessa, one eyebrow cocked to see what she would say. I knew her polite nature would have her agreeing to anything I said, and I wanted her to have some freedom today.

"Anything is fine," she answered. "Thank you, ma'am. I appreciate you welcoming me into your home."

Aunty waved away the formality but smiled; she liked helping people. She turned to me with an eyebrow raised, the tea question unanswered.

Having failed my attempt to get Tessa to pick, I said, "I defer to you, Aunty."

Aunty always knew what I needed, even if I didn't. I was sure she'd know what Tessa needed, too.

She busied herself preparing drinks before setting two steaming cups of honey lavender tea in front of both of us. As she sent them down, she lightly waved the steam into our faces, humming under her breath. The strong scent of lavender washed over me, and my shoulders relaxed. It seemed to have the same effect on Tessa.

Yes, Aunty definitely knows what we need.

We chatted idly as Aunty assembled heaping plates of fry bread with scrambled eggs and bacon. She laid out a bowl of strawberries. Aunty's garden somehow miraculously produced a conveyor belt of berries like gangbusters through the hot Oklahoma summer until the first freeze.

She seated herself, laid a napkin on her lap, and started in. Tessa, who had paused for social cues, also dug in with vigor.

The food was amazing, as always.

Tessa was all smiles, and a happy glow filled her cheeks. I felt like I was finally getting to know the real Tessa, the one who could be happy and enjoy her senior year of vet school. A Tessa who wasn't worried about money, where she would sleep, or how she would eat. It felt good to help her forget about those things, even if just for a few hours.

I wasn't a hundred percent sure she would ever be off the suicide-risk list, especially with the amount of debt she had hanging around her neck, but I'd bought her a week or two. And that was more than she'd had before.

Deep breaths. Little steps. Eyes on the prize.

As if she knew I was thinking about her, Tessa looked over and gave me a shy, thankful smile. I reached over and squeezed her hand, smiling down at my food.

We stayed at the table for over an hour in relaxed conversation, with Aunty refreshing our tea. After we cleaned up and washed the dishes, the three of us headed out for a long walk by the creek, Chula trotting along happily ahead of us.

The weather was gorgeous. We saw several birds of prey, a rat snake out sunning in the path, and the flash of a lizard escaping into the brush. And even though we'd brought three bags to pick up litter, there was almost none to collect.

We returned home in the early afternoon, kicking the red Oklahoma mud off our shoes. Tessa looked relaxed, refreshed, and—dare I say—even happy. Back at the house, she played fetch with Chula in the front yard as Aunty and I sat on the porch.

"Thanks for having us today," I said, feeling warm and happy myself.

"Thank you for coming, and thank you for bringing Tessa. She's a lovely woman."

"Yes, she is," I replied.

The good food, relaxing walk, and gentle sun had lulled me into a sense of false security. My subsequent shock over what Aunty was about to say could only be blamed on postprandial hyperglycemia.

"She has a dark cloud over her," she said in a cool, hushed voice.

Gooseflesh spread up my arms.

Startled by the dark, uncharacteristic comment, I turned to look at Aunty. Her face was neutral and her shoulders relaxed, all in complete contradiction to her tone.

Trying to brush it off, I said, "Yeah, she owes a lot of money, and she's broke."

"No. I think it's more than that," she said, eyes sharp and focused on Tessa.

I felt a trace of concern arc up my spine. The old anxiety crept in, and my sewing machine leg started bobbing.

I couldn't help myself and, again, tried to wave away her concern.

"She doesn't have a place to live," I said, sounding a bit defensive. "It's hard crashing at someone else's. She moves into emergency housing tomorrow, but that stress will still be there until her housing situation stabilizes."

Aunty pursed her lips in doubt.

"Yeah. With all that, it's understandable she's got a black cloud over her," I added lamely, my words falling flat.

Aunty turned to me, face serious and tense. "No, Josie. *Hear me.* There's a darkness surrounding her. Bad spirits. They'll wash over you, too, if you don't protect yourself."

And with those few words, all of the happiness of the weekend slipped away in the blink of an eye.

CHAPTER

EIGHTEEN

The joy from earlier bled like a wheeze from a popped party balloon as Aunty's words of warning continued to bounce around in my head.

There's a darkness surrounding her.

With my hands on the steering wheel, navigating back to Stillwater, I glanced over at Tessa. She was pink-cheeked, happy, and tapping her foot along to Cardi B's "I Like It." The wisps of hair framing her face danced lightly in the breeze from the air conditioner.

I sure as hell couldn't see the darkness.

But Aunty saw stuff—deeper shit—things that I often missed.

A thread of anxiety traced up my spine.

Bad spirits.

Chula thought Tessa was the bee's knees. That meant something, right? Dogs were good judges of character.

Cats are better judges, a nasty voice in my head whispered.

Yersi was pensive around Tessa, and their relationship seemed tentative. His eyes were always on her when she was awake, but he still snuggled up to her when she was asleep. It was kinda freaky.

I risked another glance at Tessa.

She caught the look this time and tossed me a huge grin. "Thanks for letting me come today, Josie. Aunty is great, and I love Chula."

I smiled back, but it didn't reach my eyes.

The anxiety was overwhelming, and my mind whirled. There was a dichotomy between Aunty's ominous words and the visage of a caring woman sitting in my passenger seat.

Aunty had sensed something about her was fake. But what? Her cheer? Maybe. That made the most sense, given her current financial situation. Her kindness? The idea that her kindness had been fake didn't feel right, either. The way she'd acted toward Chula was genuine; Tessa had a good heart.

I clearly wasn't going to figure this out without picking at the wound. I just didn't know how to approach it. I was also worried that confronting her would spoil the good mood. This was the happiest I'd ever seen her. I didn't want to upset the apple cart and send her back into depression.

As if she sensed my brooding, Tessa asked, "You okay?"

"Yeah, I'm good."

My hands clenched around the steering wheel, and my stomach flopped.

I'd developed a momma-bear-like attachment to Tessa these last few days. Just a few hours ago, we'd sung Lil Nas X's "Old Town Road" together at the top of our lungs, grinning like teenagers.

It made me feel awful that I was now giving her what amounted to a distrustful side-eye.

After what felt like an awkward hour but was probably more like a minute, I decided to dive in.

"Hey, Tessa," I started hesitantly.

She looked over, smiling, face relaxed. "Yeah?"

"Are *you* okay?"

Her smile got bigger. "Yep. I'm great. Aunty's place is a little piece of heaven. Thank you for inviting me."

She started humming along to the music.

Well, that didn't work.

Unable to ignore Aunty's warning, I reached over to turn the music down.

"Seriously. Like, beyond today. Like, with everything," I stumbled, trying to articulate my thoughts and failing miserably.

I took my eyes off the road to glance at her. Her smile had dropped. She turned her head to look out at the window.

The silence built in the car.

To my horror, I felt a nervous sweat trickle down my pits. Nothing like good 'ole adrenaline and cortisol to announce that I was extremely anxious.

"I just...I'm just worried about you. I'm glad you have a place to stay. That's great. And I bet they can help you get through the rest of the year." I paused, realizing I was rambling. "I just want to make sure there's nothing else going on."

"I'm fine," she said quietly, head still turned to the window. Her obsessive picking at her nails indicated the opposite.

What are you scared of?

I risked another glance at her. She was now looking down at her hands, shoulders tense, picking away at her cuticles. One had started to bleed.

Now that I really *looked*, I could see it. There was definitely more there. And it was definitely fear. When Harper first came to me, I thought Tessa's problem was all wrapped around money and a lack of housing.

Now, I wasn't so sure that was all of it.

"Are you safe?"

Out of the corner of my eye, she went still. I wished I wasn't driving so I could read her body language better without risking life and limb. I thought about pulling over but immediately decided against it; that was a bit too creeper-ish.

"Aunty and I are both worried about you. I can't help but think there is something else going on. I want to make sure you're safe. Aunty does, too."

I wasn't shy about pulling the Aunty card; it was often effective.

The silence built back up in the car.

Tessa had started crying a soundless stream of tears. She wiped her eyes with the base of her palm.

The air in the car was thick with her pain.

There was definitely *more*. Had she been raped? Did she have an abusive partner? Was it still happening?

"If someone is hurting you, you can tell me."

I wanted to reach over and squeeze her hand. But her body was tense, and I felt like any physical expression of concern or support might be unwelcome.

My hands clenched tighter on the steering wheel.

"This is a safe space. You can talk to me if you want to. You don't have to. But I'm here if you do."

What I didn't say was that if someone was abusing her, I was gonna go apeshit on the motherfucker.

I felt another protective rush of adrenaline.

"I messed up, Josie," she said so softly that I almost didn't catch it.

Those were not the words I expected to hear, and I paused to process before I stupidly said, "Huh?"

"I...I did something...and...I totally fucked up."

She rubbed at her cheeks again, almost angrily, frustrated that the tears dared to continue their watery descent.

I took one hand off the wheel to gesture between us. "Whatever we say here stays. This is a safe space."

She sniffed the inevitable tear-snot. I wanted to reach over to the glove box to pull out a napkin for her, but there was an impenetrable wall around her personal space.

"What happened?" I probed gently.

"Promise not to tell anyone. Promise," she whispered, sounding desperate and defeated.

"Sure, I promise."

Please don't say you killed your boyfriend or some crazy shit like that. I like to keep my promises.

"I did it," she said, the words escaping from her lips like gas from a nick in the abdomen of a bloated carcass.

She sighed heavily and leaned back, looking out the window again. More than one cuticle was bleeding by this point. There was a small spot of blood where it had brushed against her shirt.

Confused, I cautiously asked, "Did what?"

She rubbed the tears from her face again. Now that the words were out, I could see another layer below the fear, and it was a thick coating of *shame*.

240

"The tiger pen," she whispered.

The fry bread threatened to come back up.

"Oh, shit...Tessa..."

There's the darkness, and it has fucking teeth. Tiger *teeth.*

My chest went tight, and it was hard to breathe.

Sensing my panic, she said, "Yeah, I know. I fucked up." If anyone could sound any more humiliated and dejected, I'd never heard them.

Tessa had a good heart. But this was *serious.*

"Yeahhh," was all I could squeak out.

The steering wheel would have permanent finger-shaped dents by the end of this drive. I fought back the vomit a second time.

I took a few deep breaths, trying to push past the fight-or-flight hormones that were wreaking havoc on my brain function.

After three deep belly breaths, I was able to think more clearly. The anxiety was still there, but I channeled that into action planning. If I had a plan, I could control the outcome.

But really, how the hell are we going to unfuck this situation?

Tessa had stolen big-ticket items and could face felony charges. *A felony!*

Felony charges meant she might not be able to practice medicine...potentially forever. The decision would be up to the state licensing board. And stealing animal parts to sell on the black market was not a conviction you wanted to have on your record as a veterinarian. It was one step down from writing fake drug prescriptions for money or taking the drugs yourself. This was bad juju.

All the debt. And she might not even be able to work.

This was some heavy shit, and I just waddled right into it wearing flip-flops.

My hands clenched tighter on the steering wheel; the poor thing would need to be resuscitated soon.

We needed a plan. If the items were returned, maybe the police wouldn't pursue a theft charge.

"Do you still have the stuff?" I asked. "Maybe we could just put them back in the cooler?"

I turned to look at her. Her face was pointed down at her hands, lips pressed in a thin white line. Her head shook slowly back and forth.

"I sold them already." The words spilled from her painfully.

My mind whirled. How do you even go about selling something like that? How did she find a buyer so fast? How did she get paid? It wasn't like you could Venmo that shit. Was there a bag of money sitting in my house somewhere?

"Fuck, Tessa."

"Yeah, I know. I really screwed up. And there's no way to fix it."

They'll wash over you, too, if you don't protect yourself. Aunty's words echoed through my head.

Does this make me an accessory-after-the-fact? I tried to brush away the selfish thought.

"Fuck," I repeated, unable to get out of the loop.

"Please don't tell anyone. I...." Her voice trailed off as she wiped at her tears again.

At a loss for words, I had no choice but to let the silence spread like rancid butter.

"I need to finish school and start working," she continued, her voice laced with desperation. "I needed the money. I've got nothing."

My heart broke for her. My financial situation had been dismal during vet school, but I'd never been homeless. And I always had Aunty in the wings to keep me smiling. I couldn't imagine what Tessa was going through. She was a good person with a dream. And she'd made one bad decision that could ruin everything.

"Have the cops questioned you yet?"

She shook her head. "No. Emma said they're going to pin it on Dr. Richter. That's why they haven't talked to the students."

"Where did she hear that?" I scoffed.

"It's *Emma.*"

I could practically hear her rolling her eyes.

"Is there any truth to what she said? Do you think they'll interview y'all?" I asked.

I felt so completely out of it. The officer had asked some questions about Gerald. And I remembered him saying something about Zoe.

But my mind was foggy. I'd tried hard to block that interview out so I could enjoy the weekend. All I could remember was how much the guy had pressed me on Dustin.

Dustin.

"Tessa...I'm pretty sure they think Dustin took the stuff."

My eyes shifted from the road to catch her eye. Her face was ashen, brows creased in worry, shoulders hunched.

"They can't do anything to him without proof, right?" she fretted. "Like, he won't get in trouble because of me?"

"I have no clue," I replied. "I'd think they need more than circumstantial evidence. But that's not my thing. I cut up dead bodies. Other people worry about that stuff. Plus...Tessa...this is eating him up. Even if they don't press charges or whatever, they can make him look guilty to everyone he works with. And the stress of it all—it's killing him."

"I didn't want to hurt anyone," she said, voice phlegmy with crying.

"I know." I reached over to break the wall and squeezed her hand.

I felt like I was on the precipice of an impossible decision. I could choose Tessa or the tiger. If I kept my mouth shut, Tessa might skate out of this free and clear. But would Dustin pay the price? Or Gerald? As much as I hated Gerald, I couldn't let him be punished for something he didn't do. And what about the simple act of doing what was right? What *was* right in this situation?

"I don't know how to fix this. I don't want to hurt anyone," she repeated.

I took another deep belly breath. I could find a way through this.

"I'm not sure of the right answer, either," I confessed and then chewed on my cheek. "I've got the name of a lawyer. Would you be willing to talk to him? Get some advice on next steps?"

"I can't afford a lawyer," she answered bitterly. The tears started again.

"He's a friend of Aunty's. He'll hook us up."

I wasn't sure Ted would agree to represent Tessa, but I was going to try my darndest to make it happen if she was willing.

I risked another glance at her. She seemed to be considering it.

"I'll cover anything if he even charges you," I nudged. "He's representing me, too."

"The cops think you did it?" As if she couldn't sound more miserable, we'd now hit rock bottom.

Trying to reassure her, I said, "No. I don't think so. But Aunty insisted." After a beat, I asked again, "Would you at least give him a call?"

"Yeah...sure," she replied, resigned.

"Look," I said. "Let's get home. We'll give Ted a call, and we'll find a way through this. Deep breaths, little steps, and all that. Okay?"

She nodded and said softly, "Okay."

I tried to sound sure of it all, and she seemed to buy it. But inside, I was bubbling with anxiety. This could unravel in so many directions, and none of them were pleasant.

Aunty was right. The darkness *had* washed over me, and I'd walked right into like fucking Pollyanna. I just hoped Ted could throw us a lifeline because right now, all I saw was an impossible choice between two shitty options.

***

A couple of hours later, we were back home. We'd barely gotten in the front door before I dialed Ted. He picked up immediately. And on a Sunday, too—I was impressed.

I'd be owing Aunty, and she'd be owing Ted. Life truly was just a series of traded favors.

After brief introductions, I'd passed the phone to Tessa and slipped outside to take care of the chickens.

The sweet smell of the jasmine was almost cloying today, mocking me with its pleasant scent. Daring me to cheer up.

Even in my happy place, with the girls clucking and scratching around the yard, I couldn't relax. Before I even had a chance to start watering, Tessa poked her head out of the back door, my phone pressed to her chest.

"Josie?" she called out nervously.

"Yes? What's up?" I answered, trying to sound more confident than I felt.

"Um. Do you mind being on the call with us? Mr. Colbert says it's okay as long as I'm okay with it." She worried at the edge of her shirt. "I could use some support."

Despite my whirling thoughts, my heart swelled.

"Whatever you need," I said.

She stepped outside. Yersi streaked out behind her before she closed the door.

She put the phone on speaker. "Mr. Colbert? Can you hear us?"

"Yes, ma'am," he answered.

Tessa and I sat down under the pergola. She held the phone out between us. I leaned forward, putting my elbows on my knees so I could hear better. Yersi grabbed another chair and assumed a meatloaf position, ready to moderate.

Ted kicked things off. "Tessa provided the details of her situation. I'd like to discuss my recommendation. Is that alright with you, Tessa?"

"Yeah," Tessa answered softly, using her pointer finger on her free hand to worry the cuticle on her thumb.

Ted dove right in. "The information you have will be valuable to law enforcement, Tessa. Specifically, you know the name and phone number of the gentleman to whom you sold the items. He may have used a burner phone and a false name. But that's not for us to sort out. You also have the address where the sale happened. And most importantly, you can identify him."

I looked questioningly at Tessa, and she nodded in agreement, face resigned.

"I'm fairly confident we can exchange that information for a plea deal. I'm going to ask that the charges be reduced to a misdemeanor. I can't promise anything, but I know the DA pretty well and think she'd go for it, especially given that you have a clean record and it's a non-violent crime."

I sighed with relief.

"But," Ted continued, "if everyone agrees to this, Tessa will have to plead guilty to the misdemeanor. More importantly, she'll be asked to provide a statement and identify the person to whom she sold the items. Depending on where it goes from there, she may also be asked to testify in court, which will likely be the most difficult part."

"How do you feel about that, Tessa?" I asked.

She glanced up from the phone, eyebrows creased with worry. "I have to do it, Josie. I think it's the right thing to do. What do you think?"

I was a bit awed that she valued my opinion that much. I scrambled for an appropriate answer. I was still wrapping my head around the idea that I might not have to choose between her and the tiger.

"I...um...it's your decision," I began. Seeing her looking lost, I quickly added, "But I trust Ted."

"What other option is there?" she asked, defeated.

Ted cleared his throat. "There are other options. You could play this out and see where the chips fall. The police may not have enough evidence to prosecute. They haven't even interviewed you yet."

We all let that settle for a moment, the screaming of insects filling the air.

"However, I wouldn't recommend that," he added. "I've found the best option is to come forward early. Everyone typically plays a bit nicer in the sandbox with cooperative defendants, especially when they're also informants."

There was another long pause.

I thought Tessa should jump on that deal. It put things right, and she'd come out the other end moderately unscathed. But I was in what I figured was a support role. She needed to make the decision and *own it*.

"Would you like some time to think about it?" Ted offered.

"No," she replied instantly, shaking her head and looking resolved. "I'm ready to talk to them. Let's just get it over with. How soon can we get this done?"

"I'll put a call in tomorrow morning first thing. I have a few friends over there and suspect we can get in tomorrow. What's the best way to reach you?"

Tessa fought tears. "Um, I don't have a working phone right now. But I can call you from the dorm phone."

Ted rolled with it. "Not a problem. Just call my office around eight-thirty tomorrow. We'll have an update for you either way. Does that work for you?"

"Okay, I can do that," she answered. "Um, sir? Can Josie come with us?" She turned to me, looking hopeful. "If you're willing to, that is," she added.

"Absolutely." I gave her a slight nod of support. "Is that all right, Ted?"

"Yes, Josie can come with us to the station."

"Thank you," Tessa said, catching my eye.

"For what it's worth," Ted chimed in with certainty, "I think you're making the right choice, Tessa. I know it's a difficult situation."

Tessa took a deep breath, and her shoulders sagged. "Thank you, sir."

"Don't forget. Call my office tomorrow, and I'll have an appointment time for you."

"Yes, sir."

We said our goodbyes, with a few extra words of appreciation for Ted.

As soon as she hung up, the silent tears started.

I folded her into a hug.

"We got this," I whispered.

I stepped back to get a good look at her. She was shattered. But there was a faint hint of relief on her face.

"I find the most effective displacement activity in situations like this is watching a good flick while consuming copious amounts of ice cream."

She sniffed and smiled slightly.

"Now that that's over with, want to watch some *House of Usher*?" I offered.

She nodded.

A few minutes later, we were settled on the couch, each with our own pint of ice cream.

To my surprise, Yersi joined us, opting for Tessa's lap instead of mine.

CHAPTER

NINETEEN

Somehow, I'd made it to Monday morning.

A steaming mug of black tea rested on my desk. I stared at the wisps trailing into the air, eyes glazed over.

The afternoon sat before me like the end of a tunnel. I could see the light at the end of all of this mess, and I was *pretty* sure it wasn't a train. But I wouldn't know for sure until I'd walked the track.

If there was one tidbit of joy in this giant cluster-fuck, it was that my period had decided to bow out. I didn't need my uterus doubling me over with cramps when my stomach was already tied in knots. Tessa had an appointment at the police station at 2:30 P.M., and I'd be joining her. I just had to make it until then.

Thus, here I was. Sitting in my office. Trying to avoid contact with other human beings so I didn't accidentally let something slip.

The warmth seeped into my fingers as I wrapped them around the mug. For some reason, I wasn't fidgeting, which worried me more than if I was tapping my pen or bobbing my leg.

I'd briefly toyed with the idea of calling in sick. I wasn't on duty and didn't have any teaching responsibilities. But with all of the rumors flying around and everyone pointing fingers at everyone else, I figured that my absence would only create more drama.

Better to hide.

But I still had to get through the morning.

A pile of glass slides sat in cardboard flats on my desk; all of the tissue sections from the previous cases were patiently waiting to be slid across the microscope stage. Waiting for a final report. My normal urge to get results out as fast as possible was quenched by the black cloud that had spread over me. It was like a metastasis. I felt frozen.

Lost in my head, I barely heard the knock at my door.

My heart plummeted.

I briefly thought about ducking behind my desk so I couldn't be seen through the thin window. A modicum of self-respect kept me off the floor.

I quickly opened a flat of slides and threw one on my microscope, trying to look busy.

"Come in," I called out, channeling my business voice.

Zoe closed the door behind her, took a seat, and crossed her legs. She leaned forward conspiratorially, face eager.

Fuck.

I couldn't resist Zoe.

"Sooo," she drawled, "I met with the students this morning."

I had no idea where this was going, but I hoped it was *away* from the tiger.

"How did it go?" I asked, trying to sound innocent and interested.

She shrugged. "Oh, the session went fine."

She took a breath to start again.

"And Mackenzie? Did she ask you about careers?" I interrupted.

A confused look flashed across her face. "Uh, yeah. But that's not what I wanted to talk to you about."

She scooched to the edge of her seat and put her elbows on my desk.

Danger! Danger, Will Robinson!

"Emma said that the police spoke to her. It turns out Gerald *did* take the tiger parts."

Oh, fuuuuuuudddddggggggeeee.

I tried to keep my face neutral, which was pretty much impossible. Feeling it twitch awkwardly, I grabbed my pen and started tapping it. Though Zoe could read even the slightest change in body language, she was so riled up that she didn't even notice.

All the drama was eating me from the inside. I hated Gerald with all my heart. But I also didn't think people should be blamed for something they didn't do. I also knew that it was pretty damn likely

Emma had lied about talking to the police. She was just stirring things up, the little shitass.

I wondered how much I could share.

Nothing. I can share nothing, I reminded myself.

"I'm pretty sure Emma's making it up. Tessa has been staying at my place since Wednesday. She said that the police hadn't talked to any of them yet."

My toe was close to the line but not over.

Zoe paused to consider. "Yeah, I guess Emma could be lying. She seems like the type." She pursed her lips. "Still. It has to be Gerald. It can't be Josh. He's just a kid. And there's no way it was Dustin. No one else had access."

I knew Zoe wanted to see Gerald fall. And fall hard. So hard that he couldn't come back up again. He was cruelest to her, and her resentful anger had blinded her. I knew I couldn't convince her otherwise. All I could do was keep the gossip at bay until everything came to light.

I tried another tack. "I'm sure the cops will figure it out. I know you're worried about Dustin. But he has a lawyer now. He'll be safe."

Her eyebrows crinkled. It wasn't what she wanted to hear. I think she came in here expecting me to feed into it all. Share in the hate of our resident troll.

I felt her pull away from me.

"Look, Zoe. I'm just trying to stay out of it, is all. It's a small lab. It's a small campus. I just...." I tried to gather my thoughts. I didn't want to lose a friend over this. "I just want the cops to sort this all out and move on."

She still looked hurt. We'd always stood together against Gerald. I was pretty sure she thought I had chosen a side, and it wasn't hers.

"He always gets special treatment," she practically hissed. "Everyone just tiptoes around him and tolerates his behavior. I'm sick of it. He needs to pay for what he did. I can't believe you're letting him get away with it."

She was fuming.

A deep, tired sadness fell across my shoulders. I was caught in the middle of all this. I felt helpless, unable to console one friend without betraying another.

I regretted not calling in sick.

A sigh escaped, and my eyebrows creased. "I want to see justice, too. If it's Gerald, it's Gerald. The cops will take it from there."

It felt like a lie.

She leaned back, staring at me, dumbfounded.

"You're defending him," she practically whispered.

FML.

It was a small win that she didn't flinch when I reached over to squeeze her hand.

"Zoe, I'm with you a hundred percent. Gerald's a dick. I just don't want to crucify a guy if he didn't do it. Let's just wait for this to shake out. If he's guilty, I'll be right there with you with a match to burn him at the stake. Deal?"

That got a slight smile.

"Deal," she answered. "I'll bring the gasoline. Let the mother-fucker burn."

I forced a laugh, trying to break down the wall that had started to form between us.

After a beat, Zoe said, "You know, there's a pot going around, betting on who took it."

"Yeah, I heard," I replied, resigned. "People are losing their ever-loving minds."

I looked up quickly, hoping she hadn't taken that as an insult. I didn't want the ground I gained with the witch-burning exchange to slip away.

The comment seemed to dance right around her.

She looked pensive. "I can't believe people are placing bets on something so serious."

Relief relaxed my shoulders a tad. She might've been out to get Gerald, blinded by her hatred, but at least she wasn't part of the pool.

"It's like a bomb went off in the lab," I agreed. "I wonder if this is what people always thought of each other. And all of this crap just pulled down everyone's masks."

Zoe shook her head slowly and frowned. "Finally seeing everyone's true colors, I guess."

"Yeah, I can't wait for this to be over," I sighed.

Even though I knew it would be put to bed sooner rather than later, it couldn't happen fast enough.

"I wonder if they'll ever figure it out," Zoe mused.

A sliver of apprehension made my stomach clench. I had to be very careful with what I said next.

I settled on, "These things have a way of sorting themselves out."

"I guess. But with what happened between everyone in the lab, it's going to take a while to fix."

I felt a wave of disappointment.

She was right. Things had gotten mighty ugly. The situation with the tiger had taken a huge bite out of the tight-knit lab, and some relationships might never be the same again.

I hoped the steadfast personalities in the lab, like Sandy and Carol, could hold us all together. And once this was all over, maybe they could help mend some of the bridges.

Even if the lab healed, I knew the tiger had left a scar. And it would always be there, etched in everyone's memory.

***

Zoe's visit was enough to kick me off my ass and nudge me back to work. I was knee-deep in glass when three sharp raps on my door pulled me out of my histology zen.

"Come in," I called without thinking.

Gerald swept in and closed the door behind him.

My heart sank. He was the last person I was expecting.

He rarely came into my office, preferring premeditated ambushes in the hallway. Now, he was in my territory, and he looked uncomfortable.

I leaned back in my chair, gripping the armrests.

"Yes?" I said coolly, purposefully not offering him a seat.

He crossed his arms and frowned down at me. "Because of your negligence, everyone in the lab hates me."

Oh, bless your heart, sweety. They don't hate you because of me. They hate you because of you.

Aunty would be so proud that I didn't say that bit of nastiness out loud. Instead, I waited for him to press forward after his socially awkward, declarative statement.

He pointed his finger firmly at me and raised his voice. "It's because of you! Y'all are conspiring against me. For all I know, you and Zoe put Dustin up to it! Zoe has it out for me! Trying to frame me!"

He placed his hands firmly on his hips, face getting dark red.

The modicum of pity I was feeling was suddenly laced with trepidation.

"Did you know they're even running a racket here?" he continued, now almost shouting. "Taking bets? In this lab! As if we didn't have enough illegal activity in this hovel. And I'm on the list! With the lowest odds! Everyone here is crazy!"

Gerald was angry. *Really* angry. And it was genuine fear driving that anger—the scariest kind. It was a kind of anger that made people do stupid shit.

"And it's all because of you!" he fumed.

A fresh rush of adrenaline raced through my body.

I *could've* been the better person here. I really could've. But I wasn't sure I wanted to. Wouldn't it feel nice to let this shitass squirm a bit? Feel a tad vulnerable? Like he made all of us feel *every day*?

I heard Aunty's voice in my head: *If you do that, you're just as bad as him.*

Plus, though I hated to admit it, he was kind of scaring me. I needed him to calm the fuck down and stop waving his fist over me.

Trying to defuse the situation, I said, "Have a seat, Gerald."

I'd somehow managed to keep my voice steady despite him towering over me and screaming like a banshee.

His eyebrows shot up.

"Yeah, sit down," I commanded.

And to my utter shock, he did just that.

He sat stiffly in the chair, back straight, legs uncrossed, and hands clutching the armrests. He was still piping-hot-mad, but his face was no longer flushed.

Placing my elbows on the desk, I clasped my hands in front of me. No fidgeting allowed.

Trying to keep a matter-of-fact tone, I said, "Look, dude. You're mean to people. Most people don't like anyone who's mean to them. That's completely separate from this stuff with the tiger."

I paused to assess his response. He was deathly still, face unreadable. *Fuck it.*

With a mental shrug, I pressed on, "You know what? I've actually been defending you."

That got a response. His eyebrows raised, and he opened his mouth to say something.

"Yeah," I plowed on. "I've been defending *you.*"

Because even though you're a fucking sociopath, it doesn't mean you're a thief, I thought, but thankfully didn't blurt.

"People talk," I continued. "And I'm not cool with blaming someone until they're proven guilty. So, yeah, I've been defending you. I'm probably the only one, too."

His shoulders sagged.

"Stop being such a dick about everything, and maybe people will stop placing bets against you."

He pursed his lips and looked like he was going to say something again.

Before he could, I put my hand up. "Nope, I'm done. This conversation is over."

I stood and held my arm out to the door.

He slowly rose, face cloudy. To my utter surprise, he left without a word, closing the door behind him.

He didn't even slam it.

Heart racing after the brief encounter, I slumped back into my chair.

I felt a hint of pride, and a smile spread across my face.

Despite him being all up in my face, verbally abusing me, I'd kept my cool. I'd even managed to somehow take control of the situation.

He'd come in here with a plan to take out his anger, fear, and frustration on me. Instead, he'd left with his tail between his legs.

I couldn't help but feel like I'd just delivered a blow and had finally cracked his thick veneer. Who knew what would happen after he'd had a chance to process what just went down?

***

With all of the chaos bubbling in the lab, I decided to hide in my office for lunch.

Despite trying to avoid the gossip and the conflict, I'd already been sucked in twice. I figured that I'd met my quota for the day, so I was going to finish this last case and cut out early to meet Tessa.

Before I dipped, I needed to make sure Dustin was okay. I knew it would be risky. I had information I couldn't share that would provide relief to one of my closest buddies. But I couldn't avoid him today—that would hurt him more.

His door was uncharacteristically closed. I suspected he was hiding like I was but for a very different reason.

I knocked lightly and called out, "It's Josie. Can I come in?"

"Come on in, Doc."

I closed the door behind me and took a seat. "How you doin'?"

He shrugged. "As good as can be expected."

Bags hung below his eyes, and his forehead was plowed with deep furrows. He looked deathly pale. I'd never seen him this depressed, and my heart ached for him.

One or two more days, bud. Tessa's going in today, and this will all be cleared up soon enough.

But would it? Or would this memory hang over him permanently? A memory of a time when some people thought he was capable of theft echoing into the future. Would it settle on his soul like a scar?

I tossed him a supportive smile. "It'll all work out. We all know you didn't do anything. Ted's got your back."

"Yeah," he sighed. "Ted says I don't need to worry. But isn't that what lawyers are supposed to say?"

"Not necessarily. Aunty trusts Ted, and I trust Aunty. I'm pretty sure he wouldn't lie to you just to make you feel better. He gets paid either way."

And I know for certain you didn't do it. I know this will all be okay.

I wished I could tell him, but I couldn't. It was killing me.

He nodded slowly. "Yeah. More'n likely. It's the waitin' that's rough."

"Yeah," I agreed. Even with knowing what I knew, the waiting was agony. Never had a secret burned so hot.

"I'll make you a bet," I offered.

He smirked, but his eyes were still tight with stress.

"I bet this stuff is all sorted by the end of the week. If I win, you have to come to my place for a barbeque and tabletop games. If you win, I have to go fishing with you."

He started laughing, and I knew I'd gotten through.

He'd been trying to get me to go fishing for ages. I knew how to do it. But I truly hated it. Not like bored-and-I'd-rather-be-doing-something-else disliked it. More like, please-break-all-the-fingers-in-my-hand-so-I-don't-have-to-fish loathed it. He knew how I felt about it and what I was putting on the proverbial line.

I also knew he couldn't stand to spend his off-time bound to a chair, moving pieces around on a game board. It was an equal exchange. When all was said and done, I wouldn't make him play a tabletop game, but I was sure as hell gonna make him come over and break bread.

"Deal," he said, grinning, and we shook on it.

"Keep your chin up, man," I said.

He gave me a salute.

With a fist bump, I left him to his thoughts and hoped I'd eased his mind just a tad.

CHAPTER
TWENTY

That afternoon, I pulled into the west parking lot of the police station with trepidation.

I got out of the car, practically jumping at the *thunk* of the locks when I pressed the key fob. Nervous, I ran my fingers through my hair. The heat pressed in, and I was starting to sweat.

I'd never partaken in the lovely government decor *inside*, but I was familiar with the hulking exterior. It was a few blocks from my house, and I'd passed it often enough.

The police station crouched across the street like, well, a tiger. The front was a wall of black glass broken by two stucco panels that hugged the lower floors on each side like eyes. The entryway was a giant mouth in the middle.

If a building could eat someone, it would be this place. I briefly wondered what the architect was thinking when they designed it. They must've been inspired by the Amityville house.

I shook my head, trying to clear the tornado of thoughts, and adjusted my purse over my shoulder. In a small act of defiance, I decided to jaywalk across the street.

As I stepped off the curb, my ankle folded, and I crashed to the ground.

"Oh, my! Are you okay?" a worried, masculine voice called.

Mortified, I blinked a couple of times, trying to figure out what the fuck just happened. An inch away from my nose, a jagged crack and a faded yellow utility tag mocked me.

"Dr. Harjo! Are you hurt?" The second voice was Tessa's.

Laughing nervously, I said, "Yeah, I'm fine. I can't believe I just face-planted."

Tessa responded with a stilted laugh. Out of the corner of my eye, I saw her rush over to help me.

Determined to get up on my own, I pushed myself off the broiling asphalt and backstepped onto the sidewalk. My skin tingled with adrenaline, and my hands shook.

What the hell, Josie.... Really?

I wasn't the most athletic creature, but *still*. It wasn't like me to be such a klutz. I needed to get my head in the game. This was serious shit, and I couldn't let a malicious curb throw me off. There were much bigger fish to fry today.

As Tessa and the man joined me, I said, "And this is why I don't play sports," and added another shaky laugh.

A quick check reassured me that my clothes hadn't torn and there wasn't any blood. My hands still stung, and I had scuff marks on my jeans. I curled my fingers in and flashed a smile.

Tessa brushed her fingers on my elbow, concerned. "Are you sure you're alright?"

I felt a mixture of emotions. Part of me felt horribly embarrassed that I'd fallen on my ass like a toddler—and while trying to jaywalk to a police station, nonetheless. Another part of me felt guilty because Tessa didn't need my *Three Stooges* act today.

After a glance at her face, I realized my eating the dirt had provided a much-needed distraction.

The universe works in mysterious ways.

I put on a brave face and finally got my bearings enough to realize that the man standing next to Tessa could only be Ted.

He looked genuinely concerned. "Are you sure you're not hurt?"

"No. I'm fine," I answered, trying to brush away their fussing. "Just practicing my gymnastics routine.... Ummm...nice to meet you?" I flashed an embarrassed smile and reached out my dirty hand for a shake.

"Pleasure is mine," he replied, taking my hand lightly.

Ted stood a tad over six feet tall and was broad-shouldered. Despite the heat, he wore a nice button-up shirt, bolo tie, and fancy jacket. His long, black hair was streaked with gray and pulled into two tidy braids. He sported the fanciest set of cowboy boots I'd ever seen.

He looked pretty badass, and I was glad he was on our side. I figured he could protect us from the evil curb, the creepy building, and whatever awaited Tessa on the other side of that gaping maw.

"Thanks for helping us out," I said, finally getting enough blood to my scattered brain to form a coherent thought.

He gave me a friendly smile, the dark skin around his eyes crinkling. "Happy to." He turned to Tessa. "Shall we go in?"

The question chased away all thoughts of my fall and draped the wet blanket of reality back over Tessa's shoulders.

Tessa nodded, eyes cast down.

She was trying to put on a brave face, but I knew her well enough to see that she was freaking out beneath that mask.

At least she looked the part of a good person who'd made a single, regretful mistake. Someone who wanted to make amends.

She had completely transformed since we parted ways this morning. Her hair was freshly washed and held back with a headband that made her look five years younger. She was in a conservative dress, open-front cardigan, and flats. A light layer of makeup covered her bags. She looked ready for church.

It was *perfect*.

We crossed the street together, this time without any injury. The building still had a foreboding feeling, but I was certain we could tackle it together.

Plus, I needed to be strong for Tessa.

Ted held the glass door, ushering us in.

A rush of cold air hit me, and my arms broke out in goosebumps. I couldn't believe entering the belly of a beast could feel so *frigid*.

Inside, the reception area had generic government-building vibes. Fluorescent lights hummed, draining the life from the room. The walls were off-white with random scuff marks. Black plastic chairs sat in rows, facing a fortified receptionist desk.

Ted's boots clicked on the speckled tile.

"Have a seat. I'll go check us in," Ted said.

Tessa and I obliged.

The place was empty except for us, and we had our pick of seats. Not that it mattered. The chairs were like mini torture chambers, and the plastic bit at my ass.

I shifted uncomfortably after the first nip.

Ted's boots echoed in the stark room as he made his way to the front desk.

Somehow, the architect had managed to design the world's most condescending and threatening receptionist's area. A thick block of dark wood formed three stations. The whole thing was raised so that the receptionist was perched to look down on anyone who needed help. All of this was tucked behind a barricade of bullet-proof glass. Even Ted looked small as he made his way forward.

I leaned over to Tessa and whispered, "How're you doing?"

As soon as I said it, I wished I hadn't. It was a dumb question and would likely only make her more anxious.

She shrugged and then let out a deep sigh. "I just want to get this over with."

I reached over and squeezed her hand, ignoring the bite of my scraped palm. I didn't know what else to do.

She squeezed my hand back.

After what felt like forever, Ted made his way over to us and sat down, resting his laptop bag in the chair next to him.

Leaning forward to face Tessa, he said quietly, "We're all set. It should only be about five or ten minutes, and they'll bring us back. Remember, let me do the talking. When they ask you questions, provide yes or no answers, if possible. Don't provide more information than what they ask for."

He made eye contact with me. "Sorry, but you'll have to wait out here, Josie."

Tessa's eyes widened slightly with burgeoning panic.

"That's okay." I squeezed Tessa's hand again. "I'll be right here rooting for y'all." After a beat, I added, "Maybe we can grab an early dinner at Louie's after. My treat. Give us something to look forward to once this is all over."

I was grasping at straws, trying to give her something to think about beyond the next hour or two. I wanted her to see her life beyond this difficult point.

The offer fell flat.

She noticed my effort and smiled, but it didn't reach her eyes.

I chewed my cheek, worrying over how best to support her through this.

We sat in silence, the clock on the wall annoyingly ticking away each minute with a *ka-thunk*.

Ted seemed relaxed and confident. His body posture should've given us hope—maybe calmed us down a little. But all I felt was a low hum of tension that was slowly building. Tessa's tight shoulders and odd stillness signaled that she was feeling that strain, too, but a million-fold worse.

I uncrossed and recrossed my legs. The chair nipped my ass again in warning.

After what felt like ages, a woman in a police uniform walked over to us. Her hair was scraped back into a tight, blonde bun. She was tiny but looked tough as nails, one hand looped on her utility belt near her Taser and the other hanging not-so-casually by her firearm.

I was a tad afraid she'd tase me.

"Mr. Colbert and Ms. Eaton?"

Ted stood and reached out a hand to shake. "Yes, ma'am."

"We're ready for you."

Tessa rose and followed them as they headed to a small door adjacent to the receptionist's desk.

Ted made small talk and commented politely on the weather. Just out of earshot, he must have cracked a joke because the officer barked a laugh that was cut short as they were buzzed through to the back.

Go get 'em, Ted.

Except for the receptionist perched in her eyrie, I was all alone. I felt like I was waiting to get disciplined by the principal.

I started to sweat despite the chilled air. I wasn't sure if it was nerves or these god-awful plastic chairs creating a hot box with my ass.

Shifting in my seat, I leaned on my hip, hoping to improve the air circulation. The last thing I wanted was to get so sweaty it looked like I'd pissed myself. With the scuff marks from the fall, a wet spot would really tie the hobo look together.

My hands were barking at me, too. I unfolded them to take stock.

Dark red scrapes marred both palms. I picked the flecks of asphalt out, trying to distract myself.

It was killing me, sitting alone, wondering what was happening behind that closed door. I was worried about Tessa and wanted to make everything okay. But I was helpless out here.

I leaned back in the chair, and my sewing machine leg started up. I kicked myself for not bringing a book. There wasn't even a vending machine or anything I could fidget with.

I pulled my phone out and started surfing. Anything to keep my mind occupied. I could only survive the soul-sucking black hole of social media for so long, but it was my only option.

The minutes slowly clicked by, the clock reminding me of every single one with the same annoying *ka-thunk*. A few people came and went, but I was the only person who stayed camped in the waiting room. Every once in a while, I could feel the person at the front desk watching me.

My phone flashed a warning that my battery was at five percent. *Seriously?*

I sighed low and loud. Out of the corner of my eye, the receptionist looked up and frowned. I couldn't help but flinch like I'd disappointed the teacher.

After locking my almost-dead phone, I tucked it into my purse.

I counted the ceiling tiles.

I tried to find shapes in the scuff marks on the walls.

What was that cranberry-colored smear halfway up the wall anyway? Was that dried blood? Ewww....

I looked at my scratched hands again, pulling out the bits of asphalt I'd missed the first time around.

And, in my last bored act of desperation, I bit my nails, fussed with the ragged edges, and then finally dug out a file to smooth them so I wouldn't gnaw them bloody.

After what felt like forever, the door to the back finally opened.

Tessa and Ted walked through first, the officer trailing behind. Ted shook the officer's hand. Their expressions were unreadable.

My heart lurched, and I chewed the inside of my cheek. The tissue inside was ragged and raw from all of the worry this last week. I needed to get my shit together, or I'd chew straight through the damn thing.

It took everything in me not to rush over.

They parted easily with the officer, who returned to the back, and made their way over to me. When they reached our bank of chairs, I stood and folded Tessa in a hug.

"All done?" I asked.

She nodded, eyes puffy and red. She looked like she'd been run over by a truck, but at the same time, she also looked lighter. Like a weight had been lifted. Like the *yōkai* that had been weighing her down had finally gotten off her back.

I felt a surge of relief.

"Shall we round up outside?" Ted asked.

Tessa nodded.

We followed him out, my arm draped over her shoulder in a half hug.

As we stepped out of the building, I couldn't help but feel like we'd been regurgitated, partially digested by a Sarlacc and covered in monster goo.

We'd made it.

Ted stopped at the sidewalk under the shade of a tree, just steps away from the evil curb that had tried to fuck everything up earlier. I wanted to stick my tongue out at it. Instead, I half-hugged Tessa closer.

Ted shared a reassuring smile. "We're in a really good spot." He turned to Tessa. "Would you like me to fill Josie in?"

She nodded slightly.

Ted shifted his laptop bag to his other hand. "The officer is writing up the contract now. Tessa will provide the trafficker's information and turn the cash over to the police in exchange for immunity from any felony charges. She'll still have to plead guilty to a misdemeanor charge, but they've assured me it'll come with a small fine and community service. Nothing serious. Once the contract is ready, the DA will need to sign it—I'm certain she will; I know her. Then, I'll come back with Tessa in a day or two to sign it."

"Wow," I said reverently. "That's great news, Ted. More than I expected."

I gave Tessa a side-squeeze.

There was one more question bouncing around my head, and I fretted over the best way to ask it. I decided to dive right in.

"She'll still be able to practice medicine, right?" I asked nervously.

Tessa tensed slightly.

This was the meat of the matter, and we both knew it.

"It's my understanding that the veterinary license application only asks about felonies. If that doesn't change, she should be able to get her license. I can't speak to how individual employers may handle it. But I think she'll be fine. If you encounter any issues, you have my number. I'll do what I can."

He rested a reassuring hand on Tessa's shoulder. "I imagine you're feeling a little rung out. You did the right thing here, today."

She took a deep breath. Without looking up, she said, "Thanks for your help, Mr. Colbert."

"Yes. Thank you, Ted." I released Tessa to shake his hand, clasping his with both of mine. I didn't even feel the sting from the scrapes. "I appreciate everything you've done."

"Happy to help," he answered.

"Can I treat you to an early dinner?" I asked him.

"Thank you, but no. I gotta get back to Ada." Making eye contact with Tessa, he added, "Call my office tomorrow morning, and we'll have an update for you."

"Yes, sir. Thank you."

He tipped his head at us as he said his goodbyes.

Now just the two of us, I turned to Tessa.

"How about you? Want to get dinner?"

"Nah, I'm good," she said, eyes still cast down.

As much as I wanted to move on, I could tell she wasn't ready just yet to put all this behind her. Maybe that was a good thing. I probably would've been more worried if she happily brushed this to the side and joined me for a celebratory meal.

"I just need some time alone. Sorry," she continued.

"It's all good," I answered.

She looked up at me. "Thank you, Josie. Truly. I mean it. I couldn't have done this alone."

Her eyes started welling with tears again.

I folded her into a hug. "Anytime, hon."

"Sorry I don't want to hang out right now. I just want to get to my dorm and sleep."

"I totally get it," I said with absolute sincerity.

I'd never been in her position before. But I still understood the desire for alone time and reflection after a particularly rough spell. She'd been carrying a heavy load. And it wasn't over yet. Once she got through this legal mess, she still had to sort out a proper living situation and navigate years of debt. It was going to be a tough ride.

Despite all that, there was now something about the way that she held her shoulders; I could tell she'd be okay tonight.

"My office is always open. And you have my number. Please don't be a stranger."

A smile twitched across her lips.

"You won't be able to get rid of me that easy. Yersi likes me. And we've sung Lil Nas X together."

My heart swelled. It felt so good to hear her joke around.

On a whim, I offered, "Want to come to Aunty's with me again this weekend?"

She paused just a tad too long.

I realized I might be suffocating her.

I held my hands up in surrender. "No pressure. Just offering. If you're interested, just pop by my place Sunday morning before nine-ish. It can literally be last minute. Whatever feels right. Whatever you need."

Her smile grew a bit more, and she nodded lightly. "Sounds good."

"Need a ride back to campus?"

"Nah," she said, shaking her head. "I'll walk."

After one last hug, we parted ways. Her face was thoughtful and tired as she turned north on South Lewis Street toward campus.

After she left, I still had one more thing to do before I could get into the broiling car.

Standing on the sidewalk, I dug my phone out of my purse to text Aunty.

> Its done. Ted was amazing. Everything is going to be okay. Thanks Aunty.

She responded immediately.

> Wonderful! How's Tessa?

> Better? I think she's still processing.

> It'll take time. How are you?

> Relieved. Glad this is over.

> ...

> ...

> Hope you don't mind. I invited Tessa to brunch again.

She hearted my text.

It would be wonderful to have her join us.

Im not sure she will. I offered but she said she needs some space right now.

She'll come. I know she will. We'll do a smudging ceremony.

All will be well. You'll see.

I hearted her text.

Only time would tell if Tessa would join us this coming Sunday. I hoped she would. I'd grown rather fond of her over this last week, and I didn't want to lose our budding friendship.

Aunty says she'll come. Aunty's never wrong.

I smiled to myself.

Feeling empowered, I tossed a victory glance at the malicious curb and dared it to mess with me now.

CHAPTER

TWENTY-ONE

With the dreaded trip to the cop shop behind me, I was feeling oodles better Tuesday morning.

Tessa was settled in her new place, and I finally had my home all to myself again. I'd slept like a log last night. Feeling refreshed and waking up before my alarm, I'd bounced through the morning like Snow White, humming to myself as I fed Yersi and made a tasty omelet.

I felt like I'd spent the last week hiking up a huge mountain. Yesterday, I'd finally reached the peak, and it was just downhill from there.

Everything had landed just right. There'd be justice for Tora but in a way that wouldn't crush Tessa. It was the best thing that could've happened in a lousy situation.

It wasn't until I pulled into the lab's parking lot that I realized with a sinking feeling that I wasn't out of the woods yet. There were a couple more miles on that downhill slope, and the trail was littered with potholes and jagged stones.

The reality of the situation hit me hard, and I sat frozen in my car. Word hadn't trickled down about Tessa's confession, and I was pretty sure the hallways were going to be oozing toxic gossip.

I did *not* want to deal with that shit today.

Maybe if I sat here long enough, I could just leave at the end of the day without having ever gone inside.

Ha! Fat chance! an evil voice said.

People were going to pounce on me for intel. I just knew it. I wasn't sure how I was going to make it through the day without letting anything slip. Withholding information felt like lying, and I was a terrible liar.

I didn't have a choice; I'd just have to suck it up.

With a sigh, I grabbed my purse, lunch, and to-go tea. I pulled myself out of the car and locked it behind me. The *thunk* echoed with finality.

I figured if I could just get into my office, I could hide in there. I had enough provisions to hunker down for the day. The lunch I'd planned with Laila also gave me an excuse to get the hell out of dodge. I couldn't face everyone in the breakroom. Not today. I'd even brought chocolate chip cookies, knowing I'd be missing out on Carol's daily treats.

If I was lucky, I might be able to slink in and out of work without having to talk to anyone.

Yeeeaahhhh... Lumberg drawled in my head.

When I passed through the front doors, it was like the lab was holding its breath. There wasn't a soul in sight, but I still felt jumpy.

I fled to my office and closed the door.

Maybe no one would come knocking today. *Maybe?*

After tucking my things away and booting up my computer, I went through the motions of getting my old cases buttoned up. I opened one of the flats from the pile on my desk and placed a slide onto the microscope stage. Work would keep me occupied; I had plenty of glass to shuffle through to keep me busy.

Even if, by some miracle, I managed to make it through all of the cases on my desk, I still needed to polish up my endocrine lectures. They'd be starting in a couple of weeks, and I still wasn't happy with them yet. I'd vented enough about them that it wouldn't raise any alarms if I was busy clicking away at my computer all day.

Anything to hide from the swirling rumors.

The situation was going to sort itself out soon enough, I kept telling myself. Dustin would be free and clear within the next day or two. The lab would start feeling "normal" again. Surely....

Though the end was near, it was agony waiting to get there. My heart ached for my friend. I couldn't even imagine how he must be feeling right about now. I felt awful keeping knowledge tucked close to my chest that I knew would make him feel better.

And Gerald.... If I was honest with myself, a small part of me was even relieved that this wouldn't be pinned on him either. For all of his faults, he didn't deserve to take the fall for a crime he didn't commit. The way everyone was attacking him felt gross, and I didn't want to be a part of that. If he was going to be a target, it should be over his horrible behavior, not *this*.

The morning slugged by without a whisper from anyone. I figured my coworkers were keeping their heads down, too, waiting for the bomb blast with gritted teeth and hands over their ears.

At half past eleven, I walked over to Laila's office, glad to shrug off the intense cloud hanging over the lab, even if just for an hour.

The summer weather was starting to bow out, and it was a gorgeous day outside. A day like today—warm but not too hot with minimal humidity—was just what I needed.

The cicadas were still at it, and their loud whirring filled the air. I headed down Farm Road on foot. With each step, the fresh air and beautiful landscaping helped me relax.

I took my time making my way to Laila's, thoughts spinning.

Just another day or two. That was it. Then, I could put this tiger mess behind me. I'd done my part. I just needed to be patient—wait for everything to settle in place.

Well, *mostly* settle into place. Tessa was in it for the long haul.

Her financial situation was back at square one. She had a place to stay, but she was still broke and carried an exorbitant amount of student debt. In addition to the financial baggage, I knew she also carried a heavy burden of shame. She'd fucked up pretty bad, and she knew it.

It'd be hard for her for a while, and she'd always carry an emotional scar.

I couldn't help but feel like the invitation to Aunty's this weekend was a pivotal moment. Like a split in the road. On one path, she would join us, and it would be the start of our friendship on the other side of all this madness. It would mean that she could get past this experience and see a future for herself. The other path was shrouded in darkness. I didn't want her to go down that one.

By the time I pushed into Laila's office, thoughts of forked paths and darkness were swimming through my head.

She noticed that I was caught in an anxiety loop as soon as I walked through her door.

"Hey, Josie!" Her voice was warm and friendly, but the skin around her eyes was creased with worry.

"Howdy."

We traded a quick hug.

"You doing okay?" she asked as she shut down her computer and dug out her lunch.

"Meh."

I shrugged one shoulder and chewed my cheek.

"And that's a 'no.' Let's go grab a table and talk. Want to sit outside?" she asked.

I nodded.

We wove our way back outside and picked a table in the shade. I brushed some tree debris off the bench and sat down. I couldn't help but sigh heavily.

"Okay, so spill it," Laila asserted, back straight, unpacking her lunch in a business-like manner.

I couldn't share the details about the tiger with her—not yet, anyway. It might make a brief splash in the news in a few days. But for now, I needed to keep my mouth shut. I decided to dance around the subject.

"Remember that student I told you about who was a suicide risk and was struggling with money?"

"Yup. The one who stayed with you." She crunched on some chips, looking at me expectantly.

"Yeah. Well, she got temporary housing on campus. Which is great. But she.... I don't know.... She still has a bunch of stuff going on."

Words were tumbling out of my mouth, and she rescued me. "And you feel a duty toward her."

She pushed the chip bag over to me, and I took an appreciative handful. I crunched through a few chips before continuing. "Yeah, I guess I do feel responsible for her. And...I think the worst might be behind her. But it's still gonna be a rough go."

Laila nodded sagely, still crunching through the chips.

"I just.... It's like when you save a life, you know? You're kinda responsible for it forever? That's how I feel."

Had I saved Tessa's life?

I thought I had, in a way. Whether it was keeping the suicidal thoughts in check or helping her with her legal issues, her life was different now. And I hoped it was for the better: the sunny path.

"Her money situation isn't resolved," I continued. "She's got the rest of this school year. And then she has what may be a lifetime of debt."

Laila shook her head in sympathy and ate another chip.

"I only just paid off my loans," I continued. "And students nowadays have double or triple what I had. How's she ever gonna get hers paid off?" Dismay trickled in. "Even with the rural vet repayment program, it isn't enough. It's like the game is rigged."

"Yes," she agreed. "It's most definitely rigged. But there *are* cheats. And there are ways to nudge the dice roll one way or the other. It's just another strategy game that you gotta min-max."

She dramatically licked the salt off her fingers one by one and arched her eyebrow.

Though she had intended it as cheeky, I felt a tickle of unease.

Tessa had most definitely tried to play the game, but the dice had been weighted.

And she'd lost.

Thankfully, it hadn't been a hard, eat-the-dirt loss—that would've been a felony and maybe even some jail time. She'd lucked out this time and would probably be able to recover...if a lifetime of crippling debt could be called "lucking out."

Laila noticed the doubt and anxiety flitter across my face.

"I didn't mean to imply that y'all don't know how to play the game," she said, worried she'd hurt my feelings. "I'm just thinking, if we put our heads together, maybe there's a way we can help her. And if I want to be real sunshine-and-roses about it, we might be able to work on a better plan for students at the vet school in general."

I ate more of Laila's chips, brooding.

After a beat, she continued, "You're doing what you can for her. She's honestly lucky to have you. Some people don't have that."

I couldn't imagine going through what Tessa had all alone. At least I had Aunty for moral support.

"Yeah," I conceded. "Sadly, a lot of veterinarians are in a similar situation. Eight years of school tuition—especially vet school tuition—amounts to a crap ton of money. Plus, most people don't work during vet school. So that's at least four years without a paycheck or saving for retirement. Then, when they see the light at the end of the tunnel—they finally graduate—and they end up making peanuts."

I took a deep breath and shook my head. "It's embarrassing to have all that debt. It's just assumed students will take out loans to pay for college and then, when they do, they're shamed about their financial situation when they graduate. Even when they start getting a paycheck, half of it goes to pay off loans. Saving for retirement is a joke when someone doesn't even have enough left to buy groceries. It's hard for vets to talk about it."

Laila reached over and squeezed my hand.

"Then, they finally get the job they've been dreaming about since they were four years old," I huffed dejectedly. "And they're straining under fifteen-minute office visit requirements. Trying to meet metrics. As if it couldn't get any worse, they start to realize that clients can be downright *nasty*, whining about bills that are an itty bitty fraction of what a procedure would cost at their human medical doctor's office. Calling the vets 'greedy.' They'd never treat their own doctor like that."

All the anger and frustration at the injustice of it was spilling out. I couldn't control it.

"And they wonder why vets have such a high suicide rate..." I practically whispered, my voice trailing off.

My mind jumped to Nathan, and my eyes filled with tears.

Laila squeezed my hand again and nudged the chip bag closer.

276

I angrily brushed the tears away with a fist and then sunk my hand into the bag.

My crunching filled the silence.

As if reading my thoughts, Laila said softly, "You can't fix a broken system, Josie. But you can help the people around you. You're doing that by being there for Tessa. Even if you're just there so that she knows someone cares about her. That means a lot to people."

She was right. I knew I couldn't save the world, and I *had* helped Tessa. It felt great being able to help her. And I could keep being there for her as long as she wanted me to. It was another way to put a little bit of good out into the world.

Deep breaths. Little steps. Eyes on the prize.

Feeling slightly empowered, I opened my salad and poked at the lettuce with my fork as my thoughts raced.

"You know," I started, "I wonder if I could start a scholarship. Like to help students in her situation."

Laila clapped her hands together in excitement. "That's a fabulous idea!"

"The problem with scholarships, though, is that you have to have good grades. The students who are struggling with money issues are usually working at the same time and have to deal with that added stress. That baggage surely impacts their grades."

Her eyebrows creased together. "I'm not sure good grades *have* to be a requirement. I think, since it's your money, *you* can set the criteria however you want. You should look into it. I bet you can stipulate that the award is based on financial need alone, and grades cannot be considered or something like that."

"Hm," I answered, noodling over the idea.

"You might even be able to add something about how the money they earn from a part-time job can't be considered, either. That way, they aren't punished for trying to work hard to make ends meet."

I felt a spark of hope. "That would be pretty slick. Do you know how I go about setting something like that up?"

"No clue. Sorry. But you can probably go to the alumni center and ask. They love taking people's money."

I laughed. "Yeah, they do. Go Pokes."

The alumni center had the best marketing campaign *ever*. A sense of loyalty and pride in the school was nurtured from freshman year on. People who graduated from Oklahoma State did, in fact, bleed orange. Even as a faculty member, I felt a fierce loyalty to the school. All that pride had the added benefit of loose alumni pocketbooks.

"I'll check it out. Thanks, Laila."

She smiled to herself; helping people always made her happy.

My heart swelled with appreciation for my friend. Laila was such a wonderful person and always said just the right thing. For the millionth time, I wished she was my boss. I knew she was going to get that Chair position, and I was so frigging jealous of everyone in that department. She was going to be a rockstar in that role.

"So, how's class going for you this semester?" I asked.

And with that, the topic shifted to lighter things. We laughed as we polished off Laila's giant bag of chips and the chocolate chip cookies I'd brought.

When we finished, Laila walked me back to the lab. We took it easy, in no rush to get back to work, and simply enjoyed each other's company.

At the front door, she gave me a big hug. "You've got a big heart, sweety. Remember that."

***

After my lunch with Laila, I returned to my office feeling high on good vibes. I was ready to put this behind me and plan for the future.

Filled with warm fuzzies, I sent a quick email to the alumni center asking for more info. Then, I pulled out my phone to text Armand.

> Miss you

He responded immediately.

Miss you too.

Want to come over for dinner sometime this week?

Sounds good. Want me to bring takeout?

I can cook. It'll be nice.

I appreciated his offer, especially in the context of how crazy things had been the last week or so. But I enjoyed cooking, even if it was just for myself. I'd been so busy lately that I hadn't had much of a chance. I was eager to get back in the kitchen and return to my normal routine. And since I wasn't on duty this week, I'd have time to shop and make something tasty.

Are you sure? I know its been busy with Tessa there

She moved into her new place yesterday

I'm glad it worked out

The ellipses bounced for a few seconds.

I couldn't help but feel a thrill of anticipatory excitement. We'd be alone, and I was off the rag. I knew he was thinking the same thing.

Even though he couldn't see me, I smiled mischievously and waited for his next text.

I'm free all week. What day?

I wanted to text back, "Tonight!" Instead, I did the mental math. I wanted all the tiger business to be public knowledge. I wasn't sure I could hold the secret for much longer, especially around someone I cared about. It'd been hard as hell not to say anything to Laila today.

> How about Friday? You could sleep over if you wanted.

Or not sleep. Either way....
I grinned again, feeling my cheeks warm.
He added a thumbs up to Friday.

> Im playing football on Saturday at 10 but can still stay over

He added an emoji of a soccer ball.

> You mean soccer?

I was feeling feisty and couldn't help but tease him a little.
He responded to my text with an eye roll emoji. He added a meme with a picture of Ronaldo Nazário that said, "Real men play real football."
I laughed out loud and sent an emoji expressing that.

> Let me know if I can bring anything on Friday

My mind made a hard left to where it shouldn't go, especially at work. I bit my lip.

Just yourself

The ellipses sat bouncing a bit, and I knew where his mind had gone, too. My cheeks burned hotter.

Ever the gentleman, he politely texted a thumbs up and added:

Can't wait to see you

Friday couldn't come fast enough.

CHAPTER
TWENTY-TWO

Wednesday morning, I was walking on eggshells in the lab. Everyone still had their fake Oklahoma smiles and polite "good mornings" to hand out. But shifty eyes and scrunched shoulders told the truth about how people were feeling.

I couldn't take another day of this, and I was freaking out over the possibility that something had fallen through with Tessa's deal. I was pretty sure that the news would've been shared with Fran as soon as the ink was dry.

Knowing the best place to shop for gossip, I stopped in the front office under the pretense of checking my mailbox.

For some unknown reason, I still received paper mail. Granted, it was so infrequent that there was a layer of dust in the mailbox. And I never checked my box, so said dust also coated the envelopes resting within it.

But still.

I hoped Carol wouldn't see through my ruse.

"Good morning, y'all," I said, weaving between the desks to the mailboxes along the back wall.

"Good morning, Dr. Harjo. How're you this morning?" Carol drawled, all relaxed southerner.

Before I could answer, James jumped in, back straight and eyes excited, "Morning, Dr. Harjo. Did you hear?"

There we go.

I knew that good 'ole front office gossip would come through for me.

"Hear what?" I asked, all innocent-like.

My pulse raced as I tried to keep my face neutral.

"There's a lab meeting at ten. All hands. Fran has an announcement. I bet it's about the tiger. I bet she's gonna announce that Dr. Richter is the thief."

"Now, James," Carol chided, not unkindly.

James shrugged it off, looking smug, eyebrow arched in a *We'll just see, won't we?* look.

"Y'all know he's just the type," he said.

"Gerald may be a bit difficult..." Carol started and then trailed off, catching herself.

"There's a difference between difficult and cruel," he replied. "Dr. Richter is a nutjob. Just sayin'." Lips pressed together and eyebrows raised, he grabbed some papers and tapped them into a neat pile.

I cleared my throat, uncomfortable. I suddenly regretted my decision to collect my ancient junk mail.

Maybe I should've just stayed in my office.

"Well...um...thanks for the heads up about the meeting, James."

I grabbed the useless paper out of my mailbox and sorted through it to buy myself some time to think. The witch hunt in the lab wasn't sitting right with me, and I felt like I had to say something.

"We should probably just wait to see what the police say," I started, feeling a bit shaky. "We don't know what happened."

James harrumphed.

Feeling irritated, I couldn't help but snark. "What if someone was betting that you stole it? How'd that make you feel?"

Carol visibly flinched.

I had not intended to be so direct, but in typical Josie fashion, it came out more like a baseball bat to the face.

James shrugged again, but it was like the shrug of a kid caught with his hand in the cookie jar.

He had a good heart. He just hadn't had the life experiences yet to understand what it was like being a target. I was getting the impression that he didn't understand how much it sucked when everyone was talking about you behind your back, either.

"Sorry to be so blunt," I said, trying to smooth things over. "I just worry about what that pool is doing to people. We all used to be so tight. It's just hard seeing everyone form cliques."

"The pool is just somethin'," Carol said, shaking her head in disappointment. "Good folks behaving like monsters."

James blushed.

"At least this will all be over soon," I added hopefully. "Sounds like we'll know soon enough during the all-hands. It'll be nice having everything get back to normal."

"Yes, it will," Carol said with a hint of relief.

The bubble of tension popped with her response.

The stress in the lab just kept bubbling over, and a few more noses had been tweaked. I made a mental note to bring donuts tomorrow. A treat would be required to make everything right again with these two.

Another bridge to mend.

"Thanks for filling me in on the meeting," I said.

"See you soon, Dr. Harjo," Carol said.

They both smiled and waved.

Not wanting to dig the hole any deeper, I fled the office with a return wave.

And ran right into Gerald.

A dump of adrenaline surged through my veins, prepping me for the usual hallway attack.

Sure enough, he turned his body to block my way and puffed up his chest. Unable to help myself, I took a step back.

Stop being prey, Josie.

I stiffened my spine and looked him straight in the eyes. "Is there something you need, Gerald?"

That was when I finally noticed the worry.

Wrinkles had settled around his eyes, and he had bags. *Actual bags.* A strand of his usually immaculately slicked-back hair had even fallen over his brow. This was about as wrecked as I'd ever seen him.

"I heard you in there." His voice sounded accusatory.

"Excuse me?" I couldn't keep the irritation out of my tone.

He nodded his chin to the front office. "I heard you in there," he said, voice low.

"I'm sure the citizens of Stillwater will be relieved to know that you are watching my every move," I sniped.

His eyebrows crinkled, confused. "No."

What the fuck?

I crossed my arms. The junk mail in my right hand dug into my underarm. Having decided I'd had enough of his crap already, I tried to step around him.

He moved to block me and raised his hands. It was almost a surrender.

Almost.

"No. I mean, I heard you defend me."

Huh.

I stopped, now interested to see where this was going. I lifted an eyebrow, arms still crossed.

"Officer Watts also told me you were convinced that I didn't steal the tiger parts. He said you were the only one to staunchly defend me."

"I don't know about 'staunchly,'" I said, unable to help myself. "That's stretching it a bit."

His eyes narrowed, and he looked hurt.

Fuck.

The dude was finally trying to be a human being for once, and I'd kicked him in the dick.

I felt a surge of guilt. Then, I immediately became pissed at myself for feeling guilty. It was all very confusing.

"But yes, I defended you," I added somewhat resentfully.

I let the silence build, wondering what his next move would be.

He shifted his weight and cleared his throat. "Thank you."

I tried to keep the shock off my face.

I *had* been the only one to defend him, and I'd done so even before I'd known who the real thief was. The dude *did* owe me some serious gratitude, but I'd never expected thanks. Especially from Gerald-fuck-ing-Richter. It also wasn't a public "thank you," but it'd do.

Beggars can't be choosers.

I still felt a little sick to my stomach having defended him. He embodied just about everything I could possibly hate about a person that didn't border on a felony action.

"You're welcome," I huffed. "You can be a complete asshole and are in a permanent state of cranio-rectal intussusception. You certainly don't make it easy. But I don't believe people should be blamed for things they didn't do."

He surprised me again when he leaned back, thoughtful, as if he was considering what I'd said.

"Just try to be a little nicer, will you?" I asked.

He snorted, but it sounded vulnerable and lacked its usual *oomph*.

"Seriously, dude. You're kinda a dick. And you say inappropriate shit all of the time. Cut it out, and maybe you wouldn't *need* me to defend you."

He crossed his arms and stepped back, eyes dropping to the ground.

I couldn't help but feel like I'd kicked a puppy. It was a hard truth, and I just wasn't eloquent enough to say it any other way.

"I've got stuff to do. See you at the lab meeting." I stepped around him and went to my office, heart thudding.

I'd had an interaction with Gerald, and he hadn't insulted or offended me.

There might be hope for the world.

I was so focused on Tessa and the tiger, and the thought of choosing between them, that I'd started to lose sight of the other people affected by this mess. This situation had shaken Gerald. Maybe even in a good way.

Some people talked about silver linings. In this giant cluster-fuck, there were only silver shavings left. But seeing Gerald pause to reflect on his behavior, even just for a moment, that right there was a silver fucking shaving.

***

A bit before ten, I headed to the conference room for the all-hands meeting. Anxiety was buzzing through my veins.

The room was packed when I arrived, and once again, it was standing-room only. The air was electric with worry, and there was a faint whiff of BO. Low chatter filled the room.

I was pretty sure I knew how this was going to go down. But I wouldn't be able to relax until I knew everything was completely put to bed. The lab drama was one thing I'd be happy to see tamped down.

I slid in next to Dustin.

"Morning," I said, flashing him a smile of reassurance.

For the first time in the last week, his face was no longer etched with worry.

He must already know.

A confused swirl of emotions whisked through my mind, with relief for my friend leading the pack.

He smiled back. "Mornin', Doc."

I caught a glimpse of Gerald. He'd managed to find a seat at the table, but he was white as a sheet. His arms were crossed, and he still had that small wisp of hair that dared to fall across his forehead. He glared at the table. The people sitting next to him leaned away like there was a bubble around him.

"Ya looking at Dr. Richter?" Dustin asked quietly, nodding his chin at him.

"Yeah. He doesn't look too hot."

"Nope, he doesn't," Dustin replied, tone unreadable and his face a mask.

Before I had a chance to ask him what he meant, Fran stood.

"Everyone, please quiet down, and we'll get started. James? Is everyone here?"

"Yes, ma'am," James called out from the door.

People were still talking in hushed tones.

"Everyone, please," Fran said again, annoyed this time.

The chatter died away, and attentive eyes turned to her.

"I've received word from the police department regarding the missing tiger pelt and claws. They've identified the culprit."

She paused for a dramatic effect that came off cheesy. The audience waited expectantly. Some looked around the room, checking to see whether the person they'd put their money on was present. There were a few disappointed looks as people noted Gerald.

His eyebrows furrowed in hurt.

"I can't share the details. But please rest assured that an employee of the lab was *not* involved."

Conversations around the room picked up.

"Who stole the stuff, then?" Lenny called out.

"I'm unable to share that information," Fran answered.

Disappointment spread like wildfire. There were a few rolling eyes and shaking heads. I wondered what would happen with all of the betting money. Would they still lose if the thief wasn't announced?

No one should get it. They should use that money to make the conference room habitable, I thought bitterly.

"I also wanted to share that the tiger parts have been recovered and are en route to Tiawah Animal Sanctuary."

I felt a bolt of surprise.

They'd found the parts and recovered them. That was fantastic! It also meant that they'd probably captured the trafficker, whom Fran had either failed to mention or whom she was unaware of.

"We'll be putting measures in place to prevent this from happening in the future. More to follow on that."

From there, she moved to questions. And in the irritating way that always happened in meetings, people asked questions about information Fran had already shared. They also tried to press her on the identity of the thief. To her credit, she held her ground.

When the meeting ended, the whispered conversations continued. But there was a palpable difference. The tension that was there just twenty minutes before had been released. It was like a balloon had been deflated with a dying wheeze.

Splitting off from the crowd, Dustin and I walked back to our offices together.

"Thanks for being there for me, Doc. It's been a long week."

"Yes, it has. Thankfully, this is probably a once-in-a-lifetime experience."

He nodded sagely and stopped.

I turned to him, curious. "Dustin?"

I was sure Dustin didn't know all of the nitty-gritty details. But he'd been around the block enough times to be able to read people. I couldn't help thinking he knew more than he was letting on.

He looked at me and said quietly so only I could hear, "I know you were somehow involved in resolving all of this." He gave a small appreciative nod. "You did a good thing. Thanks."

I couldn't help but feel a surge of surprise followed by a sliver of pride. I *had* done a good thing. When faced with an impossible choice–two doors leading to equally unpleasant endings—I said, "fuck it," and chose the window.

And it had *worked*.

It'd been a tough run, but I felt like every piece shook out where it should have. Having everything sorted with the tiger didn't wipe all of the drama away, but it shoved all of the petty bullshit back into the tidy box it'd been hiding in. At least people wouldn't be placing nasty bets against each other.

Dustin and I hugged.

He cleared his throat and patted me on the back. "Gotta get back to it. There's a parvo puppy waitin' for me and Dr. Smith."

"See ya, Dustin."

He turned the corner of the hallway, shoulders lighter. I smiled to myself, happy that such a cool guy could make it out in one piece.

***

On Friday, things had almost returned to normal at the lab, and I was feeling back to my old self.

As the cherry on top, Armand was coming over for dinner tonight.

The last week and a half had been tense, and I'd been seriously distracted. But I'd still managed to hit the grocery store last night and got the crockpot going before I left for work. I could finally return to my usual routine, and it felt pretty awesome.

By the time I got home, the wonderful smell of spicy lamb stew filled the house. Yersi greeted me at the door with excited *meows*, and I had to stumble a bit to avoid squashing him or tipping anything over.

Knowing he'd be underfoot until I bent to his demands, I fed him first and then got to work on the garlic bread. About ten minutes later, the smell of toasting bread had my stomach growling. Everything had been timed perfectly; Armand would arrive any minute now.

I was practically drooling...and for more than one reason.

I decided to stay in my work clothes, figuring I wouldn't be wearing them for much longer anyway. I still went to the bathroom to fuss with my hair. I combed it out and let the slightly wavy curls dance over my shoulders. I added matching beaded earrings and a bracelet.

It felt good to be thinking about simple things again. The rhythm of getting ready calmed me.

The doorbell rang, and my stomach fluttered with glee.

Yersi must have been feeling the vibe. With an excited *merf*, he scampered to the door, beating me there.

I opened the door, and my heart tugged.

"Hey, you," I said, slightly breathless. The smell of his aftershave was damn near intoxicating.

Armand's chin was tilted down, and he looked up with a mischievous grin. He stepped over the threshold, folding me into his arms.

"Hey, love."

Yep, everything is going to be just fine.

CHAPTER
TWENTY-THREE

Yersi's not-so-gentle back-surfing woke me up Sunday morning. When I rolled over, he skittered away to the bedroom doorway and shouted a *meow* at me. I reached for the spray bottle. As per usual, he knew the exact distance from which he could demand breakfast and still evade being spritzed.

I stretched beneath the covers, feeling pretty damn amazing. The crap with the tiger was finally over, I'd had a lovely time with Armand on Friday, and I was going to see Aunty today. I wasn't sure if Tessa was going to join me, but I had a good feeling she would.

After feeding the Great Slayer of Canned Food, I cradled a steaming cup of black tea. Yersi jumped into the counter chair next to me and started cleaning his face.

"That tasty, bud?" I asked.

Merf, he deigned to answer.

I laughed softly and gave him a scratch under the chin. It was nice spending time together, just the two of us.

After scarfing down some toast with jam to get me by until brunch, I piddled around the garden. The smell of jasmine and the sounds of birds chirping filled the yard. It was going to be another gorgeous day. I smiled to myself.

Despite the chill morning, something was still niggling at me. Every little sound had me looking toward the front of the house, hoping to see the beater sedan parked out front. I realized I *needed* Tessa to come today.

When the clock hit nine, and Tessa still hadn't shown, a feeling of disappointment settled over me.

Maybe she was busy getting comfortable in her new place. Or maybe she needed to study for the NAVLE.

Or maybe you now symbolize her shame, and she'll avoid you like the plague.

An assertive *merf* shook me from my downward spiral. Yersi sat, looking at me impatiently, tail swishing with irritation.

His look said, "Get out of your head."

I dawdled just a bit, making sure I had everything.

As I was patting my pockets and checking my purse, Yersi let out an excited *meow* and ran to the front door. Less than a millisecond later, there was a light knocking.

I felt anticipatory excitement race through my body. Pulling the door back, I was thrilled to see Tessa standing there.

"Sorry I'm a bit late," she said, face flushed. "My alarm didn't go off."

As I stepped back, Tessa moved inside.

Yersi was all over her, making loud purring sounds and pushing against her legs. He even tried to jump in her half-lap when she crouched down to pet him.

I did my best not to let my jaw drop with shock.

"Yersi! What's up, buddy?" she said, laughing lightly.

He was going bonkers but in a good way. The Raven had officially left the building.

I took a critical look at her. She had true color in her cheeks, and her bags were almost non-existent. Her face was relaxed, and her smile genuine. More importantly, there was a visible difference in her posture. The load she'd been carrying looked significantly lighter now.

Yersi gave another purr-meow that sounded a lot like approval.

Even he could sense that she was back on the right path.

I felt a zing of pure joy and pride.

Deep breaths. Little steps. Eyes on the prize.

"I'm so glad you came, Tessa."

She stood and gave me a big hug—the deep, enveloping kind that speaks volumes. I hugged her back.

Yersi pushed between us with a *merf*.

"Okay, Yersi. That's enough," I chided playfully. "We've gotta head out."

As if he understood every word, he head-butted Tessa's leg one more time and then jumped on the entryway table next to the stack of books to return to Aunty.

"I'll grab those," Tessa said, bundling them into her arms. "Ready?"

"Absolutely." I grinned. "Cardi B today?"

"Hell yeah."

***

About halfway through the drive, I turned the music down.

"Hey, soooo...after brunch, Aunty has something planned for us."

I risked a glance to gauge her response.

She was watching me with a relaxed smile and waved her hand in a keep-going motion.

I wavered.

I'd thought about talking to Tessa multiple times about what Aunty had planned. But I didn't know how to approach it. I wasn't sure if she'd ever been to a smudging ceremony before. Or whether she'd think it was hokey. Or if she'd just downright refuse.

"Ummm...." I hesitated further. "Aunty would like to perform a smudging ceremony."

I caught her confused look out of the corner of my eye.

"I don't know what that is," she said shyly. "Is that like when people sage houses?"

"Um, sort of."

Not really.

How could I explain this without sounding patronizing?

"It's a cleansing ritual. It can be used on people to clear negative energy, purify them, and bless them. It's about transformation. Smudging can also be performed on spaces. But it's much more complicated than just buying a random sage bundle off the internet, lighting it, and waving it around the house."

I risked another glance at her. She looked thoughtful but was still fidgeting with the edge of her shirt.

At least I hadn't scared her away yet.

"It's peaceful," I said, hoping to reassure her. "And I always come away feeling better. Even if you don't believe in negative energy or spirits or whatever...there's something special about having someone who cares about you working to help you be in a better place."

Tessa smiled sadly and looked down at her hands.

I paused for a beat before pressing on. "Aunty was the one who brought it up. Y'all clicked last time. She likes you and worries about you. Now that the worst part is over, she wants to make sure you are set on your true path."

"Like a clean slate?" she asked, a thread of hope in her voice.

"Kinda."

"Hmm," she said, nodding slightly, like she was warming to the idea.

"Plus, it's *Aunty*," I added.

She laughed softly. "Well, in that case. I guess I have to, right?" She looked up at me and flashed a smile.

"Most definitely," I answered, feeling my heart swell.

I felt like I had learned quite a bit about Tessa in the last week or so. But there was still a lot that she kept locked away. I was hoping that, over time, I could get to know her better. She was already starting to feel a bit like family. The smudging ceremony would just be one step closer.

"I'm glad you're coming to brunch today. We might even have to make it a standing thing if your rotations don't keep you over the weekend."

It was a bold step, one I was a little shocked that I had taken. But I couldn't help feeling like Tessa was family now—like she belonged with us *every* Sunday.

I risked another glance at her.

She looked at me with one of the warmest smiles I'd ever seen. "That would be amazing."

***

Pulling into Aunty's driveway was like a big hug, and Chula coming out to greet us, tail wagging, was the kiss on the cheek.

It was so good to be here. In *this* moment.

The stress from the Tora case and my worry about Tessa seeped away. A faint breeze brought the scent of lavender, and my shoulders relaxed further.

"There's my girl," Tessa said. She hopped out of the car, dropped to her knees, and snuggled on Chula, who returned the affection with dozens of licks to her face.

I grabbed the books to return and wound my way up the path to the house.

As I opened the door, I called out, "We're here!"

Aunty bustled out of the kitchen to fold both of us into hugs. "Look at both of you! You look hungry, come on back."

We made our way to the kitchen.

"Can I help?" Tessa offered.

"Sure! Here." Aunty handed her a bowl of late-season strawberries. "Cut the tops off for me, would you, please?"

Tessa got to work as Aunty finished up the eggs. Hashbrowns sat in a skillet on the stove, already done. There was a plate of bacon out on the table. I cheated and grabbed a slice to snack on.

"How are things?" I asked.

"Oh, wonderful," Aunty replied. "We just got the book order in. There are lots of good ones. I checked out several. They're by the door for you. I also picked some out for you, Tessa. I know senior year is really busy. But you need to take time for yourself, too."

"Thank you, Aunty," Tessa said.

I smiled inwardly.

Aunty had checked out books for Tessa! She'd never done that for any of my other friends before. Between that and inviting her back to brunch, it was obvious Aunty had a soft spot for her.

And Tessa had taken to calling her "Aunty."

I felt like a friendship was blooming right before me, and I couldn't stop from feeling the warm fuzzies.

Several hours later, with our stomachs full, we sat on Aunty's porch, watching the chickens in the yard. Chula was snoozing at Tessa's feet. Every once in a while, the chickens would scuffle, and Chula would perk her ears and squint her eyes open to check on them.

The smell of lavender mixed with jasmine washed over us. The afternoon was pleasantly warm. The insects buzzed hypnotically, reminding us that we shared this earth with billions of fabulous critters.

Aunty was slowly rocking in her chair, the rhythmic creaking practically lulling me to sleep.

I was perfectly content and could have sat there until the sun set. But we had one more thing to do.

"Shall we, then?" Aunty said, her tone an odd mixture of seriousness and reassurance. "We need to clear you of bad spirits and bring the positive energy in."

Tessa sat silently, looking nervous.

The creaking of Aunty's chair came to an abrupt stop. "I'll get my things. We'll do it out back. I'll meet you out there."

Aunty shuffled into the house.

I stood and waved Tessa along. "It's all good. Don't worry."

She gave me a slight smile. "I've never done this before. I just don't want to do anything to offend Aunty."

"You're good. She'll guide us."

Chula gave her hand a reassuring lick and then trotted around to the back of the house, toenails clicking on the wood of the wrap-around porch.

We followed close behind.

In the back, the porch expanded to a large deck that overlooked the garden. Pots of medicinal plants were stacked along the edges. The chickens didn't dare come up there, and the deck was squeaky clean.

In the center of the deck, there was a small circle of chairs with a round table in the middle. This was where Aunty usually smudged, and I took a seat, directing Tessa to sit next to me.

Chula joined us, taking up a spot at Tessa's feet.

"I've never done this before," Tessa repeated nervously.

She reached down to scratch Chula behind her ears. Chula's tail thumped on the deck.

"I'll go first so you can watch," I tried to reassure her.

Aunty came out through the back door, carrying a bundle. She laid all of the medicines out on a delicately woven cloth next to a large abalone shell. With careful intention, she laid several white sage leaves into the bowl. She then added small pieces of sweet grass, tobacco, and cedar. Using a match, she lit a piece of sage and dropped the smoking leaves into the bowl. She waved the match out and rested it to the side.

Leaning over the bowl, she inhaled the smoke deeply, preparing herself. She cupped her hands and directed the smoke to her eyes, ears, and heart. Cupped smoke was also passed across her arms, along her braid, and down her body to her feet.

Having smudged herself, she carefully picked up an eagle's flight feather and passed it through the smoke. Finally, she stood and presented the bowl to the four directions before turning to us.

I rose and stepped forward. I figured it would help Tessa if I went first.

Aunty tipped the bowl and used the eagle feather to pass smoke toward me. I cupped my hands, washing the smoke over my face, hair, heart, and body. My shoulders relaxed at the familiar scent, and all of the stress and anxiety was chased away.

Tessa watched intensely, seeming to take mental notes. She respected Aunty, and I was certain she wanted to do her part perfectly.

I returned to my seat and encouraged Tessa to stand with a slight nod of my chin.

She rose and stood before Aunty, nervous.

Aunty began directing the smoke toward her, this time speaking in Chickasaw as she did. Tessa cupped the smoke, copying what I had done, and passed it over her body.

After smudging Tessa's entire body, Aunty said in English, "Walk in a good way, Tessa."

Tessa nodded slightly and returned to her seat. Her face was a complicated mix of emotions. It was as if the smoke had peeled away the layers, and the real Tessa sat before us, raw and vulnerable. But also relieved. And *strong*. Ready to continue the fight.

Tessa sighed heavily, letting the last of the bad spirits flow away.

I reached over and squeezed her hand lightly. "You got this."

***

The drive home was quiet but comfortable, the tone of the music matching our moods. When we arrived back at my place, we exchanged a big hug in the driveway

"Same time next week?" I asked.

"Wouldn't miss it for the world," she said, giving me another side hug. "I'm on radiology rotation next. So, I should be free over the weekend. Give Mr. Pestis a scratch for me, will you?"

"Of course. He wouldn't have it any other way."

She headed over to her beater, keys in hand.

"Don't be a stranger!" I called after her.

She beamed at me over her shoulder. "Never!" she called back cheerfully.

Hopping into her car, she left with a wave.

I felt a huge surge of relief. Tessa was finally on her true path, and the drama was over.

Well, mostly over.

Tessa wasn't completely out of the woods. She still had community service as part of her deal, and money would continue to be a challenge. But she was in a good mental space, and the nagging worry that she might kill herself was finally gone.

I was surprised at how much seeing her smile mattered to me. It wasn't just about getting a student through a rough spot anymore. We now shared something that would last beyond these few turbulent days.

She's family now.

I smiled to myself.

As I was walking up to my front door, I figured it was time to rejoin the real world and grabbed my phone to take it off silent. At my touch, it woke with a malevolent cheer and filled my screen with several notifications, including multiple texts, a phone call, and a voicemail.

There's actually a voicemail. *No one leaves voicemails anymore.*

I felt a tingle of worry and stopped halfway to the house to scroll through them.

They were *all* from Laila. My chest tightened.

I skipped the texts and went straight to the voicemail.

"Josie," the voicemail said; Laila's voice was panicky, like a wolf was at the door. "I know you're at Aunty's. Call me as soon as you can. My parents are coming. Remember laughing about that arranged marriage I blew off? Yeah, well, it just fucking blew up. My dad is pissed I didn't marry that guy. Now, my parents are coming here. *Here,* Josie. They've never come to visit me. *Not once.* They said they're going to stay until I'm married."

There was a pause, and her voice changed as she started to cry. "Josie...they're coming. I don't want to get married...like maybe never. I'm not sure I can stand up to them alone. Please, please, please call me as soon as you get this."

My heart dropped into my shoes, and just like that, the big, bad wolf blew the house down.

ACKNOWLEDGMENTS

Wow...Josie Harjo, Book Two is in the bag...whew.

I have to say, this book was a very difficult one to write. Depression and suicidal thoughts are something we all encounter in one way or another during our short stint on this small, angry planet. It's hard to talk about, whether you've lost someone or you're struggling yourself. But we *have* to talk about it. Taking care of your mental health is just as important as getting a dental cleaning or cancer screening. Your brain is part of your body, too. Don't neglect it!

Please be kind to your veterinarian, veterinary technicians, and veterinary office staff. Heck, be kind to everyone. The world could use a little bit more love. And you never know if you might be saving a life by sharing a smile, saying thank you, paying for someone's coffee, or holding the door for them. Little things like that might be the one thing that gets someone through a rough patch.

If you want to go a step further, I'd encourage you to learn how to help someone who is struggling and/or donate to the non-profit of your choice. NOMV (Not One More Vet, https://www.nomv.org/) is an organization that provides mental health support to those in the veterinary profession. Another great organization is the Trevor Project (https://www.thetrevorproject.org/), which provides support to members of the LGBTQ+ community. Every little bit helps.

And now to show appreciation to everyone who supported me during this latest quest.

Oodles of thanks to my copy editor, Caryn Pine. This is the third book we've worked on together, and her input has always improved the end product. Yasmine Bonatch served as proofreader-extraordinaire; there'd be a gagillion missing dialogue tags, misplaced commas, and inappropriately spaced ellipses if it wasn't for her. Thank you for catching all my typos and polishing everything up. Angela Caldwell designed the cover. It takes a village—thank you.

To my family, you're the best adventure group a non-Dungeons&Dragons player could ask for. To Derek Smith, the true neutral, bard College of Lore, goliath, who has a wisdom of twenty, I never would have completed this quest without you. Thank you for poking holes at the story until the weave was tight and the characters were strong. To Tyler Dryden, the chaotic good, battle smith artificer, changeling, who can take any concept and shape it into perfection, thank you for nudging every art piece in the right direction. Last but not least, to my hubby Justin Smith, lawful neutral, Eldritch fighter, dwarf, I appreciate your ability to weather any storm and come out the other side with a mischievous smile. I know that I'm a neutral good, wildfire druid, firbolg, who fails every wisdom saving throw, and I appreciate you all for sticking with me on this journey. One more dungeon cleared, bitches!

And to everyone who has read this far, thank you for your time. I hope you find joy in the small things, appreciate differences, and put a little more kindness out into the world. And, if just one more person can make it another day after reading this, that's a win for me.

ABOUT THE AUTHOR

Catherine Sequeira was born and raised in the Bay Area. She obtained her BS and DVM from UC Davis and completed an anatomic pathology residency at Cornell. Throughout her career, she has lived and worked in Switzerland, New York, Oklahoma, and Scotland before returning to California. With over twenty years as a veterinary anatomic pathologist under her belt, she now writes and teaches. In her spare time, she enjoys reading sci-fi and fantasy, playing tabletop games, and gardening. She lives in Northern California with her partner, son, cat, and dragon (the bearded kind, that is).

She can be found online at www.catherinesequeira.com.

Milton Keynes UK
Ingram Content Group UK Ltd.
UKHW040213091024
449407UK00011BA/193/J